out of nowhere

out of nowhere

the musical life of warne marsh

A Novel

Marcus M. Cornelius

Authors Choice Press
New York Bloomington Shanghai

out of nowhere
the musical life of warne marsh

Authors Choice Press
an imprint of iUniverse, Inc.

iUniverse books may be ordered through booksellers or by contacting:

iUniverse
1663 Liberty Drive
Bloomington, IN 47403
www.iuniverse.com
1-800-Authors (1-800-288-4677)

Originally published by Aurora Nova Publishing

ISBN: 978-0-595-51090-0

Printed in the United States of America

"The music comes out of nowhere, like the wind, and is gone."

FOR WARNE MARSH
26 October 1927 – 18 December 1987

This book is inspired by and dedicated to the music of perhaps the most inventive improviser in the history of music in the West. It is an account of his life as he might have told it: his song set to words.

In loving memory of Ike Isaacs, a very dear friend who helped me listen to my own voice.

Behind every story, there is another story in the telling and so this is for all my children:

Amaliah, Bevan, Dexter, Hassana, Iwan, Latifah, Risman

out of nowhere

part one

background music

chapter one **background music**

Finished. I never thought it would be, the music. This is like the hours after a gig in some club where you would rather not be, but where else is there to play to be heard. Maybe it's three, four or five in the morning, still dark, time on my hands. The chairs are all on top of tables, the instruments put away in their cases, the last of the ash trays cleaned and stacked; couples have gone home; some singles have made temporary couples to collaborate on an impulse. A few have approached me with words of admiration. Never paid much attention to that. And the music is as present and invisible as the air. We carry it around in us, in our ears, our hearts, our favorite tunes whose titles are like the names on files containing the flavor of moments locked up forever, granaries of life, honey sacks, earthenware pots slowly submerging under the moving sands on the ocean floor, age upon age. For most of those who were here tonight, the music was background music, an interlude to soften the blows of life, sweeten the day, permit some variation from whatever it is they do with their lives. There are a few who really listen, hear the whisper of the inner melody. The rest go home, sleep, and pick up again on their own theme, repeating the same old melody off the written sheet; for the lucky ones who know the duty to change the tune, they go searching for the melody which reflects what's new in what they see and hear and feel. That's a tough one, scary, man. I should know.

Carolyn picks up the last of the glasses, to dry it, turns the rim around in the cloth, both elbows rising and falling as the glass is turned. She really shines them. There's a clink as she puts the glass up on the shelf with the other glasses. She then hangs the cloth on the rail beneath the sink, giving it a shake first. I watch as she puts on her coat, picks up her bag and gives us a bright good night as she steps out to wave down a cab. Nice girl. Lonesome, or just alone by choice. Some play, some listen, some don't do either. Melody, harmony and rhythm, and the greatest of these is rhythm. Instruments in their cases. Footsteps on the sidewalk. Dawn. Whether you and I are around to see it or not. And come what may, let's face it, in the end it is alone, clear out of choices. Like after a gig. You have either taken the risks or taken a ride.

I have a good life, and, truly, never feel the need to complain. My own man. My own music. That's all. I am asked questions from time to time, asked, for example, where do I find the inspiration to go through the same songs and always produce melodies of such unpredictable beauty. And to that question there is only one answer: a whole lot of living. It requires effort. Everyday, I have to play it in a new way. Improvising. And if I have to go slowly, then so be it. Look around you. It is all in nature. Effort and continuity.

First up is the melody. So where does it begin, this tune, the theme, the first note, or, to be exhaustive, the inclination to sing even? In the northern hemisphere, some places the snow still lays over the earth in April I remember; though the sun is warm on a pale skin, the soil is cold under the crust of white. More or less overnight, the melt transpires and the fresh yellow or purple bud of a crocus is opening, luscious and fat. In desert lands, after twenty years or so of pounding heat, there is a cloud burst. Five minutes. A rock hollowed out to a crucible of possibilities, like two cupped hands, gathers a tepid lake of rain no deeper than the first joint of your thumb, a baptismal font, and within hours embryonic fish swim, inevitable. What we deem to be new is already old, way back. Incubation. Continuity. That's the point where it began.

There was a man some time in the late nineteenth century living in Madrid, New Mexico, an arid place. An accountant with the Santa Fe railroad, he had a son and a daughter both of whom became known in their chosen field and are now largely forgotten, which makes them no different from anyone else. The son, Oliver, had an interest in how things worked. This interest turned to typewriters because they were new and mysterious in their way, this complex system of rods and levers and round white keys, for that time quite intricate devices. He was fascinated by the efficiency of typewriters and needed to make a living somehow, so he sold and serviced typewriters and was competent in a trade that was in demand, industrious and competent, and these two qualities made the difference between a life as a salesman, with its empty talk, and the way his life in fact became what it was.

These are passing notes, incidentals and embellishments, and even as such they have import but I do not know whether they are important. Passing notes and grace notes; in isolation they do not have much gravity; in their place they add grace, like a greeting accompanied by an assuring touch.

The man from Madrid in New Mexico also had a daughter to whom he gave two names, Mary and Warne, but she abbreviated her first name to Mae - it was a custom - and hardly used the middle name at all. She had beauty and sensibility, a face that expressed tenderness and pathos, a depth of unrequited love and bathos. Her face is memorable to me because it possessed dignity and smoothness of line. Her time was the beginning of silent movies, and a company called Biograph and Hollywood. It was D.W. Griffith who recognized her talent. He was the top name then, the master.

Mae knew of Oliver's competence in mechanics and found him work as second cameraman, hoping to share her good fortune in Hollywood with her brother. Here was something even more fascinating than typewriters, and Oliver came to know everything about a film camera, regularly practicing and refining his skill by stripping one down and reassembling it out of simple curiosity, until he could almost do it with his eyes shut, until he had explored every part and mastered all its mysteries. And all this in his spare time, hour after hour. One day, on set, the camera breaks down, and the first cameraman is unable to fix it. Time on a film set has never come cheap, so the fact that Oliver could repair the camera led to promotion, to first cameraman. He was gifted in this work, understood all the options for interpreting a scene through his camera, which became his way of seeing life. He developed a style that was identifiable as the signature of Oliver Marsh, a personal interpretation of light and shade and perspective. Later on he filmed Greta Garbo and Jeannette MacDonald, as, of course, did many others, and, generally, kept to himself. Miss Garbo remembered him because he once told her she reminded him of a grand fjord. That impressed her for some reason.

His sister Mae was one of the four leading ladies of that era, and Lillian Gish, another of the four, confided that Mae was the only actress who aroused envy in her. In 1915, she appeared in the film called "Birth Of A Nation" directed by the master David Wark Griffith, one of the most powerful films ever produced. "Mae Marsh gives a performance unequalled for dramatic intensity in the entire history of the cinema." "Her work is little short of a revelation." "She was extraordinarily competent and, as an actress, gave as much as an audience could possibly want." Quotes from the records. This was the film that brought seriousness to the cinema and elevated the medium to an art form that countless millions all over the world would soon enjoy.

Some say that she was the finest silent-movie actress. For the poet Vachel Lindsay she certainly was the finest because he was in love with her, but she married a wealthy man, most of whose wealth evaporated with the Wall Street Crash, and it could be that Vachel Lindsay saw some justice in that. Mae was famous and rich, travelled to Europe and worked there and was later forgotten when silent movies gave way to the talkie. So eventually she was not famous; her name found a resting place in reference books but not in people's living memories. So it goes. To be remembered is not the point. There is a photograph of Mae. She is sitting at the end of a wooden bench, her fine hands resting one on the other in her lap, a gold bracelet high on her left wrist. Behind her is a mature cherry tree in blossom. It is late afternoon and her face is half in shadow. She is looking into the ground to her left. Her face is impassive, wistful. She is alone. Perhaps by choice but probably not, because this is a publicity photograph for one of her films. There is one shot in another film that became a classic example of the art of acting on film. This shot focuses on Mae's hands. The distressed wringing of her hands conveyed completely all the anguish of her situation, more than any words or facial expression could have done.

As for the father of these two children, whatever the facts might have been, they are lost to me, since he turned his back and disappeared and was never heard from or spoken about. He accomplished the anonymity he sought, convinced he had nothing to give of himself. But he must have passed something on. He is as known to me as the poetry of Vachel Lindsay and I have never read a single word of that, or the town of Madrid, New Mexico. Such is the line of descent, this melody line from generation to generation.

Russia. Perhaps St. Petersburg. Grand city of aristocratic refinement showing up as posturing and wealth. I have a profound bond with Russia, as profound as with Madrid, New Mexico. A century ago, Louis Marionovsky, a tall young man, rose in the ranks of the Imperial Army as a bandsman, a trumpeter; the trumpeter of St. Petersburg in ceremonial dress, shining buttons, shining shoes, played the ritual music always by the book, as the lines wheeled and turned about, marked time, step for step, every movement precise, brisk, well drilled, shoulder to shoulder, step for step. I have his name. He did not bring anything Russian with him except his name, Marionovsky, and himself. No pictures, no knick-knacks, no stories. He had heard of America and did not feel inclined to rise up the ranks any further in service of the Imperial Army. His parents were peasants, cultured peasants, but peasants all the same, and he could guess what was going to happen before long. He put off his imperial costume, hung it up in the barracks, and walked, deserted, turned his back on the country that had nothing to give him but a costume and living by the book. In due course, he saw the city of Philadelphia, which was European enough in style to appeal to him. And there he settled, and cut his name in half, throwing away the Russian 'ovsky', as the Chinaman felt compelled to slice off his glossy black queue.

And there he stood, inconspicuous as Louis Marion, not so obviously Jewish, in the doorway of a small five-and-dime store in Philadelphia, a trader amongst traders, a man amidst the American people, adapting to a new language his mouth never did learn to express without stumbling. But even Louis was too long for the new world, and folk cut that in half and left him as simple Lou. "Mawnin Lou." "Gudtamornin Ben." Literacy for Louis

Marionovsky was the unfettered joy of the trumpet which he had left behind in the barracks along with his dress uniform. For Lou Marion it was countless gudtamorninbens, every one imparted with goodwill, a friend behind the counter or in the doorway, gray-blue eyes, straight back, phlegmatic. He was trained in martial music, but the folk songs of ancient Russia were what he still heard and sometimes sang, to himself.

He had a depth of pride, and a big Russian heart. He fell in love and married and the daughter of the marriage was Elizabeth Marion, and she had music. He taught her the ways of discipline, and at a young age she was learning violin, doing sight reading exercises on the bus or subway as she went to her lessons, or humming softly to herself on the way to one of the ceremonial occasions at which she used to perform. Just before the first World War, the family moved to Los Angeles for a better life further away from Europe. The one thing she would never do was to play solo because she did not want to stand out, and that aggrieved her tutor more than a little. Around the same time that Elizabeth's father met his wife, Oliver's father married a descendant of the Brewsters, one of the original pilgrim fathers, a line now in its tenth generation, and by the early nineteen twenties his children, Oliver and Mae, were well settled in their lives in Hollywood.

Madrid, New Mexico, St. Petersburg, the Santa Fe Railroad, the Pilgrim Fathers, the Imperial Russian Army, trumpet, violin, five and dime stores, desertions, movie sets, silent movies, talkies. Names that have remained in circulation and names that survive on headstones or in indexes in libraries; in a photograph, a face voicing sentiments agitated by currents of obscured events and still able to stir feelings commensurate, if that face is seen through eyes affected by more than the image. I have a profound bond through these names and remnants with worlds long ploughed back into the soil. I am a retrieval system, knowing practically nothing of what is gone or what has gone on, childishly carefree in my ignorance and, I have to say, largely without curiosity. Over these many years, the resonance of the heart of Russia would beat in me but never does; there was resonance but it was not Russia, whose images and sounds had long been swept away like sand off a desert highway.

My own man. A good life. That was all. Background music. Rain for five minutes. Enough, for continuity. Germs of mysteries thrown back into the present I am, to be reworked in one more invention, whether to remain as anonymous as the verse of Vachel Lindsay or men from Madrid New Mexico, or celebrated; as the expression goes, who gives a shit?

I am asked questions and now I am not asked questions. Effort and a lot of experience, I said, and music in harmony and in time; your self and my self in rhythm; there is the choice, to till the soil or tamp it flat or peck and scratch at it like a chicken, and in that choice is where the melody can begin to flourish or peter out. To be as tenacious as the roots of a tree that will drill through rock to reach the subterranean lake, and find there such delicious sweetness in that cool water.

chapter two **all of me**

String quartets and carpentry and Hollywood talk.

Los Angeles is surrounded by orange groves. It is hard to imagine an easier way to live, always plenty, always time, a generous portion, never a hint of having to make do. We have a substantial house in the San Fernando Valley on the outskirts of L.A., not far from the film lots, rebuilt some years ago by a film producer with a cinematic appreciation of the grand: tennis courts, pool, and acres of land surrounding the house. It is built in the Spanish style, with arches and stucco and cool spaces. It is like a ranch. The grounds are big enough to hide in and not be found for hours. Everywhere farms and orange groves, the land of plenty.

My mother has bought me a piano accordion. My buddies can't make this out; they can't think of anyone else who was ever given a piano accordion. But they come around just to look at it and are kind of impressed. I could never ask her about it, but I find that pretty strange myself, why she chose the accordion. I prefer the piano in the library. Still, we do have some fun.

I remember Christmas, must have been when I have just turned six. The first time I performed with my mother. We'd rehearsed 'Silent Night' pretty often, she on violin, me on piano accordion, which I'd only had since October. It was a performance, the center piece of the evening, with all my father's and mother's Hollywood friends; a set-up. There was a long stairway going up from the living room to a balcony; the audience waited down below, anticipating what they knew was going to happen, ready to break out into applause and comment that was expected by the occasion, in happy collusion. Father had set up a spot light, and lines of small fairy lights along the balcony and bannister. The drapes had been drawn and a fire burned in the large open fireplace, though it wasn't cold. Atmospherics.

The whole house was dark except for the fairy lights and the firelight. My father's cue was when the bedroom door opened. He then turned on the spot light gradually, and my mother and I stepped out and I played the opening chords as we went along the balcony, followed by the spot. As we reached the top of the stairs, we started to play the melody in unison. We'd timed it so that we'd finish one verse by the time we'd made it to the bottom of the stairs. Then everyone was to sing the second verse together. I remember it as being quite moving, those few minutes; everyone had done something to make it happen like that. But looking back, it was an exhibition, a show.

The house never changed. Whenever I went back there, sometimes to live for a while, everything was exactly as it used to be, though my mother lived there alone in the end, until she sold it. It was a time capsule, a set sealed off from the influence of changes. I guess there's a stability in that.

Hollywood. A fantasy.

I imagine I am playing the organ or playing music for dancers. I like playing standing up, and you can do that with the accordion but you can't do it on the piano so well. People seem to be surprised by how I can find groups of notes that fit together in harmony, without anyone ever having shown me how; then another group of notes that sounds good played after the first group. My mother calls then chords. I hear them as easily as I guess a painter sees colors that fit. It's all in the ear already. I tell people it's nothing strange, all they have to do is listen like I do, and play around, see what turns up. But they say 'Nah, I couldn't do that'. But they could, if they were patient.

More than anything else, though, I am absorbed in learning music from the Anna Magdalena Bach Notebooks which have always been in the piano stool but which I have only now started to look at closely. There are some reproductions of Anna Magdalena's original handwritten scores composed by her husband Johann Sebastian and a portrait of him. I am attracted to these pages. My mother often plays Bach, the sonatas, at home with her friends. They make up a string quartet, all ladies, and practice in the lounge for hours around the piano. My mother doesn't play professionally any more, because of us kids. but they sound good and the music does something to me that makes me want to hear it often.

And the Bach notebooks, I enjoy reading them, turning the pages and just staring at the shapes, the patterns the notes make on the staves, like waves, or grass in the wind. It's more interesting than printed music; seeing the notes all written out by hand is like reading a personal letter in code. So I just look at them and see if I can hear the music by looking into the page, but it hasn't happened yet. I don't like to speak about this to the kids at school; they don't know who Bach is.

We often go to people's houses, people from the studios, and they come here regularly, especially when they've finished a movie, and talk a lot and drink. My father drinks, even on his own. Maybe grown folk do that, but I can't imagine why. He never used to - mom keeps telling him that when she thinks we aren't listening. I've tried some - he left the bottle out. It tastes disgusting. He never does it in front of us, so he must do it when we've gone to bed.

There's a pool and tennis courts where we mess around, and dad's workshop where we can't go unless he's in there - if he isn't, it'll be locked. The house has got so many rooms. Mine looks out down the drive and over the tomato farm across the road. It's next to my brother's. I guess we get on ok except he doesn't like me playing the piano accordion, says it reminds him of chapel. We never go to chapel so I don't know what he means. But I don't say anything; just practice when he isn't around.

My favorite thing? Getting my mom's violin out of its case. The velvet, the bow clipped to the lid, lump of resin, spare strings coiled up in small greaseproof paper packets, and the black flat bone shape of the chin rest. The way it is anchored to the strings which spread out as they go over the bridge, that reminds me of a sail. Sometimes I get it out, her violin, and try to hold it between my chin and shoulder like she does, so the violin stays still without having to use my left hand. But it doesn't fit and slips out. Maybe it's too big or something, or I'm not doing it right. I prefer my fingers moving over the buttons and keys of the accordion because there's more movement for my fingers. But whenever I see the violin case, I want to open it and just look at the bits and pieces, and the shine of the grain in the polished wood, kind of shimmering yellow streaks like gold. If I was to play a stringed instrument I would prefer the cello.

My mom is not so happy about dad drinking. I hear her talking to him about it sometimes, not being angry and shouting, just asking him can he not do it alone. I don't think he listens. He hasn't much time for music. When mom is practicing, he goes into the workshop. That's another of my favorite things, watching him do carpentry in the workshop. He's made me a fine chair and some wooden dolls for sis and a rocker for mom, perhaps for when she gets old because she doesn't sit in it. Mostly he just carves and shapes pieces of wood that he likes, and then leaves them in a box. I know them very well. They are just shapes but we have names for each one of them, and if he works on a piece and it starts to look like something else, then we change its name. He can see things in them that I can't at first, until he explains them to me and then I can see what he sees, kind of. If he wants a piece to work on or fiddle about with, he asks for it by name and I know which one he means and pick it out. Otherwise I just sit on the workbench where he keeps pieces of wood - off-cuts he calls them - and watch. He says one day he'll show me how, on the lathe too.

Sometimes I go with him to collect bits of drift wood from one of the beaches, at Malibu where we lived before moving here. He gazes at the sea and that seems to make him happy, as if he can see things out there that don't show themselves to me - guess that's the same for him as it is for me looking at the letters from Bach.

He doesn't do his carpentry if he's been drinking, says he can't afford to have an accident with his hands. He likes being in the workshop because there's people fussing round him at the studios all day and he has to concentrate and in here he can go at his own pace and whittle, because there's just him, and sometimes me which is fine by him. He told me "that's dandy; you just sit up there: that's your spot." And that's where I always sit and watch. We don't talk much. He never mentions the music but he knows that I would like him to, every so often. I tell him about how I look at the pages of music, waiting to hear it just by looking at the handwritten notes. He looks at me, smiles, continues polishing the wood.

Sometimes, when he's working on a piece, carving and polishing, he explains: If you want the best out of a piece of wood, you have to work at it, know the grain, give the wood the shape that best fits what it can be. Let it tell you what to do next. Then polish, until every aspect is smooth, and the grain starts to shine and you've worked out all the imperfections in the piece you started with. And I think of the back of mom's violin.

The players arrange themselves in a semicircle, within arms reach of each other, so that they do not feel the discomfiture of too wide a gap one between the other. As they prepare to play, they can engage in small talk in a conversational tone, even a whisper, and be heard. They also need to observe small gestures, fleeting facial expressions, to be informed through those physical movements that accompany the playing and indicate to each of them the shifting nuances of the piece. It is not just the physical comfort of being close which fosters mutual support, and even gives courage. During the playing, they respond to the feeling within each other, and this proximity of feeling happens most readily when they are physically close together. If all is well, their devotion to the playing will produce the almost liquid tremor of inspiration which is the expression of their willingness to be close to each other, as in a marriage of their musical individuality, to share of themselves without the least reluctance, which means putting aside the habitual differences, implies the willingness to shed personality and become absorbed in unison. Share of themselves, the way food is shared out among a family.

They do not congregate there in this semicircle to attract admiration or applause, nor to demonstrate prowess, nor to expose their brilliance. They gather for the simple purpose of voicing the music, which belongs to the community from which it springs and reaffirms that community's vigor or its ailing. And in the playing, this voice of the community, this music, is revitalized in one more expression, interpreted through the sensibilities of each one of them. Since they have last played together, they have lived through changes, reached new understandings, faced new difficulties through which they may have helped each other or failed to help each other. The music tells of the changes as the storyteller retells his tale and builds recent events into the telling.

So the music is the same music - they all know the theme of the story by heart - but they are different people today than they were last time and they do not pretend otherwise, and so it goes without saying that how they play, the sequence of the choruses, the patterns they discover, will have to be touched by these changes and accomplish newness. They are at the center of the event and are permitted for a brief while to be the core of the community; and the rest of the community, tribe, family, group (call it what you will) wish it to be so, and assemble to witness evidence of their corporate self, this one voice distilled from four or five or six or twenty persons. By striving for harmony in the music, they measure their appetite for harmony.

Sometimes it happens throughout, sometimes only in snatches, and sometimes there is nothing to report. There is nothing written down, notated. The music lives in memory as much as their history is part of their memory. But it is practiced, repeated year after year, generation after generation, revised not just reiterated, an echo of continuity. Every one of them learns the common song from birth, and with each repetition it is new and yet remains ancient, from way back.

The community gathers on a day. The players arrange themselves in a semicircle, seated cross legged on the ground as often as not, and then they play and discover what is both familiar and surprising and uplifting. And the scene repeated itself, century after century, anywhere from the Balkans to the plateaux of the Andes, issuing from fashioned bamboo or rosewood or the polyrhythmic cantations of the choirs of Africa or Melanesia, each voice holding the beat as surely as the planets hold their circuit around the sun. The need that compels those voices to sing is the same need that sends a Yehudi Menuhin to seek out the company of a Ravi Shankar and sit cross-legged before the community and discard notation.

I once knew a Hungarian man, over six feet tall and with a full beard. In a photograph he would have made an imposing image, but the last time I met him he was dressed in very tatty clothes, doing some rare work he had been offered by friends, to keep him from thinking about what had happened, retracing tracks until they vanish, desperate to find and hold on once again to the time before when he was carefree, a boy in a mountain village, find that link that would rescue him from madness. The work was a respite, a stalling the imponderable conclusion. He was painting a doorway, as I remember it, with brush strokes up and down, up and down with a stupefying slowness, covering over and over again the part of the door he had already covered with paint. Then he abruptly lost patience and, with a series of grunts, proceeded to skimp over the rest of the woodwork, barely covering it at all. On this the occasion of my last seeing him, with an almost princely composure, he stopped in mid brush stroke, put his brush down deliberately on the carpeted floor beside the paint tin, fingered his beard and pronounced a decree, as if he was in that place on his own: "It is time for me to have lunch". Then he strode away full of purpose and never came back.

I can only recall his name as a garble of sound, something like Cerukic. But what does it matter? He was a violinist, a master whose joy was to celebrate life through the compositions of Bela Bartok. He was surely a master and said to have been poised for a life in all the concert halls of the world, and yet it was his devotion, his love of Bartok that meant more to him than anything else life could have offered: his devotion demanded virtuosity to do his love justice.

It was some time shortly before the end of the war that he knew his life was in jeopardy. With the help of people who loved him, in Hungary and elsewhere, he conceived a plan to escape. Some railway workers in Budapest removed the ceiling of a compartment of a railcar that was bound for Italy. As I said, he was a large man, but somehow he squeezed his body into the cavity between the ceiling and the railcar roof, and the railway workers fixed the ceiling back in place, leaving enough small holes so that he would not suffocate on the interminable journey of darkness. These workers knew all too well that to be discovered in the act meant death for each of them; their love of the music in the man, however, was such that to liberate his soul from execution was a fair price, since, after all, was it not worth it to free him and so send his music, like despatching a gift, to those who would never have heard him had he not escaped. They were only letting a nightingale out of a cage.

Though he must have been in agony during the voyage over those rails, he dared not utter a sound. He had no idea who was in the compartment below; nor did he know where he was, so he was bound to be silent. On and on he floated over the countryside, like the wife of Chagall in one of Marc Chagall's paintings, without any effort at all. All he had for company was his violin, in its case, and doubtless he hugged it close to him day and night, even if his finger tips alone could touch it, even if he simply knew that, somewhere in the darkness not far from him, his voice lay still, like a child in restful sleep. Doubtless he sang his way, over and over again, through the songs of his homeland, a tireless dance with Bela Bartok over the landscape of Hungary, while his unseen fellow travellers exchanged intermittent conversation, snored, laughed and stared out of the window.

In Italy, two men were supposed to be waiting for the train to arrive. But they were not waiting because, in an incident completely unrelated to this escape, they had both been shot. The only consolation for the soul of Cerucik, more and more ready to start from this tortured body trapped in the roof of an inconspicuous railcar as time wore on, the only consolation would be the sound of Italian. Being a musical man, he would recognize Italian when he heard it. And he did hear it. But he did not hear the sound of his pseudonym - Bela - which would tell him that he had been found. Perhaps it was his good fortune that this part of the world was enjoying spring, because for a whole day the railcar stayed in a siding and the warmth of the sun stirred some warmth in his brittle body.

He was in a terror of anxiety, barely able to move a muscle by now, bewildered into speechlessness. Why did no one whisper or shout out 'Bela'? Had he been betrayed? Was he where the plan predicted he would be, or had the destiny of this railcar taken another course? In the end, some force overtook him, as irresistible as the force that projects a human being into life, and the last truly brute strength he would ever use was consumed in breaking through the plywood of that railcar ceiling. The only thought he had left was, what was he doing with the rest of his life.

Alone, very near blindness for a long while, unable to speak and without a current language anyway, he lay with his violin for all the world like a book closed on his chest as he slept in the warmth of a spring afternoon in Italy. Some children found him and brought water, and then the children's father, hearing the man only carried a violin, took courage and brought food. That is all he can remember of the past.

One day he lost his violin case. He was singing in his heart to a melody of Bela Bartok, and closed his eyes as a musician will, the better to surrender himself to echoes and eddies of his love. When it was over, he looked down and the violin case and the coins it had gathered were all gone. So be it. He acquired a sack and some string, perhaps dishonestly, and from then on kept his instrument carefully wrapped in its sack.

He became a hermit of sorts, living in the mountains in a small hut he built, and adopted the monastic silence and averted gaze that makes other people mistrust a man enough to leave him completely to his own devices, and stirs in children the art of artless mimicry. He also turned to drink, distilling his own solace.

Once a year there was a festival in a village a few hours' horse ride away from the place to which he had retired, and this was his annual appearance in society. He arrives in the village, riding an old horse bareback, his violin resting across his lap, still wrapped in its sack and tied up with string. He leaves his horse to graze; the animal loves him and so has no need of a tether. Every year, he stands in the same spot, in the middle of the square, the very core of the community, and he plays.

Every year, a widow of the village, also of Hungarian descent, approaches him, almost in supplication, for she knows the truth from past experiences. Halting no more than an arm's length away from this still unbowed, still bearded recluse, she whispers her request: please, I ask you humbly, may we hear the melody once again. Then she steps back a few paces, but not so far that she cannot recognize the fleeting expressions on his face, and the master plays. And the two of them are revived, in a brief marriage of their song. Hearing the last of it, she will weep, go to him in dignity, hold him close to her, with her head pressed against his shoulder. He neither resists nor welcomes her embrace. She looses her hold and he takes both her hands between both of his, bows his head very slightly and then leans down so that she may kiss him on both of his cheeks.

They could be lovers; returning or parting who can tell? In the ceremonial air that comes over him only here, he kneels down on the grass to fold the sack around the violin, and ties it around with the string as if wrapping up a gift. A young man comes near and studies his every movement, the way an apprentice observes a master craftsman. Cerucik, if that was his name, and the widow are full of the knowledge that the year will pass by when one or the other of them is unable to make it. It is a matter of time. If all is well, someone else will have heard the melody and ensure the continuity of the song. But it is not something that can be left to random chance.

When I was born, my father had put my name down to attend Cal Tech because that was the school if you wanted the best for your son, which I guess is what he wanted although I found out that he started drinking the year I was born. He still doesn't talk much, even less than before, and I have too much to do to spend time with him as I used to because he stays at the studios till late. We don't have quite so much land now after the flood, but even though there's a war going on we still have everything we need and dad's won some Academy Awards for his work. He'd show me and say, "You see what I mean. Just keep polishing."

I have been playing alto saxophone with the school band for a while. It was not enough to go on playing at home on the piano and the accordion. And having listened so long to my mother play with her friends, enjoying it the way she did, I figured playing with a band was the thing to do. And I like the sound of the saxophone. There was a place in the horn section for an alto. I didn't need encouragement. We'd been listening to all the bands on the radio, especially Glen Miller, and reckoned we could do the same. We love it. All the kids are white.

Lennie, I remember. I remember Lennie who taught me all I know. He had the kind of background from the likes of which you would predict that nothing good would ever emerge. But the melody will spring up where it will. He was musically gifted from an early age, and blind by the time he was ten. A white boy who obviously couldn't see differences in color so they didn't mean anything to him, visually or otherwise. It was just a question of playing. But that is not how most people saw life then, or now. Why is it that we remember black blind musicians more than we remember white blind musicians? Guilt must have something to do with it.

So nobody knows what to do with this blind kid. He's not stupid, not antisocial, not black, but nobody wants him, and all he wants to do is play music. So he ends up in an institution for the blind, run like a reform school, with a bunch of misfits, who don't want to do anything except get out and away. And he would always speak his mind and do what he wanted to do, which was play. So they put him in front of a piano, and he played. He didn't need to read music; he could hear it all. So he learned Bach by ear, learned to play Art Tatum solos faster than Art Tatum could play them, learned the discipline of classical musicians, sheer devoted effort and repetition dedicated to an honorable calling.

Nobody knew what to do with him, until someone caught on and said "This kid is a genius" and off he went to the American Conservatorium of Music. And he discovered the clubs in those parts of Chicago where white kids were never seen. And he played with the best of them, the black guys who were jazz. And he refused to accept that this new music should be holed up in small, noisy, smoke filled basement clubs that were alright for gambling or illicit drinking, but not for music. Where were classical musicians playing? Certainly not below street level at 3 o'clock in the morning. The romance of jazz had almost become institutionalized. It was jazz because the musicians were broke most of the time and slept during the day; at night they could make as much noise as they liked, and made a virtue out of being second class citizens. Apparently uneducated, and not interested in keeping a regular job. The reality was that they had no choices.

Lennie refused to buy into that one, refused to be a performing musician if he had to contend with those conditions. So he taught. He started teaching by the time he was twenty. He'd come from nowhere, against all the odds, and people were worried, the same as they were worried by Bird. What were these guys trying to do? Show us all up, or show us something? What was so wrong about playing the same way as everyone else?

Mozart and Bach and Bartok had the same problem. Like them, Lennie and Bird had no choice: they had to play the way they played, with their individual voice, to express what they heard completely. So, what's new? Club owners, record company executives, studio technicians. And profit.

And Bach and Lennie and Bartok and Bird and Mozart had something else in common: they played because the music was in them and would come out, and continued to do so whether people listened or not. A phenomenon, like the wind.

chapter three **scatterbrain**

It is a mild afternoon, a Friday, the day of the lesson. A six year old boy prepares, once again, to go to the small music studio of a man he knows as Dr. Amos. He has checked the violin case to make sure that he has not left the resin somewhere, that the bow has been loosened, and he has tuned the instrument up using the tuning fork. Before he closes the lid, he stands gazing at the violin, like a body in a coffin, ready to reverberate with life as soon as it is touched by his fingers and the caress of the bow over the strings. He loves the violin, a totally trusted friend that cannot lie: the instrument speaks the truth about his feelings, his ability and the state of his song. He does not love Dr. Amos. He has been told, regularly, as an incentive to persist with the methods of Dr. Amos, that he is indeed a fortunate child to be able to learn music from a private teacher. Even so, as he closes the lid, says goodbye to his mother, and sets off, he knows that this week his willingness to experience another quota of good fortune has diminished to the point where all he really wants to do is to go and sit in the park for an hour and then go home again.

He loves the music and he loves the violin. He does not love the sound of his own footsteps over the gravel path that is the last few yards of his journey. In a few seconds, his feet will leave the gravel and tread, almost silently, over paving stones, through an ivy covered archway and the across forecourt of this rather imposing building where Dr. Amos is waiting for him. It is an old building, built from the stones that would look quite in place in a castle. There are five worn steps up to a side door which is always unlocked, and then two flights of stone stairs. The boy stops half way up, ready to turn tail and flee: he knows what to expect. But the lesson has been paid for and he loves the violin and the music, and he trudges on up the next flight. He reaches the top, turns right, and sixteen of his small paces finds that the door to the studio is still there, with the name of Dr. Amos etched into a small brass plate a few inches above his head. It is a thick door, padded to make it sound proof.

He knocks, without enthusiasm. He hears the handle turn, then sees the same chairs in the same position as they were in last week, and the music stand precisely where it was destined to be. In half an hour, it will be over; it is that thought which enables him to sit down, take the sheet of music he has been practicing out of his music case, put it on the music stand, and get out the violin and the bow while Dr. Amos sits down at the piano, looking absently out of the window over some school playing fields. At the very moment when Dr. Amos plays the tuning note on the piano, something happens to the boy: his hopes rise, a sudden longing for the music makes him forget the discomfort he was feeling, and he prays that his fingers will dance over the strings as he knows they can and must, urges his hand to hold the bow firmly so that it does not wobble or drag over the strings and hears already the rich tones start to swell through the belly of the violin and let his spirit free.

His spirit stirs, but is quelled by the very weariness of Dr. Amos' voice, which tells the boy, in feeling alone, that this is another lesson to another pupil on yet another Friday afternoon. Fingers on the right hand a little more arched, bow hand a little flatter, elbow up, chin down, on the count of four, back straight, relax, that'll be all for today, do this for next week, and the two flights of stairs, paving stones, gravel, back home, denied again by an old man imparting instruction when what is required is tenderness and someone to hold open the door of possibilities.

So far away, so long ago. As if it all happened to someone else, or that I am looking at another person no longer familiar to me. Yet they are my footsteps, my shadows, my song. So I must own it, every fragment, all of it an unfinished piece containing moments of completeness. Rests between takes, pauses for reflection before hearing another line to follow, another vein to mine and to make mine. I could never deny it, that call to attempt everything, every last drop.

We play contemporary music, which is white mostly, not Dixieland, which is mostly black. Most of the time now I either study or practice; I enjoy study. I like to know all that I can. I swim, play tennis and go off on camps, but mainly I am happiest doing the practice on alto, learning Scatterbrain, a song that's popular at the moment, and Glen Miller and some Tommy Dorsey, dance band music and patriotic marching music for the school band. There's a war on, in other parts of the world; that's all I know. Everything's still the same in Hollywood, making movies, except Aunt Mae has gone to Europe. The movies are talkies and Aunt Mae is not so good at that, and she's gone to Europe after losing most of her money in the crash.

But there are still the orange groves and tomato farms round here, though you can still see the damage done by the flood a couple of years ago. Aunt Mae's in England and writes now and again. I never get to read the letters but I see them on the dresser now and again. Maybe the news is not good enough to read out to us. We still have servants. I thought everyone had servants, but they don't - guess you don't need them in a small house.

I think about what to do. Dad never suggests I show an interest in movies. He's real busy, hardly see him these days, even in the workshop. Meal times and when guests come around. So we just get on with what we're doing. Which for me is school and a lesson once in a while. Never took much to lessons. And listening to the radio and records and Tex Beneke. That's something, the way he plays; I wouldn't mind playing like that. It's either band music or Dixieland or classical. But I want to play what's new.

Looking back on it, there was nothing to complain about. We were comfortable. My father was well regarded and highly respected as a cameraman, and the actors and actresses genuinely liked him and how he worked untiringly to get the best results for them. It isn't there any more, but my mother still has it, a silver cigarette case that used to be on the dresser in the lounge room. Jeannette MacDonald and Nelson Eddy gave it to him after the filming of The Merry Widow, and had had it engraved 'To Oliver

Marsh from Jeannette MacDonald and Nelson Eddy'.

We all got along pretty well, mostly by avoiding each other. Never short of anything. No one ever pushed me in any particular direction; I just kind of did what I did because nothing else took my fancy. As far back as I can remember, it was all very natural and exciting. There were the beaches and lots of the kids went to the beaches, or dances, but I had too much to do.

Earl Immel, the band leader at North Hollywood High, he used to watch me playing with an odd look, like he was taken by what I was doing. He thought I might like to try my hand at arranging, so I wrote a line for the lead alto on Star Spangled Banner, which wasn't bad, looking back on it. I'd heard enough already to know what to do. Kids then kind of assumed they could do just as well as people who were well known. There wasn't so much competition, because jazz was relatively new, and there was none of the mumbo jumbo that came along later, so you just went for it if you had the inclination, and taught yourself. And the choices were fairly straight forward: join one of the big bands, or play the dance halls or get what work you could in the studios. If you wanted to play contemporary music. It was like that, looking back on it.

chapter four **requiem**

Oliver T. Marsh,leading cameraman in Hollywood during the early years of the talkies; worked in the company of men and women who were like founding fathers of the industry, early masters of their art, early examples of the star phenomenon that threatened to falsify art. He is not remembered by anyone these days.

Some credits where credit is due.

David Copperfield, produced in 1935. Director: George Cukor, who was to be one of the directors of Gone With The Wind. The cast included W.C. Fields, Lionel Barrymore, Basil Rathbone, stars of stage and screen. San Francisco, produced in 1936. Director: W.S. Van Dyke, who acknowledged that he learned all he knew about film from the master D.W. Griffith. As a tribute he invited D.W. Griffith to direct a scene in this film. No one knows for sure which one it is. Starring Clark Gable, to achieve a place in social consciousness with his role in Gone With The Wind, and Spencer Tracey. Continuity. This film confirmed MGM as the most omnipotent studio in Hollywood - Louis B. Mayer was a very determined man and not above displaying fierce anger if crossed. It had star power, a great, rowdy story, and one of the most awesome special effects sequences in the entire history of the cinema. This all worked to make San Francisco a masterpiece.

The Great Ziegfeld, produced in 1936. With Jeannette MacDonald. At the time, this was the longest film ever released in America, all of 170 minutes viewing time. Pat Nixon, the wife of a man who became President of the United States, she was an extra in this production. It was the first film biography of a living legend.

Bitter Sweet produced in 1940. With Jeannette MacDonald and Nelson Eddy. "The exquisite photography almost triumphs over some of the wooden acting." The film musical became a thriving genre for mass entertainers, as the industry aroused a public appetite for amusement and proceeded to satisfy that appetite and to make millions and millions of dollars to feed the industry. And standards slipped for Oliver T. Marsh. Blond Inspiration (1941) was described as 'pulp'. Lady Be Good (1941) warranted a reviewer to denounce it as 'meaningless drivel'. The Wild Man of Borneo (1941) failed to attract any comment, but it is worth noting that it was an early vehicle for the young comedian Phil Silvers who later achieved remarkable success as television's Sergeant Bilko. And it was a long way from Birth of a Nation to that.

A litany of names.

Take One.

It is May 5 1941. The crew are at the MGM studio early as usual preparing for the day's shoot. Ollie, the cameraman, goes through the routine checks of his camera, makes sure his assistant has enough film on hand, and questions him about all the scenes they are going to work through, and what he was up to last night. The assistant is sitting on a box beside the camera. Ollie looks over his shoulder, reading through the notes he made at the meeting yesterday evening with the director and the rest of the cast who would be used today. During the night, not being able to sleep much, he has run through every scene, imagining the various options he will have on each shot, steadily knocking back another bottle of bourbon. He's used to it. He can take the drink the same as he can take the pressure of filming, and the pressure of asking himself about the point of doing this every day. "I'm just the cameraman. So long as what I get on film is the best that I can do, what the heck. I can't write the scripts, and it's Louis' money - he must know what people want to see."

He is always aware of his part; how the actors and actresses rely on him. "How was that, Ollie? Did you get that?" Sometimes he'll give the faintest of nods and start preparing for the next shot. Other times he wants to make adjustments, to the lighting, the pacing, the rate of movement of the camera, or asks them to let him dwell on an expression for a couple of beats longer than they gave him the first time. And they'll do it again. "What do you say, Ollie?" The nod. Relax a little. Take off his cap, smooth back his hair, put the cap back on. Check the sheets and his pencilled notes. Light a cigarette. Once in a while, he smiles along with the nod, and then everyone knows there's something special in the can, footage with his signature on it, unmistakably his.

He had an intuition for what was required of him, and, through using light and perspective and being completely familiar with his camera, he could bring the mood of a passing moment to life on film, and override all the artificiality of the studio set up, and even the shortcomings of the acting. And he could play with light. He didn't need much direction, and people came to have an almost unquestioning confidence in his skill. He was a man they could depend on, and it was always good to have that kind of man around, so the events of the last few months had been a matter of concern.

Everyone knew he drank. In Hollywood there was nothing unusual about that. He was never seen to be drunk. But he did have a habit, even though he never let that interfere with his craft; he was never late, never did shoddy work, never let anyone down and was always able to concentrate on what was going on.

This morning was different. No one was about to say anything because it would have sounded rude and they all had a great respect for him. It was just before morning break. At first, his assistant thought he was checking the gate of the camera. Ollie did not have his eyes closed. He seemed to be looking at a piece of the camera that does not need to be looked at. He is looking along the beach at Malibu, ten years back, watching the kids run ahead of him, the three of them. He takes them along there every weekend, from the beach house where they live. He's not looking at the scenery. He's taking note of the changes in the light; every day it's different, and every period of the day. Ollie observes the way different light effects the colors, of the water, the sand, the skin of his children's faces, the sky. That was his training; watching and taking note. He understood what a painter sees. He is wondering whether his knowledge of light will ever be used in a way that satisfies him, because, so far, not one script has come close to really challenging his knowledge. He is mentally flicking through all the awards for cinematography that have his name on them, and not one of them means much, in terms of what he knows he could do if given the opportunity.

"You coming, Ollie?"

He hears his wife calling him. He's in the workshop with his son. Never could figure out why his wife had to call him Marion as well. Maybe music was his thing.

"Ollie, you ok?"

"Yeh, I'll be along in a minute. I'm not feeling so good."

His assistant puts his hand on Ollie's shoulder, gives it a gentle and understanding squeeze, and goes off to join the rest of the crew. Ollie stays on the seat behind the camera, suddenly feeling very, very tired, overpowered by the need to sleep. He almost wraps himself around the camera he loves, rests the side of his head against his right upper arm, and closes his eyes. He has never felt so comfortable.

That was how they found him, ten minutes later. "Ollie, what's up? Ollie?"

May 5th 1941.

Take Two

Elizabeth was sitting in the library, holding in her hands the silver cigarette case. She held it as if warming her hands. That is how she would hold his hand. She brought her hands up to her cheek, but could not bear that for many moments because she did not have the strength to weep any more just now. Several friends had rung to ask if she wanted company. She didn't. Well, she did; she would have liked Ollie's company. Ever since she had left the hospital, she had been singing a tune to herself. It took her a while to realize that she was in fact singing to herself, silently, the same tune, over and over, as the cab took her back home. She had asked the driver to take her past the studios. All she really took notice of were the blobs of orange on the fruit trees and the glimpses of red on the tomatoes in the fields, as she sang, to herself, The Roses of Picardie and saw the weeping eyes of Mary Pickford.

It was all so long ago and far away. She used to play violin in the orchestra - an all-female quartet - which helped the actors to express a particular emotion. What they played did not become part of the finished film: it was just background music. Actors had their own favorites, for joy, sorrow, disappointment, anticipation, anger, and Mary Pickford's favorite for helping her express sadness was The Roses of Picardie. Miss Pickford used to come over and thank them if the music had been especially effective; the tune always brought tears to her eyes. Elizabeth did not enjoy playing that tune at all, since she knew what it was about, but Miss Pickford was Miss Pickford and you played. And if Miss Pickford was called upon to show sadness, you played The Roses of Picardie. Elizabeth preferred Gilbert and Sullivan, nothing too serious, and she'd stopped playing at the studios after Warne was born. Was it really so long ago?

And here she was in a cab, playing that same old tune to herself when she had no need of anything to arouse feelings of sadness. Roses are blooming da diddy dee. Orange groves and tomato farms. Burbank. Home. What next? The cab drew up alongside the front door. "Could you switch off the engine. please, I want to sit here for a while and get used to it." The driver took a deep breath and settled back into his seat. Way back, in Philadelphia, her tutor had almost pleaded with her to audition for a solo part, but she had declined because she did not want to be conspicuous. It was her father's overly zealous encouragement of her music that inclined her to let her children follow their noses, so long as they worked hard and enjoyed what they did. Ollie was of the same mind. Had been. And he'd been a good example. They could be proud of him.

And they'd be home soon. "You can let me out now." The driver got out and, try though he did not to let it happen, he couldn't help opening her door with the somber courtesy of a funeral parlor attendant. He knew who she was and he knew who her husband was. "If there's anything I can do, Mrs Marsh." "I'll be fine. In a few days." She opened her purse. "No, Mrs Marsh, Mr Mayer said you weren't to pay a cent." He even refused the tip.

She had stood in the hallway and listened to the sound of the cab as it turned out of the driveway and off along Lower Canyon Boulevard, and promised herself she would not dwell on anything over much. Betty, the cook, could stay and prepare the evening meal; that would maintain the routine. She'd have to think about what to do with the gardener. Frank. He'd be heartbroken. She put away the clothes that Ollie had left on the chair beside the dresser that morning and gathered together his things from the bathroom. Strange that he hadn't come to bed last night. And the thought struck her that she had not known Ollie at all, one of those thoughts that threaten to open up issues not easily confronted simply because they've been left untended for too long. It was too late. Forty nine. He must have been sick for a long while. How could she not have known that? And she put the ivory handled razor, the hair brush, the shaving soap and the collar studs in a drawer. Then she prepared herself. She didn't know whether she really cared or not.

They'd be home soon, so she went to the kitchen and told Betty what to prepare for supper and asked her to try and not look so upset. And then she went to the library and waited. She had deliberately left the library door open so that the children would see her sitting there; that would tell them that something was amiss. It was always better to have some warning. She had had no warning at all. He had gone off to the studios before she was up, and the next time she saw him there was nothing to be done about it. Every time we say goodbye. And the next thought she had was that she would leave everything in the house just as it was, just as it had been for years. Though she would give his clothes to the Red Cross, some of them anyway. And roses blooming and a war on again. She would write to Mac tomorrow and tell her. There was a lot to do. Even his own father was still alive, probably, somewhere or other; that was one letter she didn't have to write.

The three children were coming down the hall and she still had not found a plausible set of words to use. They looked so young. No matter what words came out, they were bound to sound brutal. So nice to come home to, you'd be. May 5 1941.

Take Three.

"He's gone."

All three children are momentarily quite bemused and ask the same silent question: Where?

'Small wonder they look blank; they don't know who I mean. How can they possibly know what I'm saying? Not even a wild guess.'

"Your father's gone."

'How much can they tell from the eyes, the way I'm sitting. Roses in Laurel Canyon. May they not break down when they realize. Do they realize I'm not strong enough for that? Did he say goodbye to them before he went, this morning, so suddenly. He went this morning. So much like a camera, all the film used up, the lazy flick, flick, flick of a loose end flapping against the housing and then coming to rest, life all snapped. A hemorrhage, they called it.'

Elizabeth sat before them as they gazed patiently, the truth reluctantly dawning on them, needing more information for it to be beyond doubt. She insisted on being composed and dignified. She had hoped they would spontaneously understand what she was alluding to so that she would be spared delivery of the actual word. Dead. Roses in the canyon.

"What's happened, ma. Where is he?"

There was the off chance he had just disappeared. People did that kind of thing. Lots of people just disappeared.

"Children, your father's dead."

The words somehow refused to make any sense.

"Where is he?"

Elizabeth looked at them one after the other, holding their gaze for a few seconds. 'I know where he is, but I do not know who he was.'
"He died this morning in the hospital."

"Was it an accident?"

"No, not an accident. He just died."

And she lowered her gaze. Their mother had evidently conveyed to them all she dared, and her stillness implied she was not able to add anything. One by one they moved close to her and she touched them and they felt her remoteness. Her daughter kissed her on the forehead and held her hands and turned away and went urgently to her room. Elizabeth looked at the cigarette case. Her two boys stood by her, looking down on her hair where it was parted by the teeth of the combs; it was neatly in place. And they too went off to be alone. She thought they had gone out of compassion for her own need to be alone. But they went because they had no more words than she did.

'Your father's gone' sounded to her and the children as if Ollie had vanished unaccountably, but she could still see him walking back along the beach at Malibu, Owen on his shoulders as the other two ran around him playing some game and forcing Ollie to adjust his stride. She deliberately painted him out of that scene and her children came home and heard the news and went to their rooms, hoping that, magically, sometime around seven, they would hear wheels on the driveway and the sound of the workshop door close loudly.

After going to the kitchen to ask Betty to wake her in time for supper, Elizabeth went to her room to sleep. And she did sleep. How she slept, on a bed of roses in Picardie. 'My Ollie, you did it to yourself' was all she had left.

The song is never finished; it is passed on, taken up, every death a pick-up note.

The house is as quiet as if no one was here tonight. I sit. We are here. What are we going to do? I heard wheels on the driveway. It was the telegram boy. Two telegrams. One from Mr Louis B. Mayer, the boss of the studios where dad worked, MGM in big letters. One from an actress who was in the film he was shooting, a Miss McDonald. They were very fond of him and are very sad and will miss him and want to help if they can. I heard him go off to work, early. He went to work. We went to school. We came home and he's in the hospital. Gone. I don't know what I'm supposed to do. There are all those pieces in the workshop, some we never named and some we never started on. I heard him last night, too, talking to himself.

Do people get ready? I wouldn't know how to do that. And after you've gone? Maybe I'll go to the workshop and pick out one of the finished pieces, in case they all get thrown away. It's probably locked. He didn't even let her have a key. What a difference a day makes! Why would I want one of the pieces? I know what he meant. I can remember what he said: "Keep polishing it, until it's the finest." He never did say much, but I remember. I will do that.

He lay on his bed for quite a while, hands behind his head, patiently staring into the ceiling. 'Maybe you just wait until you've figured it out. Maybe you never could figure it out.' It wasn't that his father had gone without warning, not given so much as a hint, but more like he'd vanished without trace, like an iceberg melted. Ashes and dust.

There was the temptation to admit morbid thoughts and feelings, but with no effective way of articulating them or placing them in any scheme of things, they very rapidly created an emotional log jam of confusion. He couldn't bear that and so had no alternative but to put things aside for now and accept that he was confused and feeling strangely deceived and disappointed and caught short. To all the questions he asked himself, there were no satisfactory answers; another question came up, and another. But he knew that some part of him had become remote, as remote as his father was for years.

The family is seated around the dinner table. Elizabeth passes the food to Ollie as if he was one of the children and a dunce. They are accustomed to this ritual, a battle they watch and wait for something to change. They chatter amongst themselves and with barely disguised provocation try and create some mischief, to disturb the ritual. Warne eats too quickly and starts to gag. The others carry on eating, unperturbed. The boy's breathing becomes spasmodic as the blood rushes to his cheeks. Still nothing, except Owen and Gloria stop chewing. Between mouthfuls and without lifting his eyes from his food, Ollie says, "The child is choking," the way a child would repeat "The sky is blue"; a statement of fact that did not suggest any consequent action. It was Betty who brought a glass of water and slapped him on the back and helped him recover his composure. The child was no longer choking.

The scenes came up, one after another, and all the scenes were unsatisfactory and just petered out before he could articulate a question, while he looked and recognized a remoteness in himself that was as remote as his father was for years and ever will be. What he finally felt was a resolve, a resolve which was also inarticulate but which was a starting point, like a pick up note.

He had to do something, make some statement that he was still here. The saxophone case was on his desk. He went over and opened the lid by lifting up both catches with his thumbs - he'd done it a thousand times already. He then sat down in the chair by the desk and remembered how he used to take secret looks inside his mother's violin case, the violin she rarely played any more. He had never been convinced by her claim that she stopped playing when the children were born; that couldn't have been the real reason. For a start, she could have played to them. That would have been easy enough since they had a nurse and a cook and a gardener. Her stories about what a studio musician had to put up with convinced him that he would avoid doing it at all costs. Obviously she had made a choice which she gave no sign of regretting. So her music had run its course. He knew from his own experience that if you really wanted to do something, like play the music, you simply did just that and never had to call on an excuse. There were friends of his who played but needed encouragement to continue; in the end they would give it away because the music was not important enough, which meant, to him, that they could not have known what the music is. There is one person who will wade in the river for fun, and there is another who will look into the water and search and find precious gemstones which will then be polished until they are the finest. In his case, he had to play, just as he had to breathe if he wanted to remain alive. It was not a compulsion or an obsession: it was an inevitable consequence of his being alive. In fact, it *was* being alive.

He caught hold of the body of saxophone with one hand and lifted it out of the case, looking along it the way someone else looks along the body of a rifle. Reflection without any specific thought. He then put the saxophone on his bed, and, one by one, took the mouth piece, ligature, gooseneck, the small pill-box of cork-wax, neck strap and reed guard out of the storage compartment of the instrument case, and lay them all out on the bed. He was looking at the rest of his life, sitting there in his room at a few months short of 14 years old.

After supper, Elizabeth had related to her children what she had been told of the way her husband had finished up. And it was to that image that Warne finally returned late at night. The image of his father, whom he did not think he knew very well at all, choosing or being obliged to complete his last scene with his camera, awoke in the son an admiration and contentment that was as surprising as it was welcome. It was an image and a feeling he would never forget.

His mother had spent much of the evening writing letters and making phone calls. His sister and brother had gone to bed earlier than usual. Betty had gone home soon after the meal. Now all the lights in the house were out except for the wooden study lamp in his room. Never mind tomorrow. He just sat in the chair by the desk, looking over at the array of peculiar shapes on his bed. He had all he needed, and he slept. And that was how his mother found him, on the morning of May 6th 1941, and she did not wake him.

chapter five **just friends**

All so distant, as if it happened to someone else. This is how it is related.

The first major change came not long after the funeral. To ensure the livelihood of the family, Elizabeth arranged for the sale of all but an acre or so of the land around the house. This raised a considerable sum, which was invested wisely enough that the family never fell upon hard times. Their house, built to look impressive on a large plot, now appeared somewhat out of context in its diminished surroundings. The gardener was not required as often as before. There was still the swimming pool, tennis court, and an out-house which had served as quarters for overnight guests but was rarely used these days except by the children and their friends because visitors rarely came.

Warne had become competent on the bass clarinet, and the tuba of all things, partly just for the challenge and partly because he wanted to play the bass register as well as the treble so as to explore the principles of harmony which had become so clear to him through listening to the music of Bach. He studied classical saxophone classical clarinet. For him, the difference between classical music and contemporary music was that contemporary music had somehow lost the long melodic line and classical music had lost the improvised line. And so he was dissatisfied with both options. But the dissatisfaction was not specific; it was a suspicion that the deeper resources of the power of the music were ignored, which meant that part of him was ignored. Even so, he could do nothing about that because there was available what there was, for the time being.

The cause of the changes in music was that the dominant musical form had become the popular song which accompanied the various dances that had become popular - it was a way everyone could have fun. The limitation was that a dance could only go on for so long before people became bored with a tune or needed a rest or a change of pace. The movements of the modern dance were also fairly simple; it was popular dancing and was something most people could learn to do without having to put in too much effort. These were the early days of mass entertainment, which followed hard on the heels of the decline of the cohesive and self reliant communities which had spent centuries very often refining and refining a culture that was peculiarly local. Life, by and large, had also become confusing and the demand was for a simple culture in which the public (the community) could participate easily. The world had already experienced one cataclysm in the first world war, followed by the Depression, and was now in the throes of yet another cataclysmic war. Culture became dominated by popular entertainment.

Whereas, years gone by, an audience was all too willing to spend an entire night listening attentively to a performance which renewed a community's sense of its place in the scheme of things, and affirmed that place, the communal history that gave relevance to that performance had been lost as populations migrated and people in urban and suburban communities no longer shared a common history.

These were also the days of the first popular records. Technology had made it possible for performances to be recorded and transferred anywhere in the world. But technology had only advanced as far as giving us the three minute song, and songs were written, not to express the full potential of the melodic idea or the sentiment, but to fit the three minute format. And besides, businessmen had invested in this technology, and, not surprisingly, wanted a return on their investment, and so the offerings of the entertainment culture had to become popular, because if it was popular then it made money. Culture, in other words, was now an economical activity, another profit center: its value was its capacity to create satisfactory returns on the investment made in the technology. So people were now able to listen and dance for three minutes, more or less. The radio had an additional influence. Recorded music was cheaper, and hence more profitable than live music and the radio provided a means by which a still larger audience could be reached, and therefore larger profits. It seemed like a good idea at the time. But if an individual's art, the fruit of the culture of an individual, did not prove itself capable of creating profits, then that art remained unseen, unheard and of no apparent value to anyone except the individual who originated it. The material prosperity of the new mass culture was one thing, but ultimately it would bear little relationship to a culture that espoused values, especially the value of dignity, integrity and the profound.

Instead of referring to a common history, the entertainment culture had to appeal to specific common experiences amongst a population that did not share a common history. Things became generalized and, of necessity, there was a tendency towards the shallow and ephemeral, performances for the passing moment. Life was serious enough as it was. The world had slipped off its axis: people were thrown together by disruptive events, from the pogroms in Armenia, revolution in Russia, to potato famines in Ireland, all looking for a safer place to live and make a buck. And they were just now being joined by hoards of human beings fleeing the terrors unleashed by Adolf Hitler and Little Joe. And for many years, not a few million black people had been ferried from one continent to another for their value as cheap and disposable labor in the progressive economy that was America. Out of their bitter experience, their capacity to forgive, an ancient familiarity with and responsiveness to complex rhythms, and a joy in invention, from all this came the new music called jazz. And there were two styles of jazz: Dixieland and contemporary, also known as traditional and modern.

Warne's experiments on the bass instruments did not go unnoticed. After band practice one day, his school band director, with one of those off-the-cuff remarks that can change the direction of an entire life, offered the opinion that Warne would be more comfortable with the tenor saxophone. He bought one.

I became a somewhat antisocial boy. My exclusive interest was music and, by now, the tenor saxophone, which meant that the company of friends was not something I sought out or even thought of that often. My only ambition was to master the instrument and my approach was totally single-minded; there was nothing else I wanted to do, and it was with the instrument that I passed all my spare time. It was some consolation that this form of antisocial behavior was not unique to me amongst my peers, otherwise I might have felt conspicuous. Even so, I doubt that being looked upon as an odd-ball would have made much difference.

Awareness of this new music spread not so much by word of mouth as by the influence of the records and the radio. And it had an effect, profound enough to divide families, to polarize the young in a culture or taste quite incompatible with that of their elders. The jazz compelled and repelled.

"I won't have that kind of thing in this house! It's noise, that's all it is."

So the kid who had heard Kid Ory or King Oliver or Art Tatum or Sidney Bechet or Johnny Dodds and was forbidden to listen to it in the house in which he lived, had little choice but to go where he could hear it. This would be a friend's house or, as a last resort, anywhere the music could be heard. At that time, record stores had listening booths where you could listen before you bought. There were no headphones; the music was piped into the booth through speakers and the listener could not even adjust the volume. If you didn't buy, the proprietor did not smile at you when you left, and there was always the misgiving that you might be recognized the next time you came in. In such places young kids acquired their musical education.

Love of the new music became a new basis for friendships. Two such friends sought out each other's company. One was not allowed to listen to jazz in his house, the other was looked after by his mother - his father was at war and she worked most weekends and so he was relatively free to listen to what he wanted. Her son had heard Ben Webster, and by honest labor, delivering newspapers seven days a week, had managed to acquire a tenor saxophone and a recording of his master. There was no one around able to teach him, so he listened, hour after hour, until he knew the music by heart, and then he learned how to play it. Sheer determination.

His friend would cycle some twelve miles to listen as well, and occasionally try his hand on the instrument. If the mother was home and needed to sleep, they would walk the mile or so to a canal and take it in turns to play Oh Lady Be Good and Sophisticated Lady. Later on, the one who was not allowed to listen openly to the music would wait until his parents had gone to sleep, and then, like a thief, creep down stairs in the dark, go into the lounge room, turn on the radio as low as he could and still hear something, and sit in the dark room with his ear almost against the speaker, turning the dial in the hope that he would hear some of the music. It was often too late and all he would hear was hiss. But the effort was that important: some days he was lucky.

When I am not at high school, much of my time is spent in the library at home. The building is a solid structure so the sound doesn't travel through the house. There are heavy drapes and good carpet, thickly upholstered furniture and well stocked book cases. This makes it a good place for practice; there is hardly any echo. The very high notes make the light fittings vibrate but I can tolerate that. There is a grand piano, the same one that I used to tinker around on as a little kid, and the piano stool with the Bach notebooks and my mother's favorite violin scores. The silver cigarette case is now on a coffee table. And there's the record player.

On weekends, I come in here after breakfast. Whatever else is going on in the house during the day remains a mystery to me: my mind doesn't wander, and as soon as the horn is clipped onto the neck strap, I feel my real time has begun. There isn't anything else; just me and the music. First, there's the choice of which reed to use, so I try out three or four of those I didn't use yesterday and settle on the one that sounds best today. Then tune up to the piano. Then I'm off. Scale passages in every major and minor key over the whole instrument, increasing the tempo as I warm up, and then several scale patterns that I learned by heart from a book of technical exercises. I concentrate now on the ones that have the most difficult fingering because my aim is to master the technique, and the only way to do that is repetition. The third octave is the hardest and not many tenor players use the top of the instrument, but my thinking is that I want to master the whole instrument. So I go over phrases, maybe fifty times, until I can hear that every note is even and clean. Slowly at first, then setting the metronome at a faster tempo until I find the limits of what I can do. And I'm always pushing the limits out. There's not much point spending long on what I can do; my purpose is always to master what I can't do yet, because in the end there will be little, perhaps nothing, that I can't play.

After an hour or two, I'll have a break, give the lips and lungs a rest, and enjoy the silence, sitting on the lounge suite with the horn across my lap. I feel satisfied but still not content. Something's missing and I do not know what it is. Nothing serious, but missing, like a name that's on the tip of your tongue; you know it, but you can't say it. My sister Gloria comes in. She's no trouble, and I don't take any notice. She just sits in an armchair and reads a book while I play a Coleman Hawkins solo - Body and Soul - over and over, repeating it phrase by phrase on the piano, building it up until I can transcribe the whole solo, note for note. And then I learn it on the horn. Not just the notes; the style, inflection, tone, accents and as much of the feeling as I can. But I'm not yet a man so my voice does not have resonance, does not vibrate as deeply as the Hawk's. I want to sound exactly like the Hawk, close enough for someone listening to mistake my playing for his. I know it's a forgery. But that's not where I will stop. I first discover what it is that makes the Hawk's music his unique expression; by copying, I can tell the difference between what is mine and what is not mine, what has been borrowed, learned. And I only copy the music that I love. I do it as an exercise. I've listened to this track so often that the first record got worn out and I had to buy another copy. These jazz men, the negroes, have a different style of name to the white guys. Instead of Tommy and Jimmy or Glen or Stan, there's Hawk, Pres, Satchmo, King, Kid, Dodo, Lady Day, Jelly Roll, Duke. A whole pantheon of names the likes of which have never been heard before, like the jazz. And they have like trademarks in the way they appear, Hawk and his hat, Pres and the odd way he holds his horn. They even make a tuxedo look different, kind of up-beat. Probably the contrast. The idiosyncrasies that appeal to people, something to latch onto: 'Oh yeh, I know him, man, he's the one who holds his horn like this'. Maybe they're distractions and attractions, because they are not the way white people do things. I don't want to stand out. I want to be unknown; I am not important, the music is. So it is the music that will be prominent.

I ask Gloria to get me some lunch. I'm hungry. She goes and gets me some lunch. It's good having a sister. She comes back and wants to talk, but I don't want to talk; there's too much to do. She picks up her book again, while I go over some classical pieces, changing the rhythmic pulse of the piece. I can hear the melody well enough in my head to be able to play a counterpoint line to it. The music has a shape, like a landscape, and it has a mood. I can change the landscape and change the mood, and sometimes lose my way. So I retrace my steps. This world for me is like the ocean floor for a diver, hidden but not beyond discovery. There is the scientist in me, probing, experimenting, convinced that there is something to reveal that no one else has found. Here, in the silence, I am weightless. It's gotten dark already. Gloria must have turned on the lights before she went out. There's just me. I've been here all day, eight, nine hours, and I'm exhausted. The exhaustion will pass, a break between movements.

Tomorrow, reckon I'll spend a few hours here and then go over to Karl's place and get Andre over there too. Karl's something of a hassle because the drums aren't easy to move about. Lucky he's got a piano there too. Andre's amazing, been playing Beethoven since he was ten, and I thought I got off to a good start. A father who has things figured out, that makes a difference. The bastard drank himself to death in secret. We're just friends, the three of us,

Karl, Andre and myself. White kids looking for the music. My father, the bastard, just friends.

There they were. I see them again now. There we are, three kids from North Hollywood High, getting into the music together, and more besides, two, sometimes three evenings a week, and Saturday night down Spade Alley. You could call a spade a spade then. Never have felt any prejudice myself; the music doesn't really allow for prejudice. It was just that, at the time, they were the best, the black guys, because it was their music and they looked after it; they lived for it, their culture. Like classical music was white music, way back.

This was the big band era, Glenn Miller, the Dorseys, Duke Ellington, Buddy Rich, Art Blakey, Dizzy Gillespie, Stan Kenton, Woody Herman, Fletcher Henderson, mainly white guys in their white bands, or orchestras, and black guys in theirs. They were like travelling schools of music and they played dance halls and concert halls all over the country. It was one of the few ways negroes could function publicly in a white society, and be respected and admired. The respect and admiration didn't follow them into their daily lives when they became just another coon, but at least there was a platform. The big bands were in demand, and a young musician playing contemporary jazz started off in a high school band and then hoped to make it in one of the big bands because that was about the only secure option. But down where the rents were cheap there were the smaller bands, in clubs, and in Los Angeles that was Central Avenue, popularly known as Spade Alley, socially a very long way from 5717 Lower Canyon Boulevard, near Burbank Boulevard in San Fernando Valley and white society. That's where we used to hang out Saturday evenings and pick up on the music. And we watched a way of life that was mysterious and new, a way of talking and moving that felt almost dangerous. And may be it was dangerous down there for fifteen-year-old white kids. But all we wanted was to pick up on the music, because these guys had it. There was something forbidden about it too, going down Spade

Alley with no one's permission, no one even knowing we were there or what we were doing, some freedom not to explain, not to try and explain why we went, because our explanations wouldn't have made any sense. Truth is, I didn't think to explain to my mother, or even think it was relevant to have her know. I went to the music like a moth to the lamp.

Some of the guys who played at the halls and clubs were already masters of this new music. And there was both the thrill of knowing we were watching something the world had never heard before, which was changing music for ever, and the casual acceptance that we could do the same in our own way. So, while it is surprising now to recall that a kid called Chuck Faulkner at the age of thirteen had already put together his own band, at the time it was nothing special. Because in those days, the masters were accessible; you could sit just a few feet away and watch their hands, hear them grunting or humming in a nasal way while they played, while they improvised a new music. There was no awe of stars, simply an awe of what they played, music we had never imagined. So it was simply natural to assume that if they could do it, so could we; just a question of learning, practice, persistent practice and more practice and more listening. The music was endless and the world became eternal. We were kids, just making friends with the music.

I do not know what drove me to it, but I had to master the technique. At fifteen I had. I knew every note the instrument could play, and every finger combination for producing any note. It is true that if you want to master an instrument, to be a true master, you have to have mastered the technique by the time you're fifteen, or sixteen at the latest. There just isn't time in life to leave it any later. As you get older, other things start to eat away at the time of your day, and there isn't enough time to devote to learning the instrument. Nobody ever told me that, it was something I did without even thinking. It just isn't possible to give inspiration free rein unless the instrument is already as much part of you as your hands, so that your hands move as spontaneously as your heart beats or as your eye sees.

At that time I hadn't given any thought to what I would do with it all. I was an academic sort of guy and enjoyed study and made good grades, straight A's as the saying goes. We lived for playing, and mostly we played the music we heard, played the charts. And we tried to sound like the musicians we imitated, because we didn't know how to play our own music yet. But at best we sounded reminiscent of other people. Being yourself wasn't really encouraged in America; easier just to accept that and become another instrument in the lineup and play the way everyone else played. I never did quite buy into that.

chapter six **flying home**

I remember Lee, kindred spirit who forsook me. Lee, I will remember. Do you remember me? It is like you're in a coma, just coming round, and I stand in front of you and you look at me and I ask you do you remember me, Lee, it's me, and your eyes remain steady, no wrinkle of a smile at the corner of your eyes, no relief to recognize a face. Impassive, lumpen. I only want to play, surely you must know that, the way we do, no one else can bring that about, not the way we did, weaving lines of liquid glass into flawless jewels of sound, symphonies in miniature, because we have only a few minutes, three minutes, five minutes, longer in the later years when technology made more allowances, unerring, as if we shared a muse. We soared, we gave each other flight, we saw over the other side, there the glory, the pattern of all things, devoted to the music. Until something happened.

I am talking to you, hear me, I have no strength in my voice to talk to you when you are out of earshot. I am talking to you, respectfully, as if to myself, and you put on your hat and turn up the collar of your coat, hold the lapels together against the wind with your gloved hand, the other hand in your overcoat pocket, a short man, and let me watch you walk on down Riverside Drive, a stranger in New York City. Something happened. Something happened then, to me, as I watch you disappear for good. Something happened before then. I did you no injustice that I know of. That was the last time I saw you, the last time I presented myself, saying, (Was it only to myself?) you must have known, here I am, Lee, do you remember me, the countless thousands of hours, tell me what happened to frighten you away. I never heard you play again, not you; sometimes a guest put on a CD, what do you think, I don't think at all about that, he isn't in what I'm hearing the way he used to be. Do you remember, Lee? Subconscious-lee? I remember. Lennie would have remembered.

We were young, dedicated. Do you remember Lennie? Who was Lennie? What happened to Lennie? What happened to us? What went wrong? You did not speak to me any more. Words were addressed, but not to me. Something happened, and that was that. I am not bitter (bitterness is the rust of life), not bitterly disappointed, since I am not the judge and we have both of us walked in the shadows of the sidewalk at three in the morning. Though I am not bitter, and have no cause to complain, it has been hard, to lose. My father despatched himself: yes, harder to stomach than that. Didn't you know? Didn't you know that I could hear you? I do not know if you can hear me even now. But I never gave up, never relinquished the hope in the song. I have my blemishes, but that's not one of them.

You were in Chicago and I was in Hollywood, before we each set out.

Then I'm in a band of kids roughly my age, fourteen, fifteen, sixteen years old, and a girl, Betty on alto and clarinet, and two black kids. When we joined the musicians' union, the Local 47 - which we had to do to get work - the black kids were sacrificed, because that kind of arrangement still wasn't tolerable. Did I say anything? To myself I made note that the music, the real music would not permit this decision, this sacrifice: the real music is not beholden to ideology. Sure enough, I admit I was involved in a tradeoff and any tradeoff belittles the music. We were kids and had no say in the matter. Ok kid sign here and you and you and not you and not you, that's the way it is, come on kids, give me a break for Chrissake will you, we didn't write the rules. So who did?

Perhaps there's nothing more American than the band. Chuck, at thirteen, saw nothing to stop him putting together a band of competent teenage musicians and pulling in some work. Never gave it a second thought. And he did it. And we pulled in work, regular work. Man, we were busy, for kids still in High School, and stayed busy for the next three years: people were hungry for this music and we stayed as busy as they were hungry. We believed we were good and we were good: we'd put in the hours, and rehearsed the charts, stock arrangements executed with bags of energy and swing in our white shirts and black ties and white-boy, west coast hair cuts, smart and confident and expecting the best would happen and we'd make it big. Some of us cycled to rehearsals with instruments slung on our backs or tied to the cycle with string, others, like me, would arrive in style, in the family car.

The war helped. We played at bond rallies, to raise money for Uncle Sam. But our main venue was the Hollywood Canteen, a serviceman's club at Cahuenga near Sunset, where the band played every weekend for a while in 1943. We were more or a less a junior house band, taking sets between the established bands, and the Chuck Falkner Orchestra was renamed the Hollywood Canteen Kids, because that name had more zip, and, lest we forgot, we were in Hollywood.

This was Hollywood, the fantasy. And being Hollywood, household names were being made, and the household names in production on the studio lots turned up at the Canteen to be seen. Hollywood took hold of the appeal of child performers that had started in the music halls; it somehow consoled the older folk to encourage the kids to imitate and go through the same hoops, like apprentices, and to show personality. In a couple of years, they'd be old enough to join the major leagues and keep the machinery turning. Exposure was a major consideration and personality even more so. John Wayne turned up, Roy Rogers turned up (without his horse), Dale Evans turned up to be courted by Roy Rogers and ride off into the sunset, and we were news. All the returning and departing soldiers loved us, and the prostitutes and pimps, and the household names and the others who danced to get some joy out of life. It was heady stuff, to be urged on by applause and ovations that made generous allowances for the many shortcomings in the performance, proficient though it was. We were news and read about it in *Downbeat* magazine, June 1 1943.

Excerpt:-

"Los Angeles - Of new bands appearing on the music scene here during the past year, the one that is attracting most attention is Chuck Falkner's 'Hollywood Canteen Kids', which bobbed up at the Hollywood Canteen about a month ago and has now been signed by MCA, which has already set the combo for a summer tour of theaters, opening here on June 23.

Notice the date. It couldn't have been sooner because the members of this band range in age from 13 to 16 and can't take any steady jobs until they complete their current semester at local high schools and junior high schools. The kids have been batting around as a more or less organized unit for some time, but their first break came when MCA's Jules Stein worked out a deal whereby they have been guaranteed a small weekly stipend by the Hollywood Canteen to work there as 'house band' and fill in between the gratis appearances of named bands and service outfits. The money advanced by the Canteen enabled the kids to get better instruments, supplied them with a place to rehearse and the incentive to get in and dig.

Stand-out 'men' in the combo are Karl Kiffe, drummer, and Bob Clark, piano, aged 15 and 16 respectively. Stein will have to pay this band to work at pretty good dough or these two boys can spend their vacations with established name outfits. The sax section has an interesting feature in the presence there of an attractive 15 year old chick, Betty Churchill, on third alto. Neil Cunningham, trumpet, and Warne Marsh, tenor, both show a good conception of the hot style and promise to develop into competent soloists...."

End of excerpt.

Could this be the start of something, something out of nothing? Fresh faced kids looking into the eyes of household names and matinee idols and reckoning on the chances of what might be. Chutzpah, we had that.

The solo. The lead voice. The guy who stands up and plays a chorus of his own invention while the rest of the band sits down. For the classical musician, playing a solo is to repeat a written line, memorized, and what infuses the theme with originality, what renews it is the interpretation, the depth of feeling, sometimes the daring of the performer, the stirring evidence that every note was personally expressed and wrung from the instrument: the performer enters into the music so completely it is played as if it was he or she who wrote it and not the composer. In the main, the process is routine, because we are now talking about a profession, a job, a source of income; we are not talking about an honorable calling; in the main we are not talking about music as anything to do with the human spirit.

I am not a man to study nature. Nevertheless, I hear the birds at dawn and hear a statement, a song that I know very well since I have heard it many times before today's dawning. And, I must say, I feel personally addressed by the songbird: the song wakes me up. I am happy to hear this connection with the passing of all time, a connection between me and who I am now, an affirmation that I am at all and that there is continuity. In jazz, the solo can be the fullness of the individual voice, the individual melody, through which anyone who dares, or who must, is called upon to create spontaneously, just as Bach did - he heard what he wrote down: he could do that because he knew the essence of harmony of sound, the meaning of form, and the capabilities of all the instruments available to him. Much of what he wrote down was declared to be unplayable - he pushed out the limits. Many jazz solos, when written down, are declared to be unplayable, ever when presented to the musician who first performed them. The power of the solo in the jazz music is that it returns to the individual a responsibility for his or her own voice. What is created depends on the individual: one can scratch the ground like a chicken or dare to fly; one can rely on the conductor, the band leader, or one can have the courage to call on the self to lead the song, and the song has no limits. My life is my solo. My song, and your song, needs to be as distinguishable as the blackbird is from the bird of paradise.

A year later, Chuck left for some reason, and Karl took over as leader - he'd won the national Gene Krupa drum contest and would soon sub for Buddy Rich in the Tommy Dorsey orchestra, while he was still at high school and not yet shaving. It was a great adventure to be so close to musicians who were like family, before the days when being a so-called star made personalities out of what were in fact ordinary people given some status that made them remote.

I could already hear the melodies and harmonies in even the simplest song - the most moving often has a very simple melody - and spent a great deal of my time experimenting on how to build a melody to harmonize with another melody and realized then that I would be a soloist, or a scientist. To be a section man and just play parts would not be possible; my ear could hear too many possibilities to ignore them. I have known men go to pieces when confronted with the challenge of creating a solo, and the intensity of the demand of being a soloist has put an end to more than a few musical careers, the way some pilots lose nerve after a crash. It is all to do with confidence built upon knowledge: true inspiration is always informed. On the other hand, many people cannot face even speaking to a group, and yet can play improvised solos without hesitation.

We would go to almost any lengths to get hold of material if we couldn't find it on record or hear it on the radio. Not everyone had a gramophone then, and hardly anyone had a tape recorder so we depended upon our ears - listening to the radio and listening to our models play in person. That was not always so easy because we were under age and couldn't get into bars and clubs; so we would listen outside, and memorize what we heard. For instance, Karl wanted to hear his hero, Lionel Hampton, who was appearing in one of the local ballrooms. Too young to go in legitimately, he climbed onto the roof of the place. And from that vantage point, he listened with total concentration, like a juvenile spy, to the Lionel Hampton band's arrangement of Flying Home, memorizing as much of it as he could, and sang it to himself over and over on his way back to his bedroom where he jotted down all that he could recall and filled in the rest. Then he wrote out the parts for the kids' band. We had to be resourceful and use our ears, because there wasn't a second chance. A solo I played on Flying Home is one of my first recordings, a hybrid of Ben Webster and Coleman Hawkins and yet neither of them and not much of me either. We were at the Pasadena Civic ballroom and the performance was recorded and transmitted by the Mutual Radio Network. It's still around somewhere, a curiosity for historians, a keepsake for an old man. There's another one on a Jane Powell movie sound track, *Song of the Open Road.* All before I was seventeen. I wonder about recordings. Maybe it's better to select the best and throw away the rest.

We just happened to be born at a time when this was all new and happening on our doorstep. Audiences gave us standing ovations: no group of kids had ever been in the position to do this kind of thing. And the war was on: kids filling the breach was heart warming. There was some cause for hope in that energy, enthusiasm and zest for life, and the band swung on.

chapter seven **apple honey**

I am confused. All the fuss and admiration. It's a nuisance. I'm curious about what makes a dance hall crowd hear out a solo and roar their approval so you can no longer hear what you're playing. In classical recitals, the audience will wait until the end of a piece. Is it that, because the music is spontaneous, then the response must be spontaneous or that music has become the same as a dramatic touch down, simply a momentary thrill? I arrive home and the noise is still ringing in my ears. The musician doesn't need it; the audience needs it. Why? What's missing in their lives that something can literally lift them onto their feet and make their hands move together until they hurt, and cheer as if at some rare victory. This is not being ungracious or boorish, and I accept the applause without deference, but it leaves me ill at ease. Folk treat me differently, like I have something they admire, wish they had, if they had it then they would be happier, better people, not that, they do not want it anyway, somehow too much trouble and it touches some part of them that doesn't want to be awoken, and the applause may arise from that brief recognition, burst of rapturous awakening, sudden, ear splitting and brief still ringing in my ears, and they turn away, satisfied with this welding of the soul, spot welding moment in time, turn away, tossing back the last of their drinks, putting on their coats as they reminisce already so close not even an hour past by on a moment so far away and long ago and whose car will they go home in and who will be coming to dinner with whom tomorrow and how's Ephraim or Eliza as the kids pack up their instruments, rosy with the pleasure of being admired and appreciated, and our thin voices, turn away we all do and me then the soloist hearing in my ears wisps of melodies not yet ready to be played, shards of early morning mist, whispers of inventions still out of my reach. It is as if I have opened a door, have had to open a door but not with that intention, unsuspectingly see it and open it to pursue the theme where it leads, but who comes in, who does not see, who hears and turns away, turning down the fleeting impulse to aspire to their own, down the highway that's as it may be and no concern of mine.

A few friends then, each of us already going our own way, Karl already on the road with Jimmy Dorsey, doing his apprenticeship as a professional, on the road, bars, new town every week, and a merciful spell a while longer in a town never seen before and never again. There's an excitement in youth, but then look around the bus or the train and there are guys been doing this for years, with a woman here a woman there, like a fellow on a furlough, transients taking the message to the people, according to the stories that trickle back home and I ask myself is that me I'm looking at twenty thirty forty years from now, a section man, can that possibly be me, section man in a band that's really a travelling business, jesus will that be me, slumped over the steering wheel dead drunk or utterly exhausted on a southern night mid way between gigs life brought up sharp against a tree to be retrieved by a passing good samaritan notifying the world from a wayside phone booth that another genius - "I guess he must have been a muso. His gear's all in splinters. I was driving by and there it was. My name? Yeh, sure, but look I had nothing to do with it, I was just passing by, you understand" - a few friends gone on their way already they have.

Is that the price, to be worn out, full of stuff, full of shit, forever chasing, the indignity of being a commodity in a basement because that's where the rents are cheap and bug infested lodgings so that a man can trade in his muse for never enough unless you join the market and produce tailor made product for public taste for placebos in their ears, I am asking myself what's going on in front of me. Play that again, play it again, the lure of repetition, familiar, all too familiar, did I get this far to just hear a repeat performance of myself or do I go on beyond all that road already travelled, without tricks, humoring an audience? I will never yield to that. I would like to prove this an honorable calling, not white not black music, just all music. If they have ears, let them hear. Who is making distinctions?

There's already a problem about pace and aspiration, in the band now on radio, when the solo is called for, even in rehearsal. Hey stop stop, what are you doing, man, keep in rhythm, keep leaning against the rhythm like that and I can't keep time, man, this is a band, you trying to show us up, leave us behind, go easy, we've got a style of our own so stay in your box. They were pleasant about it, not out to cause offence. We had all heard about what was happening to Bird. They never realized that the man doesn't chose to embark on that flight: my music lifts me there and if I resist I fall to earth. At seventeen you comply.

We had uniforms, costumes or call it what you will, so that the Teenagers were identifiable as an outfit, had identity. We looked like Austrian yodellers, small high cut lapels and an emblem. Every time I put that jacket on it felt hysterically funny, hardly my preference in rituals, a parody of the concert pianist in his long tails, flicked up just before he sits down at the grand and then shoots his cuffs. But we did look organized and confident - how the machinery loves confidence because, in the market, confidence outsells competence - and arrived well presented and on time.

This was Hollywood the fantasy and we were learning the game. It has appeal. The money we were earning still at school, enough to buy a Cadillac, passable condition, enough to create an image, look like we'd made it. Yes, we got mobility. The profile, learning the profile for the omnivorous camera, which side of the face looks most becoming, caught up in the publicity machine and to perpetrate the image giving out 10 x 8 personality shots to whoever with my love signed Warne Marsh, all of seventeen and a half years of clean cut middle class well-groomed presentable photogenic white articulate college material, everything going for us. It was a gas and I tried to stay out of it, having to resist pressure from the maternal side that urged make the most of it my you look fetching if not debonair, they all love your solos my how they love your solos, so my progeny deliver forth not hiding like your father. Hiding, I rage a question: hiding? he was incarcerated, shouting, veins pulsing on the side of my neck as I slap her face. Correction: rage is wrong. I just looked down at my feet with a mild indignation through being too little au fait with the truth, too feeble a protest to deserve speech. The woman would have brushed my hair had I not been on my guard and a handkerchief for the top pocket, a dash of elegance that would be a wasted adornment for elegance I do not have.

Recognition, above all, we expected and received, lifted off the treadmill of anonymity, given identity through regular public use of the name to which I am attached, rubbing shoulders with living legends and absorbing fame by association. These, in their way, were the golden years during which life around you made decisions, other people seeing opportunities to reach the market with a competent, gifted collection of young musicians who had put in the hours and were ready to perform alongside the best in the industry and had no misgivings about taking their chances with relish. This was the foundation and it was firm.

Who remembers Hoagy now? Mr. Carmichael - 'Mr. Stardust' - singer, song writer legend and popular entertainer when the choices of mediums were radio and film and records. Such a litany of names, like a rosary of secular music for the scattered congregation, and he was one of the names, with his own show on NBC radio across the nation from the heart of entertainment. Bringing you, live from Hollywood ... how many times have you heard it. It was new then, and captivating and we really were the lucky ones to be on air, even though we had connections, a father who was musical director at the studios, a cameraman at the studios (even if deceased), a cartoonist at the studios, a tutor who was resident composer at the studios, we were well-fed, well-placed, well-motivated, well-versed in the catechisms of success and white and played our hearts out like there was no tomorrow.

I'd say there was no other teenage band of the day that launched so many successful careers in the industry: hardly a week goes by without television showing something in which an alumni from the Teenagers is involved. A forty five year legacy. It was not for me. I'd been pretty well born into Hollywood the fantasy and was not enamored with the prospects: I valued it too highly, this song of myself, and, I ask, I do ask myself questions, is this voice of mine to be trivialized. Silence is preferable to a lie. We are a community of sorts, loosely speaking, and keep contact intermittently over the years, not all of us intent on preserving the continuity of the song by any means, making the connection that will transform the song, breath life into it a while longer. It is important. I did not do it by choice; there was no other way.

Here comes Hoagy, every Monday, in his bulky orange and black coat that reaches down to his ankles, you'd have thought overdressing for a radio studio. There is the clown in him, a personality that goes over well, good strong voice, relaxed, ample confidence as if he has all the time in the world even though the broadcast is carefully programmed to the second. And the kids have rehearsed all the tunes to fit the schedule, and technology is a marvel of punctuality and accuracy but structures experience in a way that is unfaithful and dishonest - all a matter of seconds finally so some have to be done at a slightly faster tempo, solos edited before the day so that the original creation is tampered with, a best fit because the attention span of the congregation is withering, and they're ready to go. The red studio warning light blinks until we see the 'on air' light when the compere gets the show under way with the usual routine welcoming Mr. Carmichael who do we have tonight and all light hearted and a laugh here and there building up to the first tune and if you're ready for this Mr. Carmichael we'll hear the Teenagers, Hoagy Carmichael's Teenagers, ladies and gentlemen, featuring the tenor saxophone of Warne Marsh on Apple Honey. Bird loved that tune.

Forty years on. Bodily in the Penthouse Ballroom of the Holiday Inn on Pico in Santa Monica, emotionally in the memory of the Saturday night dance at the Pasadena Civic, two kids in the band, more than just friends, lean back in their chairs after the reunion dinner of the alumni of those golden years.

"His tone was richer then, not so pipe-like as it became."

"Somewhere between Ben Webster and Coleman Hawkins."

"Yes, and so distinctive all the same. Could he blow!"

"He was my idol. We went to school together, but he was my idol, not Ben or Hawk. My idol was right there beside me in the horn section."

"I remember talking, and he's telling me why he's such a recluse, and just as a matter of fact he says if you're going to master the instrument, you have to have it all under your hands by the time you're 15, 16, no later than that, and he did not want to only master the instrument. At 16, he had it all together. He was right. I didn't have it in me."

"He'd say, don't put me in your way, Bob, you listen to your own thing, you're making me nervous."

"You remember Stan Getz appeared with us once? I heard a story that he and Warne jammed together. Stan was the new name on tenor, no one really cared much for Warne. But he played Stan to a standstill. Guy didn't know what was going on. Like he was saying, well Stan you've got a name and a reputation and contracts and the bossa nova, but, can you really play. I'm glad it wasn't me, that's all."

"Didn't care at all for making a name for himself. I respect that. But what a way to run a career."

"Well, I reckon you've misread him. It wasn't a career. It was his life, every note. He lived it like he played it, out of nowhere, you could never tell what was going to happen. He could have had any career he liked. Wasn't interested."

"Glad it wasn't me."

"There's an opera singer, a dame, gave up singing in public for ten years. Know her? Black woman. Said singing so much in public was going to destroy her voice. The demand of the public, gluttonous. I have a gift, she said, more precious than anything I can receive in exchange. I have a responsibility, that's what she said. He was like that, held the music under his fingers, cherished it like water in an arid world and no sign of rain."

"Never spoke much either."

"The same with words."

"Come on, man, this is making me feel old. Let's blow. Come on, guys, let's blow."

And they blew like there was no tomorrow. Karl on drums, Bags Bagley on bass, Ollie Mitchell on trumpet, Dick Allen on electric piano, Bob Clarke on the real thing, Earl Freeman on alto, Bob Drasnin on clarinet, Bob Hardaway on tenor, at sixty years old, round about, savoring recollections of the romance of cavernous art-deco dance halls entertaining servicemen living it up while Tokyo lay blistered by a collision with the sun, chorus after chorus through the early hours of the morning, high school kids born lucky in Hollywood the fantasy. When we were young and life had few options.

Oslo October 1984

Dear Karl,

thanks for letting me know about the reunion of the class of '44. I'll be in Oslo for a few weeks yet and then back to New York. You'd be surprised at the standards over here and none of that old United States jive; feels like being back home, minus the language. Norwegian is a very lyrical language. Can't understand a word, which doesn't make a whole lot of difference. Give my regards to the boys from the band. You know I'm not much of a social animal and care even less for looking over my shoulder, but I do wish you an evening together that does you all justice. Pop a cork for me, for the memory. Is Andre in LA or Berlin or London? I lose track. Quite a collection, weren't we! Best wishes,
Yours affectionately.

W.M.

ps. Could you do me a favor and call Gerry, let her know I'm fine. I'm never awake at the right time to ring from here. Thanks. You know how it is.

chapter eight **strike up**

Life calls the changes and we call the tune. In the fall of 1945, after the end of the war and a month before I turned eighteen, I enrolled at the University of Southern California in Los Angeles, to study for a Bachelor of Arts with a major in music. There was the appeal of joining a professional band and going on the road, if only to escape from Hollywood, but I had heard enough to put me off that route, not so much because of the lifestyle - although, as I was accustomed to comfort, one nighters in strange beds was a romance I could pass up - but because, after almost three years of playing big band arrangements, I had an instinct that my voice didn't fit the environment. I always felt thwarted: it was too easy. The alternative was to find employment in the studios. I'd done two movie jobs by then and spent hours in the studios with Mr. Carmichael, and studios were not for me. (It is strange how the future often walks across ones path in the present. A tenor player I joined up with some ten years later recalled how he used to listen to me on his car radio, playing on the Carmichael show, while he was on his way to the Hollywood Canteen - "I could recognize you even then.")

If it came to a choice between using the music as an ingredient that was to be shaped and determined by a format - processed music - and receiving a salary or not playing at all, then I might decide not to play at all. At nearly eighteen years old, the dilemma I was in was not so clear, so, by default and being prevailed upon, I opted to study. Rather like my father's assumption that I would go to Cal Tech, there was now an assumption that, white and well-to-do and gifted and bright more so than the average, I would excel academically and maybe find myself on the MGM payroll and be seen in an Oldsmobile with power steering before too long, in which I could escort my mother to opening nights. She would have loved that. Then I could marry a girl with connections, maybe an actress. Nothing was said directly. It never was. I listened to Bela Bartok and studied the theory of advanced harmonic structure and produced exercises in composition. In the evening I would listen to jazz on Central Avenue and couldn't decide where my allegiances lay. I was studying classical clarinet - there wasn't that much classical saxophone material - and reading theories. But we never played live. It was all paperwork, etudes and theory. This was a very confusing situation for a young man passively expecting an entirely different treatment. The one who had shown signs of promise as a competent soloist was sitting at a desk taking notes, and copying notes off the scores.

I listened to Bach and I listened to Bela Bartok and I listened to the guys on Central Avenue and I was in a dilemma. What was it about these men, and the models I had taken in jazz, like Tex Benneke, Ben Webster and Coleman Hawkins, that made such an impression on me that my present situation is without substance? I feel like I have been left out of consideration. Having trained for the past 8 years, why I am studying at all? Well, there is nothing else to do, except maybe give up the music altogether. There is the white school of music which is studied in institutions in which music is read like history, and there is the black school of music in which the music is heard and is relevant to the present. I am fitted to neither of them and hover on the fringes of both. What are my options? I could perform in a classical orchestra where the only liberty is interpretation - there is something sacrosanct about the extant score. The composer is obviously not insisting on these particular notes (he's dead), but the preservers of the archives are. I do not mean to say that the music is not valid; it is simply not my music. I believe I can compose, though my way of 'composing' is on the instrument. What I can hear does not yet have a context, so for the time being I simply practice, in my room, hour after hour until my body and the instrument learn to become one, so that I can play instantly what I hear, what I feel, and without hesitation. I am far from that, still not at ease with myself. I asked myself, why do Bach and Bartok and Hawkins convince me that my present has no substance? They had discipline and they had form, and the content of their music, I mean their content, transcended the forms they inherited. We are all inheritors. Bach used themes from children's songs and his precursor Buxtehude, Bartok used themes from Hungarian folk songs.

I have not learned to sing. Who will teach me to sing at USC? We are not taught to sing: we are taught to read. Bach was a man with a huge depth and fineness of feeling through his faith; Bartok carried in him the song of his people. I do not have the churches and choirs of Germany, nor do I have the folk songs of Hungary. I am the son of a Hollywood cameraman and a violinist who could play any song that a scene demanded, but could not bring herself to play what her own feelings prompted. Since I do not have a faith such as Bach had, nor a people, I, a son of America America, have only my own voice, but I do not have a context.

My options? Could I then mock my self and perform on cue in the studios of NBC or MGM or 20th Century Fox, a session man, knowing that is not the best that I can do? Shall I then abandon myself, and learn the parts for arrangements to be repeated in one dance hall after another to while away the early morning hours for shift workers and servicemen and other dancers enthralled by the popular themes and attentive only to the rhythm, a section man, given occasional freedom on a solo, a bird let out of a cage on a long or short piece of string? Or shall I play the way I am the way it is from time to time? I will not be a journeyman, a musical journalist. My knowledge requires more of me than that, and yet sometimes, sitting here listening to a talk about harmonic structure as if it had nothing to do with life on Spade Alley, nothing to do with my life, sometimes I believe I am without substance, a painter without a canvas, and with time on my hands, arrested in shallowness.

End of first semester and home for Christmas.

I must be honest. I call it shallowness and yet this way of life has the substance of novelty and privilege and leisure, a euphoric idleness in contrast to the often intense activity of the previous years. And, although I am very much contained by my own privacy, I learn the ways of composition.

"As a further step, the composer may begin writing accompanying parts to soprano lines which he himself has written in imitation of his models. Gradually his mind will acquire the ability to direct a phrase which starts in the tonic to the dominant, mediant, submediant, or other destinations, as well as to extend it to any desired length. It is then that he will understand that if he focuses his attention on a definite key and beats mentally in a chosen meter, musical images will be set in motion in his mind, and the entire musical texture generated in this way. It is extremely important to practice these exercises in all keys and all rhythms so that the greatest degree of fluency may be attained. The importance of daily practice also cannot be overemphasized, for without it the bridge established between the conscious and the creative unconscious by technical exercise is soon blocked off by non-musical associations. Just as the daily ritual and prayer, as related to the intuitive realization of deity, is that of preserving the thread of connected thoughts which lead to the intuition itself, so the function of daily technical practice, as related to musical composition, is that of maintaining free the inroad to that corner of the mind from which the music comes.

As the composer continues to work exercises in imitation of his models he will be surprised to find that along with the thousand subtleties of technique he will absorb from his masters, he will discover the personal materials of his own art. From these experiences he will gradually accumulate the technical stuffs of a private creative world, possessing capabilities of change and expansion according to his expressive needs."

I value being heard: I do not value being seen. The only recognition I looked forward to was the recognition of another who could know that this song was not the result of a gratuitous inspiration, but that it was the result of effort and knowledge and deliberate experiment which created space for inspiration, a kindred spirit who could accompany me on the journey. Even the company of someone not a musician but capable of bearing witness. I certainly had no wish to travel alone.

I was alone. At my desk I was alone. In the Teenagers I was alone, to all intents and purposes much the same as the other kids, but all the time I could hear more than what I played, and as I listened to the others I could hear what could have been, an endless variety, and I was alone; I was never satisfied, and my peers, it seemed to me, were satisfied. My horizon would always be those melodies I was not yet able to catch, only because I was not yet competent and did not know myself well enough. They were still abstract, notions, notations in emergent feeling only. I am young. Just a kid. All I know is my instrument, Hollywood, dance halls and ballrooms, a little geography and science, the streets of LA where white kids were presumed not to venture, and a lack of future options. None of the available options offer very much to me. Just a kid.

That is what I mean by shallowness; the absence of a true companion in the love of the music. I read about the life of Bartok, and understand even now that there is a price to pay, and wonder if I have it in me to pay that price. After all, I have never been hungry against my will, have never considered not buying what I needed, and read of the poverty of Mozart and Bartok. What causes that poverty? Time. To create something totally mine, totally without a hint of imitation, totally honest, something that transforms the existing music into a new music, that touches the human spirit and eliminates black and white, that reaches for the finest song the human voice can sing, time is the main resource. There is no time for anything except relentlessly to explore my ignorance, my fears, my humors, my proof, knowing that it will never be finished. I never thought it would be, and I am unable to set out. So, mercifully in shallowness, I am in my second semester, a freshman at USC.

"I knew then that it was no use saying anything, no point at all. Yes, I did speak to him about it, because I was not pleased. It was not a choice of my making. The crowds loved him. You should have heard them, close to ecstatic, how they shouted for more, really brought the house down and him no more than seventeen. My God, forgive me, I was proud of my boy. Those places, huge places, full of servicemen and pleasure seekers of all kinds, and all the famous names, Frank Sinatra and the Dorseys, I did not like being there but couldn't resist listening and then drive him home in the car. I didn't want him going with the women you could see idolized him. He'd sit beside me. Many sons wouldn't at that age. I was saying that I knew he loved the music, and that he would be a soloist. He used to correct me about that Not a soloist, an improviser. Either way, I did not like his prospects as a jazz musician, they were all so poor, and did not live a healthy life. He didn't share much with me, oh a letter - he did not like to phone - and I didn't ask questions. I don't think he was happy. I can't imagine he was happy. And I always said there was a home for him and he need go short of nothing, he only had to ask. Sometimes he did, when there was nowhere else to turn to."

The student has just come home. His mother is setting table for supper.

"There's a letter on the table."

"Thanks."

He takes off his jacket and hangs it over a chair, glancing down at the envelope.

"It's government mail. Not been in any trouble have you?"

"I didn't think so."

He takes the instrument case to his room, and then goes to wash his face at the kitchen sink, and comes back into the dining room.

"I wish you'd use the bathroom to wash."

He sits down in the chair with his jacket on it, picks up the envelope, studies the front, and turns it over to look quickly at the back.

"I don't think I want to open this."

He opens the letter with a knife, puts the knife back on the table which is set for dinner, unfolds the letter.

"What is it?"

He reads the letter again.

"Well?"

"It's my draft papers. I've been drafted. Induction's next week."

"Has no one told them the war's over?"

"I'm sure the army knows that."

He places the sheet of paper back on the table, crosses his legs, right foot on his left knee, and taps a rhythm on the table with the fingers of his right hand.

"Well, you don't look like a soldier boy to me. You've only just started your studies."

"Looks to me like I've just finished."

The woman pulls up a chair and sits down beside him, putting her hand on his forearm. She is anxious.

"What will you do?"

"Pack, and go."

He smiles in anticipation.

"You don't have to. First Oliver and now you. No!"

Agitated and beginning to lose control, she moves away from him.

"I will have our attorney do something. You could finish your studies, if you like, or we could go away."

He gets up quietly and, unable to look at her, starts to leave.

"You don't have to be like this."

"We could go to Europe. Mae would help. I have the money. What am I going to do, here, on my own?"

He turns around, still unable to meet her gaze.

"There's Gloria and Owen still."

"You won't listen?"

He leaves the dining room, goes into the library and shuts the door firmly but not aggressively.

"Warne!"

Marsh. Private. Bandsman. Special Services Band. Fort Lee, Virginia. Height 6ft 1in. Weight 11st 9lbs. Special marks, none. Date of birth October 26 1927. Caucasian. Musician. Home State California. Next of kin mother. Father deceased. You, over there. Next. One set fatigues. One set dress uniform. Identity tag. Two pair black boots. Polish until they're the finest, you won't need a mirror. One tenor saxophone remains the property of the United States Army, at all times, ya'unnerstan. Show it due care and attention. Sign here, here, and here and move out. Uniform, costume, call it what you will, like Austrian yodellers, now bit players as raw recruits in a military guise in a world unfurling like a banner in a shifting wind. God bless you Uncle Sam.

Yesterday in California cosseted by the Pacific Ocean, pampered by the ease and affluence of Hollywood the fantasy where the child is choking. Presently on the army cot in a barracks in old Virginia of the founding, green blankets fit for horses, and the top sheet turned back in regulation manner, on my back, hands behind my head feeling the change in climate, all of eighteen years and six months out to sea, born on the West Coast ferried to the East coast against the Atlantic Ocean by the government in whose service I reside, two sets of uniform - ceremonial and regular - both in the locker in the deserted barracks of St Petersburg over whose cobblestones I dance at night in a rare dream, learning to darn socks and rub out finger prints left on the glossy black peak of a flashy hat. In summation, all background musings of my own man in answer to questions I am asked, answers always courteous and predictably careful to skirt the issues personal and of no concern to anyone any more.

part two

all god's chillun

chapter nine **battle hymn of the republic**

Lennie was born in the Italian quarter of Chicago in 1919, at the height of a flu epidemic. From the age of four he was finding his way around the piano and remembers piecing together The Stars and Stripes Forever. An attack of the measles in his sixth year weakened his already failing eyesight and by the time he was eight years old, he was in a one-room school for handicapped with kids from seven to eighteen years old, all learning side by side. He excelled.

At nine years old, his parents sent him to a state institution for the sightless, in a small Illinois town some 200 miles from home. Being unable to see was the only criterion for admission. The place contained all manner of children, from the near mad, to no-hopers, to those who were going places. It was run like a reform school out of a Dickens novel. Lennie excelled, especially at mathematics, saxophone, clarinet, piano and cello. At eleven years old he had set up his own band and before long was playing at local bars: he knew all the popular songs inside out. Finally his music teacher placed him at the American Conservatory in Chicago, where he completed the four-year degree course in three years, including all forms of composition, from symphonies to dance-band charts and jazz string quartets, and then did a year of his Masters degree before leaving to play professionally. He was a familiar sight in the black ghetto clubs of Chicago, where the presence of white people was almost as unthinkable as spitting in church. Color didn't have any bearing on him: you could tell more from tone of voice than you could from complexion of skin. He did not have sight, but he could hear. And what he heard was a future which embraced the classical discipline and form, and the innovation, energy, currency and the personal voice of jazz. He could hear it in his head.

He put aside the tenor sax that had been his main instrument, in order to concentrate on piano, which he did to such effect that he was playing Art Tatum pieces - "rifle them off" is how he put it - faster and more accurately than Art Tatum could play them. There was nothing he couldn't play.

His music was completely new and made absolutely no attempt to pander to prevailing tastes or vested interests. This did not endear him to the owners of clubs where jazz could be heard. He even got paid on condition he did not play. One club owner interrupted him at the end of the first half of the first set. "Look Lennie, you're not to take this personally at all, I like you, you play real well, but people here think your music stinks. They wanna hear the old stuff. Yeh, sure I know it's the old stuff, but, Lennie, look, I gotta make a buck. We don't get no govamunt subsidies for promotin culture. This is downtown Chicago for chrissake, not an Ivy League lounge room. Here, that's the three days I owe you for. That's good money - you only bin here two owas. No hard feelings? You promise me? I knew it. You're a gentleman. Give my love to your wife. She's a sweetie." Another guy came up to him at the end of a session. All the customers had already gone. "I'm telling you, Lennie, I've had a bellyful of musos and I'm going to open up in a more secure line of business, a deli. You can count on people being hungry."

Market forces. Different today perhaps than they were over the centuries, but life, for all its liberations, still did not welcome changes in form with open arms. Changing the form demanded effort and intelligent listening, which was too much to expect in a bar in Chicago in 1945. And it's fair enough: if you want to make a buck, you'd better make a buck, and the surest way to make a buck was to be fashionable; fiddle about with the details but keep your hands off the form. Bartok was already dead after spending much of his life in America in abject poverty. Them's the breaks. America liked to back winners and winners were popular.

In the summer of 1946, a year after marrying a singer called Judy Moore, Lennie was invited to New York and the two of them went. They had already heard about him in New York and they were going to hear some more. He was an articulate and very determined man, especially determined not to take crap from anyone, and in regular letters to magazines he had already made known his opinions about owners of clubs who were only interested in music if it promoted bar sales, and about owners of clubs who never would give a thought to the finer points, like acoustics, and some degree of comfort for the performers; in short, he wanted to know when anyone was going to show a little respect.

Because night clubs did not offer an environment in which musicians were allowed to perform at their best, and because record companies wanted sales more than they wanted to discriminate - let the public be the arbiter - the only place to play freely was in private. This gave rise to rehearsal bands. Lennie had assembled one in April of 1945, a sextet. To play well together, jazz musicians were no different than other musicians: they had to put in the hours together, to get to know each other, because the better they knew each other's musical thinking and feeling, the richer their work would be. And before you appeared in public, you rehearsed. It made so much sense people had been doing it for centuries. So they rehearsed until all hours, and never appeared in public because there was nowhere to perform where they could create their best. Generally speaking the best happened in private. There are some recordings, for what they are worth, and they are not in the hands of the record companies.

Lee had been playing publicly around Chicago since he was 15, with the Teddy Powell band and the Claude Thornhill band in which he started to learn bebop. He had also become one of Lennie's pupils in Chicago and soon followed him to New York. He was a flash eighteen year old jewish kid who happened to be playing alto saxophone at the same time as Charlie Parker who, at twenty four, was giving jazz a new definition almost singlehanded. Lennie, at twenty seven and nobody's fool, got to know him.

There must be some explanation. I owe you one. My wife, talking about her. But there isn't one. We liked the same kind of books, enjoyed scrabble. Scrabble was an obsession. So was chess. The challenge of endless opportunities, reducing with the passing of time. And the playing of the music made you happy. We had fun. On times my style of living caused you some embarrassment, made you wonder about the wisdom of your agreement. Does it matter that I would go to the store in my fur lined slippers? Not everyone does that. But does it matter? Not at all. You didn't mock me for it - though you didn't let it go without remarking on it - or say I won't be seen dead with you in those slippers. And we made out, got by, with help. Dependable is not a good description of me.

You were dependable, always. Dependable you. So there must be an explanation. And there isn't one. I could not have asked for more complete acceptance; you never once thwarted me or laid any kind of blame. So that's not it. If you had played too, that might have made a difference. Yet I doubt that. It is something else. There is no excuse, so there needs to be some explanation. Come's a time when there's no help in these matters. And then I play. That is what I am here for. Even in art there is danger, like the maidens on the rock for Ulysses.

It is so personal, the music, always without final form. I play for the glory of God, I said to you by way of explanation, because I seek infinity and look ridiculous in my fur-lined slippers on my way to the store for some bread or a toy for one of the kids, or somewhere else to seek help in other things that, how well I know, provide no help nor answers nor explanations of any kind, yet they do put off the ignorance, prevent close scrutiny, but in such short shrift that the dose must be repeated with interminable and welcomed frequency. Not a man wholly of my own making by any means, I aid and abet, a contributing factor for sure without even knowing how at the time.

In the living, it all happened through a never predictable sequence of coincidence, choice, collusion and absentmindedness. In the playing of my brief glorias, I divine infinite variation in which every note has purpose, relevance, consciousness and aspiration. Were these notes you and me, we would be in paradise or at least well en route. Instead we sit looking into our cups of instant coffee between breaks in conversation remote and exposed amongst the sparse secondhand furniture after the kids have gone to sleep, hoping for a spontaneous explanation.

I will try again another day. Perhaps you will hear the words then that even I cannot unearth, an archaeologist with broken finger nails. Perhaps what I have left behind will have to suffice, despite my sure knowledge that it has not been and will not be the sufficient explanation that I owe you.

Born in the cradle of Hollywood, white and carried along by the tide of the American dream, never felt the rough edges of loss of dignity, in a social sense, and hardship was as personally known as a scene in a movie - it was something you saw. As she said, I only had to ask: trouble was, I did. Reared to presume sufficiency, I was finding that insufficient. I had been inured.

Always contradictions. At college there was all the time and all the facilities but never the occasion to respond personally. Here, in Fort Lee - I mean, the word 'fort' says we're still in cowboy and Indian territory - my presence here demanded by regulations, I once again have all the time and all the facilities. This is a camp for bandsmen, because the army needs bands, for ceremonial occasions, and we practice all day. There's no marching, no training to use a gun, just practice and keeping the place neat and clean and peeling potatoes and washing dishes. It's a joke. We're all immaculate in our white t-shirts showing at the neck under sand colored shirts, brown belts around sand colored pants. This is the first time in their lives some of these guys have been well-dressed and clean and well-fed, every day. I have to ask why the same generosity can't be shown in other situations, why it has to be reserved for institutional life.

And there's a strong camaraderie because all most of us want to do is play. We're not playing what we want to play, but it's good practice. And at night, we do what we want, in our private sessions, something that didn't happen at college. And friendships are made that will last a lifetime. Courtesy of the American government which won't give a cent to a musician out of uniform or outside some kind of institution. So I conclude that the purpose of music is not understood and that I'm not going to learn anything serious here, except the discipline of practice and the art of sleeping on an army cot.

Teachers of jazz were pretty well unheard of in those days. It was all picked up as you went along. And because of its origins, I mean because it was the creation of black people, the form was not taken seriously, not the way white art was taken seriously. How could you take black art seriously when black people were not taken seriously? Unless, of course, they were popular. Then you could make an exception, grudgingly, on the face of it. Being popular was almost as good as being white. So if you were to teach jazz, what were you going to do, teach people to be negro?

Scene:

One of the rehearsal rooms at Fort Lee. A young man who would still look in place in high school, in regulation army casuals, on his own. It's a hot summer evening and the windows are open. A manuscript pad and pencil are on the table, beside which is a music stand with nothing on it. There are some thirty chairs in the room, in untidy formation from the last band practice. The soldier gets out his trumpet and an envelope. He takes a letter out of the envelope, unfolds it, flattens it out over his knee, and puts it up on the stand. It blows off. He puts it back, and secures it. He concentrates on the contents of the letter, like someone studying.

He then runs over a few scales, in various rhythms and patterns. After that, he plays the melody of Round Midnight, several times, each time evoking more feeling from the melody, and each time in a different key. He then sings the words of the song quietly, with not so much confidence as he showed on his instrument, struggling to find notes that are outside the immediate range of his untrained voice. There is a stark contrast between this now vulnerable human being and the austerity of the army camp. His singing is sincere for all its flaws, bringing a touch of femininity to the scene.

He then sings the first phrase of the melody, followed by a harmonic variation on his trumpet. He repeats this process several times as well, until he finds a phrase that satisfies him. He repeats it again on his trumpet, and then writes it out on the manuscript pad.

Another soldier has been watching and listening at the doorway. While the trumpet player is writing out his phrase, the second soldier stubs out a cigarette, and comes in. The trumpet player looks up, startled.

"Shit, man, you scared me."

"Some soldier!"

"Where are the guys?"

"Chasing arse. What are you doing?"

"Ah, just fooling around."

"Hey man, I've been listening. You're not fooling around. What you up to?"

"Just my lesson." He's apologetic.

The second soldier sees the letter on the stand, picks it up and reads it, appearing to have forgotten the presence of the other man.

"How did you get a hold of this guy?"

"Friend in Chicago told me. Does jazz tuition by correspondence."

"You serious? Who is he?" He points to the signature on the letter.

"Pianist. Used to play classical. Now he's doing jazz in New York and taking students. Knows Bird and Pres. Great country this.

Bird's a junkie and Pres an alcoholic. Two of the country's leading musicians, both broke and who gives a shit."

The second soldier reads the letter again. In anticipation of having an ally in a fellow student, the first soldier asks, almost reticently, "Interested?"

The second soldier puts the letter back on the stand.

"That's the first thing I ever read that ever made sense. How long you been doing this?"

"Ah, couple of months already."

"New York you say. I don't like doing correspondence but how old's the guy?"

"Mid twenties, and he's blind."

"What's his address?"

o———+———

The letters were too slow in coming. For the first time in my life I could feel enthusiasm, had heard a hint of something most definitely for me. New York was too far away. The army looks so efficient, so inflexible, and yet it only takes a good operator to get the system to respond in a delightfully helpful way. I wanted to get to New York, or at least a lot closer to it than Virginia. It was Fred who came up with the idea.

"It's simple. Leave it to me."

"How in hell you going to do that?"

"I'll get myself transferred to administration. Don't worry."

He got himself transferred. Then he simply located my file, and wrote on it "Transfer to Fort Monmouth, New Jersey" and forged the appropriate signature. Within a couple of weeks I was in New Jersey, a short drive from New York City. From time to time, life conspires in your favor, and this conspiracy was the single most important favor of my life; for that, credit where credit is due, I have to say God bless America. But to be honest, it took me a year or so to realize just what had happened. So much of life is hindsight; so much of the calling is reading ahead.

chapter ten **52nd street**

I took the train to New York, changed at Penn Station, found out where to catch the train to Flushing and before long was sitting in a crowded compartment looking out over a city I had never seen before. All I cared for at that moment was a slip of paper with a name and address on it, and my instrument. Everything was superfluous, especially the blur of the city, every moment no more than a shortening gap between me and the address in Flushing. So foreign was the place that I may as well have been in another country. There were no orange groves or swimming pools and no lots. There were tenements and the elevated, and people starting to dress down after winter.

I was nineteen and no doubt looked as conspicuously out of town as I felt. Curiosity and intrigue drew me on. You only know what you're looking for when you find it, and I was willing to take the chance that what had made sense to me in the letter was going to be confirmed by meeting the man face to face. I had never spoken to a blind man before. I had never made this kind of journey to a teacher before, and the whole of my life up to this day, this train ride, receded like a mirage. And then it struck me, quite forcibly: this was the first time I had ever been alone, finding my own way with no input from anyone else.

The street was not very far from Flushing station. In fact it was all too close to the railway line. I looked at it, a small tenement block, so far from Laurel Canyon, even after the flood. I had never been inside such a building before, and had no notion of what to expect on the inside. I would adopt the attitude of the man waiting in there: it would be as if I could not see anything. That felt good, because I would better concentrate on him.

I was in there for an hour. The aftermath took some getting used to. I was neither elated nor disappointed. I was moved, that's the only way to put it. He shocked me, took me by surprise. Perhaps the authority with which he spoke; straight forward, to the point, unequivocal. He said he did not teach but maybe he could show me something about myself. That came as a shock since no one had ever been that blunt with me, no one had actually addressed me directly like that. Then he asked if I had brought my instrument and I said yes I had, and then he said well you do not need to bring it next time, but since you have it there, play me the harmony you have composed in the style of whoever you choose. I mean there was nothing petrifying about this; I had played on radio, in dance halls, practiced for hours every day for years, and thought I knew what I was doing. But there was something so direct and personal in his approach that I could not respond straight away.

I felt that he had revealed an unsuspected shortcoming: I knew how to play; the problem was I did not know the why of what I was playing . And then he said, if you are serious you can come back, and added that I should listen to Bird and Pres, in person as often as I could. I asked what he meant by serious, and he replied that what he meant was that he wanted me to be completely honest with myself and respect my craft. That was it. I didn't know what he meant, but I nodded. Nodding of course signified nothing to him. He smiled as if he knew my face. It was late in the afternoon, yet he was wearing a deep plum colored dressing gown. Had he been sick? He saw me to the door and didn't wait more than a second or two before closing it behind him.

I had not kept up with him. Unaccustomed to such energy and plain speaking in so few words. Try this he said and try it I did and the difference was plain. He listened, intently, serious and attentive. Serious? Could I be? And welcomed. You don't have to say much. The first human being to whom I spoke and was heard. The train stopped every few minutes and people brushed passed me but I was still in the room. I cannot hear you, he said, you are telling me what you have picked up by hear say. Do you wear other people's clothes? Of course not. Acquire knowledge and intuition, he said. You may come back. It is important, to show respect. Why have human beings played music for thousands of years? It is not to make a living, that is not the purpose.

52nd Street was to contemporary jazz what Basin Street was to dixieland or Broadway to theater or Hollywood to fantasy. There was an excitement just saying 'Let's go up to 52nd Street', and that's what we did as often as we could, to listen to Bird and Pres, sitting within feet of men who had mastered their art in this new music. There is a beautiful informality about jazz, a generosity that is missing from classical, in my experience. You can turn up to a club on 52nd Street, and, if you can cut it, you join in with whoever's there. A few times I sat in with Lennie and Lee and with Bird, just to get the feel of things. They were heady days. And Pres was my man. He never wasted a note, every note selected with the same care as if he was picking the choicest fruit, nothing second grade was good enough. Bird opened my ears, Pres opened my heart and Lennie, well, Lennie became my closest friend.

After spending an evening at a club on 52nd Street, I'd stand on the street and wonder what was going to happen. There was a whole new range of options now. And then someone told the army that the war was over, and the GI's were discharged. It was like reaching the end of the line, suddenly finding yourself entering a world that is totally new, uncharted, enchanting and disturbing, with my instrument at my feet on a platform at Penn station, half expecting that someone would walk out of the crowd and address me by name and give me an explanation, or at least directions. I felt that, with no effort on my part, I had been thrust through all the constraints that had withheld me and even so I was exhausted and invigorated.

I became very homesick. Life was beginning to demand decisions from me and I needed to go back to the familiar and figure things out . If I went back to the west coast, college was due to start and I could re-enrol and pick up where I left off. I was all undecided. It was a question of survival. How would I survive in New York? In a tenement block beside a railway track? I didn't know if I was that serious. You know, sometimes someone can be offering you exactly what you need, and for some reason you can't see it. Lennie was like that, making me an offer I didn't have the courage or the understanding to take up. Yet what else was I going to do?

Lennie and Bird and Pres and New York had, together, brought me up sharp, and I had to ask the question, What are you doing with the rest of your life? Well, I was born in California; worse than that, I was nurtured in the cradle of Hollywood and it is not easy to be serious about life and art in such a cultural desert. New York and New Jersey and Virginia had given me my first taste of European culture, about which I knew nothing whatsoever until now. It was natural that I returned to Laurel Canyon. They were surprised when I knocked on the front door: I had not remembered to let them know I was on my way. Nothing in the house had changed and the workshed was still locked: I could have been gone for a single night. They wanted to know what it had been like in the army and there was nothing I could put to words so we just got on with things. I was persuaded to re-enrol at USC but never showed. For days I lay about and revisited one memory after another, a bee in a field of flowers in summer, heard again one conversation after another, studied one solo after another, always ending up on the train back from Flushing sitting opposite a man in a deep plum colored dressing gown, on his way, he said, to perform at Carnegie Hall because there was so much more space there than in his tenement flat.

Lennie explained the dilemma along these lines, more or less:-

Classical music started off in church and made its way into the Courts of Europe, where the guys had money to support it, and it always drew on the themes of common songs. Jazz started off in the streets and made its way into dance halls and bars, where guys sold alcohol to make the profit to support it, but it wasn't long before it became a way of stimulating trade, which is not what music is about. It's not possible to create serious music in bars, so for a serious musician that can't be a long term option. Jazz was the first new music for hundreds of years, and once again drew on common song, the astounding outpouring of the American writers of the early twentieth century. But no matter how new the music, the foundation of creating has to be knowledge and intuition. And knowledge implied understanding the history, by listening to the music of the last three hundred years at least and figuring out what's going on and then using that knowledge to create something new.

Jazz has done an amazing thing. It has liberated the individual from the composer. With jazz, which is improvisation, the individual creates his own music and it's not written down: its heard, through knowledge and intuition. Further than that, it has brought about a situation where a group of people can all create at the same time completely in their own individual manner and yet in harmony with each other. Now that doesn't happen from casual acquaintance: it happens through knowing each other, musically speaking, being at ease with each other and respecting each other, and, finally, inspiring each other. That means you have to spend time together, a lot of time, like people used to, and that's very demanding. And why is the individual voice so important? Because we have a world around us that constantly bullies us to 'fit in', to copy, to imitate, intimidates us so that we do not have the courage any longer to express our own feelings freely and competently. We have built around us a system that makes so-called stars of the very few and audiences of the many. It was not always like that and it's very unhealthy that it is like that. It's a terrible weakness and we're paying the price.

Lennie said: "This cultural revolution of jazz, Bird is the originator of all that. Let me put it to you this way. Number one, Bird was a genius. Whether he'd been born in China, Czechoslovakia or Russia or the United States, whether he'd been white, black or whatever color, he'd have been a great musical genius. That's number one. In the second place, the intelligence, the brilliance that you could sense from Bird, you can hear in the way he put his material together. You see, thousands of people copied every note Bird played, but they could only play it the way he did, except Bud and Fats; in other words, in their brains someplace it was reorganized - that combination of intelligence and intuition. Bird is the originator of the whole scene - I'm talking about music. One of the things people say is that the blacks got together and turned everything around so that whitey wouldn't know what was happening. Which is bullshit.

It all came from Bird who was influenced by Pres, musically speaking. Pres did his great work in 1935 or 36 which is when Bird was fourteen years old and just started. The revolution really started with Louis, through Roy, to Pres. That took time, during the middle and late 30s. But it was in the 40s people began to realize Pres was a great genius. and by then he was deteriorating. Alcohol for one thing. And for another, Bird turned him around. And I talked to Bird about that. I said, Bird, what do you think about Pres? He said, Oh I love Pres, but Pres hates me, in fact Pres threw me out of his room. I don't know whether that's true or not, but that's what Bird told me. And when I hear them together, Pres sounds like he's about to cry.

And then you can hear Bird, on 'Yardbird Suite', sound just like Pres, same kind of vibrato, same kind of punch, same kind of legato attack. And then for a long time we hear people being influenced by Pres and Bird, playing Bird's material with Pres' sound - yeh, I know, that's an oversimplification.

And Bird got put down for years. Black and white people put him down. And you know, it's incomprehensible to me that Bird got his habit when he was fourteen. And I blame society, not only for what they were doing to black people and what they are still doing to black people, but for not either making it legal or helping him, helping him control it, because when it was controlled he was just great. During the 1930s and early 1940s before I came to New York, I used to hang out in the black ghetto in Chicago, which is about the biggest black ghetto you could find and in those days I was the only white person for miles. And one of the things that happened in Chicago was that they wouldn't let Bird into any of the clubs - he was just too far ahead.

I didn't hang out with him, but I saw him a lot and we got along just great. I knew him over the years, eight years from 1947 to 55, and we saw an awful lot of each other. I loved Bird. People say they loved Bird, which is bullshit. There was that dog arse of a funeral of his, a farce. I was one of the pall bearers. And the benefit concert, that was another thing. It was Diz who called me, to tell me Bird had died, and he wanted to put on some concert, and I said no, not some concert: we'll do it at Carnegie Hall. And he said, ok, I'll do it with you. And you know, I couldn't get money - you had to put the money up front for Carnegie Hall or they wouldn't talk to you - I couldn't get the money from anyone for a benefit concert, not from anybody. In the end I put the money up myself and raised $15,000 for his kids. I was alone in my studio when Diz rang, and after that I did something I rarely do, played the blues, for three hours, and out of that came Requiem, a requiem for Bird. And you know, nobody said a word to me about it, especially black people. I think a lot of people were actually glad he was dead, I mean musicians. It's true.

Now, twenty years later, just to survive, it's a question of being commercial. But through the commerce you lose an awful lot so it's not worth it. When it comes to writing music for commercials, like Freddy, then you have to know something's wrong. So I chose to teach. People said I was crazy to turn down so many opportunities to play. But I'm not interested in that way of doing things, so I teach. And almost everybody in the world, except black people, like to say they studied with me (Laughs), so I hear it said.

No, I'm not bitter in any way that I didn't make it, as we say now. No. I had the best opportunity of anyone to make it because I was the only one not copying Bird. (Pause) I just didn't want what was on offer. I've turned down more work than I care to mention, and still do. It's my prerogative. After all, it's my music; I can play my music wherever I want, however I want with whoever I want wearing whatever I want because music means a great deal to me and I won't trade it in.

People generally find that hard to understand, but people generally know so very little. For instance, I have small hands. That surprises people. It doesn't surprise them that I'm blind and play as I do. But the size of your hands has nothing to do with it. First of all it's knowledge and intuition. Then it's to do with the flexibility between the knuckles, how relaxed the musculature is there, that's what makes for the span of the hands. Most people think it's the distance between the thumb and the tip of the pinkie. It's not."

So three new words come into my life: knowledge, intuition and serious. I was twenty and have been brought up sharp and lie for days on my bed waiting for a blind man dressed in a deep plum colored dressing gown to step into view, his forehead as smooth as a white clay mask, eyes closed. Then I hear a voice call out, "You going to lay around here another day?"

chapter eleven **back home again in laurel canyon**

A period of rest. Restless. Look over the land we used to own. Play tennis. Swim. The pool is not well maintained. The way it is and the way it was. Not quite Beverly Hills. The house is eerie, traces of old smells from another lifetime. Mother plays bridge. I, saxophone. Laugh, the incongruity of this woman and my current activities; laugh which I do on occasions. More at home with a smile though, ruminative. That elusive smile of someone preoccupied, a smile that has time on its side. This is an exceedingly complex house. We reminisce. And that time, you remember, how could you have done that, your very own brother, and he the younger one, unable to fend you off. On the lawn, pinned down at the wrists and ankles, your own brother on the croquet lawn pinned him down with the croquet hoops. The earth must have been soft. He cried for mercy when you turned on the sprinklers. Spreadeagled like the human target for a knife thrower, only not spinning, except in his own panic, and you would not throw the knife. He knew you would not torment him longer than it took you to weary of his impotence. It was not malicious. Calculated. Not to wound or inflict but to assert. Assert what? It required imagination to see the opportunity, I am tempted to commend myself for that flash of inspiration. And a most unnameable anger hidden within such boyhood mischief. Not excusable, all these things you are and you, part and parcel of the human lot. I am talking to myself. How we take pride in our perversity, no longer having the excuse of a wanton youth.

In my recollection of that present I am, at the time of the idyll that was North Hollywood at its face value, I am an ageing man many years hence as I walk, nay glide, serene and silent above the rolling landscape of my history sometimes covered by cloud, other times exposed to me alone the true witness, and can happen upon whatever moment I choose from amongst those hidden or those made public, never one to discuss personal matters, except in general terms, holding to specifics enough to create an outline, a semblance, like the cartoonist who with the skimpiest touch of pen to paper animates an invisible face.

'My mother was a classically trained violinist who played on film sets and at the gatherings of the wealthy members of the Hollywood scene. My father's mother was a tenth generation Brewster, the Pilgrim Father.' In so many words, over and over again, I lay claim to lineage, as becomes the publicist depicting a public image, and the culture that was never present and always a lack. Artifice. That was my attempt at public relations which I never did have the stomach for. The journalist would nod and reflect and publish the stuff because people like to know. But it never appeared that I said know me know my song. Or may be I only thought that. Who's to say? Possibly, very possibly just thought it and left it at that to decline the risk of stimulating a further line of enquiry as to the meaning which people as a whole prefer to have explained rather than be left holding ambiguity. So much unsaid for that very reason and absolutely resisting words, the inchoate stirring of the ever unresolved. It is easier by far to read the visible than to pluck wisdom from the sound of wind passing through the branches, a blind man for a guide. A sincere attempt at public relations it was, believe me, and not faithfully reported, - after all I had nothing to gain, for who will listen the more intently given a few facts that have no bearing. The truth is, the world is deaf with its own noise.

I stake no claims, not having to, since the finest of sound, the purest is as out of earshot as a bird let from a cage, unless you will fly with it, and me an ageing man called upon by he the younger one for the first time in all those years - he had endeavored to summon me but, alas, I had not heard him, absorbed as I was in my own pursuit - and time has stood us on our heads and here, long hence, it is I, the indigent, pinned down the first time, on my public hospital bed, by cardiac arrest, catching sight of the sprinkler above my head and smiling elusively which he interprets as recognition which it is but primarily and essentially of an association I do not deem worthy of mention to him despite his intimate part in the enactment of that moment and how far we have travelled since then and he the caring one and I did not know how much. It is with this purity that I aspired to imbue my voice,in such wise as I could, given the tools at my disposal, gazing at me it is now through the eyes of Owen, the younger, a prince amongst men and I the shabby one.

These months it took to gather breath, mull over the turning of the years, the changes, set myself in context before a future quite without incentives, visit the old haunts, nod to familiar faces concealing lusts and inclinations within the veil of courtesies. I was a well known face in those parts and I suspect many privately whispered their doubts as to whether I would come to any good. Was it not strange that he showed no wish to join the stream of things, opportunities waved under his nose and he pushing them away as a dignitary easing folk out of his way as he walks through a crowd. Did they have doubts? Well, I had doubts and make no judgements.

But credit where credit is due, I was handsome, had presence, did not suffer fools gladly and kept my own counsel. The photograph I have in my hands is some two years old, an early publicity shot. The tenor held across my body looks enormous and my ears are larger than I realized, the left one substantially higher than the right, a blemish I did not notice at the time. Dress shirt, black bow tie, tuxedo, with a graceful cut to the long lapels, hair swept back up off the forehead and my left shoulder lower than the right. All in all, not a symmetrical arrangement. It seems that I am happy, but the half-smile is made by tense lips and there's the look on my face that I'm not enjoying the sitting. I have a long head and a long jaw line tending to pointed. There's an unsureness about my posture and a confidence in it to, noticeably in the way my finger tips are placed on the mother of pearl keys. I could be thinking, 'I'd far rather be playing this thing than holding it like this so don't take too long about it'. I am lean but not thin, and perhaps stoned. There is also the suggestion of someone adventurous, charming, stylish, professional and remote. It is dated three days before my seventeenth birthday, and signed 'To Joy, with all my love'. We were sweethearts. It came to nothing. I am back home in Laurel Canyon, rummaging through my few things. Restless. The perilous ignorance of youth.

It is my eyes which emanate clues as to my whereabouts, pensive without being intellectual, sensitive without proper defence, pupils enlarged, iris clear as crystal, the clarity of an eye of an owl without the stare, washed clean, a proclivity for reflection in those eyes of mine which, looking at them from a place much removed, remind me of the readiness in which I held myself for some greeting from the world yet to declare itself in its true colors, a world changing before your eyes even as you approach what you had set your sights on to see the object of your focus undergoing incessant metamorphosis from which is to be learned that repetition is to ignore the truth beheld, to withstand which is to be like Canute (that much of history I am assured of) stamping his petulant feet at the power of the moon in the rising waters. There is in those eyes of mine the affirmation that I will weave the melody of my self with threads of gold and silver melodies into a constellation of sound forever to hover there a diadem in space. I can even detect hope, a kind of aristocracy without title except that I am alive, a subtle hope. And not the least, I do believe I was feeling pride in my intentions to pursue an honorable calling (the word vocation might be considered cocky). For sure, I am not seeking congratulation. Knowledge and a lot of experience, right from the beginning, mostly self taught initially, never self-deprecating and for sure not a person to pretend false modesty.

"He was truly a great improviser, a genius of improvisation, and he did not realize how great he was. He knew how good he was, but he did not know how great he was."

That was one opinion possibly misquoted. But all these opinions, especially those that regret this or that, are wide of the mark. I mean to say, what does it matter because the music speaks for itself (there was ample opportunity and still is, to listen and draw whatever conclusions seem valid). I mean to say, who gives a shit? The point is, not that this one or that one achieved some relative greatness, whatever that means, but that the music was played like that. That is what is important, and, fact is, the world is deaf with its own noise. But the noise will subside, one way or another, and the evidence is there to be heard, my voice amongst many, for the world needs to hear the finest, and in the end the finest is what is filled with compassion and contrition and tenderness and, through its very intricacy, asserts the wonder of life against all the odds.

I never did plan anything, and these months in LA were no different. It was back down to Central Avenue and to the Downbeat Club, and the Red Feather just out of town, but mainly the old haunt of Spade Alley. Round midnight whenever I felt like it there'd be the chance to blow with Dexter Gordon or Wardell Gray. They were already acknowledged names, but, in the manner of some musicians, not all by any means, they were generous enough to make space for people like myself to test ourselves out, find out whether we could cut it with the best. How else was a young man to learn? It was a privilege.

Having dropped out of college, I needed to earn a living. Well, actually earning a living was not my principal concern, which was to be active regularly rather than just sitting in and becoming a musical vagrant. First it was the Butch Stone band. It was hard for me to take initiative in securing work, and others frequently took it upon themselves to compensate for this deficiency for which I am grateful but in all honesty largely took it for granted. Hal McCusick persuaded Buddy Rich to give me a place in the horn section of his band which was still playing the Palladium Ballroom in 1948, a place where I'd appeared as an adolescent, old haunts revisited, advising me as to how much progress had been made by the music, by me. But even then my style was getting me into difficulties. I was developing a very individual sound, a sound that I could honestly claim as my own, and a very individual use of rhythm, learning how to play across the rhythm and to improvise the rhythmic feel of a piece, a bit like juggling three eggs each one leaving the hand at a different speed. Buddy had problems with all of this, because in a section of horns the idea is that they all play as one. I simply couldn't contain the need to sing with my own voice, and we know already that America does not subscribe to the authority of the individual. My solos seemed to cause some friction also, mainly because I never felt I had finished a solo in one straight chorus, usually too short for me, and being intent on playing what I heard I evidently took up too much time: gradually

I was allowed less and less time to solo and was moved closer and closer to Buddy Rich, who thrived on the sheer physical exercise of drumming. The band went on tour and ended up in New York.

While I had not been able to forget my lessons with Lennie, and the compelling logic of his approach, I had still not come any where near making a deliberate decision about moving to New York or staying put. The easy way of life in California and Laurel Canyon had taken a hold of me. That, and the growing realization that the life of a jazz musician is not a very attractive one and that I was not looking for security of tenure. By the time we arrived in New York, Buddy had moved me right in front of his drums, in the direct line of fire so to say It was more than I could tolerate, the more so because, whenever I did solo, the drums effectively terminated my flight before I had left the ground. From that time on I never did find it easy to get along with drummers. And it was more from a wish to get away from the din than to do anything else in particular that I let Buddy know: thanks, no thanks. He was relieved. I to find myself telephoning Lennie, who said, "I've been expecting you. Come on over. You know where we are", like it hadn't been two days since I was last there. Playing with Buddy was like living at the buffer end of Grand Central Station. Flushing had to be an improvement, musically speaking. I had my pay from Buddy, and the band went its own way. I had a suitcase inherited from my father's estate (never was finally resolved), my saxophone, clarinet (which I held on to as a fall back and because it was refreshing to play a different instrument now and again), some determination, a stack of arrangements, and no fixed address. But I had optimism, a belief that I was right not to practice my art where I would have to prune it to some marketable form. There really wasn't a choice, and I felt happy. First up, I walked along 52nd Street which is so different during the day, just another street with the customary refuse of city life and city people. Walked along and remembered how it had felt listening to Bird and Bud and sitting in with Lennie and Lee, and kicked myself that it had taken this long to get back. I had stepped out of the desert.

chapter twelve **pennies**

"My ideals were formed by the time I was twenty, I'm sure. I'd heard Bach and Bartok and Bird and Bud and Lennie and Pres. It stayed for life. I was totally committed. I abandoned myself to the music when I got back to New York. And for five years it was listen to music and play music day and night. So that's not going to leave a person. It never did, and my standards have stayed pretty much the same throughout."

That's something I can confirm that I did say, verbatim, because it was recorded and broadcast on the radio. With the press it's often a different story, and facts, emphasis, implication, all distort as the material is tidied up even before the editor cuts and pastes, taking minor liberties.

"The best way to think of Lennie is simply as a very well informed musician. Of all the musicians I met, he was the most articulate about applying twentieth century classical music to jazz."

That's something I can confirm that I did say, verbatim, because it was recorded, a telephone conversation with a young man called John, maybe a student, who was genuinely curious, I believe and of course I may have misread that one. He was very nervous, calling up, at considerable expense, interstate, out of curiosity - he really wanted to know how it was then. Nervously excited. Perhaps he was overcome by the fact that I was willing to talk with him, not knowing who he was - America's full of some very weird people - but he was genuine: he kept the information to himself. It was important to provide an accurate account, so I spoke. I really believe in that, giving an accurate account, of the music, and I wonder, as I speak, whether the one who listens really wants information to act on, to verify by listening to the content, or whether the one who listens is collecting snippets, like newspaper cuttings that fill space but don't imply much. Now that I think about it, John may have been a high school student researching a project, and, as far as he was concerned, had a scoop.

Yes. I really believe in applying the information or don't bother to ask for it. There was a responsibility I felt too. I mean, there were so many people beating up on Bird and Lennie in private, and publicly not saying much. We were never into maintaining a profile, I mean a high profile, you know, the star syndrome and all that crap, about air play and exposure, courting affection and cultivating a manner. No, we were adamant about playing it all straight ahead, no chaser. What's popularity? What's success?

So I like to reflect while I talk, to say the thing clear, straight ahead, no bullshit. Bird was like that too. He'd say, it's all in the music, so what are we going to talk about, publicly I mean. Privately we talked a lot, as friends do. Developing a public personality, I mean, to the extent that the personality overshadows the work. Art does not need PR, and it is not true that the finest will always survive. Sometimes the finest is never even voiced, and people end up pillaged and defaced. In the end we are not talking about the physical object: we are talking about the human spirit and the timeless. It is not the book, or the painting, or the architecture: it's the integrity of the action, and what's personality and exposure and money in the bank to do with that, I ask you. Our approach was very simple, very straight ahead, and there were things we would not do, musically speaking and commercially speaking.

I always said the same thing, over and over again, until even I was tired of it, publicly speaking, and had no more to say. Though if someone asked genuinely, then I made an effort to provide a genuine response. I'm not a difficult person, but I live economically and talk sparingly, at that time and for a long time hence. Not a difficult person to talk with, if I have something to say at the time, and often I don't but sometimes I do and I quote:-

"It's probably uh the fact that er we're also classically oriented I think, Lennie, Lee and myself. Lennie is er a graduate of Chicago Conservatory and he quit in the final year when he decided that he'd uh had lost interest in the classical and was meant to be a er jazz musician (pause) or an improviser really, but he brought all his knowledge with him and he uses it in his teaching. It's a classical discipline (pause) the way he teaches.

I have to say that (those years were the good old times). Charlie Parker was still alive and an immediate influence on American musicians' lives and the late 40s and 50s was uh the very uh best in American jazz I think. No I don't mean to be separated, I mean uh uh personality to be subject to character (pause) character is what decides uh how a musician is going to live his life (pause) if he is going to be uncompromising and uh seek only to express what he really feels (pause) that, as opposed to a musician who is concerned with putting on a show. That's the distinction I wanted to make. (Do you agree style is the man himself?) Absolutely. A great musician doesn't think about style, Charlie Parker didn't think about style, Bach didn't think about style, but they create more style without even thinking about it than someone who tries. Yes.

The immediate future is uh uh besides being my first appearance in Europe which uh I'm enjoying thoroughly uh Lee and I are going to work together later this month and uh I even suspect Lennie is to begin performing again since he's been teaching for about ten years straight without (pause) getting out and working at all, so uh anything can really happen. I hope at least to work with Lennie again and I now know I'm going to work with Lee."

And it was years later, many years later I had this to say, I had to say this, in Denmark it was, I was in Denmark doing a summer workshop, teaching, like master classes, in Copenhagen it was, years later and time running out. But be that as the case may be, I mean time running out, the words chosen after deliberation of many years and conveyed in a slow, almost ruminative manner, giving the subject my full attention so as to express the meaning fully, neither embroidering for dramatic effect nor diminishing in order to stimulate a fascination in a mystique. Someone once called this kind of thing 'his 1000lb phrases': take that to mean I was to the point.

And many years earlier I said to John the student or whatever he was, "Don't be afraid to look backwards. All the major influences are behind us, and we learn, finally, from past experience." He then became anxious about his phone bill or his tape was running out, something like that, and he said thank you very much and hung up, reluctant to pass up a taste, or beside himself with glee at his good fortune. I was in California again and he was in New York, someone looking for answers, or possibly the other way around.

Digression, looking back on it, the influences, you know how it is, a penny for your thoughts.

The penny, finally, had dropped. To my mind, there could not be a finer teacher in the country, any country. For me, that is. No one more knowledgeable, more gifted as a teacher. In one sentence he could tell me all I needed to know, more than a good many people had told me in five years, in fact, because no one had told me anything over the years that I had not already discovered for myself. No one, black or white. And don't forget, by then I had listened to, played with or heard everyone in jazz who was leading the music forward without much of a care for the consequence, extending the form to new relevance, and that includes Bird and Pres, both from Kansas City, now best known because of rock and roll, such is the ignorance thrust upon us. In one sentence on Wednesday he would tell me all I needed to know. In one sentence on Saturday running into Sunday morning he would tell me all I needed to know, week after week. Some say I idolized him, others say that he was a father to me. We were, it is true, a family, this small band of men, and the occasional woman later on, and too many women later on, which is another story, Lennie holding the conviction that women active in creative expression would bring a new dimension and open up some untouched aspect of men and somehow set off changes in the world which would change the world in its entirety. There was Lady Day already and others, who were singing with their own voice in their own style from their own deepest feelings and not with a voice adopted as a result of the influence of men desiring a woman to perform in a way they desired, a truly independent woman, as valid in her expression as any man. He was way ahead of his time.

We evolved into a community, some men with wives, others not, living for the music, and not to sell it but to learn, through study. The School, it became called that, The Lennie Tristano School, which was not a place but an attitude, a commitment to revealing the unique individual voice, and not stand-alone, but together with others on the same journey for the time being a harmony in difference, while it lasted. Of course, we never thought of it as a school; we were friends, some closer than others, finding our direction in circumstances not available anywhere else in America at least and perhaps nowhere else in the entire world. This was a personal training in individual competence and separateness and group harmonics. We became very close, musically speaking, some more than others, relying on each other, helping each other, spending the better part of each waking day together, in different combinations, in different places, according to who had space available. I just fell into it. We were young and made space for each other as only young people can; as the individuality blossoms so do different lifestyles, preferences, habits, obligations, and all that leaves less space to share. But at this time we were young, with one or two exceptions, and with an appetite for this experience of taking music seriously and being taken seriously without having also to contend with the pressures of commerce industry. It was a question of willingness to find the deepest feeling and the deepest knowledge, of the nature of music, the finest resonance of the self through the chosen instrument and striving for a union in which conscious knowledge opened the doors of the intuition and the subconscious, to work ones way to the threshold of inspiration. And I mean work.

We were all welcome. He was not so much a guide whom we idolized, that's not true, as someone who cared about us as people and who sought to assist us in releasing all our capability. A teacher in the true sense, he made each one of us equally welcome and demanded competence. He was big on competence, believing, and I am of the same mind, that a jazz musician had to have the same degree of competence as classical musicians, even more so since there were the very strenuous demands of improvising. Lennie did not believe in accidents, in flying by the seat of your pants, in the hit or miss approach. It was partly because the music was black, in origin, that no one took it seriously, as an art form. It was presumed that it all happened by random chance. It didn't and it doesn't. It was partly because he was not black, and none of his so called students were black, that he was not and is not taken seriously, even now. He is not alone in that.

He rarely spoke in more than a sotto voce, a slightly husky voice that would not be out of place in a film actor, a voice that called for your attention and held it. It struck me quite forcibly, the only thing that's going to satisfy this cat is if I turn myself inside out, if I abandon myself to the subject, creating music, that he would accept no less than the utmost I could do and that if music could mean so much to him and be so profound an influence on what he chose to do with his life and what he chose not to do, then there was no reason that could not mean the same things for me. It was like being given permission to be serious, not to take the matter lightly. But do not be misled by the sotto voce: he was also most definite, in a considered way, willing to listen, willing to stand up for his love, and not willing to tolerate bullshit or halfheartedness. There are not many men like him around these days. And he was not always like that: we all have our prime.

So much of what was played, he could distinguish, was derivative, a patchwork quilt of ideas garnered from elsewhere, from somewhere other than the wellspring of the individual's experience and feeling.

So much of what was played, he could distinguish, did not have the levity to rise above the emotions, which are short lived, like a hot flush. If I want to witness emotion, he would say, I can visit the nearest State asylum, there's plenty of emotion there, raw emotion without form or direction or fulfillment. If I want to feel emotions, then I can watch sports or street fights, but there is little place in music for indulging emotion, which is too shallow for such a precious gift.

There were exceptions and he encouraged us to follow their example, Lady Day, for example, and Bird and Pres and Roy and Fats and Johnny, people who created music to express the subtlest feeling and claimed that feeling as their own. That is not easy, and, as I said myself in answer to a question, to feel requires a lot of experience, a lot of living, and sacrifice, and discrimination and the capacity to distinguish between what is me and what originates from somewhere other than the wellspring of my own life.

People beat up on him, less now because the moment has passed, for being intellectual, but those people are the very ones who cannot distinguish between emotion and feeling, they are that lacking in subtlety, and the rebuttal is in the reality, namely that if you listen to what he played 40 years ago and more, you will find it as fresh, as current, as surprising, as successful as the moment he played it, in some ways more so than a lot of what Bird played, because Bird often played in circumstances he did not feel happy about but had to because he needed the bread, and Lennie never did that, never allowed himself to land in that kind of situation and you can hear the benefit of the choice and we experienced the benefit of the choice, because the making of it brought him to teaching.

We are talking about my life, and talking about my life necessarily involves the solo, which is the substance of my life, and that makes me no different from anyone else, it being only a question of degree, extent, adamancy, persistence, assiduity, sedulity, the depth of the capacity to hear and take note. And this necessarily involves eschewing the urge to ingratiate, gratify, succumb to the tickle of ease. Sound also has gravity, and levity, and poise between these two points may inspire an alchemy of refinement and elegance which conspire to add a burnish to the dross. And that poise does not happen by accident, without effort, and cannot be left to random chance.

Bach, if you like, as composer, devised extended solos on a theme, a fugue of feeling through many voices, and performers replicate those solos, occasionally resonating again, hundreds of years later, with the original power of his glorious design. But the world has changed. While Bach created the music for each voice, by which I also mean each instrument, in an ensemble nowadays it is possible, given freedom once again from notation, for each individual to create the music for their voice, their instrument, simultaneously and spontaneously and accomplish a renewal of the song, a current statement of the present I am, now revived and replenished, sung into life, each one for himself or herself and always the one answerable to the other, always within arms reach, jointly creating the form, revising the harmony of the community.

It is not the notes which are the song, just as it is not the facts which are the story. But the fact is, we studied, firstly at Lennie's apartment, the few of us, Lennie and Lee and Billy and Arnold and Hal or Denzil and myself, abandoned ourselves to the training, night and day, only rarely performing in public - the time was dedicated to the training, with the intention that when we performed we would not just pass the time of day, but make a valid statement, showing some respect for the audience and for ourselves, not a privilege many musicians were willing to insist on. Gestation, it was that. We were in a minority. It takes time to create, and it is simply not possible to 'produce', as the saying goes, every night of the week and maintain a standard of relevance, personal devotion, as well. If you really need an example, just reflect on what happened to Mozart when the primary pressure was to 'produce', for the bread. You end up with crap, ingenious crap but crap nevertheless, and there is a superfluity of crap in the world these days, so why add to it.

If you still need further amplification, reflect on the method of preparation undertaken by a chamber orchestra. To prepare for a concert, the orchestra will rehearse - prepare - for weeks, until they are one unit, until they are so replete with the spirit of the pieces they are going to perform, so intimate with every note, that, on the day, with some luck, the performance will bring to them and the audience a joint experience which has the capacity to change a life.

Our desire, if you like, was to create music that is as relevant to our time as the music of Bach or Mozart was to their time, as valid, as innovative, and as worthy of attention, not only on the night, but for years to come. So we prepared in earnest, and declined easier opportunities.

We were preparing for a specific occasion, a recording session for Capitol Records. Over the months, we became totally familiar with each other's style, phrasing, tone, coloring - for sound has color too - and feeling, and relaxed by playing Bach Inventions at ever increasing tempos, to push ourselves to the limits of our technical competence, without losing the spirit of the calling. Lennie insisted, and I understood why, that we would not play with anyone outside the group in the meantime; it is no different than a group of actors preparing a play: for the duration, the ensemble must be given all the available energy. It is the effort of preparation that is important, almost as important as the result, because in the preparation, if it is serious, something new can happen, something vital which, in fact, contributes to the health of the community at large, like another year's harvest.

And if you are still in doubt, ask yourself why it was that the singer who put his love of the song, his love of his place in the community above the rewards of commerce, would walk the streets of the town and respond joyfully to the requests of the people to hear him sing, even as he walked along with them: they were his people - in whatever town he happened to be - and word about him had spread, that he sang in a way that touched them more deeply than any other singer. His spirit was as generous and as gregarious as the wind. He was never recorded, and nothing is lost. I have told the story of Cerucik, and doubt that you really listen. We are so dispersed now that word of mouth is not enough, so it is important that the evidence is extant, even if the flame is so weak that the candle must be kept out of the wind. You know how it is.

On the day against which we prepared (it was a Friday in May 1949), we gathered in a studio of Capitol Records, the six of us, early in the evening, as part of the contract, and record companies are no benefactors. We used to rehearse in a small room; piano, guitar, alto and tenor saxophone, double bass and drums, all acoustic instruments, like the human voice. (It will have to be acknowledged, sooner or later, that electronics ruin everything, because the music will not be tinkered with.) Six human beings in a family living room, one blind son of Italy, one balding, one short and with glasses like Trotsky used to wear, one with pale green eyes that never would see the grandeur of Mother Russia and slightly taller than the others, one eager as all drummers are, and the other a retiring man, all cheek by jowl, braces, rolled shirt sleeves, jacket, pullover, second hand suit jacket (the pants got lost somewhere), at home with each other.

And here we were gathered on a day, in a vacant studio, a neutral place and inhospitable, standing before an array of microphones on bleak metal sticks, which would have been intimidating had we not brought with us a total faith in each other, a total confidence in the mutual trust established, like a plant's roots, through continuity in one place and purpose.

This was going to be an experiment. Lennie was through with coyness. We were going to play without anything set down, no theme, no key signature, no chords, nothing. First question: Where's your sheets? Answer: We don't need sheets, we know it all by heart. Second question: How long's this piece? Answer: We'll find out. Third question: What's it called? Answer: Call it Intuition. You could tell by the way the sound engineer looked at us that he thought this was a dangerous assignment, that he thought we were crazy sons of bitches, nigger lovers.

The only prior arrangement had been about which instrument would start and then the order in which the others would come in, one by one. And that's how it was, and it worked out quite incredibly, creating the form as we progressed without any hint of faltering, and I did not experience that same depth of union in spontaneity again, except once, fleetingly, in Berlin, which is as close to Mother Russia as I reached. We had already done a couple of sessions for Capitol. In one of them, the engineer turned off his machine, absolutely refused to comply, as if he had been appointed censor of whatever incomprehensible rubbish it was that he hated to say he was hearing. Eventually he gave in, but he was obviously quite distraught; maybe he thought we were sending him up. He took it upon himself to erase a couple of takes. That's what contracts with record companies were like then: it was the musician's music, but the commercial transaction gave ownership to the record company - the buyer. If they didn't like the product, they could throw it away. The executives at Capitol - commerce being the new patron of creativity - then not only refused to issue the recordings, they also refused to pay Lennie the contract fee (Lennie's Pennies). But Lennie did have influence, and pressure was brought to bear. Symphony Sid got hold of a set of dubs and played the shit out of the recordings on late night radio, and Barry Ulanov wrote articles declaring that the work brought jazz to a new frontier. Capitol eventually capitulated and the printing sold out. Lennie later bought the tapes, and did very well out of them around the world, and they were still selling forty years later. One of the recordings was not heard for another fifteen years. You had to put up with that kind of thing. This was America America, where to be popular even made being black tolerable, as long as there was money to be milked from the commodity.

chapter thirteen **136th and broadway**

Those sessions made a deep impression, my first taste of controversy and my first taste of total satisfaction. They also left me with a lifelong distrust of record companies, and affirmed my trust in Lennie. It was hard enough staying alive without record companies withholding your dues. Our enthusiasm left little energy for making a living under the conditions that prevailed then. A deep enough impression for me to write home. Dear Ma, we've done our first recording with Lennie. He's an extraordinary man; there's nothing, musically, that slips past him. Capitol don't understand what's going on. It beats me why those tin ears are in the business if they can't hear what's going on. There's articles in the magazines and newspapers, and Lennie's dead set he's not going to be treated like this and will probably start his own record company. My weight isn't what you'd like it to be, but I am taking a half pint of cream each day to compensate for the meals I rarely have time to eat. He's also planning a venue of his own where we can play and be heard without all the hassles you have to contend with in the clubs. You can still send your letters to Lee's address. I'm still there, part of the family in a way, and get to use the kitchen when they've all finished. It's tough being a student and having kids. We've played a few of the clubs, the Clique Club was one of them, not like the dance halls in LA. Otherwise, we're always busy, practicing and doing clerical work at the Post Office. Thanks for the money. My life is here. I can't help that. Maybe the scene will pick up in LA one of these days. Owen still chasing his chickens? Regards.

Something like that, every intention of being dutiful but life kind of thwarting the intention. Things didn't work out as they did in the regular world; if you wanted to play your own way, then you had no choice but to create a life style to fit and take the rough with the smooth. It was living on the fringes and I wasn't complaining; I could never get enough of it, being your own man, more or less, and calling your own tune. It is true that I could not afford a place of my own, but that was not unusual for a student, and we saw ourselves as students, apprentices. It wasn't so much tough or a hardship as necessary, at least that is how I saw it, and that's what brought me and Lennie close together I suspect, because we were natural allies, had the same outlook for the duration.

With Lee, it was different, the outlook. But we were, musically, ideally suited. We heard the same things and knew what the other one was hearing. But it would not have happened if there had not been a Lennie to keep us together, day after day challenging us to deeper and deeper knowledge of the furthest reaches of our imaginations, through a finer and finer knowledge of the basics, harmony, melody, meter and form itself. It was his inexhaustible energy and love of music, for which it was worth sparing no effort, worth refusing to commit one false note. It was extremely rare that such a group of people were able to spend so much time together: it was a unique creative process. Being together so often, learning and then exercising our knowledge together, all other influences were gradually eliminated, which meant that we began to perceive each other very clearly indeed, to intuit each other also. It reminds me of the young boys who are apprenticed to a zitar or tabla player from four or five years old and over many years achieve a mastery of the art that can be acquired no other way. Time, as they say, is of the essence.

This prolonged, intense and profound experience in the end sets me apart. We sought to discriminate between a profession and a calling, between commerce and art, not self-consciously, but looking back on it that is what we did, a self-sufficient combination of free spirits not inclined to accede to the pressures of the buck, that single most distorting influence which obliges people to compromise their standards, their aims, insisting that bums on seats is the final arbiter, which in the material sense it is, and that is why we had no truck with it, because in the artistic sense - the calling - it is the finest possible evocation of individual feeling and perception which is the paramount goal, the ascent to unattainable perfection.

There was the question asked, "Why don't you guys record more often?' to which the answer was twofold, one, we're not ready yet, and, two, why record if there is nothing new to say, or, I do not seek to repeat myself. Rather than become prey to all the hullabaloo that goes hand in hand with becoming a public figure, a personality, a showman, a contract man, beholden and at beck and call, we would always prefer not to make commercial recordings, though we would record, and sometimes destroy the tapes to thwart the bootleggers - you'd be surprised at the opportunists in this industry. With a couple of exceptions, we managed to avoid the big name labels and threw in our lot with the independents, guys who threw in their lot with us and never did get rich but had the satisfaction of recording in circumstances we all enjoyed, as friends, in lounge rooms; private studios in converted garages, that kind of thing. Relaxed, no hype, no swagger, no posing, a sunny afternoon and a few beers between friends, guys who trusted each other. I learned a few things early on in the piece.

This training was absolutely what I sought and one which I embraced without reservation. I had always had the inclination, way back in the library which I usurped as my living quarters, back in that collection of rooms called a house, each of us left to our own devices, just earmarking territory with impunity, because the only things that ever happened were what the three of us initiated, generally, and the woman withdrawing behind a closing door. I was well versed in not being answerable to anyone.

Our first campus was a basement on 136th Street and Broadway, rented, a dump pretty much, Saturday nights. All night we played out what we had been practicing through the week, learning from each other, learning to play counterpoint, two, three, four part, often until dawn on Sunday, until the place got busted. From time to time we went public, at the Vanguard or Basin Street or the Clique Club, and occasionally played Bach. Such was the prejudice of the day that when we played Bach - and Bach with a jazz feel is just beautiful - we would not mention the source. People loved it, it really knocked them out. But had we said, by the way, that's Bach's Invention Number 13, the response would have been something different. As it was, audiences heard something new. The Bach was loved because people didn't have a clue what it was. And Lennie must take credit for being the first in jazz to perform Bach. The public memory recalls the Swingle Singers and the Modern Jazz Quartet who played Bach for elevator audiences, only because they became popular and became popular because they played Bach for elevator audiences, reducing the grand architecture of Bach to a cardboard cutout, dainty but not magnificent the way it was. Who knows, perhaps one day credit will be given.

If not bohemian then the lifestyle was certainly spartan, a half-pint of cream, kitchen privileges, earning just enough, scrape by, with enthusiasm applying ourselves to identifying our unique voices and imaginations. Every day a fresh attempt, and the only way to make progress was to face yourself and dig deeper and daily to further improve technique and facility. Competence, Lennie was big on that. The industry is supported by press men, those who like to comment, amongst whom there are a few honest men and women who also have ears. Many of them, however, are prejudiced, ill-informed and seeking to make life easy for themselves and do not understand at all. They love categories and they love comparing; what cannot be categorized and what cannot be compared leaves them at a loss. So, in despair and hoping to put the whole effort down, some ass created the term 'cool' and we were tagged the 'cool school'. It stuck. And in the process created a prejudice and a category that never existed, doing no one any favors, neither the us nor the public. The power of phrases, like pre-bop, be-bop, post-bop, folk-rock, rock-bop, funk, fusion and confusion. Those who like to categorize have the ears of filing clerks, and mistake the pigeon hole for the pigeon.

Well, the truth is, those guys were so dumb they couldn't hear the what was happening, because there weren't any familiar patterns, couldn't label the influences and decided 'cool' was a smart phrase to coin. And typically, they missed the point, as they always will, and, as they always will, their audience listened and mistook prejudice for discrimination, in the non-racial sense of course.

It makes me angry even now, angry in my own way, which is more disappointment and a stern gaze, to remember how a studio technician, who just turns knobs and presses buttons, and sits behind a plate glass window with headphones smothering both ears, how this guy can assume the right to interrupt when we're playing, because he reckons it's intolerable. I mean, who is he, this technician? [Can you imagine a client commissioning a work by Monet and interrupting him while he's working on the water-lilies, and saying, "Hey, Claude, for fucks sake, they're all out of bloody focus, goddamit. I'm not paying for that!"] After that experience, no self-respecting individual would set foot in a studio again, not for a name-label contract, where the company executives dictate what is to be created. As I said, a lot of experience. And worse was to come.

The great opening of Birdland - the only club to be named after a living jazz musician, and where Bird was later unable to play because at the time you needed a special license to play where alcohol was served, and Bird was being hounded by the law and couldn't get a license. I remember we played Lennie's Pennies. A moment of history, in the musical scheme of things, broadcast by Voice of America on December 15 1949. And what happened to the tapes? Lost. 'Ah, jeez, we must a los' thum.' That's about all you'd get out of technicians. I've even heard that tapes of Lady Day were wiped over because the radio station was running short of tape and wanted to economize. This is the industry as it was back then, and things may have improved in terms of efficiency and production techniques and tolerance, but things haven't changed much for the better.

Interlude. A student comes to Lennie's early afternoon in winter. An hour passes, and it is starting to get dark. The student is embarrassed to say anything, but minute by minute it's getting harder to read the charts. Lennie, of course, can't see anyway, and doesn't need to because it's all in his head. Finally, the student just clams up, still can't bring himself to ask where the light switch is. Lennie is puzzled, asks what's up, maybe the guy has lost his nerve or something. Student says he can't see the charts. Can't see?

You're supposed to hear it, man. What do you mean, you can't see it? Ah, Lennie, it's dark; where's the light switch?

Lennie cracks up. There, behind the piano. I never use it. Why didn't you say something sooner?' And otherwise, there we would be, down in the basement on 136th and Broadway, every weekend, all night and often way past dawn, intent, not casual affair, striving for the finest, best part of two years, until the place got busted, and Lennie put an end to that. A tight knit group and a more complete training could not be had anywhere else in America, perhaps in the whole world, at least in the jazz. So we got to know each other pretty well, at Billy's house, his kid and his friend listening in the other room, and at Lee's place and his kids, and at Lennie's always music, except when someone was reading a book to him. And for the wives, not an easy life, unless they loved to listen, and even then not an easy life. Spartan, for sure.

There we were, Lloyd and Billy and Joe and Arnie and later on Sal and Red, once or twice, and Ted and all the others preparing to put dedication to the test. It was ok in the studio and amongst each other, but attitudes on the scene didn't mesh with ours.

Fashions were setting in. And not satisfied at all by the ambitions of the record companies and club owners, Lennie had a vision of looking after our own interests by presenting our music the way we wanted to present it: if there was no venue that suited our style, then Lennie was ready to create one. He would say that jazz is best presented in the late afternoon to early evening - why should a musician be obliged to play until two or three in the morning mainly to create cash flow - in an informal and relaxed setting, away from alcohol. If you want to drink, fine, do it later, if you want to meet friends and talk, fine, do it later, but if you want to listen, then listen and enjoy it. Maybe even feel something, be moved: music is not an opiate. He had in mind a concert situation, jazz as chamber music but far more relevant and without the white anglosaxon formality. There is no need to be precious. But he wasn't a business man, and there wasn't the money.

As for recording, well, set up a private label. It couldn't be worse than the deal the record companies had on the table. Bird would have loved to have recorded with Lennie - he wanted to do something different and saw he could do it with Lennie - but Lennie couldn't afford the kind of money Bird could get from the companies, and he needed money to support his habit which no one was doing anything to help him with, except to make it worse, so he never did get the chance to create what he could have created. In a paternal sort of way, Lennie was trying to protect us from having to endure the totally chaotic and unhealthy lifestyle that was imposed on jazz musicians, and which, with few exceptions, the musicians themselves did little to resist, especially with the lure of stardom.

Scene: We went to the airport together. My wife again. I'd been in the public hospital in L.A. after the heart attack. She'd come down from Santa Cruz, to see me. This is June eighty seven. I am tired but just holding up, and mostly silent today. The prescription was to abandon the calling because otherwise it would kill me, but I had always been of the disposition to burn out rather than rust out. There was not much time and where to begin anyway, now, after all that's happened, and me a very private person. My effort is to maintain at least a resemblance of dignified bearing, the more readily achieved without bedroom slippers on. Perhaps in my overcoat and with my drawn countenance and hooded eyes and graying hair, perhaps I do look like a Russian, without the severity or the coldness.

We wait. Who will broach the subject. How did this come to pass? No answers up my sleeve. I look. I see her. She has a plane to catch so why set off a conversation that cannot be finished to the satisfaction of either party. How am I? Tired, but I am well. Will you keep playing? I shall attempt to follow the advice given, after all they are professional men, but I am a musician and without .... The momentum of the years spent without common experience allows us only to sit hesitant across the table in the departure lounge, not dissembling indifference, inept and haplessly naive;

yes, that, but indifference, no. I cannot hold her hand but do ask, out of a genuine and simple courtesy, whether she will eat anything, if there is time of course. The words straight forward as between two who knew each other but are currently lacking an explanation for the events that did take place and came to nothing very much, speaking from my point of view. People were always so anxious to ask for reflections on past accomplishments and I had to say, well, that doesn't interest me at all, that was then, and I am here now looking towards what I am doing next: I am a different man now, with the challenge of today, not so many liberties to play with but still seeking to voice my present feeling about life, which the song celebrates, I believe.

Those rambling thoughts circulating through, and me not able to say a word. Speechless I am not, but I am all fresh out of words, presently, now, looking at the plane on the tarmac, and too tired to take another step, too tired to open up the discussion which ought to take place, for she deserves an explanation, yet, finding myself not in possession of even an inkling, my silence perhaps conveys that I can go no further, not through incalcitrant obstinacy nor self-reproach. Words do not fail me: there are no words left.

Flight details flick over on the departure board. People boarding her flight start to pick up their plastic bags and souvenirs and knock against our chairs as they squeeze past, double check for things left behind and laughter and tears and the excitement of children which I can remember clearly and privately and obedient to a schedule stand in line and pass through the doors. It is neither necessary to encourage her on her way nor to restrain - and I remember Cerucik - because there are forces in motion that in themselves override such gestures, no matter how well meant.

"Love to the boys." It is all understatement, that 1000lb phrase, mostly silence as the time-lag between gunshot and the sound that it detonates. "They asked me to tell you they don't hate you anymore."

We look at each other, apparently ignoring the inevitable lapsing of time on this occasion, and I manage a perceptible smile with which to conclude this scene.

I am alone by the lofty plate glass window, hands in my pockets, and watch the plane reverse away from the terminal, my own man with the conundrum of his life. And I recall how I used to feel standing on 52nd Street or coming out of the basement on 136th Street on a Sunday morning in a New York dawn, young, my own man, setting standards. We played the standards, the songs of the day, and when we first met I had said to her or would have said It's You Or No One. It had the ring of Hollywood about it, a touch of Bogard.

As the plane taxis away, I am impressed by the sauntering laziness of its passage, prepossessed and me dispossessed. I turn and find myself shuffling through a clutter of irrelevant memorabilia, mental snapshots of the dog-eared novels we had read, the spaces we had never managed to fill with the stability of quality possessions, wondering if she still had the one object we did buy, that drab green sofa, the fabric worn into patches of obscene nakedness at the end of the arm rests, naked like a chicken's arse. I hear the engines roar from E flat through a seamless chromatic glissandi up to a B and the ground trembles slightly beneath my feet.

End of scene.

chapter fourteen **317 east 32nd**

After losing the basement, we quickly found a new home, an old furniture showroom at 317 East 32nd Street, on the lower East side between 1st and 2nd Avenue. There was a garage below that did servicing, run by Italians, and nothing above, an ideal place for us but not somewhere you'd take your mother to make a good impression. This was April fifty one - so much happened in Aprils, I remember, the cruellest month, so it has been said.

It took the next five months to convert the place, putting up partitions and reasonably effective soundproofing, and acquiring chairs. A real community effort, (I don't know of any other group of musicians who were putting in the same kind of effort in those days) and that was, by and large, the only physical work I ever did, fitting studios and occasionally building some furniture.

Lennie was an inspiration and you would be surprised at the number of highly respected and wonderfully gifted and competent musicians who studied with him and repaid the debt in turn by providing an inspiration to another generation. It is still going on, and he is largely forgotten. Well, to be remembered is not the point. His very remarkable capacity was to inspire confidence and a respect for the history and to impart knowledge, and to demystify the nature of improvising.

Improvising is still considered to be something out of the blue. And yet the opposite is true: it is a deal more demanding than composition because you're creating and performing simultaneously. He wanted well trained musicians - his word was "competent" musicians. Well trained classical musicians two hundred years ago were better trained to improvise than today's jazz musicians. Just the discipline, so the student can perform the raw material and hear harmony, and feel and hear meter and rhythms and can perform them. And beyond that it's every individual's creativity. The idea that he was trying to turn out carbon copies of himself, that's preposterous. In fact the opposite is true: he insists on a student doing his own thing. He'll settle for nothing less. That's one of the first feelings I got from him.

We were watching Bird deteriorate in what was becoming a nightmare and a circus, Bud dissipate, and the life of Pres melt into a slurry, their lives like the flaking facades of buildings gnawed at by acid rain. The calling was one thing and the lifestyle was another, but the club owners and the record companies were making a buck so the personal fallout was an acceptable part of the deal, ugly if you took the trouble to look, and sad too, but acceptable to the makers of deals. It was a tradeoff, and, especially for the blacks, another slavery.

In addition to our weekly lessons with Lennie, we would meet up two or three times a week at Sal's or Red's or Peter's apartment to play and also rented rehearsal studios - Nola's or Malin's, often recording what we played, then listened, and worked on always improving, getting closer to the feeling a melody moved in us and which we wanted to substantiate in our song, experimenting all the time to find the way to release the individual's voice, in harmony with another's, in all its fullness. Lennie only once saw Bird really angry. It was the Metronome All Stars session in January 1949. Lennie had introduced Bird to 'Victory Ball', sort of a composition of his, showed him the sheets. Bird said, yeh, play it, and Lennie played it, and Bird took to it. So first up they did the large band numbers, took six hours over that, take after take after take, and Bird all the time is getting impatient because he wanted to get to the small band side. Finally, they did. And they played Victory Ball and Bird got a hold of it, played the shit out of it, no not just a hold of it, took it to his heart and played it like it was his life in there.

They were beginning to get to the real feeling in it, and the record men said that was it, they'd have to finish. After fifteen minutes, and they'd spent six hours on the other stuff. Bird was incensed, like he'd been treated like shit, so angry he just screamed at those guys to go fuck themselves, and then he split in a rage, and didn't come back and that was the end of that session. That was a story - Dizzy was there and Kai and Buddy D. and Shelley, Billy, Eddie, guys who knew what was going on. And then we had our own experience with Intuition. Record companies are still the same. While you make money for them, the record companies love you, and when you don't, they find someone else to love. Commerce.

The teaching method is so simple, there is no mystique. It's a question of knowledge and application, but not knowledge in the theoretical sense, because, knowledgeable though Lennie was, and more so than any other musician I ever met, he didn't teach theory; it was all practical work. I have used the same principles myself. And if there is any doubt about the efficacy of what Lennie passed on, then ask yourself the question: how come so many extraordinarily gifted and inspiring musicians came to him? When I start students off on this path, they often say, "How come this is not the way we are taught in college?". To which I can only reply, "Give me an explanation."

"This new jazz of Lennie's is a profoundly moving music to hear. It is, of course, even more satisfying to play. For it rests upon the pillars of all of music, the great supports which buoyed the polyphony of Bach and gave depth to the elegance of Mozart. It marks a strong parallel to the development of the twelve-tone structure in classical music in the twentieth century, a parallel but not an imitation. Whatever the limitations within the present three-minute form on records and only slightly longer elaboration off them, these performances represent the fullest possible unfolding of the resources of the participating men. Here, after all, are improvising musicians, who are sufficiently disciplined on their instruments to give full expression to almost any idea that they may think or feel, sufficiently free to vent those ideas together, with a beat, without preliminary map or plan. Here jazz comes of age."

The first step was to sing. To sing a solo by Bird or Pres, from memory and unaccompanied. You learned to listen and hear accurately. It's hard to believe that musicians generally never use their own voice, which is the most direct, the most vital expression of what we feel. It's as if they hide behind their instruments. Lennie would have none of that. "Whoever heard of a musician who couldn't sing?" The point was not to copy, but to attend to the feeling. And it was important not to learn the solos on the instrument, because that way the fingers didn't adopt the patterns, because once they do, the patterns are hard to break down and you end up imitating. After that, we played the solos in a style and with a feeling that was demonstrably our own. After that we would write out variations, in the classical sense, based on the melodic line of the solo and the harmonies suggested by the chord progressions, as many as we could imagine. It was all training in liberating the imagination, or, as Lennie would say, going beyond the brain.

The school was organized, it had to be because there were now some thirty students, all professionals. Sessions were held on Wednesday and Saturday, and after a while on Sunday as well, and which one you went to depended upon the level of competence you had reached. The first part of the lesson was with Lennie, in what was called 'the control room', and the second part was playing together, straight away given the opportunity to put ideas into practice. And that was training in true ensemble work; there wasn't room for personalities to dominate: jazz is people relating harmonically to each other.

And we played the Clique Club, the Vanguard, the Top of the Gate, Birdland and Carnegie Hall in New York, the Blue Note and the Silhouette Club in Chicago, the 421 Club in Philadelphia, recorded in Toronto, recorded at Birdland - we were constantly returning to Birdland - and did casuals in Brooklyn, New Jersey, Long Island, Westchester and elsewhere. There was an audience for jazz in those days and New York was overflowing with good music. And the writing was on the wall nevertheless.

"It's not just that something new has been added; jazz has regularly benefitted from the administration of fresh ideas, fresh sounds and direction. Rather, something as old as Western music has been brought alive again: the contrapuntal form which underlies the great years most clearly identified with the music of Johann Sebastian Bach has been revivified. In the process, a half-dozen men have made a rich contribution to jazz and jazz has been brought to a point where it can make the richest of contributions."

"Warne Marsh was a little short of amazing. His tone was constant, beautifully controlled, matching color with thought, charming in his frequent simplicity. He gave the group some of the warmth that Billy Bauer used to contribute. This was the highlight of the evening to me, Warne playing better than he has for a long time. Lee Konitz, on the other hand, was playing exactly as he had about six months before. In an ordinarily good musician, this might be cause for jubilation, but Lee has such tremendous stature as a creative musician that it's hard to imagine what could suddenly cause him to stand still and to play only a few great things during the course of an evening. Lennie, of course, was superb. It seems so strange and yet, perhaps, it is so obvious, that only when Lennie plays alone does his music reach its final fruition. Only then, stripped of the ensemble figures which were strangely mechanical this night, and assorted sounds, does it make consistent sense. And only then can it be seen for just what it is."

You have good nights and you have the other nights.

I mention these things because it is quite obvious that musicians nowadays just do not know the history, have no idea of the roots, by and large, and one thing we learned from Lennie was that if you don't know the history by ear then you have no points of reference; a mariner with no knowledge of the stars can only hug the shore.

This was not college. This was the education of life. And we were experiencing first hand how the music was being treated by society, especially by those in a position to do better - the recording companies and the club owners. Frankly, they didn't care a damn. But word about Lennie had gotten out anyway, as far as Europe, and guys like Peter and Ronnie came from England to study with him. There was a thing then, and there still is, that jazz was black, that only a negro could play jazz, and on paper they were idolized, but in reality they were treated like shit, many of them, including the two leading voices in their field, America's greatest contribution to the world of music. To Pres, a lyricist like no other, they more or less said, go straight ahead, motherfucker, swill another fifth of bourbon, we don't care, and to Bird, a musical genius who surfaces may be once every hundred years or more, they said, go ahead motherfucker in your white suit, hold that spoon over the anxious flame and go to hell because we don't give a shit, because you owe us anyway. In Kansas City, where they both spent years of their lives, people didn't even know who they were, and still didn't thirty years later. But in Europe they do, which is why so many American musicians left America and went to Europe, not just journeymen either, no, the very best.

We saw Mingus who wanted to make politics with music. He, the one later on, in his wheel chair on the lawn of the White House, with the President of the United States, Jimmy Carter, who genuinely meant well, resting a comforting hand on his shoulder, Mingus mostly paralysed and shaking with tears at the cruelty of this public gesture of recognition when he could play no more. Mingus comes rushing up the stairs at 317 East 32nd Street, bellowing in a fit of rage, wanting Ronnie's blood for something or other, just won't go away. Lennie the blind man hears the commotion and comes out and asks hey man what's the matter. Let me get my hands on that mother, I'll loosen his teeth - Mingus had a habit of punching people in the mouth, especially horn players: he was quite overwrought about the music on times. They're eyeball to eyeball and Lennie gently lets Mingus know that any more trouble and he'd get Lennie's knee flush in his groin, and what then? are you going to punch a blind man in the mouth? Mingus went.

We saw Miles, all set to milk the commodity for everything he could suck out of it.

We saw Bird. Bird had had enough. Everywhere he went he was hearing repetitions of himself, only just the notes, the discarded peanut shells, and he wanted to quit. But he couldn't quit because he had contracts and owed some. He wanted someone to show him where to get to next so he could stop hearing his old notes thrown around on the squalls of popularity, even setting up a meeting with Varese, the composer, who knew Bird had the gift. And he knew Lennie and he could share something but they couldn't afford to. They got along the way friends do.

And we played with Bird and Bird would sit and listen, and Bird said to Lennie, "Watch that kid. He's got it."

I never did have the inclination to hustle. But Lee did, and he got us recording dates. I came from Hollywood and always had a fallback and Lee came from Chicago and had this jewish thing and had to hustle and he had five kids to feed and I was single. He was already teaching his own students, and wanted to perform with whoever he chose to perform with, and Lennie would like us to stay together, the same kind of paternal instinct that Duke had, and some could make the commitment and some couldn't. And Billy was getting tired of the scene. Peter was full of energy and enthusiasm and wanted to get a scene of his own going. And Sal was the aesthete and didn't want any of the rough and tumble stuff, all the jive.

Fragmented impressions. In July fifty two, we played Toronto often criticized for playing cool overly intellectualized music Live in Toronto dispels view.... Consider 317 East 32nd, Tristano's anthem on Out of Nowhere....swiftly intone fragile tentative lines.... cool yes bloodless no....You Go To My Head.... reeds in stately cadences....April opens bright reeds harmonically bowing Bird's direction....Back Home (Tristano's Indiana) saxophones nearly scream Tristano burns and sparkles and certainly not without passion.

Then Lee joined Stan Kenton's band in fifty two, and slowly the whole thing broke up. Christmas that year I went back home and made my first recording in my own name, largely by accident, happening to bump into some guys at The Haig on Wilshire Boulevard in Los Angeles, and someone decided to record the session, though I don't know if I ever got what was due to me for that, financially speaking, there was too much going on to keep track.

And fragments of my youthful voice out on its own, earliest examples of extended improvisations on Live in Hollywood....Bob Andrews, a migrant from Wisconsin small Pentron recorder and single microphone he and the musicians bringing you 'live' in Hollywood far cry from days of Hoagy this recording vivid example inventive ability mine gold continually inspired without empty gesture moving music if this isn't emotional what is....a peak graceful dancing crisply ethereal free eccentric molten gargantuan and will endure as does all great art....fragments to make of them what you will.

Lennie got places by remembering how many paces there were between various points. It is the same with the music: you get to know the relationship between sounds, the distance between them, and which sequence of sounds voice what you are feeling at the time. And the feelings are always changing and so the music changes, the tone, rhythm, accent, melody, texture, attack. use of vibrato, volume, tempo and shifts in tempo, modulation in key, inflection and on and on. And the people you are playing with are going through the same process, which makes it highly complex, and yet, when there is an advanced degree of mutual sensitivity and honesty, then it is strangely easy - the music starts to play itself. And people wonder why Lennie kept us together and wanted us only to play, for the most part, amongst ourselves.

But those days were retreating and the strain of staying on the scene was taking its toll on a lot of musicians. Then came the chance to record with Pres, my master, and Roy, another one in my lineage, on the Metronome All Stars session of fifty three. How High The Moon was my center piece. Pres passed his best and fading into darkness like the smoke above a flame, cocked his head to one side in a gawky posture as he breathed on me between takes, say, kid, there's nothin lef in me cept a great deal of discomfort, so you gonna be the Pres from nah on, you heuuh, and you can tell them that the Pres tol you so. He who threw Bird out of his room, the man he called Lady Bird, mischievous like.

The repertoire, I want to talk about the repertoire. This was all before the first crushing impact of rock and roll and the avidity of an audience schooled for lusting after constant and rapid change in the musical menu, their atavistic tribal chant for more. American song writers were creating a body of melody, a national opus, a proliferation of song, men and women who still had an ear for harmony and melody and knew what subtlety is, who understood the word nuance. The common characteristic of many of these songs is that they provide enormous scope for improvisation, in their harmonic structure, the form, as well as the melody itself. Bach had his local material to draw on, compositions of contemporaries in which he saw greater possibilities than did those who wrote the basics. And we had ours. And, as with people, the only way to discover them is to spend years with them. And from these songs I drew my repertoire: my inspiration, they have never failed me.

Lee had gone. We all have to make choices. It hurt. Or was it primarily a disappointment, looking forward to so much? Or sadness, the departure of someone who has shared everything and walks away, even if of necessity, the pressures of life. Perhaps I was naive, having a fallback. He says he wasn't ready for such a commitment, a devotion. With me, it was the same old story: I didn't have a choice, even without a fallback when I needed to ask. My voice was my instrument, and I wasn't willing to sacrifice my voice, not at any price.

Not long before Bird died, he was to play at Birdland again. Bud was in a foul mood. Bird was out of his depth completely. Mingus was ready to preach gospel. Lennie was sat at a table, and Bird joined him, wanting to know what Lennie thought he should do to shake Bud out of it - Bud was refusing to play the piano, refusing to play with Bird because there was a fearsome animosity burning in his belly. Lennie repeated, in a few words, that this was the kind of scene jazz just had to get out of, which didn't help Bird any because he'd already decided it was time to die. Bud hollers at Bird that Bird can't play shit, and then hammers his elbow down on the keys, smashing a few of them. It all came to a head. Mingus apologized on behalf of everyone, ladies and gentlemen, this isn't the jazz, this is some very dee-sturbed people, begging your indulgence. But the ladies and gentlemen had left.

Requiem. Bird died. Lennie cried for hours and wrote his requiem and helped carry the coffin. Bird didn't want to be buried in Kansas City. He was buried in Kansas City. Some of the pallbearers were drunk and a blind man wrestles to stop the coffin tipping over. The priest had never met the deceased and buried him as Charlie Bird and there was some laughing at that. He had wanted them to play a Lennie composition at the funeral. Fat chance for a living legend. For what it's worth, Mozart was interred in comparable disgrace. America loves the images of Hollywood but fights very hard indeed to avert the truth. But there was a memorial concert in New York, some dignity in the end, and Lennie played his Requiem.

Lee was on the West Coast and didn't forget even if he was looking in a different direction. I had some paltry quarters and there wasn't much work to be had and with Lee gone there was disruption and no more Tristano sextet or quintet or quartet as there had been. So there were some adjustments to be made. He called me, to say he'd set up a recording session with Atlantic Records, which we did in New York. Then he called me to say there was a job he'd landed at the Hollywood Bowl which he wanted to share with me, knowing my inadequacies. He was like that, I must say, at that time. I just lit off out of New York, and left everything behind in the room, except a few clothes, some books, a scrabble set, a chess board, a deck of cards, my tenor, clarinet - which I hardly ever played - and several records. Ted had given me a few things, things to furnish the vestiges of comfort, and I quite forgot and the landlord took everything I didn't take with me, part settlement for rent he said I owed which I hadn't kept track of, never did pay much attention, so maybe he was right. It's not easy to come out ahead if you don't keep score.

chapter fifteen **dixie's dilemma**

In the middle of my life, casting my mind back to the library, and only the woman in the house, the evening the telegram arrived from Mr. Mayer, Louis B., now a mogul, Louis B. Mogul, my grandfather's name, Lou, many Lou's in my life but only one Lee and only one Lennie.

New York is now background noise behind Lennie's voice on the telephone asking what made me leave. I am prodigal and profligate, ascetic and spartan by turns. Everyone needs a change. Cast my mind back and see myself sitting on the train to Flushing. He asks me why. Must have felt betrayed, the two of us taking off, young men, prime, at a juncture, deciding. Owen the younger had flown the coop, didn't want a bar of this loafing about, no way, a self made man and what he owned he had earned.

Deliberating how to organize the my affairs in a manner befitting what I have to call art, which will endure as does all...he, myself, falling back within the shadow of former days, eschewing fame and fortune, yet with the flicker of a will not to relapse without the succor of the rigors of a mentor or the distress of having to witness the descent in dissolution of Pres and Bird's dog-arse funeral or the steeling of the mercenary edge to NYC and the hype and the dog eat dog hunger and the commerce in lives.

Home sweet home.

Lee entreats me to show greater application, in my best interests he did so, and I am grateful for that, even if it had no effect. I am who I am, and have been adequately warned about the bitterness of the limelight, and I am not an entertainer, cannot tell jokes, do not derive any satisfaction from being the center of attention, which is again not even half the truth, because I do, which is to say, by which I mean that should my joy elicit in the private heart of whoever listens the joy of attending at a moment of subtle creation, approaching the subtlety of creation itself, then I have the satisfaction of speaking to one of God's children, when it is not I who am the center of attention but the center of the heart of one of these who will endure this life as does all great art in the making of which I am of no account.

As I said, I am who I am and I have, once or twice, been called to account for my blemishes, as this story will illustrate. What are termed creative people - whether painter or sculptor or writer or dancer or con man - exert a cloying fascination over women, often not by intent but as surely as the lamp draws the moth into its orbit, in the nature of things. And there is no fault in that, as far as I can see, though there is in capitalising on the phenomenon. Young women often dote, recklessly, on the charisma of the personality of the creative one, for which the only explanation I can think of is that these men affirm in the women the primordial power of their own creative force, so that they feel acknowledged and assured, in a way in which life these days rarely graces them. Dixie was one of these, what we now term groupies. There are many dangers even in blowing a horn.

She seemed to be genuine, if somewhat hasty, in the two days we knew each other, in which time our affections were consummated. She then lost interest. Her success became a matter of boasting and came to the attention of her parents.

One evening, we were playing at some club, Jazz City or Bill Whislin's place, "Whislin's Hawaiian", yes, the Hawaiian it was, on Sunset just west of Vine. I didn't notice them come in, but several of the guys paid more attention to detail than I did and were obviously feeling uneasy. What's shaking down here, I ask, and the indication I get, with a surreptitious eye movement, is that there are two goons sitting at a table right in front of us, dressed like they stepped out of a Mickey Spillane novel or Raymond Chandler, one with his hat tipped back on his head, over-worked and world weary, the other with the brim of his hat almost covering his eyes, so as not to appear prominent, despite being at the very front table and obviously not here to listen, unless they've wandered in here by mistake, in the false anticipation of some strip tease. We play a couple more numbers after they've taken up their positions, and it's the end of our first set.

In my white dress shirt that is too big because my body is too thin and I give short shrift to fashion, I am at least presentable. I'm removing the mouthpiece from the horn and sticking it in my pocket, when these goons come up to the edge of the stage and introduce themselves, almost off hand, as representatives of the Los Angeles Police Department, which one of you is Warne Marsh, and, unsuspecting while under suspicion I say that is me. Maybe my mother's died. Then I hear 'rights' and would I like to come down to the station because they want to charge me, as if they were doing me a favor. All I can think of is the incongruity of charging me for going down to the station, and I almost ask How much, but instead I ask, out of curiosity, what the charge is, but they seem embarrassed to say and encourage me to accompany them. I explain that I'm at work, which causes them to share in a facetious smile and then ignore me completely and ask would one of you guys explain to Bill that Mr Marsh has been called away on urgent business.

Next thing I'm behind bars. A complaint had been brought against my person, statutory rape, which is serious, they tell me. Rape? I question the use of the term. Who? Dixie. Penetrating a person under the legal age of consent. I would have laughed, were it not that for some reason I thought that such a charge, if proven, carried a life-sentence. In fact, I mused, if I was black, in some States of this my country, then I might well be facing the death penalty. Farewell, My Lovely. I could make a phone call. That I called my mother struck them as something woefully short of a John Wayne approach to such a dilemma as I was in, and come to think of it not many of us have the opportunity to confide in our mother that we are sitting in the city jail, charged with statutory rape, and requiring the services of a lawyer rather urgently or someone to post bail. The allusion to John Wayne is not accidental; he who, as a rising star in the saddle preparing to uphold the fictional laws of Hollywood the fantasy, requested of the teenage Betty Churchill, ingratiating himself, that she permit him to tootle on her clarinet, was also a distant family acquaintance, and appeared with Aunty Mae in her penultimate film, Donavan's Reef, which was set in

Hawaii, and here I was just after the first set in the Hawaiian. This was, besides, another congruence of my life and that of the dominant figure in my lineage before Lennie, Pres, who had also spent time behind bars, and with as little provocation to the laws of the land of Uncle Sam, but with an equivalent weakness to the laws of human nature.

It was already late and I had to spend the night in the holding pens. Dixie, I was to learn, had been getting to know a broad cross section of the local jazz community, and the charge against me was reduced to a misdemeanor, in view of the fact that I had obviously been seduced and was a former student at the University of Southern California and white and friends of the family included Mr Louis B. Mogul and Greta Garbo and John Wayne. I was humiliated, but consoled by my mother's lack of interest in talking about the subject ever again. She collected me from jail the way she would have picked someone up from the airport, and drove me to the club for that night's performance. It was like the old days, and I wondered what she thought about in her room all the time. She ate alone, mostly, and also paid the $100 fine and the legal fees.

Lee was right, I really did need to get to grips with my affairs. He seemed to have things nicely under control, except for a few personal matters which are none of my business, but word gets around. I was disorientated, finding it hard to fathom why events were transpiring as they were. After all, we had spent the best part of the last seven years reaching such a refined understanding of each other and were capable of creating in a fashion no other two men could rival, we were like brothers who have to fight now and again, that close. Or, as Owen the younger would say, I love him but I do not like him. Why throw all that away. That was for then, he'd say, I want to find my own way, can't live like siamese twins for ever, and I want to get established, and in any case, your attitude and mine differ substantially. But, I said, we can discover what comes next together, to which the response was that audiences didn't have the patience to listen carefully unless things were simplified a bit, packaged. That all meant compromises.

It was perhaps his taste for making a name, working up a public profile, a touch of the showman, and that implied editing the inspiration. I was a perfectionist, in my occupation, and that was demanding enough without all the additional hassles of catering for the public, becoming accessible, releasing a modified version of my song and a well timed piece for the press. Not a chance. It was all a matter of taste, preferences and ideals, and the immutable force of my gift - some people would call it genius but that is a word that I cannot apply to myself, since I make no claims. I had worked assiduously for fifteen years to perfect my art on my chosen instrument and my singular goal in life was to liberate my gift from all influences, such as financial interest, personality or ego, popularity, admiration, fear, to arrive at that experience where whatever I express is absolutely what I know, feel and hear, where the beauty leaves me and my listener poised, in perfect if temporary equilibrium between eternal silence and the diminuendo of the last note. Intractable. Jazz had the same potential for enduring art as any other form - that was my profession, I mean that is something I profess. This was not an entertainment, an interlude between drinks, idle chatter, gossip, an exhibition. This was my life I was delivering. I am playing for my life. Lee felt he couldn't take it that seriously. I accept that, and make no judgements. I am who I am, one of God's chillun and we all got our own personal rhythm.

The lease on 317 East 32nd had expired and Ronnie had come out west, married a black girl - an Englishman married a black girl, was that ever defiant of the American way. Ted was soon to come out west, he was already married back east, and his wife a gifted singer who wouldn't risk herself in public. The momentum of the school had faltered with these departures, and Jeff had come out west, married to a sculptor. All educated and nurtured by Lennie. And there was sometimes Don and Ben. And me. Piano, tenor, drums, guitar and bass. The first regular performing unit since my days in New York City. No alto. There was only one other alto player I had any affinity with in these days, and that was Art, who was a delight, full of lyrical playfulness, ebullient and tragic and in and out of jail and sanatorium, not too reliable a partner and already half covered with tattoos. And nobody was helping him either, yet, so the country wasted a lot, though there is no point in talking about what could have been: we are in the present reality for ever. Art had his own lineup, but we jammed together whenever we could, and I always missed Lee, I will always miss Lee, substantial-lee, there will never be another you, it said. I am like Pres without Herschel. And there is a part of me that is sloppy and a part of me that is shabby.

Donna Lee. Dixie. Farewell, my lovely. What's in a name? That evening, after my release from custody, I called for All The Things You Are and titled the ensuing composition Dixie's Dilemma. The inventions we created. Inventions based on a theme but, improvised though they were, with hours of preparation by way of prior experiment, they were frequently, if not always, complete, self-contained works in their own right, stimulated if you like by an existing melody, and marking an occasion. The spontaneous song is for now but invested with such care and vitality that it can be for all time. Far from random. It truly does not concern me if the audience does not listen now; that is up to them. I can tell you the condition of my life: consciousness and conscientiousness inform my delivery of the evidence and bestow form upon it, rendering the art of work a work of art.

But I make no claims, not even of modesty. To know me is to know my songs - I say that to myself. Some time before Ted came back, we did a brief sortie into the South, with Lee and Ronnie and his black wife having to travel separately because the South was what it was then, and how can you express your self if you have to be surreptitious and creep about in the South at night, not daring to be seen with your wife in front of the wrong people who are likely to jerk one of you up short, and all that was hardly a success and the South is one part of this my country which I do not need to see again and never did again venture into Dixie.

After that we gathered at Jeff's garage in Pasadena - oh, the garages I have known, no churches or open space for music in our age - and labored towards affinity, a smooth working unit capable of surprising each other, and I would far rather do that in a garage with a bottle of wine between sessions than in a company studio, with some guy waving a production schedule under my nose and fretting about the cost and how many more records they would have to sell for every extra hour we took. No joy in that, but the industry was developing a pattern of what the professional musician had to do, by which it is understood that we mean profitable musician. And when we had the measure of each other's rhythm, we went out and played, at "The Lighthouse" in Hermosa Beach and a regular spot at the "Hawaiian" on Fridays and Saturdays and some Sundays and then some Thursdays, for five months, the first time I had an income from gift almost sufficient to live by. They were happy days, optimistic, all of us finding our feet, and finding that there is a limit to how long you can play a joint before the rot sets in.

And we made records, Freewheeling and Jazz of Two Cities, because we were freewheeling and playing the music of New York in Los Angeles, and a session with Art, all in a couple of months, plenty of activity, even though no one heard the session with Art for another sixteen years, like a message in a bottle. And there was a kind of following, people who could listen.

And some made comments, of which these are flaking fragments.

"....disc unavailable many years after which collectors have lusted with intensity STOP Marsh at fulcrum of conventional quartet subtlely turning the session into a veritable tour de force STOP his almost uncanny ability to sustain a flow of rich improvisational ideas STOP one of the most important rewarding reissues of the 80s one not to miss STOP a master"

"....probably one of the most spontaneous of his recorded efforts STOP one of the most highly sought after collector's items in jazz STOP really You Are Too Beautiful and the master of the subconscious."

Music For Prancing we called that, with heavy irony and twenty eight years to surface this message left for you, and that speaks for itself. And we acquired a following, mainly young people avid for the new music before the first crushing blow of rock and roll and looking for alternatives to the suffocating weight of middle America the world holding its hand over its ears nigh on deaf, no muse inviolate, young people almost revering and embarrassingly so, but listening and hearing some of the message between silence and eternal diminuendo as I said can you hear me Lee not talking about Jerusalem but this my methuselah in which the song will not be contained and I an old man harking back upon a day against which there was no preparation all morality a puff of ash in the wind then as enmity and judgements disintegrate and crumble like fabric desiccated by sheer age which we hold in our hands a thread barely retaining any color in the balance between something and nothing the recorded song released and unheard except by a few. Choirs of angels shall attend. Fade out.

Young people mainly, at that time, rebels looking for examples of finding a way out from under the weight of middle American irrelevance bearing down upon them and the noise impending and the silence to which the true history had been relegated. There was an intimacy which the big band didn't allow for and for which the small combo, the ensemble, gave ample allowance. There at the Hawaiian, they attended as often as they could, compulsively, seeking assurance and possibly illegal substances around the tables with the black coffee and bottles of vino and the gaggle of glasses atop stained coasters, chins in their hands, the young men and the young ladies almost out of college, some as attentive to the melody issuing just ten feet away as Karl had been lying flat on his stomach on the roof of the dance hall or as I had been at the doors of the clubs on Spade Alley, straining to hear live music come alive in me. Inspired by and infatuated with the creative one, a young lady gazes in the dim light hoping to catch my eye. Bohemians, hipsters, drop outs but tuned in.

She made the pilgrimage to Laurel Canyon, with a friend, to visit the immortal one in his temporary lodgings owning up to the first signs of encroaching dilapidation. Some surprise then to watch the door open and see not the god like form of my humble self but my mother standing there, my mom. The visitant was speechless. Life is never the same at midnight as it is at noon, in the patently work-a-day world of mom who does not like to be disturbed by a young girl, the supplicant at the front door altar of her son to whom there is little left to say of any great significance. The one remarks, First Dixie and now this! The other remarks that there is The Myth and, somewhere, the reality.

She came bearing gifts, a basket of tokens such as a devotee might offer the departing soul in China or Egypt as sustenance on its endless journey. She was in love, in the sophomore manner. A basket to feed my every sense: incense, jelly beans, wind chimes, prism, a silk handkerchief. Could she, this jewish mom of San Fernando Valley, with her hair dyed and sprayed, please hand this my votive offering, could she, to your son, he who has inspired this gesture of, this, uh, thank you. Blush. It is easy to love?

Later on, she presented a simpler gift, something recognizably personal and straight forward, and so delightful, a small dime store turtle, cute but honest, and I said to her just how big will this little fellow grow. I had it with me for a long while, a memento of the spirit of that era amongst those looking for inspiration and zest for life beyond the shallows in the cultural desert that was California.

And there was Leroy, big and black, and there was Red who said we appreciate your appreciation, to the assembled congregation who appreciated being appreciated, and there was me who said very little, living on the night side of life, into it perhaps too far to get back by morning or ever.

Once you have embarked upon the journey there is no turning back if you have a mind to complete it. Improvisation is like that, sincerely brand new, a fresh creation for a fresh day already history, not a note borrowed or tossed up flippantly, everyone as precise as the settings of a jewel, nothing just for the sake of filling time, always the effort to leave behind a new experience, to exhilarate and, in our fashion, to reflect the glory of being alive, which, under the conditions, was little short of miraculous.

This meant that we did not play for barflies, or those who came to be seen or those who were not prepared to listen intently - the invention of canned music saved a whole lot of people a whole lot of wasted effort. We weren't taking any short cuts, so it was reasonable to expect that our audience would not cheat either. Reasonable maybe, but far from the case.

In March fifty seven, it was said, in part, I read it in down beat that myself "and Ted and Ronnie and Ben and Jeff been together almost a year one of most clearly individual groups in jazz anticipating the other's ideas to a degree suggests telepathy and audience response uniformly favorable as the tenor unison lines unfold intricate patterns on Smog Eyes, Long Gone, or Topsy, performers' uncompromising conviction they play own unique brand of jazz for thoughtful listeners so much happening between ensemble voices demanding unqualified attention indeed unique jazz unit should hit the college circuit and really make it."

But that would have been too predictable, and spontaneity demands the unpredictable, and demanding attention led to its not being required any more. Still, it was a good run, those months of youthful optimism and reasonably good money and good wine and good company, and where was there to play and be heard, in California. If you play too often, particularly at a price, it starts to wither, so I'd rather play when I feel like it, not have it be like I'm turning up at a job. The lifestyle wasn't that attractive.

Then the phone rang, long distance.

chapter sixteen **i remember you**

Scene: I'm in the library, practicing, in the early evening. Mother is in the lounge. watching tv while she practices her bridge. I've promised her a game when I've finished. The phone rings. She answers it, comes to the library door and knocks.

"Warne. (I hear but continue: I do not enjoy interruptions.) Warne! (I block out the voice calling.) Phone call. Long distance. From a pay phone."

She walks away, knowing what to expect.

I finish, unclip the horn and set it on the stand and wander in to the lounge, still working through what I was playing, singing it through in my head, a theme from Bartok.

"(Tentative) Lennie? Ah, Sheila! (She's never rung before) Where are you calling from? Sure I remember. It's not that long ago. You singing there? Uhu. On piano? It has to be Horace. It is? You see, I've kept my ear in. You think we just hang loose out here? Ah, Ronnie, Jeff, Red, Joe (coins dropping into the pay phone cut the conversation) Ted, Art, Don; yeh, it's been busy, a lot of fun. Yeh, a few casuals. Oh, you know how it is, enough to live by. How's the scene in New York? He wants to work again? Actually, I'm bored with LA. Why doesn't he ask me himself? Tell him I'll be up. Oh, a few days."

"You never move that fast for me."

"It was a message from Lennie."

"I'd never have guessed."

I set off back to the library.

"And when are we to enjoy this game of bridge? It's late already."

"Half an hour?"

"Just wait until you're an old man! You'll be glad of a son."

"You're only sixty."

"Fifty eight. And that's fine. I can manage."

"Half an hour."

It must have been three in the morning when I finished and she'd gone to bed and left all the lights on.

It was not easy to bring friends back to the house, so I would go visit, which was a habit that had started in my teens, finding someone who liked to blow for hours. I derived more pleasure from dropping in on friends than I ever did from playing in public in America; always informal, often unannounced, there'd I'd be, horn in one hand, scrabble and chess sets in the other. No need to cut a figure or make conversation. I was always on the look out for friends who could come at that, and there weren't that many. Don was one.

We'd done a casual at a dance with Buddy, who played bass, and took a shine to each other, having similar tastes. He was one of the few on the West coast who knew Lennie's work and appreciated it and wasn't out to make the scene or play house band piano forever or do the vogue hip thing. Sometimes we'd blow, sometimes we'd despatch a bottle of vino over a game of chess which would go on for hours because I liked to take my time and ponder all the options which existed at this move and calculate what options would be available after this move, in the context of all the options that Don would have after this move, plotting two or three moves ahead. He was patient. What was the hurry? Relaxing was essential to good improvising, and this was all training in relaxation. I can't tolerate impatience, there's so little room left in life to savor the passing moments, and ruminate.

I had my room in that anachronism of a house and a few things and kitchen privileges and the past always encroaching. He had an apartment in Echo Park where I became a regular visitor: it was neutral ground and a relief. Those nights I looked forward to, in an apartment that was comfortable, not spartan, nor with the woman behind closed doors. Private, secluded in its way, definitely nothing to do with my own history. Going there was like a security, a safe place. I could never imagine having such a pad, all the trouble it must take to maintain. We had always had a cook and a maid and a governess and a gardener, and that never left me, the expectation of being looked after, so I was totally unmotivated for that kind of effort. And besides, to play was my living; for the rest, I would make do. I was also careless, no matter how well-intentioned. Perhaps I deserve the excuse of being absent minded. One evening I turn up with the vino, and, in a party mood, make a great show of the maitre D uncorking the bottle, only to watch the cork fly in a delinquent trajectory straight between a gap in the drapes and then clean through the glass of Don's living room window. Fortunately no one was passing by at the time. My prior thought had been to avoid smashing the lamp shade at all costs. I did. It was as stunning as getting a birdie in golf, blindfold. I can't remember if I offered to pay for it or not, but next time I arrive, Don's had it fixed.

It became like another regular gig without the audience or time limit, minimum or maximum, an opportunity to try the impossible with impunity: if it didn't work, we'd have a good laugh at our failed audacity, and try it again, until, often, it came right. We even worked up part of Bartok's Concerto for Orchestra into a new kind of ballad, and tended that until it was our own thing, a curio. I think he felt privileged to witness what he said was a level of music that isn't heard that often these days, and to be kept on his toes.

Our Bartok invention had one public performance, its world premiere, in a stylish club in LA, 'the' place to go, where the house band had established a clique of its own - the leader was the pianist. Now Don was not an accepted face, not being set on making the scene or taking any bullshit and prone to the jitters. I sat in for a set and was hustling the pianist to let Don sit in. And when I was given the chance of a ballad, I say, well, this ballad there's only one pianist in the world can get over and that's Don. So there we are, introducing our ballad on a theme from Bartok's Concerto for Orchestra. It was a show stopper. No one knew Bartok's Concerto for Orchestra, but they knew a fine ballad when they heard one. I think everyone felt set up, especially the pianist. It was enough to make a point, though our intention was merely to play something different.

Actually Don had little stomach for public performance; he got stage fright and was always terrified of panicking, but you'll have heard some of his compositions on television. I've seen that so many times - Billy had lost his nerve, Ted's wife had no nerve, both brim full of talent and rich in imagination - and yet when I put the horn to my mouth I feel powerful, alive, relish every second like I'll only stop playing when there's no more air in the world. Odd how it goes.

A friendship like this was a sanctuary for the two of us. Don had permission to play at his most daring and without fear (because there is fear to be overcome in music) and I had the space and time just to be myself and be accepted for that and to blow away cobwebs in sympathetic company. Neither of us had anything to prove, no egos to preen or pride to polish, no quibbles about morality or personality, and the vino and the joints and scrabble - I was an unwilling loser - and tolerance without impatience. Was I demanding? I don't think I was demanding. But I had a fallback and he didn't and he got the jitters and I didn't and come December we each headed off to wherever.

New York City. Back to a fitful experiment in continuum. Search for the authentic I am. My style my life, this peripatetic shunt between West and East: the pacific cradle of my birth a narcosis I cannot start to wrestle with, the atlantic germination of my song the loyalty I cannot satiate. We were a scattered tribe assembling, for another tilt at what was not to be, a family more retrospective than advancing and held together by the irresistible tension of differences and contrary motion, like a slow divorce.

The scene had changed so much. And we were older. The Manhattan studio was a history becoming folk lore remembered only in song and the 'school' had fragmented into a rearguard action. Lennie was teaching on and off, playing rarely in public and recording even less often, except in his home, which was now in Palo Alto Street in the suburb of Jamaica on Long Island. A new generation of jazz was emerging from the big band era which had been terminated by economics - and once again the emphasis was black (John, Thelonius, Quincey, Miles, Sonny R, Sonny S, Ornette, Sun Ra, Art and Dizzy in his prime) and the voice of Africa was sounding and very fashionable and very marketable it was.

The age of the showman had really arrived and jazz was now called modern and mainstream. It was a time to be current and ignorant of the history, and jazz began its amoebic proliferation into marketable tastes. But the greatest of tastes was rock and roll, that wraith-like behemoth, which was the greatest of successes for the industry and creators of merchandise, and, frankly, wreaked the greatest possible damage to the art of listening. And competence and honesty departed underground rather than acquiesce with the passing mood of the times, and I, plain to a fault, prepared against the days of my descent, confident that after the fire had scorched the earth there would be, still, the germ of life in the crucible. Jazz had held onto space in Manhattan and the Village, but it was starting to move out of town, and was not even a pale reflection of the glorious days of 52nd Street when New York City was a compendium of jazz. (My nostalgia for the sessions with Bird, just casuals, but just beautiful, the way his life yearned for beauty, exquisite and unassuming, this nostalgia would continue to assail me for years.) I camped at Lennie's house for a while and then found a room on West 76th Street, somewhere to sleep and practice - I was not an entertainer - a few yards from where I had lived with

Lee and his family a few years back, close to Central Park. Peter had stayed on with his recording studio and bass, consistently dedicated, inspired, and gaunt, and Sal was still studying and later on Lee came back and Ronnie. And it was not like old times.

I had a small room - charm is not a quality it had -• with a secondhand sofa bed, coffee maker, my instrument, metronome and suit case. And a chair. This was a gift from Betty, one of the new faces, but it didn't stay long because Lennie was short of a chair. Things got passed around; that communal spirit lingered on. And I gave lessons, taking students Lennie could not find time for.

"I first heard him at the Half Note. That changed my life. I swear no one had ever played like he did. As soon as he took off on a solo, something happened, to him, to the audience and to the other musicians, something indescribable. I was only twenty and missed out on hearing Bird in person, or Pres at his best. But I have never had anything approaching that experience listening to anyone else. The only word that fits is 'revelation'.

I had not heard him before. A friend had told me to catch him if I wanted to know what inspired improvising was. Even forewarned, it was all so completely unexpected. For a start, there was nothing about him to suggest that he had anything going for him at all. He looked just plain ordinary, made no kind of impression; dressed this side of drab, on the street you would not have noticed him if he passed by twenty times, a real ordinary face in a crowd, a school teacher or store keeper, an average Joe. So my first impression contradicted what I had been led to expect. And I thought, 'This guy is inspired?' Well, if you don't know what it is, I guess a bomb looks fairly uninspiring - until it goes off.

Then I noticed two things. His eyes first of all. He was taking everything in, concentrating without effort. His gaze was not penetrating; it was absorbing, discriminating. Impassive but not remote. You could tell from his gaze alone that this man knew what he had. Shy without being timid. And next up, the way he held his horn. Utter assurance. Like the instrument (an old Conn) was malleable, surrendered to him, like a child in the arms of a father in whom he has complete trust. Affectionate. Just the way the thing was rested against him. The way his hand lay over the keys, resolved, like the hand of a priest on his breviary. They were intimate friends who had no secrets from each other; the master and servant who had discovered equality of dependence. Baptismal, that was it.

He put the mouthpiece to his lips and gave a couple of puffs, gentle nudges of air. It was You Stepped Out Of A Dream. But it wasn't. As he moved into the solo, it started to happen. The whole feel of the man changed and as he changed so did the atmosphere in the room and something in me. Bewilderment, disbelief, love, admiration, hope, appetite, the shock and delight of witnessing an unsuspected beauty and tenderness. Above all, the awakening in me of a new sensitivity, a first taste of true subtlety.

There was a grace about the way he played, modest but commanding, a sensuality veiled by discretion, a daring that did not need bravado or posturing. He loved what he was playing. I could almost see the shape of it, and could not help but listen more and more attentively, as phrase after phrase surprised me. The music danced. And as if to make sure that it did not get out of control, he would occasionally sway ever so slightly or lean back as if to give the music an upward push, where it hovered in the air almost beyond the reach of gravity. There was no force, only a man singing of the freedom from intensity.

I am left with an impression, as if I had seen a painting that so affected me that it stayed in my sight even when I closed my eyes, an impression that will never leave my hearing. Optimism in the long flowing lines, the caress of an exultant piping, rapid phrases, triplet upon triplet peeling off like the squeals of laughter of children in spontaneous innocence or the bubbling of water at a spring, the song darting upwards into the alto register, then a swoop down to pluck out a succulent plum of a note at the bottom of the tenor's range, all in one unbroken graceful movement.

I hear him sing out, chuckle, the song ebb and flow, swell, surge, dip, linger, flutter like a humming bird while he lets his body catch up with the melody running ahead of him, while his feelings fill the space that the song creates in the relish of discovery. All so generous, asking nothing, a giving forth without hesitation, occasionally a reining in followed by release, probing and amplifying the change in feeling, every phrase obliging what came next, until the whole design is brought to completion in the contentment of perfect form, all coming to rest like the sea on a calm day in an expanse of silence.

I am not so much impressed as grateful, satisfied, awake, to have witnessed such a superb, flawlessly relaxed technique stripped of any pretension even at quite extraordinary speed; what was questionable was not whether his technique was sufficient, but whether the instrument was sufficient to voice all the ideas, that it might burst. More than that, I realize how pertinent this invention was to the theme of the song, how apt and sincere.

It was architecture, musical architecture, crazy unpredictable melodies, fresher and more exciting than anything I'd ever heard. And the rhythm of the playing moved in eddies, shimmering like a mirage. And every note so controlled and poignant, the performer and instrument in perfect balance. I can still see it all now. He hardly seemed to hear the applause and certainly didn't seem to expect any as he spoke quietly to the pianist about the next tune.

For the first time in my life, I had been shocked by finding that I was more alive than I had been aware of. I stayed until the end of the session, by now quite insatiable, alive, as I said, in a way I had not been before, and decided to ask him for lessons, which took some courage. He said he'd have to check with Lennie and asked if I could leave my number. He didn't ring, so after a few weeks I rang him, several times, and eventually got through. And that was my second shock - the lesson."

O——+——

Back in LA I had gotten lazy. Lennie remarked on that pretty soon. Once again he took me in hand, demanded discipline. Improvised solo was my form. I started putting in the hours again, undistracted, grateful for a task master.

Lee was back east and wasn't hitting it off with Lennie. They had constant disagreements. Lennie resented Lee's playing the field, getting to perform with all manner of people, which Lennie considered to be a poor way to develop a unique style, because there were too many influences, and what about the quartet we had put so much of our lives into. Lennie was performing solo more and more, and recording on his own in his house. They rarely played together. and talked less and less, except to argue. Lennie and his wife were arguing. It was a madhouse. Which is why I ended up on the west side.

Lennie also accused Lee of cashing in, seeking to get himself known and sacrificing purity in the process. Lee took offence. I could see Lennie's point of view but still found playing with Lee allowed me to perform at a level of spontaneous creativity that just didn't happen with anyone else. For that reason more than any other, I kept my opinions to myself. I mean that I did not allow them to make it impossible for us to play together. Lee was ever the hustler, so we did tv and radio, an album with Jimmy Giuffre, appeared once in a while at Birdland and regular spots at the Half Note. He was in the business, while I still only wanted to be living on my own terms, which meant still turning down work if it was just for the money. We were different, no getting away from that.

And we argued, mostly with few words and I was watching part of my life flake away, but not before we had produced works together that are the best I ever did. And from then on I am in search of my counterpart, which I need more than I need an audience, and which I had found but could not have. So I would be looking for my counterpart, even though I knew I did not need to look. And finding an audience required an energy I didn't have - it was as simple as that: I could play for 20 hours a day, but finding an audience was quite beyond my strength. In this regard, I confess to being inept, unable to push myself forward, always needing someone to take the initiative on my behalf. We all have our weaknesses. I would rather teach than hustle. And I would rather play than teach. And I would rather wear out than rust out.

O——+——

"As I was saying, the second shock. Partly the lesson, but initially the place where he lived. There was nothing in it bar the barest essentials: a rather tatty couch that unfolded into a bed, his saxophone and music stand. And a tiny porcelain turtle and a few books on the shelf above a fireplace that was long out of commission. I supposed there were other things in the cupboards, but it wouldn't have surprised me if they were mostly empty. In one corner of the room there was an old cooker and sink. The space was so bare that, once he'd invited me in and closed the door, I felt like an intruder. Neither of us had called each other by name. He gestured towards the couch and asked if I wanted to sit down. But if I sat down, he would have to remain standing. Or if he sat down, then I'd have to stand there on my own in the middle of the room.

Neither alternative would rid me of my awkwardness, so I stood where I was and waited. He went to the window and looked down onto the street below, saying nothing for the moment. I looked around me. A typical rent-controlled New York room. Still looking out of the window, he asked if I knew New York very well. I told him I was born here. He sighed and said 'You're lucky'. Sure it was small, but convenient and clean by New York standards, and there is nothing more you could say about it except that it presented a paradox that still baffles me.

What the hell was a guy whose playing was so full of life doing living in a place that was practically devoid of evidence of a life in progress? A student I could understand, but a successful musician could surely not be so poor. And from the way he was acting, he gave every indication of being quite at home: he was comfortable here. I would like to have asked him some questions, but that would have been difficult; for a start, he had his back to me.

He turned around, put one foot up on the arm of the couch, looked at me as if to get the measure of me, and then the lesson started.

"I'd like you to sing the A-minor scale."

I stared at him.

"Just one octave, or two if you can manage that."

I carried on staring, wondering what was going on.

There wasn't a piano in the room.

"I can give you the A if you like."

I nodded. He sang out the note A, making a clear 'la' sound. It was done quite naturally as if everyone could do that.

"Do you know the jazz A-minor scale?"

"Yes, I do, on the instrument."

"That's not good enough. I'll sing it, then you repeat it."

He sang it, slowly, going up and coming down. La la la la la la la la la la la la la la la. I started out and struggled around the 7th note. He helped me out. He waited. I repeated it and got it right after stumbling pathetically once or twice. I had never heard my own voice before. I was close to running out of the room.

"Now I want you to sing the scale 1 3, 2 4, 3 5 and so on. Up and down. Just one octave."

And so it went on, every combination of pattern you could think of. Patiently, relentlessly. And as the process unfolded, I started to really like the man and to realize what the purpose of the exercise was. He shared in my growing confidence. Then, all of a sudden, he stopped and went back to looking out of the window, for several minutes. And my confidence drained away. Maybe intuiting this, but I suspect not, he turned around and started talking as if we had been in conversation all along.

"Rhythm is so important. We can get on to harmony and melody, but first of all you should be able to sing your scales, and at the same time cultivate your sense of rhythm. You are not relaxed. And to feel rhythm you have to be relaxed. Sit down."

I went to the couch and sat down.

"You might like to keep your eyes shut. Beat a 4/4 rhythm with your left foot. Any tempo you like. Ok. Now set up a 2/2 rhythm with your right hand on your knee. Ok. Now switch them over."

My foot and hand stopped, paralysed. He gave a short, tolerant laugh. Since he said nothing, I tried again, and again and slowly improved.

"Ok, keep that going, and now set up a 3/4 rhythm with your right foot."

He was leaning back against the window sill, demonstrating, his face quite impassive. It was totally impossible for me. Despair was welling up to engulf me. He saved me.

"It takes a lot of practice. Keep working on it. After that, we'll learn to keep four rhythms going independently and move them around from hand to foot to foot to hand and back again and from left foot to right hand and right foot to left hand, until you can do it any way you choose, on demand. It puts the brain back where it belongs."

He moved into the middle of the room. That was obviously that for today, so I stood up and paid him.

"Can I come back next week?"

"If you've made progress, yes."

I was thrilled, and horrified of having to face my own ignorance. He opened the door and I shook his hand and had already taken a few steps down the corridor when he called me back.

"Jack, you've forgotten your horn."

He used my name as if we were equals, and I had the irrational expectation that we would become friends."

My element is water. The oceans, clear out of sight of any land. I do not venture where there is no light, and only occasionally do I break the surface. I am the wanderer, go anywhere I please, preferring the faster currents and temporary shelter in the idleness of warm lagoons. I am fish. Not glamorous tropical fish, nor of bulk, nor the hunter, nor the host, nor the parasite. I do not seek company and I do not shun company. I hunger neither for conquest nor for arrival anywhere: I explore and prove the oceans endless. Movement is my language.

I have encountered friends and enjoyed dialogue absolutely free of vagueness and bluff as we moved consorting and mercurial through this elixir of life, sprightly, deft, itinerant, precise, delving into motion, contrary motion and resolution with eloquence and honesty. Until we each have slipped away, concurrent, often with much to be thankful for, sometimes with a sadness that beauty is inconclusive and elusive, a rainbow limned in vapor.

In still waters, I am inert, awkward, disaffected and irresolute; in turbulent waters, in distress. Therefore I choose, where I can, the manner of my passage, my passing through, even if it is beyond my power to hold off the tribulation of the straits. In constant motion, I am inconstant and faithful nevertheless.

Music is my element in which I thrive and in which I had immersed myself. I could not abide by discord and was without the knack of coping with it. And all around me I see discord. My aim is to leave a legacy free of sentimentality, pride, preening, any vestige of personality, and refuse to employ music as a means of self-advancement, as bait for flattery or incitement. And all around me I see arrogance parading as knowledge, fads masquerading as competence, and the enormous maw of the industry disgorging a slurry of noise and amplification into the ears of the attendant droves. Am I to be a peddler of wares, string about my person pots and pans of every conceivable moderate quality, and, beating upon them, jocular and gap-toothed, go to market? I think not.

No. I would go about my own business in my own time, with associates of my deliberate choosing, in my own context, wherever I felt at home and unharried by the executive mob, somewhere just plain ordinary but of my own choice, perhaps, in the end, of my own making.

There was less and less work available, unless we accept a tv show, commercials, weigh in with the new popular culture, produce, produce, produce, even if there was nothing to say, record, record, record, in order to fulfil contracts. You may as well clip the wings of a bird of paradise and cage it in a shoe box.

Because people had to take their pick of the options at that time, there were fewer friends to perform with, even socially. Lennie's ambitions were in tatters, and he all morose, and here we were at the sorry end of a story that had begun with such aspirations.

There were recordings, some of them personal hallmarks, snatches of life for me at the time, vibrant with an affinity between companions that was to dissipate, a prelude to my own dissipation, recordings that remained unissued for sixteen or seventeen years. That they existed was enough, for the song was never recorded of old, just as it was never notated, written down. There was no need for such substitution because the song was sustained in the heart of the community, the tribe, and my belief is that time has not changed that. The song will always come to life, so long as there is life in the community, though, as I have witnessed, there is a forbidding silence which does not augur well. I am faithful nevertheless.

The best was live, not in the commercial studio, because in the intimate context there is a community alive in the present and the song is touched by that presence. And, being live, most of the best is held in memory only. Perhaps what is left is sufficient as a testament to the spirit of the occasion, a spur, a reminder that music is the deepest expression of the very soul of man, and an honorable calling for that. Perhaps, at best, the recorded moment is tremulous evidence lest the art of the true song peter out: to uphold this unison in the history ....

Dear Bill,

We've mastered the record. Since the editing is about perfect, McLeod got nervous having nothing to do and suggested slower fades beginning before the ends of choruses, but I calmed him down. So give Lennie the editing credit.

I've been trying ideas for liner notes that would put the art of improvisation - a splendid title - and jazz and classical in perspective with each other.

I get as far as describing improvisation as a new genre - not the improvising of a solitary great composer in Bach's time - but ensemble improvising as an art form; however, to estimate the role of improvisation in classic music, particularly in its inception, when I'm convinced improvising was the motivating power, and to estimate improvisation in jazz, obviously considerable, but rejected by traditional thought, or at least suspect as art ... I'm trying to put into words....As ever, Warne. (4 February 1974)

There are snatches, always annotated, of the evidence, by necessity out of context being after the event, a kind of verbal notation, fumbling and imprecise, which nevertheless testify to some permanence in the song of my life, set down many years after the events which, faint echoes though they be at best, have some art in them, some love, and is not all art strangely present, as if nothing has intervened between the present of its coming to be and the moment of its fresh utterance, as if we did elide the years ....

So these words not mine concerning what I did own most thoroughly, knowing that I had spared no effort nor forthrightness, and surrendered because the moment vanished with its completion, not to be held onto like a collection of trophies to be admired in old age ....

These words remembered in snatches for the record (Volume One) wonderful sessions at the Half Note....all the solos distilled essence of improvising, among his highest achievements mesmerizing, reached a peak here never issued a more important recording, seldom obvious without cliche some marvelous vistas if you can stay on the saddle....It was Bill who said that and of Volume Two three years later he added....Warne is a giant, the equal in stature of Bird, Coltrane, Dizzy, Satchmo and Pres....and comparisons are odious so who am I to agree or disagree.

The fact that there is anything left at all is very much the work of others, none of them seeking credit. But the memories did evoke comment, in words that are like the paint flaking off in a harsh wind.... phrases that resolve miraculously, incomplete solos of great richness, flowing mastery, from lyricism to intricacy serenity bursting with feeling invention and rhythmic life....

The soloist is what I am, preparing, unwittingly, for my descent from the peak only seen from the valleys ahead many years later. And there was Bird ten years earlier saying watch that kid he's got it and Pres passing on his laurel in a tender whisper before he slumped dear Pres and no one inclined or competent to do anything about that and I did not ask them to commit those words in fact never did invite comment because I knew time would tell much more clearly.

And I had watched them fall, no one grieving, only lurching from one fiasco to the next, quite ignoring his requests, I refer to Bird buried like a dressed doll in a shoe box, and his bequests in the spirit in which they were given, watched the machine grind on, and standards fall in slow motion like an insidious disease, knowing the consequences as I did and wanting no part, speaking when invited but otherwise holding my tongue, and watched Lennie court despair and his wife shouting at him, heedless of the fight he had put up against the light going out and that he failed to see that times had changed.

Thank God for the friendships. You can keep the accolades, the flashing lights, the teetering gantry bolted together by the executive mob and the descendants of Mr Mogul which would surely collapse under its own weight in the fullness of time because it was becoming fashionable to ignore the basics, the fundamentals, and I had no wish to be amongst the debris, an Ollie slumped bleeding to death while the crew munch on heavily buttered cinnamon toast and fat sausages. And I determined to play just for friendships.

A sorry state of affairs, really, run out of puff, last gasp of an epoch, that August in New York before my descent. Yes, I had harbored expectations of something different, in my fondness, and yes, they had gone unrequited, except for the friendships, and at thirty two staring into the wilderness of Broadway from my window, a young student behind me, waiting patiently in the middle of the world for some guidance. Maybe when I turn round he will have gone already.

chapter seventeen **descent into the maelstrom**

Bird played a spontaneous invention on the Ray Noble song Cherokee (1937) and called it Ko-Ko (1949), an entirely new contribution, absolutely the creative work of Bird, his song, but descended quite deliberately from a specific source and not just plucked out of the air, happenstance. You can see by the name he gave his song that Bird acknowledges his source - he has borrowed two letters - the same way parents name their children after ancestors. A kind of musical humor. I could hear other possibilities in Cherokee and found my own song in it, my own melody and my own time signature, and called this Marshmallow (1958), extending the play on words - a nice cup of cocoa has a lump of marshmallow in it - and cocoa of course is brown and marshmallow is white, and the harmonies prove a point which life itself most often doesn't, except in feeling perhaps. Artistry is an intense process and we were having a little fun: a marshmallow is some jump from a Cherokee Indian.

We played in basements, living rooms, occasionally in brothels and a concert hall, converted storerooms and garages, and you have to draw the line somewhere if you are serious about standards and the standards my word they were our education our lineage and raising the quality and self-respect and respect for the gift and knowledge and competence and an honorable calling after eighteen years of assiduous effort and devotion by the kid who's got it now thirty three years after the cradle on the porch of the beach house in Malibu loved but not liked and not even loved and become philosophically resigned but not deterred nor yet interred as luck would have it with the job to be done far from complete even if dejected on times and popping pills by the fistful to ward off something or other a realization dreaded heavy hearted and travelling light he my unison departed silentlee nothing resolved except in that which is my element like a divorce never named as such there being no litigation yet devised to cover such eventualities which are not eventualities but processes like evolution or absolution and where is andre now buddy of my youth to whom I handed my copy of sweet lorraine under the hands of Art Tatum rifled off he used to say you know the blind man young pros that we were all of seventeen andre and karl and me recording our interpretation of how high the moon out of which the bird hatched ornithology and our adolescent effervescent stompin at the savoy still extant in someone's cupboard these many moons down the track is there for me a sweet lorraine the name the names sweet sweet the names oh herschel oh herschel I hear pres cry yes he a man too and black overtly weeping as if he had lost his own child cradling the sweetest memories of veritable bliss in his thin arms and his head twisted gawky to one side a gentle man and black too and not sophisticate look look there they go mr young and mr herschel boys in long trousers off to their communion in sweet hymn sweet lorraine and oh sweet jesus shall we sing a lullaby or at worst a smattering of southern gospel for bird in his box dressed impeccable like a child off to school for the first time fresh and neat but parcelled up in fact for the train ride back to kansas city a most unplanned outing here we come surprise surprise toot toot to take up his position as a fallen pillar of the community if only they knew the truth and sighs of relief from all over the place after all is said and done a line of descent is drawn such as I have specified and a line has to be drawn somewhere and that is where I shall begin my descent

into the maelstrom that is the consummation of my destiny along the long flowing lines something along these lines I have played an aristocrat without title tilting one more time at the unattainable because this gig we call existence is not long enough for one man to complete the journey through the continuum that task calling out for a lineage of journeys from duke and his train to john and his trane and cerucik on his train the entire history of the song in train all of us fairly chugging along chasing the unattainable bar in snatches caught on the hop time and time and again confounded by the erratic bounce of the pigskin of human events time to call on fred and carol the wife of the same though now he too deceased but not then of course he never ceased to be among the friends who would have the pleasure of my dropping by never that is until I dropped you remember him don't you remember fred who in the army the impostor to effect my posting to fort monmouth yes you do remember so it's time to call on fred

because we are back in la now no no no not as in la la la lesson one but as in los angeles at a loss in los angeles spic and spanish in los angeles with fred during this descent this descant contrapuntal of the pigskin going haywire with the rest of my life what am I doing calling on fred hi fred hi carol 'sonly me the door's always open they recognize my voice

staying for an indefinite engagement with mom meting out the inheritance of shekels piecemeal drips and drabs one only had to ask probably calculated how much at a time to eke the sum out so that in a final crescendo the last shekel will fall on the beat as I drop my mortal coil until the last of my days like an actuary she was not generous this rent free arrangement with the old woman as part of the deal struck between silent partners in this hand life's dealt me or the cards I tease from the deck taking each one as it comes each day as it comes one more hand of bridge over these very troubled waters constraints torn asunder no complaints I said good no lump sum son she said some son I exclaim tight lipped never could bring myself to let out the word bitch and why that is I do not know because it screeched right through me and no complaints I said this life good anyway fred was the salt of the earth and we could have been old campaigners back in arms again carousing together and carol his lovely woman a sister to me drawn into the bosom of this family scene with fred and carol and me gathered here today around the table benign company as always the door open to the balmy air of california and me wolfing down the food and a discrete belch for good measure and no stern looks the kind of childhood I would have had had I not had the childhood I have had no choking here no sirree I am wolfing it down with relish popping pills like hundreds and thousands and out of control like the bounce of the pigskin on a blustery day

there is a reason for the way it goes with me and that is to alleviate the unbearable silence in the wake of elusive beauty and fighting back that one word certainly induced a disorder which the stimulants and destimulants keep in check but more than that because that was a minor ailment yes more than that it was the sheer isolation between the elusive beauty of the work and the deadly silence of the hum drum down to the drug store in my slippers practicing the banal wanting to be plain ordinary but denied that by the insistence of my inspirations and me in a torment wondering whether if no one can hear there might be no point perhaps then easier to leave the faithful old conn in its case and the pads dry out and crack and the brass slowly corrode and putting that notion to the test I am

fred calling you comin' man can't sit around on your arse all day re-arranging those chess pieces you've moved them around so much they probably know how to play the game by themselves by now and think about what the hell is happening to your chops so he would cajole me and off we'd go to the body shop or some such burlesque joint past sunset one set at a time

once or twice just for the shekels stripped of every vestige of the dignity of the calling and with little other work available sorry fred I haven't the heart to do this not nice work even if you can get it no matter how delectable the body in the flashing lights all silky soft blue yellow and green glittering stars upon her nipples and the second hand g-string by turns this gogoing dancer a doxy in dixie's dilemma and all the things you are for so many in the groin of America

fred calling you comin' man yeh man there's work in vegas got a call from don you're kidding man you can finish the goddam book in vegas so persuaded I heave myself out of the couch and grab some shekels that were my due and toss in the overnight bag pick up the horn and off to fill up the tank with gasoline while the kid does an express job cleaning the windscreen with a sponge and a squeegee then go go on go on up the highway cruising a mile at a time down the highway to vegas elbow out the window in the coolness of the desert night going back over the old stories laughing ourselves silly like the old days down the alley when we were young one day at a time so long ago long ago and sharing the driving but he did the most part because I kept falling asleep during this descent into the valley of fire it's like this I said by twenty knew the history of johann bela lennie bird pres and eine kleine wolfgang and I got myself standards man and that don't leave a man and never did man simple as that and fred got calls strip joint sure man I'll be there MGM studio job I'll be there wedding I'll be there counting my bills for a man has to live and that was fred the regular professional with no compunction and grateful for all the casuals he could get and I got calls from fred and say sure fred

I'll be there but in the end most often I didn't show and he knew the score and he had his standards too and we were as thick as thieves never planned anything never kept track of anything who I owed who owed me past caring about the banalities in no way articulate in my relating and not deterred by this forced descent into the valley of fire to flirt with the pleasures of the flesh and dereliction of my duty to uphold the standards by way of experiment like what if what if part of me relishing every mouthful relinquishing my hold on the untenable in this maelstrom of contradictory messages meted out by ours the modern age just to find out for myself what the standards mean to me and I must say I was enjoying the drive careering through city of baker

baking in the sun towards the end of the highway across the mojave (pronounced like mu'hahvi) to vegas before which is the city of baker with its neat green lawns laughing at the desert that is my wilderness in this the years of my wandering and us turning a deaf ear to the present predicament laughing ourselves silly as we cruise past these outposts of seductive stability which oh how my simple soul hankers after that unattainable predictability and I wondering within my contortions of laughter whether this is not all too high a price but my incessant inspirations without which I stop breathing and sink and breathing is kind of vital and so in the final analysis no cause for complaint and good I mean that's good isn't it fred

it was fred who saved my life door always open never objected to my failing to show not a word said ever the willing partner in the endless games of chess knowing perhaps that this was for me a way of holding on in an oasis of the loveable hum drum not to be found anywhere else no questions asked always welcome day or night one move at a time until I just got up and departed again and until I returned again through the door of friendship always open as if I had only been gone long enough to check the mail box and call out hi fred and how he knew the sound of my voice hi carol hi fred what's cooking 'sonly me sure I'll be there and come through I did I guess with help such as this at a loss in los angeles groovin high throughout this descent into the valley of fire and a few lost days in vegas and nothing more to say about that now or ever

chapter eighteen **loverman**

no more vegas no fred no more body shop for a long while been sunk in this couch gaping at the conn in its case and not ready for anything else just yet but some new inevitability no doubt looming

listen to the phone ringing day after day while the stubble grows rougher on my chin and the muscles around the lips sag like a woman's stomach muscles after birth

no motivation no discipline no point no more casuals for a long while no thank you because it's not worth this dejection as after self abuse gape at the conn in the case slouched in the couch day after day listen to the phone ringing and the woman invites her coterie around for another hand and turn towards her to decline the invitation to preview the onset of old age

a small advertisement had been placed in the paper issued by the musicians' union local 47 to which my membership dates back to somewhere around 1942 and this had triggered off an irregular flow of students wishing to know improvising and that paid for the paraphernalia of daily living at 5717 laurel canyon boulevard in the san fernando valley where this body lounges within spitting distance of the folk lore of hollywood dotted amongst the orange groves still clinging to the hills beyond my window through which I do not bother to look for my eyes are fixed on my finger tips each one a window into scenes of former hours in this 10 x 12 box of a room

at an address not mine but at least an address for the few who arrive and peer around this dark and secretive repository of so much left unspoken and stole away within this time capsule and half my life along with it during the lesson some enthusiasm returns sufficient impetus to hazard a flurry on the clarinet and see a face not unduly impressed by the post-maelstrom lack lustre effort of the master of his art which will endure

only to subside again once the visitor's car has accelerated off down the road leaving us in a silent motionless world with the conn in its black case of secrets

slowly it came back I mean the enthusiasm and the fundamentals passed on with authority won from half a life of tireless effort listening and my own voice incanting the steps through learn the tunes and sing the tunes and play the tunes with conviction and write harmonies on the tunes and play the tunes again in the style of a singer of your choice and hear the tunes in your head and accompany what you hear with your own melody in your own sense of time present time past and practice hearing chords and naming them and practice playing chords and arpeggios of the chords and inversions and extensions and alterations and playing worn out records on the cheap phonograph and talking about art and standards and maybe the students did indeed help which was a smart move to have taken the trouble like fred said to put it in the union paper because the serious ones are sure to know who you are

and slowly it subsided tumescent then limp and then languid and then lounging in the couch listening to the phone ringing day after day transfixed by the windows on my finger tips in a process reaching through the months of wondering for why had I progressed this far and what was I going to do with the rest

and the knock on the door that said phone for you and my silence punctuated by tight lipped snatches of hot air and nothing mattering much in california with the beat generation getting into its stride with the beards and bangles and whimsical revolution and the woman explaining that he's out

and can she take a message and it all sounding a very long way off because this was a long way down on the other side of the door

did you ever pause to consider how fragile the path of your life is with all those unheralded intersections with other lives some of which exert a resonant influence that changes everything until long after you've gone and we think we can plan things

never planned anything and never kept very good track of anything you know uh the balance sheet which is why they said no definitely not a detail man except concerning the standards which was true by and large

and then in one split second it's all different and will always be different because of that one split second erratic bounce of the pigskin against the run of play you decide to do something uh go somewhere for no reason just an impulse feeling uhu why not and in that mode of why not because maybe this couch is getting uh too familiar and the walls are like the inside of my eyeballs man

so on a whim it was off to the Outrigger in Carmel Valley just to sit and listen again hanging out incognito amongst the audience in this arty cafe all atmosphere and creative with the surf not far away and beatnik becoming a word to lend some people the feeling that yeh man like they belonged

and there it was in the little gallery before you go into the cafe where local artists held exhibitions to sell a bit and pay for some of the paraphernalia

and me with my hands in my pockets having a glance around quite out of character because the mood was for something against the run of play like I was being set up and my eyes fix on this portrait of a young woman not long out of college at a guess and I'm interested uh it caught my attention and that was not a frequent occurrence but I hear my voice asking of no one in particular who this young woman might be and hearing reply that she just happened to be here and if you'd like to step inside you can hear the band too which is what happened

she was sitting at a table and not obviously in company so I approach the table without her noticing me and with a smile on my insides and my expression very here's looking at you kid and sit down like I hadn't noticed her either and sit myself at an angle with one arm resting on the back of the chair to facilitate my looking at the band or looking discretely at her without letting on that I'm fascinated she's not flashy and not hip and has an air of the impetuous about her even a little of the gipsy and I do not fail to notice her looking all innocuous in my direction and of course I do not register any acknowledgement of this intrigue because for one thing I'm trying to suppress my own fascination

then the thought crosses my mind that maybe she simply recognizes me as being a name and that changes things for a minute or two and then I'm back where I was looking at the portrait

time for some applause and we smile at each other like good entertainment wasn't it yes not bad considering I'm not paying much attention and then she left looking kind of pleased with herself and I found out who she was and all that and the couch didn't seem to want me in it after that and laurel canyon was a dead end

and that was october 30 1963 as she was inclined to remind me being the romantic sort and enjoying the happy memory she had and this is the one to whom an explanation is due and not forthcoming even now

the next time we met was by prior arrangement at big sur with the surf up and strolling along between bars and I'm thinking don't say it come on man what are you saying while the words tumble around inside jostling for the exit and what happens but there I am never very nimble on my feet in these circumstances chasing the pigskin and saying do you want to be my wife and have my children and she just said ok with a perky shrug and that was good enough by me and that was good enough by her and nothing more was said about that and I took her back to her mother's place in Pacific Grove outside of Monterey and not a word about pa and not for the last time and went on to another game of chess with fred and every so often I'd laugh without taking my eyes off the board because maybe this was the turning point in my free form tumbling through months without the glimmer of a future or because I knew I had fielded the pigskin on impulse

you know how it is

chapter nineteen **east side swing**

She must have had second thoughts because she rang to ask was I serious about the offer and I gave her the affirmative and waited but she never did ask the same questions as did a couple of others who were more amused than serious and smiled and alluded to the matter of my not seeming to be such a hot prospect at feeding the kids what with half a life of effort and little else to show for it besides a box of a rent-free room and some novels and a chess set and a passion for scrabble and a deck of cards and an old phonograph with records to match and a saxophone and a second hand clarinet and a beat-up Volkswagen and a suitcase and overnight bag and a clutch of bad habits and an impeccable record for upholding the standards and the purity of the art which was all very commendable but what was there to eat.

Here was someone who never so much as thought up such a question and wanted to travel light and have a companion to travel with and that was enough for the two of us and every other bridge we would cross when we came to it and off we went like a couple of abandoned children who have found security at last compared to the lack of which everything else was a vista of enchanting tomorrows we would savor at our leisure.

Though having given some thought at least to what on earth was going to happen next she did ask well what are we going to do then since there you are too old to be still at your mom's and here I am at my mom's and we don't have no place except the Volkswagen and I said well let's throw caution to the winds once in our lives and just go straight ahead with what we've got and on that note we chucked our stuff in the back of the car one afternoon because she had collected a couple of weeks' pay and I had successfully put in a request for additional shekels without specifying the intended application of the funds and that was what we had apart form the hand luggage and we hit the road cool as you like.

Some way out of LA we paused to give further consideration to the road ahead and decided - each of us for the first time making a mutual decision - to honor custom and introduce ourselves to our respective families which necessitated a detour through Missouri driving mostly at night while she read Shirley Jackson ghost stories by the light of a torch sometimes turning off the main beam to frighten ourselves in our little capsule of privacy threading our way through the middle of America and not a soul knew where we were and we were thrilled by that seclusion like children in a game pretending they are the only people left in the whole world comforted by the throaty drone of the engine behind us and the mysterious silence of the road ahead in all its darkness.

And we told stories that we'd not told anyone else and I even mentioned Dixie and we'd sing the melodies and talk a bit about the history and then we'd be quiet for a while and she'd doze off and I'd be thinking and we'd stop by the wayside at an all-night and order root beer and greasy food and stretch and go on to fulfil the custom. We were fugitives, elopers, and every time we crossed a State line we'd turn to each other and smile like there was no tomorrow. At a gas station a couple of hundred miles out of town, she phoned ahead to warn of our arrival and we spruced ourselves up in the rudimentary rest rooms and had a few doubts as we headed for Houston all the way out in the middle of nowhere.

Houston, a town of some 1500 people in Texas County, Missouri, in the middle of America, not that far from Kansas, and there was Los Angeles all the way back west and New York City all the way back east and Chicago all the way up north and New Orleans all the way down south.

And there we stood in the parlor of a clapboard house in a sleepy town of 1500 souls in Houston, Missouri, all helping with the washing up and singing four part harmony with her aunt and uncle and getting along just fine until, embracing my arm with both of hers, she mentioned that her aunty and uncle had the privilege of meeting the man who some say is the greatest living exponent of the art of improvisation, right here in Houston, Missouri, helping with the washing up. Aunty played competent self-taught piano and rose to the challenge and insisted on hearing some of this art, and so I had to go to the vee-dub and dig out my horn in its black case of secrets and watch the pigskin ricochet towards me yet again.

And we played a few choruses of How High The Moon. Then she turned from the keyboard and admonished me with a look that asked a host of questions and said:

"Don't you think you're blowing a mite too much air through that thing?"

School band, Canteen Kids, Carmichael's Teenagers, Special Services Band, 52nd Street, recordings, Birdland, Metronome All-Stars, Carnegie Hall, Hollywood Bowl, film studio, tv studio, radio studio, concert halls and brothels, the kid's got it, you're the pres, the Half Note, more recordings from the alumnus of the School, a most dedicated student, unheralded visitor in the parlor of a clapboard house in Houston somewhere in the state of Missouri, all that way and many thousands of hours of assiduous effort only to be brought up short against the wall of truth by aunty turning half round on her piano stool like a concert pianist far from satisfied with the competence of the orchestra, and offering, not as a statement but as a simple question:

"Don't you think you're blowing a mite too much air through that thing?"

My life is a sequence of specific moments about which the ebb and flow of my affairs has turned, pin points of change, and hearing that question was one of them, equally as profound as first hearing Bird or standing in front of Lennie, because in that moment I was cut free.

I became just an ordinary man living my ordinary life and would go about it in an ordinary way. Except to the friends who would always recognize my voice, there was nothing to distinguish me from anyone else in Houston or anywhere else for that matter, apart from this gift I had and that, all said and done, was largely by the by and meant nothing at all if a simple woman could hear something that didn't add up and turn around to half face me and say:

"Don't you think you're blowing a mite too much air through that thing?"

It was like the moment of impact of that cork against Don's pane of glass, a split second after which there is only a pile of debris on the ground and the wind blowing through a hole in the silence.

Much to aunty's surprise, I was gripped by a spasm of laughter in which I became child again, free of the elaborate scene-setting of a Christmas long ago, free of awe and admiration, free of the need to resist, free of the pressure to perform, free of the slightest wish to be acknowledged, the child on a work bench who could not communicate in words but could hear an incessant melody and only now realizing that there was nothing and no one preventing my voicing that melody except me.

Full of motherly concern, she thought I had choked and came with a glass of water. The following morning we set off for New York, to meet my half of the family. She who was travelling with me had never met a blind man and I took advantage of her gullibility and explained that the blind man would want to feel her face in order to acquaint himself and when she took over the driving on the freeway on the last night of our transcontinental odyssey I demonstrated how the hands would explore the curves and recesses and apertures and protuberances of the front of her head at his leisure and exclaim Wow! as his fingers concluded their interpretation of the striking beauty of this San Francisco girl and she panicked and swerved out of her lane that was nearly the end of us and we laughed about that for a long time and we never again knew each other as well as we knew each other then.

On the outskirts of New York she plucked up courage and asked about where we were going to stay so I pulled into a gas station and made a call and got back in the vee dub and told her everything was arranged which in a manner of speaking it was for a man not given to looking after the details and she took me at my word and carried on singing the best thing for me is you and in that spirit I turned off the ignition outside a three-storey house on Palo Alto Street in Jamaica, Long Island, and we looked at each other and traced the steps from Carmel Valley to Big Sur to Houston in Missouri to here and when she caught sight of him standing in the doorway in his Noel Coward dressing gown, her hands went to her face in apprehension and I had to give her a little push and say Lennie I'd like you to meet Gerry and it dawned on me only then that she wasn't a musician and he put out his hand for her to take in greeting and I'd never introduced anyone to him before and she was visibly relieved when he took her arm and led her inside to inspect the house and she glanced back over her shoulder with a vengeful look and I made a face and went to fetch our bags and that was our first home to which I had returned from out the wilderness and we had honored the custom which we had set out to do and the pigskin bobbed gently out of play for the time being.

She settled in without a murmur and cooked and cleaned and read War and Peace to Lennie and curled up on the sofa in the lounge while I practiced in the basement which was our quarters and Lennie practiced on the top floor and she curled up with a detective novel on the sofa happy to have been spirited away into this musical box as she put it. There was space because Lennie and Carol had recently split up and the kids were with her and their rooms were empty and Carol wouldn't let them come until she heard about Gerry and then they used to visit and Gerry would go out with them and sometimes with them and Lennie too and it was all family again in a makeshift way and we played

And she loved that because it made her happy and she would have put up with anything to sustain the efforts being made and tried to make peace between Lee and Tavia who were there on and off and always arguing in a petulant tug of war and Lennie had hopes again after three years of not doing much except recording in his own in his room at all hours of the day and night while Carol tossed and turned and lost the stamina to cope with a blind man who played piano and talked about the miracle of the instrument which after all was only a conglomeration of bits and pieces akin to a pile of junk and how every note had to be struck like your finger went down to the very bottom of it, nay to the very depths if you were to play from your soul and not just the extremities of your hands and she struggling to take care of the kids and was glad to get out in the end for peace of mind.

And it was Gerry who brought a stable heart to the place because she was satisfied and just took everything else as it came and went out to work when we couldn't get enough work of our own without anything being said until one day Lennie took me aside and asked, hey man, what are you two planning, to which I replied that we had no plans as such and he said well, man, look after the kid because she loves you and all you are and deserves something, like does she want to get married and I remembered Big Sur and we made the arrangements.

We joined the queue at City Hall. It had that much atmosphere that we could have been putting in an application for a building permit and even the ring wouldn't fit and that was in April of sixty four and so much happened in an April I remember and it was all over in sixty seconds for better or worse and we repaired to a local bar to celebrate and Lennie was the perfect father giving us both away and Lennie had always wanted to drive so he got settled in the driver's seat and off we went in the car and I steered while he did the gear changes and we hadn't been so joyous or felt so prosperous in all of the past fifteen years.

It was uncanny. I mean Lennie was totally blind and yet when we got back home he asked Gerry whether she still had the marriage certificate and she looked in her handbag and realized that she had left it on the bar counter and he put it down to intuition and I had to go back and try to find the place which was easier said than done and by the time I made it back to Jamaica the reception was in full swing with Betty and Lee and Tavia and Ronnie and his wife wearing next to nothing which was fairly typical and there was a knock on the door and it was Jack come for a lesson and he looked kind of surprised and I don't like to disappoint people so we went down to the basement and he kept looking at the top of my head and in the end I gave my hair a tousle and rice pattered onto the floor and I had to explain that I'd just become a married man but that didn't mean we couldn't go ahead with the lesson even if I did have to lean against the wall.

And Gerry really wanted the scene to come good and turned up at all the clubs and though she wasn't trained she could tell who was on and who was just fooling around and who was preening their ego and who was playing for a living and who was playing to stay alive. But most of all she loved being in the musical box; I'm in heaven she would say. And Lennie liked to go for a walk with Betty along the beaches of Long Island and she'd read Walt Whitman poems to him while Gerry looked after her kid and day dreamed about her own.

Occasionally we did a quintet, at the Half Note again, and in Boston and Toronto, and it was becoming more and more of a struggle even to turn up at the clubs. Personally, I was still willing to travel anywhere with Lennie, but he and Lee had less and less in common, what with Lennie believing he could get back into the past and Lee trying to push ahead and each of us now more firmly established in our own styles it was sometimes like bending over backwards to reach each other. But for all that, when we turned it on, there was a thrilling magic about the outpouring; you could tell by the way the audience went quiet the way an audience does at the circus when the high wire act is at its peak.

And just for the shekels I did a recording session to please Lee; perhaps ashamed to acknowledge the work or to avoid the Internal Revenue, I took the name Rawen Shram and performed a piece called Ougadougou Blues for a Tahitian pianist in Port Au Prince, which all sounds very exotic but it wasn't.

Lennie accepted an invitation to do a short concert tour in Europe, and I filled time with teaching. It was still winter and not many made it to the door and those that did looked around at the army cot as neatly made up as ever and the record rack that demonstrated my aversion to collect recorded work and at the padded section on the wall - put there to cut down echo so you could really hear what you were playing - and gave a silent wince when I declared that if they wanted to make a living then they would be better off learning from someone else. I'd light my pipe and drift of some and in the end they'd be gone, and I'd fall prey to the dreadful isolation of the journey I was on and then go upstairs and watch Gerry and pass her the pipe and realize that no one knew any answers and there was only one way and that was to go down to the depths of every note in order to penetrate beyond - or was it within? - the extremities.

Lennie returned, Lee went off again, Sonny's wife wouldn't let him come out to practice at Lennie's preferred times which were generally the hours of darkness. And so I'd go off and play with Sal who was becoming a recluse like Lennie, whom I couldn't bring myself to desert, until Gerry became pregnant and wanted a home. So in the Fall of sixty six we loaded the things back in the vee-dub and headed out west. And she asked where were we going to live, trying not to make the question sound like an accusation. I only knew one place and wondered if I had bitten off more than I could chew.

chapter twenty **god bless the child**

It would be like a dream from which I would never wake up, and I was a stranger to myself:-

They were on the last leg of the journey and Gerry was suffering the first bouts of morning sickness. He was struggling to come to terms with everything that was happening to him. Even at thirty nine, he was not feeling competent about being a husband or a father. Circumstances in New York had shielded him from the full import of marriage: Lennie had provided the home and a common focus which kept the advances of the interpersonal world at bay. The months had passed like a honeymoon. And now they faced each other as they had last done on the way towards Houston, Missouri.

But now, cramped in the vee-dub, tired and uncertain, chugging down the freeway into LA, there was just the two of them, and he was like Cerucik falling out of the ceiling of the railway carriage, albeit in slow motion. As a singular man, it had been fine to drop in out of the blue whenever he chose to; driving his pregnant wife into town, fighting off the nagging thought that he had no idea where they were going to live, found him wanting. Somehow or other he would have to come up with a solution, and, if he maintained his present speed, he only had a couple of hours, so he slowed down and went over the only options that came to mind. Carol and Fred's place was not a possibility, Owen never had shown much sympathy for his life style and would not want to have much to do about this predicament, Don only had a one bedroom apartment, and where else was there. And in amongst all his rambling thoughts - all of them cul de sacs - the same foreboding request turned up again and again: whatever you do, he thought to her, don't ask me where we're going to live.

She sat up in her seat, as if woken up by a sudden noise. "Where are we going to live?"

The uncharacteristic urgency in her voice meant that the simple and honest answer was not going to be the best response. To gain time, he just ignored her question. That is, he did not say anything out loud, but to himself he started repeating the question until it sounded like a mantra in his head, a question as persistent as flies around a cow's eyes and no way of fending them off.

All was not lost He remembered that they still had a little money left. And with that consolation, the pressure on him eased: he would buy some time and book them into a motel. Cheered by this respite, he accelerated, almost as if he was now in a hurry. She glanced sideways at him, discomforted by the impetuous change in pace, and asked him if he was all right, fearing that he might be on the verge of a nasty turn. The last time it had happened, she had been convinced he was dying.

They were playing badminton in Lennie's back yard. Nothing serious or very energetic, nothing more, in fact, than having some fun. She would shriek with laughter at his efforts to reach the shuttlecock, wondering at the childlike lack of coordination in one so totally together when playing the saxophone. Without warning, his body started to writhe with alarming, jerky movements, all haywire and in slow motion, like a haunting memory; she thought he was play acting, and laughed her head off, until she saw the eyes in their frozen stare and the mouth rigidly open as the body convulsed in a spasm and hit the ground like a rag doll thrown down in a tantrum.

She ran to him, screaming his name. Lennie was playing piano on the top floor but stopped when he heard her scream and went to the window to listen to what was going on. Without hesitation, he went to the phone and called an ambulance, and then ran down stairs and out into the yard, straight to where her husband lay still twitching, and made sure the tongue was not blocking the throat. The ambulance men arrived. It hadn't been a heart attack. They administered a sedative and his body went limp and the lids closed over the eyes and they took him off to hospital and pumped out another stomach. And after that, she made sure she knew what he was taking, and tried to persuade him not to, and because persuasion had no effect, she started to join him, and that was her first mistake. These were the days of Timothy Leary and peyote parties and magic mushrooms and the doors of deception.

She asked him the same question again. He looked at her in his usual ruminative, considered, remote way, and she was so reassured that she forgot she had asked him a most pressing question, and dozed off with her head against his arm.

When she woke up, it was early evening and dark and she was alone in the car, which was parked facing the open door of a motel room. He came out, saw she was awake and opened the door for her. She was tired and stiff and thirsty and hungry and grateful for a clean place to have a shower and looking forward to lying down full length and going to sleep between fresh sheets with her head on a soft pillow. He had a shower as well, and then ordered room service and brought in the few things she needed from the car. They were both relieved to be back close to home.

o———+——

He left her asleep in the motel room and drove over to the house in San Fernando Valley. The place was starting to decay and looked decidedly tatty in comparison with the homes of the new elite of Hollywood, with weeds in profusion over the driveway and trees left to grow wild. It was a dark place and seemed to have shrunk.

"Where is she?"

"We're staying in a motel for the night."

"Is she looking after you?"

"She's pregnant."

"You could have done better than that. She's only a San Francisco girl."

"We need somewhere to stay. Until we get settled."

"And when might that be?" She paused so that he could savor the uncertainty. "And how are you going to support a wife and a child."

"It may be twins."

Elizabeth stared at him. He hated her but she was his mother.

"There's the cabana. That would be enough."

"Oh my, I don't know where you'd be without me." He looked at the floor. "Yes, of course you can stay in the cabana. But remember: I'm an old woman, not a nurse." She smiled at him and went to her room without another word, so he did not have to say thank you.

He drove back to the motel. Gerry was still asleep. When he moved into the bed, she stirred enough to ask him where he had been. He told her he had found a place to stay, but was prudent enough not say where it was, and she fell asleep again, a peaceful expression on her face that made him feel guilty.

After Lennie's house, bursting with activity and people coming and going and arguing and laughing all hours of the day and night, she found it difficult to relax in the gloom and silence. Elizabeth rarely made an appearance, and when she did she always said the same thing: 'I must be getting old,' she said, 'and my memory lets me down. Tell me again where you are from?' And Gerry would repeat the same answer: Carmel Valley, Mrs. Marsh. 'Ah, yes, Carmel Valley. Well, there are valleys and there are valleys. I guess we don't have much say in where we are raised.'

She only came into the main house to eat and to listen to him practicing, and the acerbic exchanges with his mother made even those visits an endurance she had never imagined she would have to go through. Most of the time she spent in the cabana, feeling outcast, or wandering around the garden, and more often than not she was on her own.

He had taken it upon himself to acquire some practical qualification, with a view to earning a living. Since that moment in Houston, Missouri, the path he would have to follow had become very clear to him, clearer still after the two years back east, and that meant playing the music in circumstances where he was free to play all of what he heard, at the time there wasn't any such place and there was no telling how long the situation might continue. So he studied rudimentary electronics, enough to work as a tv and radio repair man, to be responsible. It was accurate work, and delicate, and totally beside the point.

He did it with a willing resignation. And for light relief, he would occasionally clean swimming pools for the neighboring Hollywood set - his mother gave him introductions. He could at least enjoy the open air, and no one bothered him, and it gave him the opportunity to sing quietly to himself.

Gerry became sickly and the doctor called by more regularly as she approached her term. She was carrying twins and the doctor became concerned and insisted that she spend the last few weeks in the hospital, which had to be a public hospital because the old woman was not of a mind to assist further than she had already.

Her husband came to visit, usually on time, and looked at her and wondered. One day, after he had returned to the cabana after such a visit, he got a phone call telling him to come urgently because his wife was in labor. When he arrived, she was in intensive care, and for the first time since he was a child, he felt helplessly bewildered. For what seemed like years, no one came to tell him anything. He was not one to ask, so all he could do was wait and smoke and wonder if he wasn't just now out of his depth.

In the end he sat down in a chair that was not very comfortable and must have fallen asleep, because he was woken up by the touch of the doctor's hand on his. It was that quality of touch that prevents any movement, that helps you prepare for an event for which there can be no preparation other than stillness. He watched the doctor's eyes. If he had been a man of few words prior to this, he was now to be a man of even fewer words, more carefully chosen.

"Your wife is still under sedation."

He swallowed hard and thought he understood.

"When you feel ready...."

The rest he heard well enough but he was cut off from the words, isolated in his own turmoil. He walked along the corridor that was a swoon of all colors, as happens when one is about to faint, but he was firm on his feet and knew in those few paces what courage was. And then he was standing by a bed on which his wife lay, barely breathing and looking gaunt and buried within weariness. Beside her, in two tiny plastic cribs, were the two baby girls for whom they would never need to find names and who lay arrested in a terrible stillness. It was as if his own life had expired.

He was not aware of anyone else near at hand, and even if there was anyone, they were certainly not near. He took a chair and sat between his wife and the twins, and stroked his wife's fingers and remembered how the ring would not fit because he had bought it not thinking that he had to pay attention to details like the size of his woman's third finger, and he regretted the oversight.

He was empty, listening to an eternal silence as veils came down around him, when something made him stand up. Like a man who has returned home late from work to find his children already asleep, he stepped quietly to the cribs, and, bending over, kissed first the one, and then the other, on the forehead. He slowly straightened up, put both hands over his face in anguish and heard something in him say, "God bless the child", and then he felt his heart break.

It frightened him that he could not weep. He turned around and said to anyone who was there to hear, "You will have to tell me what to do." At that moment, his knees buckled, and the last thing he remembered was someone catching him before he hit the floor.

A few weeks later, he was out at work, and his wife was resting on a deck chair on the veranda of the cabana, trying to let the sunshine lift her spirits. The old woman came out of the main house and walked towards her, something she had not done before today.

The young woman said 'Hello' and gave the old woman a puzzled but not unfriendly look: she was possibly coming to make her peace. The old woman stopped a few feet away from her.

"I have held my tongue out of respect, but there is one thing I want to tell you and that is: nothing like this has ever happened on our side of the family. I hope I have made myself clear."

And the old woman must have derived some rare and thrilling satisfaction from her own performance because as she rounded the corner of the house, she broke into a short laugh and a girlish skip.

When her husband came home, she could see straight away that the work was making him very unhappy, and so resisted the temptation to mention her own ordeal. She did raise the subject months later, but by then it had become little more than a joke in extremely poor taste, and they were beginning to get back to normal.

One of the questions I was asked was, "How do you manage to work such constantly fresh and surprising improvisations from the same melody?" And the answer I always give is simple: a lot of practice and a lot of living. But I guess there's something else to it besides that.

part three

the song is you

chapter twenty one **how about you**

She recovered, by and by. And I was a working man. Not that I worked with any enthusiasm; the activity was more of a therapy. I'd sit on the edge of a swimming pool, mid way through cleaning it, enjoying a cigarette and the fresh air, and a wave of nausea would creep over me and before me appear two children floating motionless on the water lapping at my feet. And in my hallucination, I waded in and plucked them from the water and revived them and saw them open their eyes. That was the worst of it, that I'd never looked into their eyes, never heard a sound from them. And then I'd have to get on with the job, to get the picture out of my head, and go on to the next house.

For several months, I had fits of weeping that came on without warning and stopped of their own accord, and, thankfully, they happened when I was either on my own or in the cabana. The impact of such a loss makes you sensitive to the hidden things in life, and puts fame and prominence and self-seeking all in perspective. I was never meek, but through all this I got myself humility. More importantly, I learned, right there and then, that art is selfless and yet springs from the deepest firsthand experience: it makes no claims, expects nothing in return and can never be constrained or modified. And it is, paradoxically, the most personal of gifts that can be exchanged between human beings. It is made as if for ever and is of value only to the spirit, remaining only abstract if it is not dedicated to the community. And it is not possible to reach or strain for it, because art will find a voice where it will. But what it demands is constant readiness to admit the unexpected and follow it boldly. And a lot of living, and by living I do not mean intensity but depth of feeling.

My interest in everything had diminished as if I was in hibernation in the shelter of the cabana. We were content just to get by and keep out of the old woman's way as much as possible. And we read avidly, mostly detective novels and Arthur Upfield and Elmore Leonard, enjoyable chaff, until we couldn't keep our eyes open, sometimes falling asleep in the lounge and waking up stiff half way through the night, and one of us would say to the other, "My, is this a fine romance!"

But slowly we revived, like the earth after a hard winter, with the crocuses and snow drops already in bud under the thinning mantle of snow. During the week I was doing shift work on the assembly line of an electronics factory, testing components. I never complained to Gerry but she could see all too clearly that the work was depressing me, that I was wasting my life. She was back to herself by now and was missing the hours of music she used to revel in when we were in New York, not to mention the company of other musicians and their wives. So I continued cleaning the swimming pools and she found a job in a local bar, and that gave me the opportunity to practice on my own more regularly and also make contact with a group of LA musicians who rehearsed together.

I started turning up from time to time, it was at Ace Lane's place. Never said much: so much talk ends up in ill-considered discussion. But, attentive to the call of a kindred spirit, I always listened closely to the way they played, how sensitive they each were to the others, who had real courage and grace and who leaned more to ingratiating themselves. By this stage of the game, I needed confirmation several times before I'd be willing to commit and that is really why I kept turning up, apart from the fact that I was happy to be playing again, knowing that my heart was mending.

I believed that if someone had something to say, it was best to give them the benefit of the doubt and assume that they would be more satisfied by a reply which showed some effort had gone into it, than by a reply which was shot from the hip. Very often a comment didn't warrant a response at all. In either case, I kept my peace, for a while, maybe weeks. My outlook was very much like Bird's: what good's words when we can say it in the music. Apart from those who really did know me intuitively, my style of conversation was mistaken for haughtiness or cultivated remoteness - some folks will always put you down no matter what you do, so as to keep the superficial attention on themselves. I guess that made me feel uncomfortable. On the other hand, the closer we are, the less we have to explain, and the more we love someone, the less we are careless with what we can take for granted.

Initially, I would pay no attention to people. My whole attention focussed elsewhere: and I would read people by listening to what they played, what shape their ideas took, how much was borrowed and to what extent they dared to be themselves. So I could say, well, the second tenor is like this, or the lead trumpet is like that, without really having much of a notion about what they looked like. However, I was not the type of person to make advances, content, after all I had been through, for life to open or close doors for me, unlike Lee, for example, or Miles, who had reached the point where they compulsively had to race around the world, always for a fat fee, just to keep the whole machinery of their own publicity spinning along, like the juggler with ten plates on the ends of thin sticks. To have charisma seemed to be worth a hell of a lot these days. Or the Modern Jazz Quartet, all classical players, but trapped by their own success, so that they constantly had to play what people expected them to play, and that shut the door on the principle rule of art. So the crowds roar for Django, or Take Five, and they have to play that, and the audience and the musicians have cheated each other and no one's ready to admit that.

With me, it was different. A popular favorite was My Funny Valentine. Occasionally I'd get the shout for that, to which I would whisper, "I don't know that one". Or, my favorite story, the time when we had reached the end of a set somewhere and were fairly exhausted and the drummer bathed in sweat and somebody, who couldn't tell one style of outfit from another, starts shouting "Donna Lee, Donna Lee, Donna Lee", to which the reply was "Hey, big mouth, f..k her, we're going home."

"My name's Gary Foster." I waited because I didn't recognize the name. "You were at Ace Lane's the other day, with Lou . I wanted to introduce myself. I was alto. I thought we had something going, you know. How about you? Just wanted to check it out with you, see how you felt."

There was an alto I had clicked with here and there. "Are you the large guy with the glasses and beard?"

"That's right. My name's Gary."

He had a gentle voice, with a caring quality you don't often hear in America, and a fine sense of humor.

"Yeh, Gary, I like what you play. What do you suggest?"

"Well, I don't like admitting this, but I play in the Keith Williams Dance Band. One of the tenor section's pulled out and I said I'd see if you were interested. It's fifty bucks. He doesn't want you to play anything, just sit there and mime. All you need is a tux and your horn."

I'd been turning down casuals for months because there was no way I was going to slip back into that. But he must have sensed that I was falling for the chance to mime away 6 hours and collect fifty bucks. It seemed too ridiculous to pass up.

"If you get yourself over to my place, I'll drive us down."

"How far?"

"The Balboa Bay Club. Maybe an hour."

And that's how we got to know each other.

I was paid to mime, but I thought, well, if I have to wear a tux then I'm going to get one chance to shift some air through this thing, and dear Keith looked like he could have murdered Gary when, despite my better judgement, I lit off on a modest solo. He should have known better because we'd been together in the Canteen Kids twenty five years before. Not an easy guy to like, he never gave me the chance to help him out again. On the drive back, we took some pleasure in the joke and then talked some and got to feel at ease with each other. He knew the history and had a great respect for Lee and Lennie.

Back at his place, I climbed into the vee-dub and wound down the window to thank him. He crouched down to talk eye to eye, and asked in a courteous way if I'd be kind enough to give him some tuition. Well, he was already accomplished and perhaps only lacked real belief in his ability. I gazed at the wipers on the windscreen, wondering how long it would be before the remains of the rubbers finally fell off.

"This is just my opinion, Gary. You're good enough to be able to figure out for yourself what you need to know."

He laughed, "Thanks. That's better than 'no'" and slapped the roof of the car. And that's how we left it. And he waved and went indoors and I drove back to the cabana.

He hadn't given me his phone number and I had forgotten his address, so when, to my surprise, and partly with Gerry's encouragement, I wanted to contact him again, I found myself going to more trouble than I had since making the railway trip to find Lennie. Even returning telephone messages was usually an irksome chore. What made me change my mind was that I liked the man and appreciated that he had not hassled me and had taken my opinion to heart. He was pleased to hear from me again and would very much like to come with his wife for the meal Gerry had been planning.

After we'd eaten and finished the wine, we went into the kitchen and I sat and watched him put the alto together and try out a couple of reeds while I pondered what to do. It was a long time since I'd done any teaching. Maybe my approach appeared to be rather haphazard: that wasn't the case. The lessons certainly were not planned specifically; after so many years of playing, the secret was to find something new that would challenge a particular student. My starting place would always be: where is this guy weakest? It is a very poor teacher who offers congratulation.

He was ready. Probably had been for a while. I decided to use the situation as an audition, find out what his powers of invention were when playing unaccompanied, what prospects there might be for teaming up. So I ask him to play a ballad, maybe it was Here's that rainy day again, but at a tempo much, much slower than usual, like the ponderous flap of a large bird's wings through heavy air. If he could breath life into that then we had something going for sure. The slower the tempo, the more the greater the command has to be of every aspect of musicianship, especially in sincerity of feeling, mastery of tone and quality of relaxation, simply because everything is more noticeable: like looking at someone's face up real close.

We saw each other more frequently after that, the two of us alone, and our families together for meals, and we enjoyed the friendship, and the games of bridge and scrabble, but Gary didn't have much time for chess so I went looking for Fred once in a while. And the two women talked a lot. Never would understand what they could possibly devote so many words to. And my tone was changing, losing the edgy sound it once had, becoming milder and more lubricated, less tense.

We'd been working at some Bach pieces, one of us taking the continuo part while the other improvised and then switching it around. It was exhausting work but our appetite was insatiable. We were having a coffee, and I was enjoying a cigarette - which Gary tolerated reluctantly but constantly, because I was always smoking, even between courses of a meal.

"The guys at the shop have asked me to organize the teaching side of it, build it up into more of a professional school."

I was concerned that he was then going to tell me that there would be less time to spend rehearsing together. "They want to cater to all levels, from ten year olds to experienced professionals. Seems like a good opportunity - there's not so much serious work around these days."

"LA's full of pros, but I don't know how many good teachers you'll find."

"Who would you suggest?"

I lit up another cigarette and appeared to be reflecting, while in fact I was assessing how good a judge I was of other people's effectiveness as teachers when I didn't know any of them well enough to be able to say.

"Man, I don't know. You're going to have to ask someone else."

Gary had this strange capacity of enticing something to happen if he wanted it to. Not forceful. A kind of generosity.

"How would you like some regular work and get the smell of chlorine out of your nose?"

"How regular? Every day, like a school teacher?" I recalled the tedium of USC. "And did you say kids? I've never taught kids."

Obviously he'd elected to phase me with silence and watch me talk myself into a deal.

"OK, man, let's be to the point. How much?"

"The best I can do."

In a few months I was looking after twenty to thirty students, most of them once a week; high school kids, university students, and the odd session player who'd heard I was in town. So four days a week I'd turn up at the studio rooms which were the Barry &

Grassmueck School of Music above the Barry & Grassmueck Music Store in Pasadena, and blew the smell of chlorine out of my nose for good. Some of the students lived closer to San Fernando Valley than they did to Pasadena, so I struck another deal with Gary and took their lessons in the library of the big house. I felt more comfortable with that arrangement. Another teacher was Don, the trumpet player at the army camp in Fort Lee who'd introduced me to Lennie twenty years ago. What with meeting up with Keith again and then working in the same building as Don, the past began to look a lot tidier than it had been, as it tends to when you arrive in your middle years. The stability was foreign to me but starting regular teaching was the best decision I ever made, and I probably wouldn't have made it had Gary not been the man he is.

That was another question I was asked: With so many musicians far less gifted than you making a very good living on the University circuit, how come you haven't found a place amongst them? Answer: No one has asked me yet. That was true, but the real answer was that I had no time for agents, who arranged such deals, or for having my name on a door in the wall of a corridor of doors. I could cope with the informality of Barry & Grassmueck but I'd rather test electronics components than compare notes in a staff room.

There was yet another brush with the past. CBS records were looking for a replacement property for Andre, to whom I had given my copy of Sweet Lorraine, and who had been the CBS jazz star for a while but had now started the move back into classical music. Claire Fischer had been spotted as the new talent and was making a recording at the CBS studios on Sunset Boulevard. They'd finished the material for the first side and were preparing to start work on the second side when the tenor player decided to go back to Las Vegas. I'd been rehearsing with Claire and he offered me the seat that had been left empty. It was just reading charts, big band numbers like we used to do with Hoagy, right back where I started from. The marketing men lost interest in Claire as quickly as they had found it, and sold the tapes to Discovery. I didn't get a mention on the album, so of my first two 'public' appearances in a long while, on one I'm paid fifty bucks to mime and wear a tux, and on the other I am anonymous. My previous recording - one track in Haiti - was made under a pseudonym. It still makes me laugh. Musicians would use such devices to enable them to break contracts with recording companies and escape the Internal Revenue, but I had no problems with either of those institutions. So there I am, mime artist, anonymous and Rawen Shram.

We went over to Gary's for a meal one evening and left the vee-dub parked at the curb. Maybe we'd play some later on, but that wasn't clear so I left the horn on the back seat. We were all in the lounge room at the front of the house, with a clear view over the front lawn and up and down the street. We'd been drinking and were some way into a game of scrabble, when all hell broke loose. It was like being trackside at Daytona: the scream of a car engine still out of sight and the squeal of rubber trying to hold on to the road as the driver took a bend too fast. It was all over in two seconds. One moment there was just noise, and then a sedan came into view, wriggling along and then darting across the road straight up the back of the vee-dub and then two cars joined together sliding along the street in some violent mating ritual. When all the latent energy had been expended in the final collision with a telegraph pole, there was one vanquished vee-dub, visibly shorter at both ends, and one macho sedan letting off steam with the hood all twisted and no driver to be seen.

All I could say was "That's my car" and the four of us sat and looked at each other in disbelief. The two vehicles just lay there, consumed by the passion. Gary said, "Better call the police," which his wife did as the two of us went out, ran - which was very rare - across the lawn, jumped over the low wall - he was a bigger man than me but I was finding it hard to keep up - and then we're staring in at a heap of clothes and hands and legs in disarray across the front seat. The drunk became aggressive as soon as Gary touched him, all pompous and indignant. "Whajuhdooatfor? Cahnyuhseee?" And his chin flopped over his chest. By the time we'd got him up the front steps, the customary two police officers had arrived. (I had three encounters with the police in my life, and this was the most fruitful of them.)

He was too drunk to stand up, but one officer insisted on taking a statement. "I swear (flop) uzaz I shay (flop) thiz drunk (pointing at me with an arm that was too heavy to hold up) veeered shrtraaayt croz my ride o vaaay, like thizzz." And he brought both arms out as wide and high as he could - some way below his shoulders - and slapped two puffy palms together so that they bounced off each other and both arms fell at his side as he slipped down in the chair and the other officer had to prevent him spilling all over the floor. "Heeaee werz tryn overtay me on rong sytharow...." and he sniggered and fell asleep. The interviewing officer wrote it all down, trying not to laugh. And after that we had to give our version.

Formalities all complete, the official trio went on their way, carrying the drunk like an injured sportsman between them, and we sat down to finish the wine, amidst spasms of laughter that threatened to paralyse me. When all of a sudden, I sat bolt upright and realized. "My horn!" My voice rose into a thin whine, like a grieving Latin woman. I was rarely demonstrative.

The Conn was wrecked. Totally, as if it had been dropped from about a hundred feet up: I had never seen anything so absolutely unlike what it had once been. Gary just said "Scrap". No one dared even to smile. I was so proud of that instrument, avowed time and again that it was the best instrument that had ever been made, had poured so much of my life into it. "Scrap."

The insurance came through. The vee-dub had been written off too, but that concerned me hardly at all. It's easy enough to replace a car, but my instrument had taken years to master, and now I would have to go through the process all over again. Gary suggested I borrow his Selmer. I scoffed. I tried it out. I spent hours with it. We played together. I then made an astonishing confession to him.

"You know, that old Conn was out of tune: I've been playing a liability all these years and would never have known. That guy was a godsend. How much do I owe you for this thing?"

"How would you like to play at a fancy dress?"

"Me? Are you serious?"

"Have some fun for a change. It's a Mexican evening. Local musos and their families and friends. Choose your sidemen."

"But I only know And the Mexican danced on his hat."

"You could make that last all night, no trouble."

Maybe it was at the club called Bach, Dynamite and Dancing on Half Moon Bay near San Francisco, so called because one evening some local hood decided to try and blow up the beach with a stick of dynamite while a string quartet was playing Bach in between some dancing. Very California. My wardrobe hardly catered for fancy dress - some say I dressed as stylishly as a beekeeper: prosaic is accurate enough. But my father had had a certain flare, proof of which had survived in the darkness of a chest of drawers behind closed doors in the top room of an old house which was gradually decaying.

There I stood, on a hot evening, with a quartet I trusted and respected and whom I could call friends, in my father's purple silk shirt all of forty years old, and looked out into the faces I was getting to know because they had started to follow us around. You recognize the people after a while. I was a local at a local club amongst local people who knew how to listen. The perspiration started to cover my shoulders and collar bone and chest. The sleek fabric clung to my flesh like the gossamer wings of an insect trapped by a film of moisture, and as I swayed, feeling like a grand tree in a tropical forest breeze, or bent down to pick up my cigarettes, so the fabric started to pull itself apart. Because it was already like part of my skin, I didn't even notice when the sleeves parted at the shoulder seam and the whole of the sleeves fell away, except for the cuffs.

The shirt slowly melted away. As I played, I realized that I had been granted a new freedom, as the now flimsy restraints of the past dropped away. How unlike Samson I was, how unlike Icarus as the shirt fell away like tattered wings and I soared through How High The Moon and could respond to that beautiful suspense in the audience as they followed my flight, the vibration of the sound, the delicacy of the development of sparkling melodies, daring thrusts of imagination releasing in each one of them a deep stirring of the beauty of life that bound them together invisibly. How unlike the pied piper, because now I knew what it was not to play before an audience but within it. I do not know if I was, but I truly felt like the voice of the community.

All of us were thrilled and proud of each other in that moment. But it didn't last long because everyone burst out laughing. I must have presented a most unprepossessing sight, with scraps of silk about my feet and bare from the waist up except for the cuffs about my wrists like broken manacles. And there I stood in my sandals and pants and, absurdly crowning glory, my huge sombrero. And the Mexicans danced on their hats. I was back to my best.

September 1969. Over a number of days, we made a recording. It was Bill's idea. Bill was an ornithologist by training but loved the jazz and for the love of it set up recording situations that put the comfort and ease of the artists first. It was beautiful. He'd known Gary since they were students together, and by now we all knew each other socially. So the recording was made under the most favorable conditions, amongst friends, at a friend's house, everything done by mutual agreement and at leisure, and when we felt ready, we played until it was finished. Bill said it was the most successful record he ever released. We all did it for each other and for love. For such a moment I had waited until the hope of it happening had been forgotten. Then there was myself and Gary and Dave and John, and Bill. And his wife made the coffee and we called it Ne Plus Ultra.

"Many jazzmen have been underrated, but few have been so badly under-appreciated.... his work is unknown (or virtually so). He is a master improviser."

"For a decade Marsh had been out of the limelight and the recording studios - but the Revelation set confirms that his talent has not withered in that period. He is the same highly original and gifted improviser we remember from the 1940s and 1950s, and this last example of his work has the same timeless quality....coherence, artistry and beauty....that a country can produce such an artist and then offer him virtually no opportunity for employment or reward is a shocking comment on contemporary America...."

"....one of the greatest saxophonists of all time, one of the finest improvisers, and one of the most distinctive, easy to recognize voices on his horn...."

chapter twenty two **bird on the moon**

Verbatims:-

1. "It really is curious the way jazz is underrated in its country of origin. Part of it is that its significance is overlooked because it's a black art - in spite of the fact that it has produced significant black musicians, by any standards. Charlie Parker is a major artist; if you put him up alongside Bach or Bartok, he still is substantial. In America, though, there's the question of who's a first class citizen and who isn't, and can a second-class citizen produce fine art? And automatically the assumption is, It's folk music, it's not art. That is more or less the attitude: the American Negro has produced the folk music that's called jazz, and that's that.

By this time, you would think there were enough white musicians who have made a career of what the Negro started to give the lie to that. But they're not working. There's really no organized jazz community in America that is pointing the direction, to enable you to say: 'That is contemporary jazz'."

2. "The small group, of course, became the vehicle for improvisation; the big band no longer offered the challenge that a small group does. As for the big band, I've always felt it's an elaboration of the thinking of two or three people. The real strength of Basie's band, for instance, in those days was Lester Young - that justified the band's existence, to me. Ellington had two or three soloists like that. As did all the good big bands: Tommy Dorsey had a couple of good soloists; Artie Shaw had Roy Eldridge. They were the kingpins of the band; and, more than that, I think they were real emotive forces. It goes back to Bix Beiderbecke; you have one outstanding musician who stimulates or gives character to a whole band. The only other people who are that influential are the composers, or the arrangers; if they're really good they can give character to a band too. I think the same thing about a symphony orchestra - just a few people control it."

There were, and maybe still are, two styles of venue for local jazz music: the club which regularly features local musicians and which does not charge much, and the club which places greater emphasis on 'touring names' and which has to charge higher prices to recoup the higher costs.

(The acid test of the strength of jazz in the community is not how many records are sold, but how many people turn up at clubs and concerts, regularly: jazz is essentially a 'live' music and a communal experience, deriving much of its vigor from the feelings which flow between the musicians and the people listening who often inspire the music in a way that is not possible in a studio situation. It's a physical and, at times, a spiritual thing.)

To my way of thinking, the first style of club is the most important simply because it provides somewhere for the young musician to develop his or her gifts and for the musicians and the audience to get to know each other over a period of time. That's the point: the relationship can develop over a period of time.

It's no accident that musicians find partners with whom they perform for many years and, in their way, grieve when the partnership is broken, for whatever reason. That is why Pres wept for Herschel and why I would always miss Lee.

It's no accident that for hundreds of years, maybe thousands, musicians have felt most comfortable when they are close together, often in a semicircle. and perform for an audience amongst whom there are people they know and love or can't stand. If you look at the old amphitheaters, they were two semicircles; one for the performers - who were members of the community they performed for - and the other for the audience, the two semicircles forming a completed circle. The experience, of the music or the play, transpires, then, not as something given by the performers to their audience, but as something which is completed somewhere between the two and fills the circle.

My audience can be one person, particularly if that person is also a fellow musician with whom I feel a depth of trust and affection and who presents me with a constant challenge. It is not the number of people that matters: it is how attentive each one is, how responsive to what is happening, and not just attentive to what is happening in the music but to what is happening inside themselves. What can you tell about a house without looking inside? Music is the same. Inside the music there is me, and something else besides.

For the audience it attracted and for the attitude of the owner, my favorite venue had become Dontes in North Hollywood. The people cared for the music and showed their appreciation by nurturing a community of local musicians who had little time for all the jive surrounding 'names'. It was the spirit of the place: I could just be myself.

We became regulars, Gary, John, Dave and myself, making occasional appearances at the Ice House and the Gilded Cage in Pasadena, and once in a while at the Lighthouse in Hermosa Beach. Apart from that, we rehearsed regularly at the house next to the cabana where I was still living. The walls of the swimming pool were cracked and sprouting weeds, the tennis court was overgrown and all but a few flecks of white paint had long since parted company with the now grey timber of the umpire's chair, its legs standing in a clump of wild grass a foot high, like a lifeguard's perch in a high tide. So much of the atmosphere of a deserted studio lot hung over the place. But the guys loved to rehearse there, and would comment on the absence of the woman of the house who never appeared.

Out of the friendships with Gary and Bill and Fred and the rapport with the regulars who supported Dontes, and listening to my students, watching them progress to the stage where they had the confidence to sing as individuals, I arrived at a deeper and unshareable part of myself, which I never talked about. Ever since I first fiddled around on the piano as a young kid, already assured of an intimacy with the music and completely absorbed in the process of discovery, I had had a natural wish to be devoted and to spare no effort. But lately I was given to mulling things over from a fresh perspective.

What was I now? I was a typical middle American, far from remarkable in outward appearance or imposing in demeanor, having some presence but nothing to command attention. I was a musician who had been playing professionally for more than twenty five years. I was a family man with an equally unremarkable wife - who would soon have our first son. Prosperity was not my current state of affairs, even though our situation had improved to the point where we felt secure. I was a teacher of music, on the only instrument I knew, the tenor saxophone. I had lived in New York and Los Angeles and visited a few other towns here and there. I was remote, preoccupied, eccentric in minor ways; placid, pensive, a man of few words, yet courteous, and pleasant company for some.

There was only one situation in which I was evident and that was in the music, if I was playing, teaching or talking about the music. There was an aura about me. Many people have mentioned it, and I could feel it very clearly myself, a command or authority which came upon me, so to speak, and what came out of me then had an effect which people said was profound, and I felt profound myself, without any intention or effort. It just happened. I had had that experience myself, with Lennie and Bird and Pres, so I understood what people meant when they said 'Why doesn't this happen with anyone else?' I could only offer a scrutinising gaze and reply, 'I don't know, man, you tell me'.

Far from feeling flattered, I would allow the comment to slip by and press on with what to me were basics, but more and more it dawned on me that this capacity I had - to inspire others - was not an accident and not trivial. It brought with it a responsibility precisely because it was so highly valued. Oh, not by so many; but those who did put a value on it put a very high value on it, a very deep sense of gratitude, and affection even, which surprised me because I never considered myself an affectionate person. (In many ways I think people found me disinterested and irksome preoccupied and off-putting. But in the music, all that changed:

the wonderment the audience felt was no different than what I felt; I listened to the music as if I was part of the audience because if they were hearing the music for the first time, so was I.) And this conscious awareness of a responsibility spurred me on to find the absolute limits technique, imagination, expression. The music of the tenor saxophone was, if you like, my Cistene Chapel. And I was prepared to go to the very limits, which I guess is why Columbus first climbed into a boat. To do that meant that I would have to pay the greatest attention to detail.

So I began to look for additional ways to challenge myself, and one way was the metronome. That sounds really quite ridiculous, that the plain metronome can be a challenge. I mean, look at a metronome: such a small thing that can only keep repeating the same noise at the same precise interval. But it also sounds quite ridiculous that something so apparently simple as tapping four four time with one hand and two four time with one foot, and swapping the two over at will, can lead to mastery over rhythm and then over polyrhythm. But try it for your self, and then add further complexities and see what happens. However, do not just try it and give up; keep trying until you have it under control, without the least trace of hesitation. And that takes discipline and repeated effort, believe it or not, over many years. The simpler something sounds, the harder it often is to accomplish to the point of mastery.

I choose a song and set the metronome at twice the normal tempo and then play the song at twice that speed and slowly increase the setting of the metronome until my fingers could not keep up. And I'd repeat the exercise until my fingers could keep up, going over and over it again until, in the end, I was comfortable. And the purpose was not to achieve brilliance to impress, but to be so much in control of the instrument that my imagination was free to respond to any idea no matter how fleeting or complex or unexpected. More than that, I wanted the ideas to flow as unimpeded as the breeze over the surface of a leaf. I mean, watch the sun rise over the horizon: it appears to swell slowly but that sight is happening at phenomenal speeds. I sought to master my technique so that the music, even with note following note at the fastest possible speed, had the same feeling of stillness as that sunrise.

And my other exercise was to play duets with myself. I record the music I play against the metronome, and then improvise against that and record the result onto another tape and then listen to the result over and over. It was the best way I could find of coming to know my own music. And mastery of these techniques, amazingly enough, leads to the situation where the most complex harmonic and melodic lines sound paradoxically simple and inevitable and beyond analysis. Someone said genius is ninety percent hard work and ten percent inspiration. That's about right. If you have any doubts about the virtue of practice, exercise, then look through the notebooks of Leonardo da Vinci.

I even had the idea that if I learned another instrument, I would hear the nature of the tenor saxophone more clearly. Gary offered to give me lessons. But very quickly it became pointless. Everything about playing the flute is so different from playing the saxophone, and I had to put it aside. The public tend to admire musicians who can play any number of instruments. But, for me, the truth is that there is simply not enough time in a life to master more than one instrument. Sure, I could dabble, for fun, on the piano, the clarinet, the flute, the tuba, the drums, and in an average outfit hold my own quite comfortably. But, for whatever reason, and I was not looking for the reason, my goal was to achieve mastery with the tenor saxophone. And my conclusion is, to accomplish mastery, one instrument has to be the most important thing in a person's life and that one instrument must be given complete dedication. That is why I still refused to play casuals. I refuse to be casual. That's how I am. And the responsibility I now felt about the capacity I had, but had never cultivated, to move people profoundly (some would say to me, 'You have changed my life'), obliged me to spare no effort.

Of course, there are contradictions. In regular daily life you could say that I was not only casual, I was careless. That's a point. I guess it comes down to priorities. It doesn't bother me unduly: making criticisms about a lifestyle ignores the fact that, at the time, I was doing what I had to do, as a result of which there is a body of evidence to be heard for as long as the music is valid. Mozart couldn't do much to control the demands of the music in him even when the consequences were truly chaotic in terms of domestic stability or orderly behavior, and Beethoven couldn't control the urge to walk across meadows singing to the cows. No life is neat and tidy. Bach was having continual problems with his patrons. So criticisms never did make much of an impression. I was too busy.

This chapter is called "Bird On The Moon" because this period was another watershed for me, an opportunity to pay tribute to one of the most important people in my life. Bird. The poetry of "Bird On The Moon" has to be explained. That's a shame, but it does have to be explained, like Ko-Ko had to be explained. I explain it, fully aware that all explanations are anticlimaxes, whereas realizations are not. Never mind, it's the last of the explanations. I have no more explanations. Not even to myself, and hardly ever looked for them.

Bird took a tune called How High The Moon and out of the raw material of the original melody created a masterpiece in miniature. (We live in a miniaturized world, sadly. It's in the economics of air-play, and it's in the training we have all received to pay attention for a short span. The more complex and confusing the world around us, the less we can attend to complexity in art in more than small doses). And Bird called his improvisation Ornithology - a study of the bird, in this case in flight. Bird unlocked the musical imagination the same way the first manned flight to the moon unlocked the popular imagination.

And for a few years, I studied Bird in flight, as part of my training, part of my study of the history. The band or jazz orchestra was called "Supersax".

Clippings.

3. So I'd like to speak about Supersax, with which my involvement started nine months after Buddy Clark and Med Flory had been rehearsing. The original arrangements and the reason for them came about when Med, who's a lead alto player and a band leader in LA, just got tired of having nothing to play in the sax section. The saxophone parts are as dull as the brass parts; anybody with any taste for improvisation or jazz is going to be bored to death by big band charts. So he wrote out Just Friends and a couple more of Bird's solos, orchestrated them for the saxophone section, added brass, and made big band charts of them. That was back in 1960; the idea had remained dormant, but ten years later Buddy Clark suggested making a library of Charlie Parker charts - for just the five saxes; no big band - just for the fun of rehearsing it, seeing if it could be done. It wasn't originally intended to be a working band; it was a rehearsal band.

So they were going through one Hollywood saxophone player after another. I think the order of saxophone members of the band was Med, Jack Nimitz, Jay Migliori, and Bill Perkins; they were the original ones, and then they were trying different tenor players and second alto players. I was a success as soon as I played the book, because I already knew all the Charlie Parker; it was only a matter of playing harmony. Joe Lopes replaced Bill Perkins about the beginning of that next year, '73 - in the middle of a record date, as a matter of fact. Bill was offered the job with the Johnny Carson Tonight Show; it was too good to pass up and it would have been a conflict.

Certainly I think the concept of scoring Bird in this way is a valid one. I mean, when I think that it was 100 years before Mendelssohn brought Bach's work back to life - and here we've resurrected Charlie Parker after 20 years. It's remarkable. It's great music of course; it's a challenge, and once in a while we really play it well! It's hard as hell. In America it's been an immediately successful undertaking, because there is that generation that loves his music. Many of them never heard it live. We worked a yearly festival in

Kansas City, his birth place, at the Charlie Parker Foundation that they have there; we appeared there the third year that this festival had taken place - and people were telling us it was the first time they had ever heard anything Charlie Parker played. Here's a foundation established in some kind of trust in his family's name, but they'd never heard one of his solos. The Supersax presentation was the first Charlie Parker they'd actually heard. I get black students, in Pasadena, California, who don't know who he was, amazingly enough. So the real reason for the great success of this band, I think, is Charlie Parker.

There are three Supersax albums so far. The next one is going to be made with Dizzy Gillespie, under a different label. We've parted ways with Capitol, since they don't seem to have any real interest in sponsoring jazz. The one and only reason we got in there was because one of the executives of the company loves Bird. But they've invested no time in popularizing the band, distributing the records. People can't get the albums...all kinds of hassles. I haven't even heard that the second and third albums are available here.

As albums, they capture what we do. With one qualification - you won't hear any improvisation on the albums except for the trumpet or trombone. But in a concert or night club, the whole band does a good bit of improvising - all of the saxophone players for example. There's been a lot of criticism about the lack of this. Yet the thinking, particularly on the first and second albums, was: it's going to be demanding enough to get Charlie Parker fairly represented, without adding our own improvisation to it. Well, it's a good argument - of course, it should be as well done as possible - but frankly, I think you would have gotten a better idea of what Supersax is doing if you could hear a live recording, at a club or concert."

Our first performance was at Dontes and after that the band went all over America and then around the world. Three occasions I remember above all others. Not that they were musically exceptional evenings as far as the orchestra went. For other reasons.

At Dontes one evening, we did Scrapple From The Apple which was Bird's way of expressing something left unspoken in Honeysuckle Rose. Before I started my solo, I swear Pres came and sat down behind me, the better to listen. And the whole solo was Pres, the way I stood, instrument at an angle, so relaxed and loose and lyrical. At the end I could not remember having played a single note.

During the interval, I sat with Gary for a drink. He looked at me for a while, as if he was trying to figure out something that had got him beat. "You know, man, you sounded just like Pres, even looked like him. It was uncanny."

"I'll tell you something, Gary. I thought I was Pres. For those few minutes, I was Pres. He loved Bird. Bird thought Pres hated him. Pres hated the waste, hated to see Bird let himself be used by everyone, made a joke of. But Pres loved him. I know. I could feel how close they were."

Another time, I can't remember where we were. Somewhere on the road. The scores had been left behind somewhere so we were going to have to play from memory. Now I tell you, those scores were hard enough to play with the music in front of you, even after a year of playing them. One lapse of concentration and you were gone, like missing your footing on an almost sheer mountain face. Without the scores, it was climbing without a rope and with your eyes shut. But we didn't have a choice because the audience was already waiting. We had a new baritone player and this was his first night. We was terrified and his legs went to jelly and he couldn't stand up. The fear actually made him sick. In the end we had to more or less carry him on and prop him up in his chair, urging him on all the time, persuading him he could manage. And somehow we did, and without any mistakes as far as I could hear, and I had pretty keen ears then. But I think we all aged a few days in those long hours.

And after that, there was the visit to Japan. That changed the rest of my life. I had been expecting a scene worse than Kansas where Bird was born and whose people had never heard a solo of his played live until we arrived. But that was not the case. The jazz audience in Yokohama knew Bird better than most people in America, and this was twenty years after Bird died. The people in Japan didn't have the same problem that Americans had about second class citizens and folk music. Wherever we went in Japan, they were over the moon.

The only reason for my involvement with Supersax was Gary. Buddy Clarke had asked him if he knew of a tenor who could replace someone who had left at short notice. And Gary knew how well I could read the Bird Book. If he hadn't made the suggestion....well, I guess there's no telling what might have happened.

And wherever we went, Harry came too, with his tape recorder. I think he recorded pretty well every concert we gave, but I never heard any of the tapes. It is odd how an individual assumes a mission, and Harry created a mission for himself to record every solo I played in public. I don't suppose he ever asked himself what he was going to do with the tapes.

There's a guy who had a bundle of tapes I'd given him and tapes he'd made of gigs I'd done around LA and San Francisco. I saw him a few months ago. He asked me, "What do you want me to do with all those tapes?" Tapes? Why did he ask me? It wasn't as if I'd asked him to look after them for me. He'd gone to all the trouble of making most of them, so I couldn't figure why he was asking me what he should do with them. "Hell, I don't know. Throw them in the river?" He just shook his head in exasperation. He's probably got them in a box still, like butterflies on pins in a glass case, resplendent and stuck there, baubles of elapsed time. I never saw him or spoke with him again. People went in and out of my life like that. Except for a very few.

You know how it is.

chapter twenty three **you stepped**

Out of a dream. That's the way it was. And we hardly noticed: for years we hardly noticed what was happening. By the time we noticed, it had already happened. There was never any question of trying to resist. I cannot explain it to myself, so how could I explain to anyone else?

I was creating the finest work of my life.

I was at last the complete master of my instrument, technically speaking; I had the technique down, as they say, to a science or a fine art and I knew there was nothing more to learn about technique.

I was secure, and had been for a couple of years, with regular work playing music I loved and more students than I could handle - I was having to turn them away because if I didn't then I wouldn't have had time to practice, and the hours of practice were sacrosanct, and ever will be, for ever and ever.

I had a house of my own. Hard to believe now, but I did. My own mortgage papers, which Carol typed up - she worked for the Pasadena realtor who was handling the sale. And equity, that magical word for the common man. Oh yes, I had equity alright. I had arrived at the epicenter of Middle America, and could have been in Houston Missouri. Not a fine house, nor really a charming one, but it meant I was worth something, in the bankable sense.

I had two fine sons, and a wife who adored my music and acquiesced to the whims and addictions of the artist she loved. (That was her second mistake; inevitable, but a mistake nonetheless, in hindsight. Well, I don't know; maybe not a mistake: a fact open to interpretation.) And we were established members of the community of Pasadena, recognizable faces for the local supermarket checkout girls and fellow middle-Americans of the neighborhood PTA, restaurants, bars, gas stations and doctors' waiting rooms. A car in the driveway and a lawn to mow and school reports in the desk drawer, and something of a charlatan.

Still couldn't afford new furniture but we at least had a place in which we were answerable to no one.

And I had plans too. Oh yes, for once I had plans. For a studio that would be custom made by me and for me, my inner sanctum, a most private place that was going to be built into the garage one of these days. I was drawing up my meticulous plans whenever I had a quiet moment to myself. So hard to believe now, but it's true. I can see myself at the desk late at night, poring over the plans, desk lamp etching shadows into a face no longer young, working with the concentration of a draughtsman, consulting manuals on soundproofing and acoustics, costing materials, rolling up the plans and storing them on the top of the bookshelf away from the hands of inquisitive children, switching off the lamp and going up the stairs to bed. So long ago, so far away. Echoes of a father.

And you stepped in. Alan sent you. He was from New Zealand and you were from China - we talked about doing a tour there, talked our way through many nights, working out a tour in the imagination: we even had a name for it, because these days a tour had to have a name to make it marketable, and we called it "The Great Wail of China". The two of us, it was going to be; just friends, as we were by then.

All I knew was what he had told me: you were a classically trained pianist, thoroughly disenchanted with the attitudes and approach of the classical school, and had wandered from clique to clique in the jazz school only to find yourself thoroughly disenchanted with the posturing and bullshit and hype and small talk of the LA scene which was too close to Hollywood for its own good. A serious student he said you'd be, and there weren't so many of those around.

You were my first woman student. I had long held the belief that there were no true female artists, no women who had changed art in the same way as men had. Find me the female equivalent of Bach or Bird. I mean this has been going on for hundreds of thousands of years and it's not going to change because a few women get political. Attitudes may change, but the facts remain the same: find me the female equivalent of Bach, Wren, Michelangelo. There is nothing that doesn't have its roots in the nature of things. We would argue about that, until you would get into a rage and cuss. Sure as hell, women are powerful, but they don't bring anything truly original into art. Just an opinion - I did have a few.

I am going about my business. There's a knock on the door. I open the door, having totally forgotten you'd rung to make the appointment. In fact, you were lucky I was at home. Or was I lucky? There's no telling. Heaven knows what I was thinking about, but it wasn't a lesson. And there you were, hands clasped in front of you, long jet black hair, a little nervous through a half smile. Just a shrug of the shoulders as you said, 'Well, here I am'. As if I would have remembered. And because I didn't say anything, you added, 'You were expecting me, weren't you?' Then it was that I remembered who you were, and you stepped into my life and sat at the piano in the studio I was building, my sanctuary, world without boundaries.

I was very matter of fact. You played Lennie's Requiem, which was surprising because not many people bothered, and told me what you felt about the jazz scene. I just listened, and occasionally studied your face, enough to know that you were going to be serious. At the end I think I asked you to work on All The Things You Are, a song I must have played ten thousand times. After the hour was up, you met my wife and the boys. And then you left.

There is no such thing as 'might have been'. There is what there is, and there was what there was, and the present is like a sound carrying into the distance, and we are what we have been.

I went back to whatever I was doing before you arrived, Gerry cooked, and we ate and the boys went to bed, and I unrolled the plans to add some details as I listened to Gerry fall asleep reading. While I was concentrating on my work, I would hear you playing: hear just the snatch of a phrase, like the trace of a fragrance quickly blown away by the wind. It was not pronounced enough to cause me to think about you; I only heard the sound. Or, to be honest, I was conscious of no more than that. How did I feel? Amused and pleased; amused by the earnestness of your style, and pleased that Lennie had not been totally forgotten. But I was far too absorbed finishing the plans to be distracted for more than a second or two.

chapter twenty four **two part invention part two**

Part One

Plane to Europe. Voyage overseas number two. First one to the west, this one to the east, according to the compass. First one to the East, second one to the West, according to the politics, the two part invention on the one world. The students, I wonder how they will manage while I am away, especially her, long black hair and a hint of pudginess about the neck. Not an arbitrary journey. Time to weigh and consider, there is still time during the next few hours aloft. Do not subscribe, no, to the school of random chance: this timely journey, about which, in my own scale of things, I sense epic proportions.

Once again life has played a wild card. I am the fisherman who draws his rod behind him and, with a flick of the wrist, casts the weighted line out into the stream. The line is invisible: the suspense of waiting to see where the line will enter the water is the suspense of waiting to see where the theme will emerge. I have called this the bounce of the pigskin. There's no telling the direction it will take. I have not managed my life well: rather, I have not managed my life at all. I am no more than the accompanist to the solo that is my days. Try it; flunk it. Try it again; flunk it again. Yet again; and yet again miss it. Keep trying, and then, one great day, there is the oyster that contains the pearl. At a moment's notice, always unforetold, life calls a change.

Hear Don in the barracks. Change. Stand in front of Lennie. Change. Return from school one day in May. Change. A young woman plays a requiem. Change. Stand in front of a portrait in Monterey. Change. Gary. Change. Bill. Change. If you are listening, you hear it. Some change's irresistible, and, if you have a choice, some better ignored. That's life: knowing the difference.

A phone call, a glance, a whim, a letter, a piano in the background during a telephone conversation between Los Angeles and New York. Nothing planned, always the same, even at the last, because that is the only way I can live. Preparation but not planning: suitcase, instrument case, a bag full of charts, here we are, ladies and gentlemen, cruising at an altitude far above the Atlantic Ocean, reminiscing on thirty years of training. I am on my own again, and no idea about how long I'd be gone. There are clouds a few feet above my head. A plane load of people in a tin can of intimate isolation, all with a theme. If we could hear it, we would hear the noise of an orchestra eternally tuning up, unbearable cacophony, bedlam. And, behold, from the sanctum of the galley, that high-altar of travellers by air, enter the stewardess with the stainless steel trolley, gliding down the aisle inclining to one face after another raised in anticipation of some communion, a wafer of human contact, fragment of silence amidst all this unheard din.

Three months, six months, or for ever. I had little appetite for knowing. All I had to go by was that this was all expenses paid: I just had to show up. Somehow word had got about in Europe that I was alive, after spending the last ten years in Pasadena, picking the kids up from school, doing the local scene, and travelling around with Supersax, recording almost nothing and making no effort at all to seek any kind of exposure beyond southern California. Years of relaxed improvisation, students, playing where I wanted to play - rarely far from home - and getting on with converting the garage into the kind of studio I wanted to have, my own very private space.

When I read the invitation, my initial reaction was to pass the offer up. I had some thirty students to consider, and the studio was close to completion. Why, at close to fifty, start touring overseas? Then I thought about it some more. These guys in some small jazz clubs in Europe had put their heads together and raised the money to bring me over. How could I turn them down? I was honored, for sure. And how could I decline the opportunity to play the old book with Peter again; I hadn't seen or heard him for nearly fifteen years. And Lee was in Europe, and I hadn't played with him for more than ten years. (I didn't consider that they might have changed.) The prospects were exciting, and Pasadena or the studio couldn't compete. If a promoter had put a tour together, I would have declined. But the thought of a handful of guys putting their own money up front, without any guarantees....the difference was that they weren't in it for the business.

So here I was in an aeroplane seat that was too small, trading the ease of California for the rigors of a European winter, emerging from a decade of relative seclusion to accept a cup of coffee and two biscuits wrapped in cellophane from a woman who was as close to me as I was to her. High heeled shoes and lipstick, she too all wrapped about in cellophane.

Ted had given up performing and was programming for IBM. Don never did master his stage fright and was happily writing scores for tv. Art was in and out of gaol and in and out of sanatoriums, inspired and self-destructing by turns. Fred was still having his love affair with casuals wherever they might be. Bill the ornithologist had been farewelled at The Barry and Grassmueck Music Store near on two years ago, off to Florida with his heirloom of unreleased tapes in a box and a heart full of precious memories. Not long afterwards, Gary had opened Nova Studios, a cooperative where local musicians could practice or rehearse any time of the day or night to their hearts' content. A couple of men holding their hands around a candle lest it blow out. What an absurd age, where a few people of limited talent, a surfeit of charisma or greed and a dearth of integrity pile up unusable fortunes, while thousands of others more gifted can't find a place to practice or can't afford good instruments and can't find work that does them justice. Fame, never knock on my door, because I do not have the stomach for such a paradox.

Chess set on my lap, I ponder the next move as the plane begins its descent towards that moment when the lot of us will scatter every which way, and some of the noise will find its way out.

Part Two

From the tour of Europe, 1975-1976.

"Covent Garden Community Theater, London, England [18.12.75]

Recent appearances in Britain confirmed that he is one of the few players since Parker's death to have risen to the challenges posed by that departed master. At the first recital, on December 18, Lee was also present, so it was inevitable, I suppose, that the music should have something of a nostalgic cast, though the rhythm section, powered by the indefatigable bass work of Peter Ind, who was flanked by Dave Cliff on guitar and Al Levitt on drums, evinced a multidirectional complexity that would have been unthinkable in the Tristano circle of the late 40s or early 50s. Wow opened a program which included several other items associated with the school, notably Background Music, You Go To My Head, 317 E. 32nd, and Subconscious-Lee; all featured impeccable ensembles and solos whose harmonic and rhythmic subtleties went hand in hand with razor-sharp enunciation and real tonal sinew.

.....he came as something of a revelation ... bounding aggressiveness and remarkable rhythmic flexibility of his playing ... tremendous facility of execution, unprecedented control in and beyond his instrument's upper register and extraordinary tonal consistency throughout the range ... ability to articulate phrase patterns of very considerable length and dense rhythmic content, often implying double time yet also running his lines over and across that very implied beat further to intensify the solo's substance ... the speed of his invention evoked ... palpable excitement ... When one thinks of the multiform pressures to which jazz musicians are exposed, especially in today's climate, it is not in the least surprising that so many eventually dilute their styles, either by jettisoning hard-won individuality so as to conform to a fashionable stereotype in their field, or, perhaps more understandably, by grafting commercially useful procedures to their own medium. That Marsh has compromised in neither of these ways, but instead has worked assiduously over the years to broaden and intensify a truly personal form of expression speaks as eloquently for his integrity as it does for his musicianship."

At the Warren Bulkeley Hotel, Stockport, UK, March 1976

"Stockport is a small satellite town, joined umbilically to Manchester in the North of England by a labyrinth of industrial byways, rather like Duquesne and Pittsburgh. And it's no prettier. Somewhere off the beaten track, at the bottom of a steeply leaning cobbled street, deep in the inky shadow of a now-lifeless power station stands the Warren Bulkeley Hotel. In daytime, it is an ordinary public house, a favorite haunt for local newsmen. But at night, it shelters an intriguing jazz policy behind its beer-and-meat-pies image. Recent visitors have included Stephane Grapelli and Bud Freeman.

. ... encountering (his) extraordinary talents in such a place was redolent of hearing Charlie Parker in the flesh, as one still slightly incredulous witness remarked. This love, tinged with an awe which Marsh engenders in too small a slice of the jazz audience, is not out of place, however. Only three other living tenor saxophonists are capable of making music at the inspired level currently inhabited by Marsh. And his talents remained undimmed this night, despite a nearly 200-mile dash by car through English fog during a whistlestop tour that zig-zagged the country in a manner that would daunt even the most energetic White House incumbent in election year. As a founder-member of jazz's longest running underground movement, Marsh cannot have been too surprised at the actual venue - a cellar room cut into a subterranean tunnel whose history no doubt stretches back to the early days of Europe's Industrial Revolution.

Despite the rigors of a long journey, Marsh arrived fresh and dressed smartly, looking as though he had just stepped from a California golf course ... always a subtly complex musician, his style has developed continually ... now more emphatic and exultant than it was ... his tone more umbrous, even gritty. He also develops greater tonal flexibility and his sense of swing now floats less than it swaggers.... Much of the program comprised standards - a throwback to Tristano's dictum that musicians should play things the public can recognize and hang on to, however well disguised. And each one was given a thorough examination that often plumbed the farthest reaches of orthodox rhythm and harmony. The Way You Look Tonight was taken for a thrilling scamper, Warne's solo brimming with bold splashes of color. I Want To Be Happy boasted a torrential statement at the tempo level where bassists can scarcely breathe ....

The two most memorable spots were reserved for slow ballads. Crazy He Calls Me was a breathy lush performance, exhibiting a rich, brown tone at the bottom and a lambent, bell-like sonority at the top. It was an exquisite creation. So, too, was God Bless The Child...."

"Queen's Theater, Sittingbourne, Kent, England.

.... at Sittingbourne the spotlight was deservedly on Mr. Marsh, one of the finest tenormen of his generation and a pure improviser ... showing an almost Pres-like relaxation ... brisker than the Bird recording ... virtuoso stuff ... ample confirmation that you can never fully appreciate a musician until you see him work in person....One is left with the memory of a dedicated and astonishingly creative artist at the peak of his powers. It is a poor comment on the American jazz scene that Marsh is appreciated by all too few listeners in his country of birth. The man is a master of his instrument and within his chosen style is incomparable."

INTERVIEW: Part One

"The concert at Camden was a high point of that tour we did - an excellent room, and the audience was great. It was the first time in eleven years that Lee Konitz and I had worked together. And it's as if we've accomplished something now that we never really did in the past - working effectively together....I'd say the reason for this is maturity. We had associated mainly as sidemen in Lennie Tristano's quintet, and...well you could say we had never grown up individually to the point where we could work as partners together - that's certainly the way it appears. Until now, our paths were divergent.

On that particular concert (at the Camden Festival), that's the best I've ever played, I've got to say. And this particular quartet, having the antecedents that it does - it's mainly scholarship with Lennie; Peter Ind, Al Levitt and, of course, Lee and myself, we're all students - it comes together nicely. It's a disciplined quartet; without any special effort to work things out, we already have a lot of things in our background that work for us.

We needed very little refreshing on that material, when I think about it. Before we started work in Denmark, Lee and I spent a couple of days going over lines, but there was very little that we had to re-learn. Well, we were taught in a way that makes forgetting almost impossible - which is great. All those lines we learned, we dictated to each other; we just sat down for a few hours and composed. Lennie would dictate phrase by phrase, and we'd learn them, to play them, and go on to the next phrase. We weren't reading music, in other words; by dictate, I simply mean he played the phrase, and we learned it by ear right there and then. And although it seems like it would take a long time - in two or three hours we had completely learned a piece of material. It's practically impossible to forget that way, I think. I haven't had any trouble remembering any of that material.

As for Lee's playing now - it's the best he's sounded to me in 20 years. Because he's with me? I get that feeling this time....his strength to me is exactly this, and it always has been - that is to say, the straight - ahead music we were getting into when we were in our early twenties and Lennie in his early thirties. No there haven't really been copyists of it - I think they would be pretty hard put to do it. Well, it's really highly improvised, and that makes it hard to duplicate.

Lennie, certainly, was the real impetus; except for two or three of Lee's lines, he wrote all of the material. He really put that band together, the first one. My feeling was that I really was still in a student capacity. Since then I think I've been consistent, and just gone in one straight line. Any successful student of Lennie's does that, because by the time you've spent three or four years with him, your future is more or less mapped out....

I have done some things in the colleges, but I don't like interfering with American college curriculum. Although they are approaching the point where they hire us professionals, because they have no recourse - they can't teach the subject. Mainly I don't like teaching a class; the subject of improvisation is too demanding and personal to treat it on a class level, usually. Unless you really had a system worked out in a school, where you had nothing but jazz students in it; then possibly it could be taught in a classroom situation. But Lennie doesn't like it and neither do I. I don't like teaching by mail, or any of that. It needs to be one-to-one for effective teaching....

As for the limited appeal of jazz, I would just define it as serious music that's going to appeal to the same people who seriously listen to classical music. It's the same audience."

Sampling of the journey. Holland: Amsterdam in concert, radio broadcast from Hilversum. Sweden: Stockholm - concert at the House of Culture, and performance at the Fasching Club. Denmark: From Aarhus in the north, to Copenhagen in the south. Back to Holland, on to France, to England and Scotland, in concert halls, theaters, pubs, underground caves, day after day: Stockport, Edinburgh, London, Kent, Whitley Bay, Copenhagen and Aarhus again, to America for the Newport Jazz Festival, Chicago with Supersax, England to do Stockport and Hull and towns I have forgotten, Italy to play in Bergano and the day after that performing once more in London at the Camden Festival and at the Ronnie Scott's club in Soho, London. Back to America to play with Sal and Lee again at Storyville, and Europe again for the Verona Jazz Festival in Italy and the Aarhus Jazz Festival in Denmark, wearily back home again to do a recording in

Hollywood, and retracing my steps to Europe for a radio broadcast in Denmark and another appearance at Ronnie Scott's. Over a year of continuous travelling, playing, rehearsing, teaching, practicing, giving interviews here and there, appearing at places the names of which I cannot pronounce.

The people were just beautifully attentive and the music took flight because of that. Often, it seemed, they could not believe their ears: they had not heard music like this before and the younger ones were taken aback to learn that the music was thirty years old and now even more stirring than it was originally, perhaps because so many musicians had taken roads going nowhere. When we played, they could hear the continuity and the fruits of years of constant study and assiduous practice. This was not jazz or classical, bop or bebop or cool or blues: this was the creation of individual voices functioning together, unique and beyond imitation. Does the nightingale need to imitate the wren?

There were awkward moments, questions of priorities. Like the evening where the two sets were to be broken up unevenly to fit in with the licensing laws. Sorry, I said, I didn't come here to boost bar sales. Forget the intermission. Let them drink now, and then we play, straight ahead.

And there were disarming moments. We played, Lennie and me, a Bach two part invention, just as we did with Lennie back in the clubs in New York in the forties. Flat out, straight ahead. They hooted with delight, incredulous, whoops of amazement. There was so much I wanted to say, like, hold on guys, that was written over two hundred years ago, you hear what I said, two hundred years ago, and is it new or not? You get my point, this is the music, no gimmicks, no electronics, pure mastery and joy in the solo voice. You respond with almost ecstatic enthusiasm because the music brings you to life. Feelings really, and no words would suffice. I just stand there, words breaking around my feet like crystal glass, and I look out with something of a sheepish smile. Next number. Disagreements with Lee. Regrets for Lennie, who perhaps never would get the credit for the part he played in all this, slipping as he was into the bed of indulgence of disappointment, surrounded by a coterie of parasitic women keen to prey on his genius as if it could be syphoned off. And an occasional afterthought about Pasadena so far away, like that era had evaporated, like I'd not be able to fit myself back into all that.

Everywhere we went it was the same mixture of disbelief, delight, euphoria, amazement, and real listening. And for me, always the same surprise, that people here in Europe were more familiar with the work of Lennie and Lee and myself than people in America were. I could have stayed and taught for the next thirty years and never run out of students or places to play at. People weren't interested in the hype either, they just wanted to sit back and pay attention and show their appreciation in the way they treated us like ordinary human beings and with respect. And I realized that, in Europe anyway, people wanted to hear about Lennie and so, after years of saying nothing because no one really wanted to listen, I started giving interviews; people were, at this time anyway, genuine in their interest and serious in their questions. I mean, what they were witnessing was a phenomenon they just hadn't expected and every phenomenon passes, some more quickly than others.

INTERVIEW: Part Two

"The fact is that, at that time (the 40s and 50s), New York really had a well-developed audience for jazz. Now, any big city has that kind of an audience - if it's organized, if it's focussed, if it has a music to center itself around, like bebop in the 40s. But since then there has been no great movement in music like that. You have a much more focussed audience in Europe than we have in the States, I feel. Perhaps you have more of a cultural history than we do, and you simply pay more attention to art than Americans are in the habit of paying.

As for the free formers, they have done great harm - to themselves, and to the people, who regard them as authorities. In that sense, it's harmful; it's distracting. It's a random approach to improvisation. And, being random, it can accidentally produce some valid music. But it's not to be relied on; it can just as accidentally produce chaos - and it does: I heard some chaos the other night, that I don't even want to think about.

Certainly, a money motive exists for this. That's where the money is - so there are musicians who simply commit themselves to playing whatever is going to bring them an income.

I mean, I know some serious musicians who get into this electronic thing - but I don't know where their heads are at. For example, I don't see how you can improve on the sound of a good instrument, with good acoustics. Of course, part of the reason for electronics in the first place is amplification. Which is a reflection on how bad the acoustics are almost everywhere in the world that jazz or popular music are presented. We're talking about a nightclub that is a rectangular room - which is the worst possible shape for acoustics. And it is aggravating to a musician to go into a room like that and not be heard, of course. It's aggravating for a piano player to go in and have to play on a piece of junk - that's another problem that has encouraged the use of the electric piano. Mostly, though, I think it's jive, man. Amplifying a saxophone and a trumpet and the rest of it is just jive. It's not necessary, with even a moderately good PA system And as for the defence of it on the grounds of providing variety - that really makes it jive. The variety is not in the sounds, it's in the music - it's in the melody and the rhythm, the same way it's always been. The imagination of the player - that's infinite. But electronics is not going to produce anything infinite, or eternal, in music. No, that's not where it's going to come from. If there's substance in a player's music, it'll be heard, no matter how it's disguised; a good listener is going to hear the substance and not the package. That's so old a truth, it shouldn't even need to be gone into - but there it is.

....I've had some homework to do recently, writing some new material, in my new studio that I had just built. It's a large double garage converted to a soundproof room, for recording or whatever - every musician should have one."

It was the garage that drew me back and that slight pudginess about the neck.

chapter twenty five **worn out**

"There is nothing that has happened since 1950 to improve my understanding of music or to raise my standards. They were raised as high as they would go by the time I was twenty years old. My growth has been a steady and consistent evolution."

We played in bars all too often. That in itself was a challenge; to completely override the atmosphere, play as if we were in quite another place, like a prisoner who creates a palace in his own dignity. Sometimes I was overcome by an inspiration that did not recognize place or time, a refusal to be denied. And voices fell silent, glasses remained untouched on formica topped tables, and the mystery of the music filled the room until the air itself vibrated with anticipation. The audience sat hushed and spell bound, as if in a cathedral, while I exulted in another hymn to the harmony of life, not the visible trappings, no, the unattainable bliss when the music utterly gives form to the feelings within the heart of my existence at that moment's passing. I could feel the quickening of my spirit, and the force and thrill of the power of spontaneous creation I recognized as the surge of life beginning in an instant and already in the throes of death. That is what I mean by playing for the glory, and my cathedral is my own soul, my inner sanctum and a very sacred place. I am the meditative kind, not given to small talk or show. It is probably true that in my comings and goings I am boring. But in my music I feel triumphant, because I have had the courage to play only what I hear, and I have not sidestepped any challenge the music has asked me to face.

And now I was back in the converted garage in Pasadena. Waiting for her to arrive, wondering if she would notice the difference in me. I loved the place. And it was a good place, beautiful in fact, a place I had built with my own hands, with great attention to detail, and after over a year of not having my own space, it was good to be in the silence of that garage in Pasadena. I am reminded of the hours in that capsule of carefree abandon, the vee dub droning on through the night across the farmlands of Missouri, pale headlights occasionally stared out by the eyes of a living thing. The family are very happy to have me back in town, and presume life is back to normal. I guess it had been pretty straightforward for ten years. As I sit and wait, I know changes have taken place but do not know what they are. The journey through Europe has whet an appetite, opened up new opportunities. I am restless.

That year gave my life impetus, a renewed courage and assurance, confirmed what I had believed from the very outset, not the least because during that year I knew I had played better, more definitely, more unrestrainedly from my own inimitable voice than ever before. At the peak of my powers? It must be, because I knew by now that I would not live into old age. I had said, to Betty I think, that I would rather wear out than rust out. And it was clear to me why I had played to the limits of my powers: for the simple reason that people in Europe listened more acutely than people in America; more than that, they were touched by what they heard, and Americans, by and large, do not like to be touched, because then they are vulnerable and in danger of having to acknowledge that their lives are simplistic. America is no place for the individual.

While I'm sitting there, I'm kind of making up my mind. I had phoned Lennie many times and eventually managed to speak with him. He had succumbed to the overweening attention of some of his women students who were treating him like the last surviving sample of a species, and guarding him, keeping the real world at bay, and killing him in the process. It was as if they were jealous of his gifts being shared with anyone else. Certainly one of them always answered his phone, and Gerry, who used to talk with him often, was now forbidden from doing so. Sometimes it was obvious that he was drunk: you could hear him in the back ground, protesting about not being able to answer the phone, and memories of Bird and Pres in their decline came back to haunt me. He'd heard about the success of Europe and told me to leave Supersax. I did. He told me he thought it was my time now to return to New York. I knew that New York had little to offer but I agreed with him, for reasons that were more to do with respect for him than with seeing opportunities for myself. Anyhow, New York was closer to Europe than LA, and that in itself was a good enough reason to move.

She arrived, and we talked without prefacing what we said, and we played without purposely trying to do anything. And after that she came more frequently, not just for lessons but because she had become one of the family since I'd been away. We both understood that the easy affinity between us would not stay inarticulate for long. It was time to move.

I had worked it all out in my head but had not really discussed it with anyone else, not even Gerry. I had contacted a friend in New York who had said he would let the family stay in his house until I got settled. And then I made the announcement. "We're going back to New York." They all thought I was mad or stupid.

Not long after returning from Europe, and performing more often with Lee, I made another recording. I knew then that if I was to develop, then I'd have to let go of everything that was familiar. Part of me was indeed worn out.

It is called "WARNE OUT". I played it as a testament to all the things I had been. I am not abashed to note some phrases:- One of the most inventive communicators of the last four decades ... beautiful sound, faultless technique and lightning stream of ideas leave one breathless with admiration ... an utterly marvelous set of performances ... constantly tests and challenges himself in all manner of ways ... the finest distillation of his current level of achievement ... What is so satisfying is the phenomenal top-of-his-game consistency ... this perfect album contains some of the most exciting, commanding, utterly astounding music ever heard ... destined to become a classic ... "

Be that as it may be, we sold the house, had a farewell party and Gerry broke down and sobbed in the kitchen - she loved the place - and the kids were confused and I had $30, 000 in my pocket and felt like I'd started living again and I don't think anyone ever forgave me and I took one last look around the studio and we all said our last unfinished sentences. It was so long Gary and Jim and Fred and Allan and Lou and Fred and Carol and Art (I wasn't to see him again), Monte, Nick and Pete and all the old haunts, and Susan (who rang, just a goodbye, she said), and on the way out of town I took the keys to the realtor's office and we headed for the freeway.

chapter twenty six **requiem number three**

Once again it was back to New York, once again to lodge with a friend, a benefactor. Those months in Europe had made it very plain that I would have to keep moving, live if not on the run then surely as a vagrant, a displaced person, the wandering Jew. I had discovered something that I had never once expected, that my audience was not in one place, not in one country, but in many countries. Not a large audience: an attentive, keen audience, like pockets of resistance to the noise, the jive, the hype, the chaos, the cults, the coteries. the flamboyance, the megabucks, the racism, the posturing and fine tuning of personality, the mannequin parade of short lived, glittering, seductively merchandised names. (I had a standard piece of advice for any prospective student: If you want to make money from this, you better find another teacher.)

I did not relish the prospect of travelling constantly - it's extremely tiring, and would have been unfair to the few students I did have - and yet I did not relish the prospect of being without a musical partner. Out of the hundreds of people I had played with, there are only three or four who can evoke a better performance out of me than I could give were I playing alone, and they happened to live in different countries. And the students, they were in different countries, and keen to listen and learn. They couldn't come to me, so what choice did I have but to go to them. I owed a great debt to Lennie. That is why I came back to New York, or at the least it was the deciding factor. I needn't have done that, the same as he needn't have spent the most vital years of his life passing on all he knew and understood to a small group of students. Now, basically, he had lost interest, become embittered and hardly ever went out. He could still talk in an inspiring way, but he wanted to have nothing to do with the public. He was genuinely delighted with what had happened for me on the trip to Europe, and asked about Peter and Al and Lee and Red the way a father would, and with the same mixed responses. But the situation he was now in was such a far cry from those incredibly hardworking years in the late forties and early fifties: not the gracefully ageing master visited with respect; more the recluse who had lost heart, almost convinced that his lifework had been a waste of time. He was not alone in that: Bartok died in abject poverty, hardly acknowledged for what he was, and Bird had become a laughing stock by the end.

A small group of people, mostly women, had adopted him, jealously, and guarded him against visitors who might take up his time and so divert his attention away from them. It was weird how he had let that happen. It felt imprudent to ask him about it, and I rarely asked personal questions anyway. In the end it was too much of a hassle being with him, not because of him but because of the aggravation from these sycophants. We used to record some of our sessions, and he would talk about issuing a record, in short spasms of enthusiasm which didn't carry much conviction.

We had made an appointment for such a recording session some weeks ago. I turned up, rang the bell on the intercom: silence. Waited, and rang again: still no welcoming buzz. I knew he was looking forward to playing together - he always did - I knew he didn't go out, so I figured that the women had finally taken complete control. When I got back, there was a message on the table. "Lennie has died." November 18 1978. He died in his dressing gown. There was a memorial concert a few weeks later, at Town Hall. Much of the tribute was truly awful, quite without substance, emotional, self indulgent and false, and it was a terrible struggle to endure it to the end, the only compensation being that he wasn't around to hear parts of it. Lee didn't show up. I guess he had his reasons, which, on the evidence of the evening, may have been well-founded. Dear Lennie, goodbye. Words and even feelings are not enough to express how I felt. It was all such a mess.

Some months previously, Susan had moved into our new home in Connecticut, a small, typical middle-American family home, complete with white picket fence and large lake at the end of the back garden. She had wanted to study with Lennie. Now he was gone, she leaned more on me for tuition; after four years of discovering the meaning of improvisation and coming to terms with the very real demands it puts on a person, she was still not yet ready, in my opinion, to play in public. She trusted me.

There were so many students now who gave up because they couldn't find rewarding work or couldn't afford the tuition. And there were some who were willing to continue, albeit without any real chance of a return on their investment other than the satisfaction of knowing they were espousing standards that would last a lifetime. They were a very small minority, and, to me, a very important small minority, and it was to them that I would devote the time I had available. I do not consider myself to be a natural teacher: I would far rather be performing. But there were not that many opportunities to play regularly, so it was always going to be an uneasy combination of teaching and performing when the chance arose. These days you had to push yourself into the public eye, give out handbills, and accept that club owners would not want you to play in the one club for much more than a week every few months, because audiences demanded variety, as distinct from quality, which is what happens when society starts skidding around on the surface.

In Connecticut, there were very few students I wanted to teach, so I took a room in the Upper West Side of Manhattan, at the Hotel Bretton Hall on Broadway, and taught from there, commuting three days a week. The house by the lake looked to me like the house of someone else. I had started building a studio in the spare room, a project that would never be finished. More and more, I needed space to myself. In truth I only wanted to play with the kindred spirits I knew, and they were not many either, and in fact a diminishing number, through death, personality differences, incompatible values. A performer without a kindred spirit to perform with is as impossible a situation as a painter without a canvas. At least a painter can beg, borrow or steal a canvas, but kindred spirits cross your path or they don't. Admitting to some distress after Lennie's death, and in need of being pushed to my creative limits again, I borrowed the money and flew to Sweden just to spend a few days with Red. We had been in the same Army camp and studied with Lennie at the same time, but didn't get to know each other until years after that, one of those friendships where little needs to be said and where you can be out of each other's company for years, meet, and pick up where you left off.

Were it not for such events as that, I do not know that I could have held out. I was frequently being advised to take greater interest in what was happening to the recordings I had made; to see to it that royalties due to me were in fact paid - and often I knew very well that this was not the case. Sal helped me, a guy in Europe helped me, just as Peter had helped me, Gary had helped me, Bill had helped me, but I couldn't follow through. Just wasn't interested, because the music is here and then it is gone and I wanted to be in the present and looking forward to the future, not doing a reckoning of the sales value of past efforts. Letters would come from England. I knew what was in them: details about sales, bootleg releases, record companies using bankruptcy as a means of avoiding paying artists their fees and so on and so on. It wasn't worth opening the letters. Nothing much about business had changed in the past thirty years: I didn't need confirmation of that.

I was speaking to people less and less, because what there was to talk about was too complex and too personal, and people always wanted answers and there were no answers, or wanted explanations when there is no explanation, which in itself is the larger part of the fascination of living. I was speaking less and less to my wife, who was still in love with the music, and that was the point, there is a point there, in love with the music that was from me but where was I, a point there that I was beginning to grasp, no, grasp is far too gutsy a word, so there is no single word but there may be a picture, say, you must know this for yourself, a dirty, humid summer night during which you cannot settle down to sleep and just when you do, in the darkness the piercing whine of a mosquito which you can't see but the noise of which is bigger than the room, the point was making itself to me as persistently as that mosquito makes itself heard in fits and starts, that the music was adored but not the source. I was absent, a ghost in my own body.

That was the start of it. I spent more time at the Hotel. Susan spent more time at the Hotel. We played and talked and read and walked amongst the crowds on Broadway, stopping for a breakfast of a slice of pizza at lunch time. And she would go home to Connecticut and I'd stay in Manhattan, making the long walk down the corridor to the communal bathroom at four in the morning in my dressing gown and slippers, every inch fifty three years of my age.

Lennie was gone. I was having trouble coming to terms with that. He had been the most valuable person to my life and Lee had refused to participate in the memorial. Sal was around and a staunch friend and we spent hours together in his studio. And I needed to get away and flew down to Beverly Hills for an engagement and couldn't get back fast enough.

And there I was in the Hotel, on the army cot, and there she was on the second floor. in the room next to the kids, with the lake at the end of the garden and Gerry cooking breakfast for all of them and at the weekends I'd be there too, giving the kids lessons and all of us fooling around by the lake when it wasn't too cold and the kids missing California and me missing Lennie and everyone missing the point.

chapter twenty seven **star eyes**

Now if a recording contract says today's the day, even if you've nothing of value to say, in you go. And you'd better get there early so the engineers can get their hands on you. By doing that - recording at short notice and without the musicians getting to know each other - we hurt ourselves, and we don't do our audience any favors either.

Which is why I would rarely deal with record companies - they were not to be trusted - and chose to record at the home or studio of my friends instead. It's simple: doing things this way, we were always relaxed about recording, did it in our own time, had no one to answer to, and decided for ourselves what to offer the public and what to throw away. It all comes down to responsibility and freedom. The offers of money meant nothing to me at all; I would far rather sell 300 copies of a recording, confident that it was a true expression of the best I was capable of at the time, than sell 3000 copies of a recording I would live to be ashamed of.

I had always believed and always will believe that the finest music is performed live, and the experience in Europe proved that once and for all. So many people who had heard recordings of mine were simply blown away by hearing a good live performance, incredulous at the extraordinary difference in feeling. It is not hard to explain. I mean, there is a great deal of difference, isn't there, between talking to someone on the phone or in a letter - and I hardly ever wrote letters, and used the telephone as little as possible - and being in that person's company. In that case, you have a living memory, you have shared a moment in your lives personally. A recording is already abstract and cold, even the very finest. So when I play live, I am conscious of giving a part of my life to the audience, and whether they know it or not, those people give something of themselves to me. In a live situation, you remember the atmosphere, the presence of the performer, the physical impact of the person; it's a rich experience. And I'm convinced that one, just one special live performance will have a lifelong impact on a person, far deeper than can happen by sitting at home by the record player.

And the very finest has gone into thin air. That's beautiful. It's joined the world totally unimpeded, like bird song or the sound of the breaking of the waves. Absolutely nothing physical left. I hold my old tenor in my hands. Isn't this incredible. A piece of metal fashioned into a very odd shape, an amazingly intricate piece of craftsmanship in leather and brass and mother of pearl and steel, with an ebonite or metal mouthpiece stuck on the end, together with a sliver of bamboo, also highly crafted. And it is silent, like the house at night. A friend comes in with his double bass, another extraordinary instrument, and rests it against the wall. I put my tenor on its stand and we have a drink or two and talk and play scrabble or chess. And there the two instruments rest; patient, silent, beautiful to look at - really beautiful like a truly beautiful woman - and endless. Left alone, they demand nothing. Dare to become one with it, and you enter a limitless world, of discipline and inspiration, simplicity and complexity, thrilling success and desperate failure. More than that, you plumb the depths of yourself, to which there is no end.

Whatever else it might be, music is not live unless it aspires to a oneness with the majesty of the universe. And you don't need recording studios or record companies for that to happen. You don't need recordings. So after we've got to know each other again, maybe by two or three in the morning, I put the neck strap on, clip on the tenor, moisten the reed and set it in place while Red prepares his bass. Finally we make sure that not only are we in tune with each other but that the instruments are in tune with each other. And then we find our harmonies for that night, the melodies and the rhythm of these moments in our lives. Maybe no one hears us, and it doesn't matter, the same as it doesn't matter if not one soul hears the bird song. What matters is that the event takes place. And while I play, I am back in Houston Missouri where I learned humility. And the majesty of the universe has nothing at all to do with egos or personality or charisma: go past all those and you're maybe getting somewhere. It's not an easy road, and the valleys will be roughly as deep as the ridge of the hill is high.

I'm not a disciple of Lennie's, or if I am then I'm also a disciple of

Bach, Bartok and Parker. Lennie inspired rapport and staying together, artists functioning. There was the painting Van Gogh wanted to share with Gauguin. Like that. Social conditions don't encourage functioning together, feeling together.

I was not out to make a name. And success finally was due to studying the same thing for 30 years. Well, I was working towards personal ability, and that took effort. You have to learn to discriminate. It has to be done nowadays. In the 40s everything felt like one big happy family; it was a whole community more or less having the same goals. Nowadays everyone's up tight.

That feeling was still current between many of those with whom I spent time. Sal's studio burned down. A number of us had used the studio extensively, so it was natural for us to put on a benefit concert to raise at least some of the money Sal needed to set up another studio. It was an immediate and spontaneous wish.

Betty hadn't sung in public for years, having had a family, and wanted to perform again. I heard about her plans and wanted to take part, turn up at least and may be accompany her if that would give her confidence. The old spirit persisted.

Increasingly I wanted to look after my students, help them find their way through a situation far more complex and confusing than it had been back in the forties. It was not easy then, but it was far worse now, especially in regard to questions of integrity, standards of competence, personal courage and achieving a strong sense of your own voice. Colleges were turning out thousands of students, only a few of whom had a strong enough love to make genuine sacrifices to maintain its purity. Consequently many of them lost interest when they discovered what those sacrifices were, and many more caved in to the array of temptations presented by commerce.

My purpose was to establish in the students who stayed with me a deep sense of the uniqueness of their own voice, and the determination to work at developing that. Seeing what the situation was in the world at large, that felt to me an immensely important purpose, which I would carry out as fully as possible for as long as possible, passing on to another generation what Lennie had passed on to me. Continuity.

I told all of them, don't be afraid to look backwards. All the major influences are behind us, and we learn, finally, from past experience. The final training is to sing in unison of feeling with, say, Bird or Lady Day or Pres, then to sing the song your own way, and then to play it as if you are singing. Then you can start to improvise, because you already know a great deal about yourself. You can't improvise from a state of ignorance.

After getting set up at the Hotel, I got busy, teaching and playing at Peachtree's and the Village Vanguard, and travelling. It was a full year.

April and May:- Copenhagen, Denmark: Oslo, Norway: Stockholm, Sweden (for a concert on Swedish Radio) and recording an album with Red, just the two of us. Then back to Copenhagen.

June:- New York, at Sweet Basil (with Red) and the Vanguard (with Sal). Since Lennie's passing, I was wanting to work as much with the people who had been fellow students with me over the past thirty odd years as I wanted to work with my own students. And I didn't mind giving interviews now, because people were starting to realize that what we had been doing for the past thirty odd years had outlived most of the so-called innovations and avant-garde, free form, electronic stuff, and it seemed important to speak up and reiterate what the fundamentals. I think every interview I gave said pretty much the same thing.

July:- Master classes in Norway.

August:- Back in America, performing in California and New York City.

October:- Europe again, for the Berlin Jazz Festival, with Sal and

Lee. The response was the same everywhere: enthusiasm to hear more and to learn. And those who make their money out of music were getting interested, even publicity agents, because, here, they thought, is a promising commodity. I suppose it was almost flattering, to have persisted over so many years following the same line and to be vindicated finally. But that was enough. Even though I had made it consistently clear that I had no intention of becoming a name, a man with stars in his eyes, or even of being a figure the jazz public would recognize and say, Hey, that's you know who (friends joked that I was known as Warne Who), the agents nevertheless couldn't resist having a crack at me, thinking they were doing me a favor with their plans for recording contracts and playing the college circuit, getting organized and carrying on in a businesslike way. As if I needed someone to manage me. Fact is, I preferred to operate in my own way, exactly as I had been doing since I was twenty. Some people found my approach infuriating, though I fail to see what it had to do with them. I was just myself, and whoever that was, well that was my business.

I am not at home much. Susan has her own key to the room at the Hotel. I teach. I play. In the playing, and sometimes in the teaching, I find a taste of peace and a marvelous communion. In the other hours I am sometimes at a loss.

There are contrasts and contradictions. I am now doing what Lennie could not do. Maybe there was something of the father and son in us. I am drawn equally between the young students and my old friends, between America and Europe. The calling is more important to me than my family and yet I love my sons. I have not chosen solitude: the way of the world has made me solitary. I am not an easy man to become close to, and yet I need closeness. I teach and I play and find some communion and in the other hours we keep each other company, fellow travellers in the forest.

chapter twenty eight **love me or leave me**

You don't know what love is. What is this thing called, love? What? is this thing called love? Is this thing called love? Can this be love? I can't believe that you're in love with me. I can't give you anything but love. I can't believe that you can give me anything, but it's you or no one, lover man, the man I love when I'm in the mood for that thing you don't know, so love me or leave me she said.

So many tunes I had played with love in, many hundreds, even thousands of times during my life, and never once had I repeated a memorized theme. But I had never asked myself what love was. I had my suspicions. I knew what devotion was. She was very devoted, and I wanted love after all. I needed space, private space. Right from the beginning, if you remember, I had shied away from adulation; better to be appreciated. Adulation is fashionable and fashions come and go. Appreciation tends to persist, and perhaps blossom into what this thing called love is.

The loss of Lennie, the reception in Europe, and the spontaneous understanding between Susan and myself were all as unprepared against as were the consequences, and they all happened more or less at the same time. Before those events, I had come to terms with the world, well, behaved as if I had, because in my heart I could not escape the knowledge that I had not come to terms at all. After those events, my relationships with just about everything changed: nothing was reliable. It was like being part way through an improvisation and realizing I had forgotten something as basic as the tune the improvisation was based on or the key we were playing in At times I didn't even recognize myself any more.

I knew I had played better on that tour of Europe than I had ever played before, which made the future very frightening. Would I ever play so well again, with the feeling of being totally expressed, of having heard the beauty I had always striven to hear, of there being nothing I could have expressed in a more satisfying way? Where every single sound .... How could I possibly go beyond that? I mean, this was a very disturbing question for me. Taking comfort in what I had done never had been my way; I was always looking for what was next, and you can't go higher than the top of the mountain. There was nothing I could do to improve my technique or to extend my knowledge of the essence of music. I had mastered the art of breathing so that I could play for five, eight, twenty, thirty minutes of uninterrupted invention. I had experimented with every conceivable combination of mouthpiece and reed, over the years, and there was nothing more to be discovered about any of these things.

I became quite dejected. The jazz scene in New York was just horrible, I mean a simply terrible way to live. No one really cared the way we used to. It was all novelties, indulgence, and trying new theories, and all the stuffing had gone out of it. The functioning together, where had that notion gone?

Very little pleased me, except the progress of my students and the companionship of Susan - we had a lot to give each other, not the least the willingness to listen without having to give an answer or an explanation. Are there ever any real explanations? My family life displeased me, so I distanced myself from them, and even that displeased me and, of course, was a major disturbance for them. No one could understand what was going on, and nor could I.

The difficulty was that my dejection and displeasure did not show on the surface. I was still courteous, quiet, withdrawn and thoughtful, but despair and confusion and impatience beset me every day. My life became a series of dislocated moments, lacking in continuity.

I had a new student, George, about the same age as myself, a mature student, a pianist. We never played publicly, but in private we had a gas. I am grateful for the light relief of such friendships, where people take you just the way you are. We saw a lot of each other - that's relative, because there were very few people I met with socially on a regular basis.

We'd been out for a meal, and were happily the worse for drink, enjoying the liberation of the libation as Red might have said. It was a bitterly cold night, way below freezing, and the first flakes of a snow storm were drifting down. Gloved hands, heavy overcoats, collars turned up. We happened to be walking along a section of Broadway where the city fathers had chosen to set plaques in the sidewalk commemorating the major figures in American music. There was one for Bird. Despite the cold, we stopped at each plaque and deliberated on the contribution each figure had made. George gave me a hug and pronounced that it wouldn't be long before there was a plaque for me. I told him it was likely to be many years before anyone even realized I had died. Then we came to the one for Bird. That sobered me up a little, and with genuine heartfelt love, I knelt down and kissed the freezing tablet, because this was someone I loved. I felt that, at last, I had paid my final respects. Fortunately my lips didn't stick to the metal or I would have kissed them goodbye too.

George wanted to cheer me up. He arrived at Bretton Hall - that sounds aristocratic; add 'Hotel' and it's a different matter. He had brought a gift, a small porcelain cat playing a saxophone. Gerry's going to like that on the mantelpiece, he said, and I said she wouldn't ever see it because it was going to stay right here in Bretton Hall, next to the dime store turtle which I had kept all these years. (I am not a sentimental person, but I do allow for modest tokens.) He gave me a quizzical look. He had met Susan. I just put the cat on the mantelpiece, and we left it at that. I didn't think there was anything to add.

Gerry rang every so often. She couldn't go on living like this, she said. She sounded hysterical. There wasn't enough money to pay the rent on the house with the white picket fence and the lake out the back. Then I heard she was in the hospital. I didn't know what to do. I took her to a concert and she convinces herself the woman singing is my mistress. It was all beyond me.

Bretton Hall Hotel is a building full of musicians, dancers, actors, all trying to survive, like a ghetto of displaced people. My room had been occupied by a musician who had nailed sections of quilted brocade padding all over the walls, to deaden the noise. It was stained, and the colors had faded. I was getting too old to live like this, but just now I had no options. Work was as spasmodic as ever, and record companies must have lost my forwarding address. Or it's possible I never gave them one.

After one of George's lessons, we were talking, over a game of chess, about what quality is it which makes some music remain a deeply moving experience for centuries. I heard every word he said, but carried on studying the board. He talked away for a while and then, figuring I wasn't listening, started reading a book. Before long, Susan came home with some food, said hi and set about cooking. George put the book down and said he was going out to get some wine. I heard him, but didn't say anything until he was going out the door, and then I asked him if he minded me making his next move, if he hadn't come back by the time I'd made mine. He laughed and said why should he mind when he only moved the pieces I told him to anyway.

During the meal we didn't talk much. Then it occurred to me. The quality is feeling: it's a fine feeling, common to every human being, and expresses the nostalgia for a more peaceful and compassionate world than this one we live on, and simultaneously acknowledges the splendor of this world. And at that moment, I knew where the music was leading me. It was the feeling of compassion and gentleness and hope that must inspire me. In New York, that's not easy. After the meal we entertained each other on the piano almost until dawn. I recalled the Saturday and Sunday nights in Lennie's first studio, and this was not the same thing at all.

Gerry phones again. She's started drinking and says she is going mad. I sit there with the phone in my hand. She's not making any sense. Nothing makes any sense. Help? Me? How? May be you should go see a doctor. I meant to speak with concern but the words sounded like the beating of hammers on a hollow iron post.

I had recorded an album with one of my students a couple of years ago. He authorized the release of tracks I was not happy with, but he's arranged the contract so he has the final say, he says. It still rancors me. The record is not something I am happy about, not something I had agreed to, and yet it exists, and people will listen to it, but against my wishes, and what can I do about it? Nothing. Not what I call functioning together? Hard to believe a student of mine could have so denied me. And I never did make peace with him.

I am stubborn and single-minded, but not usually prone to anger. I notice I am feeling more anger and impatience. Maybe almost forty years of refusing to deviate from my own way, often out of sorts with the mainstream and most of the tributaries, is taking its toll.

At a performance the other night, there's a young guy at the front, recording with a pocket recorder, one of those things battery operated things. He keeps fiddling with it and I become more and more upset. At the interval, I stride over to him and try to take the thing from him. He resists, but I snatch the thing away, take out the tape and unwind the brown ribbon as fast as I can until it's a tangled mess at my feet. If I only get one chance to play the music, you only get one chance to hear it, unless I say otherwise. It's like theft, unless I give you permission, so you don't get this thing back. And I stuff it into my jacket pocket. I had surprised myself. I was starting to let it all out. One thing I absolutely hated was people taking my music away without the decency to ask first. What so annoyed me, above all, was that they were cheating themselves: the sound quality on those things is very poor, so when he listened to the recording, what was he going to hear. I told him I wouldn't allow him to record, absolutely not. If he wanted to learn it, then let him memorize it, the way Karl used to, flat on his stomach on the dance hall roof. This was not the same at all.

A group in Norway want me to spend some time with them. I go. After all, there's only a week here and a week there in New York. And they're a gentle people, the Norwegians. And their standards are high.

Play the Vanguard with Sal, and the West End with some of my students, to give them at least some professional experience. Lee and I are invited to play in Copenhagen again. A taste of a time gone by. We barely know each other any more.

A Dutch journalist has been after me for quite some time. I don't like giving interviews unless I can see what is going to be printed. It's happened too often: what I actually remember saying and what is printed are not the same thing at all. He doesn't want me to read what he's going to write. I'm depressed and figure a visitor may fill the half hour between lessons. In he comes, reckons he's got somewhere by making it through the door. Sits down, note book at the ready. I decide I'm not going to listen to a word, and go and open a bottle of wine. He might be thinking I'm acting out of character and being the good host. He fires off a few questions about my circumstances. No doubt he's taken note of the ambiance of the room and its padded walls, drum set, piano, Susan's clothes, the mess in the kitchen, the furniture I've made, the fresh white pine so contrasting with the decadent monastic drabness that to this guy is no doubt off-putting or, worse, romantic. The Dutch are very clean.

I pour him a glass of wine, red wine from France, and go to the window and watch the cars and the pedestrians, and remark, "It's easier to organize cars than people." Perhaps he thought he had misheard, because he stared at me, confused. He asked me, How would I define my approach to music now? I said, "When you've played it, it's gone, just like the wind. It comes out of nowhere, blows through and is gone. Can you remember what the wind was like last Tuesday?" It was good wine. He agreed with me, and had another glass.

Noise was another problem. Everywhere noise. I walked round to a club to set up a gig. The waitress went to fetch the manager. There was a juke box, just for the noise - without the noise there'd be nothing happening. I couldn't tolerate noise and left before the manager appeared.

I couldn't pay the rent on the house by the lake. I took Gerry and the boys back to Santa Cruz to live with her mother. It was a long drive and I don't want to think about it. The boys hardly said anything. I loved them. For the last time I spent the night at the old house in the Valley, borrowed some shekels from the old woman in the morning and flew back east, wondering what was going on in Houston Missouri.

The thirty thousand dollars I once had in my pocket had gone long since. Here I was back in New York, fresh from Los Angeles, as I had been when a young man in 1949, clean cut, noble aims, bright smile, when the notion of functioning together was current, and this wasn't the same thing at all.

While trimming my beard, back in the bathroom at the end of the corridor at the Hall, I looked at myself closely in the mirror and beheld the face of a man who is not looking well and had to ask myself when I had last eaten. Something was wrong. I remembered those half pints of cream I used to consume, gaining strength from the dignity I felt setting out on an honorable calling, and felt sick at the thought. Things were out of control, everywhere I looked.

Phone call. "If you've got any bookings for the next few weeks, cancel them. You're going to Denmark and then Holland." And, all of a sudden, I was not looking at the padded walls in the Hotel Bretton Hall, I was in Copenhagen, almost gorging myself in a restaurant, and then playing at a jazz festival with Sal.

Interview: "What sets my music apart from that of many other jazz musicians? Well, let me put it this way. That's the difference between an artistic approach and the approach of personality. The artistic approach doesn't mean you yield self-expression, but it does mean more emphasis is placed on talent rather than on personality. Certainly emotion of feeling is still at the base of playing. Putting it another way, it's a matter of how one's ability, one's talent is used either with complete integrity and artistically or primarily as a means of maintaining a 'personality', by which music is used to express personality rather than as an expression in itself. Artistic playing is economical, where every note functions within the structure of the improvisation."

Susan rings from the padded room. She misses me unbearably much, playing together, walking the streets looking for work, just hanging out. I promise to bring her with me next time. Could be I was in love.

Conversation in Copenhagen with record producer who'd travelled from Holland to meet me. He'd like to offer me a recording contract when I'm in Holland. I say I have doubts. Why, he'd like to know. Well, I only want to make records with my students, on my own label. He says such an idea won't work commercially. Hard to argue with that. Hank Jones, he says he'd like me to make a record with Hank. I say I will only record with musicians I know well. He's in a hurry because Hank has to go somewhere or other, so why don't I go and listen to Hank, who's apparently the most sought after pianist in New York just now, which is supposed to make it easy for me to agree: but I don't know where the guy's at these days. I go and listen to Hank and we end up making a record.

It worked really well, may be the best I'd played in twenty years, a powerful and profound lyricism new for me because things were not the same at all, and in the chaos my only hope was to find a purity of feeling. Hank and I looked forward to playing together back in the States; we could function together.

A few weeks later, there's a couple of performances with Lou Levy, at the Chicago Jazz Festival, and I hadn't played in Chicago since the early days with Lennie. I think George had a hand in setting that up because he had grown up with Lou. And we could function together too. I was beginning to feel optimistic, the way people were trying to get things to happen for me.

Then back to Hollywood, always back to Hollywood, for a recording session with Gary, who I hadn't performed with for years, but who hadn't forgotten, and with Alan who had introduced me to Susan and asked after her progress.

I did some club dates too. Gerry must have heard I was back home. After one of the gigs, there she was in the club foyer, huddled in a chair, desperately drunk, her mendicant eyes daring to look up, at me. A nightmare. I asked the manager to make sure she got home. I could hear her saying love me or leave, and the drone of the vee dub's engine was still ringing in my ears as the headlights occasionally picked the eyes of a living thing from out of the darkness.

chapter twenty nine **kc initially**

Lesson 3.

It is all so simple, and it drives me crazy: no one seems to be listening. Ask any of my students, whether they had only one lesson or many, and they will say the same thing: learning this way utterly changed their feeling for music - not just jazz - and opened up a world they would not have encountered because they did not know it was there. Simple. But the simple truth is steadily ignored; that's how much the true spirit of music has been lost during this century, mainly since the advent of commercially successful noise. And all I ask is to be able to work four or six months of the year in the place where I live - playing - so I can survive, and stay close to my students, so we get to know each other. But it's not possible. I have to travel to survive. I suffer, my students suffer, and, though no one has noticed yet, the public, the community, suffers too.

The simplicity is this. Improvisation, or releasing the individual voice, is based on feeling and the human ear. The way to train the human ear is to listen and the way to release the feeling is to sing. It is not surprising, therefore, that my students must learn to sing with their own voice, not imitating someone else. This is the way music was taught for thousands of years, and nothing has changed in our time to make the fundamental laws suddenly ineffective. If we think otherwise, then we're fooling ourselves.

It will be obvious, I hope, that to sing means to be able to listen carefully, with a sensitive feeling. Singing is intensely personal: it engages the whole body and the whole spirit: breath. And you have to reveal yourself. We are taught in western society to be afraid of ourselves and to imitate - that's the way to make money. None of what I am saying is new; it's just been forgotten and so needs to be reiterated. I've been reiterating it for thirty years, quietly, whenever the occasion arises, to my students, in interviews, patiently repeating myself. And I do not enjoy repeating myself, but if we can't remember the fundamentals then we're in dead trouble.

To be able to improvise also presumes a solid foundation in the basics of theory and history. And I do not mean written history. I mean aural history, a thorough knowledge of the masters, achieved through listening to them. That is all for the intellect, which has no role to play in the art of improvising: the intellect is solely a storehouse of knowledge. When improvising, the only faculties you use are your hearing, your feeling, and your imagination. It can be a very straight and lonely path. But art is like that.

I have had students come to me with a head full of theory, just total chaos in their heads, and when I ask them to forget about theory except for the basics and ask them to sing unaccompanied and with confidence and feeling, even something as rudimentary as a major scale, they can't do it. It is easy then to ask what is the value of these theories, the intellectual approach. After the inevitable breakthrough, then we can start to make progress.

Much more difficult to convey is the difference between self-expression and indulgence of personality, between emotion and feeling. Listen carefully and you will discover the difference.

End of Lesson 3

Music is ninety percent of my life. That's just the way I am. It's the way I share my life. I need people close to me who are equally close to the music. There are not many. Susan was one. And that accounts for a lot. We sang together, unaccompanied, or one of us sang and the other played piano. We played duets on the piano, four hands. We played duets, piano and tenor, piano and clarinet, piano and voice. And it brought a new quality to my life, this inexplicable unison of feeling, a lightness and delicacy.

An audience is fifty percent of my music which is why, generally speaking, I do not like recordings. And the only way to find an audience is to travel abroad because the audience in America only wanted to listen to 'names', and who was I? So, once again, off to Europe, for four months, this time the two of us, and a continuation of the journey with Lou Levy.

Holland, France, Holland, Belgium, Holland, England, Norway. Two more albums. Record producers are one of the great mysteries of my life. The recording with Lou has been described as 'one of the great ballad albums of our time'. I have said that the audience is fifty percent of my music, and it is well known that my imagination is most fertile and daring when I am playing to an attentive audience (namely people who are listening to the music and not to each other). And yet, even though I have played many thousands of hours 'live', on only the rarest of occasions did anyone have the initiative to arrange permission to record when I was playing at my best. Which says a great deal about record companies: they always want control. They talk about fidelity, but they are ignorant about music, truly and disgracefully ignorant.

I hear my music referred to as music of subtle joy and noble concerns. To me it had at last become affectionate, and forgiving as well, in spite of everything that had happened over the past forty years. This is my favorite review, not because it is flattering (I know what my talent is) but because it was written after hearing a live performance:

"With a tone that has the mellow silkiness of a cello with lines that show an astonishing continuity of invention, and with a mellifluous legato delivery, he combines originality with a supreme and sinuous melodic gift ... What really sets him apart from other jazz soloists is that his creative extemporization is almost seamless: his music is constantly creative. Where other players would bridge an invention gap with a favorite cliche or simply a tacit couple of bars, he continues to explore the changes, setting delightfully fresh and unhackneyed lines against the framework of the tune.

.... one of the quickest harmonic minds in jazz ... a tremendous assurance (and) a flawless sense of structure. He builds solos into winning compositions, starting and ending phrases with scant regard for bar lines, spinning off fresh inventions with apparent effortlessness but always staying true ..."

Norway. Another album, and a few master classes. To hear five or six talented 'professionals' sing their improvisations for the first time in their lives, and witness both their sense of wonder at the modest results and the courage it took to achieve them, always made such a journey worthwhile. Even more gratifying was the bond the experience forged between us. Yes, I would rather spend a hundred hours in private sessions imbued with a feeling of mutual care than spend one hour in the studios of a record company. On the other hand, I also need to eat.

In Paris, Susan and I made our first public appearance. It had taken ten years of playing together before we were ready to present our work: we were willing to wait twenty years. Preparation is not to be taken lightly. Following the real music is sometimes a lonely and always a straight road, usually uphill, but I know of no greater joy in life than the bliss of being in harmony with another human being, which is the moment at which life truly begins. We are not talking about box-office, royalties, appearance fees, rave reviews, public approval, being a name. Even the slightest submission to those crudities is to dip your wings in oil.

And part of me is tired. On stage in Rotterdam or Paris or London or some small town, I ponder the desirability of spending the rest of my life like this, wandering from one kind person's spare bedroom or hotel to another, and whether I have any choice. Or during a lesson, I am looking at the student, Dutch, French, English, Danish, Norwegian, wondering if I am to spend the rest of my life watching a succession of barely known faces look at me with a mixture of terror and bewilderment as I ask them to do the most obvious exercises no one had remembered to mention. Then I can feel their wonderment at the journey opening up before them, and so I repeat myself.

An impresario once said that he could not figure me out at all. Most musicians were demanding to be paid almost by the note, yet here I was preferring a private jam session to a paid gig. But the reason is simple: I try to play only when the situation does justice to the calling, and never will forget the story of Cerucik.

I liked to have a base. You get to know your audience real well, and the performers get to know each other and then wonderful and exciting things can happen; nothing of lasting value happens if it hasn't evolved over time. The one night stands so loved by business men are the kiss of death to music. In the thirty years since playing at the Half-Note with Lennie and Lee, the only base I had had was at Dontes, and that was already ten years ago. I did not choose the way of the vagrant: it was thrust upon me.

There were very few places where I actually wanted to play, for a number of very good reasons: acoustics for one, and the attitudes of the owners for another. I had found two places in New York, the Village Vanguard and the West End Cafe. But the owner of the one would say, "If you play here, I can only let you stay for a week at a time, may be two. And since you're playing at that other place, then I can't let you come back here for another three or four months. The audience wants variety. We got to have names most of the time." And the owner of the other place would come up with the same logic. And these guys had a sympathetic attitude. So there it was, four weeks work every four months at the most. It is simply impossible to build a working group under those conditions, unless every member is rich or can cope with hunger and homelessness. So you do what you can.

For a start, you can isolate the causes and accept them. And the causes are the impresarios and the marketing machine, which says 'Hey man, we're just delivering the goods the public wants' and you can say 'Hey man, you're full of bullshit, because the fact is you're only in it for what you get out of it: shekels. Period.' And then you live with that, best way you can.

A base is not only the venue, it is also the people you perform for - how a priest must love his chapel. It takes years to cultivate a closeness that can produce the best that's humanly possible and so do justice to the honorable calling. And it also takes the courage to not turn away from each other, but to learn to function together, through thick and thin. Lee had let me down, let the music down, let himself down, and I was always ready for things to change. I spend my time with people who were willing to take years. Why do you think the Indian student of the tabla starts studying with his master when he is three or four and stays with the same man until may be he's thirty? Forgive me if I repeat myself, but don't be afraid to look back because all the major influences are behind us and we learn from our ...

At least I had a makeshift base, and, the economics of the industry being what they are and my values being what they are and always will be for ever and ever amen, the best I was allowed to do was to concentrate on a small group of serious students and feature them at the West End or the Vanguard. It was not easy: the audience demanded names, and the names I knew were John and Randy and Kevin and Mark and Jim and Pete and I recognized their voices once they understood that they could sing. And, for their part, they did not understand what I said: they heard what I meant. I have no reason to complain.

So what better name for the next recording than Blues For A Reason, with Chet Baker; trumpet, tenor and rhythm section. He had a name and record producers were trying to help me by allowing me to record with names, never mind what that implies. I made the recording because Chet knew what was on. I am told it was my best selling recording - I really don't know.

Chet was in bed in Paris, in the middle of the day, which is understandable because musicians are still expected to play through the night. The phone rings. His woman answers it. Sure Mr Baker is here, but he's asleep. C'est important? Alors ... and she wakes him up. Chet needs shekels badly, like Bird did, and in his half sleep all he hears is the offer of shekels for a recording session with a guy he's never played with before. Contract? Sure man. April? Sure, man, I'll be there, trust me. The guy on the other end of the line says a whole lot more and Chet keeps agreeing and falling asleep and waking up when his woman shakes him and the voice asks him to confirm the deal and Chet wants to go back to sleep and just says sure man, that's all confirmed, just send the contract.

A few days before the session, it dawns on Chet that he's in Paris and the recording is going to happen in Holland and he doesn't have the money to make the trip and he needs the money for two tickets because he won't come without his woman. They both turn up, right on time. We had never played together before and we were never to play together again. One night, after a gig, Chet was enjoying a cigarette or whatever, leaning back against the railings around the balcony of his fifth floor hotel bedroom, enjoying the night air and the sight of his woman sleeping. He had forgotten how tall he was and how tired he was and toppled over backwards. Maybe he'd fallen asleep in his contentment, because throughout his fall he didn't utter a sound. Blues for a reason. Bounce of the pigskin. Or how the industry cares for its properties in disgraceful ignorance.

By then Susan and I were a long way away, via Rotterdam and Paris and Oslo, hotels, airport lounges, railway terminals, pianos people think you can get to know in a couple of hours, audiences who know you for two hours, three hours and having to make the best of that, through parks and cafes and spare bedrooms of kindly friends, and me making scrambled eggs on toast and fresh black coffee, discovering the limits and the limitations as we learn over and over to relinquish with as much grace as possible, so much to be thankful for, struggling against the intellect's appetite for explanation, so deeply grateful, facing the choice between personal need and the demands of the honorable calling, enough of a choice to tear you apart if you lack courage, and on and on, each one up their own mountain or down into their own valleys which are not the same things at all, and paths cross, paths join, paths divide and sometimes come together again and sometimes not.

Back in Hollywood. In honor of Bird, we had called one of our sons Casey, after Bird's invention, KC Blues. But it was the other son, Jason, who could really play, played trumpet like an angel. He was playing in the High School Band, as I had done at his age, and I had come to listen, on condition no public mention was made about who I was. (I do have a sense of humor.) And I sat there, surrounded by proud and enthusiastic parents, with my legs crossed, elbows on the arms of the chair, hands folded under my chin, my fifty seven year old eyes closed. And I knew he was playing not to please me but to address me. And there's nothing more direct than that.

After the session, I sat and watched the kids pack up. Some of the parents came across to greet me, but thankfully most of them had no reason to recognize my face. Then the hall was empty, except for Jason and three or four of his friends. He'd kept his word.

They came over with their instruments, pulled up chairs, sat themselves down and waited. Jason introduced them one by one and we shook hands. One of them asked, "Sir, what is jazz?"

"Jazz," I said, "is a misunderstood word," and asked if I could borrow his alto. I played a Bach Invention as written, and then improvised on the theme and then improvised on the harmony.

A small crowd had gathered at the doorway.

"Initially," I said, "it's simple: you have to learn to sing and your audience has to learn to listen."

He wanted to know if I gave lessons, and looked totally crestfallen to hear me say I lived in New York. Then he took a deep breath and asked for the address.

"86th and Broadway, the Hotel Bretton Hall."

The caretaker came along to usher us out.

The kid followed me out to the car-park. "Somehow or other," he told me, "I'll get there."

And not long afterwards, to my surprise, he did.

chapter thirty **alone together**

"There is a force in music that unites people and draws them into the musical experience, a total willingness to be in time and harmony with another mortal. In this confluence, the dancers become the dance."

Not possible continue New York longer. Cannot yet change, knowing the score out there, lie here on couch reading, resting limbs. Students, a handful, work in clubs, makeshift arrangement not part of the calling. No longer the strength, inclination to resist the tide drawing the music into the becalmed waters divorced from great ocean of history. Study the history, even your own.

Call a truce, then. Pointless, even for an ardent stalwart, to speak gently amongst the great din of amplified opinion and groundless experiment. Protestations, not one have I. Ghostlike, mouth moves correctly as if delivering words significant, all in working order, but mouthing only. Ah well, and turn the page. Have striven these many years.

Good book, put aside the aspiration. Pull back and consider what is prudent. Old now and conserving the energies remaining. Turn the page. A book better than wine, now and then.

The room is finished. Padding all renewed, clean fabrics picked up from jewish stores in doorways of which stand men still closer to the past than the present. Happy hours looking here and there, turning over piles of cloth and fabrics, holding up the pieces that caught the eye of either one of us. Some rugs too, from China, wall hangings, the stains of old expunged. Wandered too far afield we did, absorbed in the playful fun of it and hail a cab to get parcels rudely wrapped back home. Even the walls and ceiling rendered in colors to bring calm and make the most of what little light there was in New York. Homely she called it. Some dignity restored, as after the turmoil of a wild storm's passing.

The desk and table in every detail wrought from skills derived from watching hour after hour when he came home from the studios. Just for my pleasure, these artifacts, the work of many months.

She at the piano. I'd hear something she had passed over, rest the rebate plane on its side, dust off my hands and sit beside her on the stool and work the feeling through that had come to me, continuing for I do not know how long, never having thought of duration because it is the form I look for, and she no doubt thinking I no longer realize she's there, but I do, and then we go over it together and find something secret in common.

I go back to my work, or pick up a book, and she pursues the new feeling for herself. And the breeze through the wide open windows flips the pages over in a second.

Nothing to hide, nothing to fear, nothing to withhold, nor to gain or lose, as equally known as unknown, a perfect sameness in mutual difference, each moved by the other in exact measure in this levity of spirit.

We share an affection for the music such as a mother and father feel for the child. A comparably innate affection and tenderness, all coarseness put aside. Rare and brief such a gift, timeless and boundless, and passing, as the clouds must pass across the sky or as the tide must turn.

The tide is turning. There is a stillness at the turning of the tide, a moment of sweet rest, a pause between movements. Always looked for the changes, tried all kinds of things, all kinds of approaches, all kinds of combinations, and finally the duet, no greater challenge than that.

There was a man of Hungarian descent. The bounce of the pigskin, using the device of war and persecution, saw to it that he came to live in Manhattan. Truly the hermit, he called himself a rabbi. In nature he was, but too free a spirit to be held down by orthodoxy.

He lived in the penthouse, as he called it. This was a very splendid place on top of one of New York's tenement buildings. No one realized he lived there, and no one would have thought of living there except someone who could find no other place to rest on the earth.

You have seen such structures, from the outside, on detective films, box like structures around the stairways that lead out on to the flat roof top. His penthouse apartment was about ten feet square. Inside, it was a blend of synagogue and woodcutters hut. He had lined the walls with pieces of wood he'd scavenged from demolished buildings and fashioned to a wonderful beauty, creating a tapestry, in which the different grains in the wood had been composed into a dance. I tell you, it was a splendid place. There was a small wood-stove in one corner. In the roof, he had set two large stained glass windows, and they allowed his only natural light. At night he used oil lamps.

He was walking the streets one night and happened to pass the club where I was playing. The music drew him in and held him there until we finished, around three in the morning. With a confidence that was unusually direct and courteous, he came up to me, introduced himself and asked that I teach him. What made me agree was the air of civility and respect that was extremely rare. We set a date and he gave me his address, insisting that I meet him outside the building and that I bring my instrument.

He made me some coffee and while I was drinking it he took the thick cushion off the chest he used as a couch, and took out something wrapped in a sack. He put the cushion back on the chest and sat down, putting the parcel on his knees. It was done up with string. While he undid the string, he neither looked at me nor said a word. When the string was undone, he wound it around his hand and then put the coil neatly beside him. "I will show you something," he said, and carefully unfolded the sacking, to reveal a very old and beautifully kept violin. "Over a hundred and fifty years old." He took the bow out of a thin box he had obviously made himself, tightened the bow and tuned the instrument.

He played one Hungarian folk air after another, may be six altogether. "There, you hear I know the music, but I want you to teach me." I stayed there for weeks on end, only coming out on the Sabbath. The bargain we struck was that if I taught him the music, then he'd teach me the way of my fathers, as he put it. I learned more about music from him than from anyone else I'd ever met, except Lennie.

It all ended as unexpectedly as it had began. One day he met me outside the building, and insisted, in his persuasive way, that we went for a meal at one of his favorite eating places. He was obviously well known there because he had his own table. "You must leave this city," he said, "before it destroys what you have left, and, if I am to be straightforward with you, my honest advice is that you should learn to keep the Sabbath, in whatever way you can. For my part, I will look after you. Believe me, I do not have to live like this, but I cannot live any other way. I am sure you know what I mean."

O———+——

Give away most of the records I had, keeping two or three of my own and the Bach, and Bartok. One of my students was hard pressed so he was glad to accept the electric fan and a rug, in the same spirit as I received the chair from Betty when my face was clear and the eyes looked forward rightly not taking account of the forces opposing.

Susan ready to answer the changes, by now accustomed to responding at the very shortest notice possible. We had our plans for a recording and continued to work on those, finally settling on the name Newly Warne which seemed kind of appropriate.

Stayed with Fred and Carol back in LA until I found a place of my own. So there it was, me in my house on Runnymede Street in Van Nuys, mother around the corner, Susan in New York and sometimes LA, and Gerry in Santa Cruz. The old house was gone by now, at auction for a tidy sum.

At intervals, irregular but timely, money arrives from the Rabbi. Presumed it was him. Forsworn clubs, in effort to perceive where it is that the music deserves to be made public. Students were accepted, on recommendation only and after passing a kind of test which were more to measure sincerity and willingness to persevere than anything technical. Rhythm, I could only teach students who could feel the dynamics of rhythm.

Test: I will play this tune in waltz time, and you play it or sing it in 5:8 time, or at least try. Test: I will play a melody and you play a different melody but one which shares the same chord patterns. There was no method, each student taken as an individual, and that's not possible with a method. I had thought about writing a book about teaching, and then realized that there was no book, just as there was no book of the music we made with Lennie, all of it learned by ear, completely by ear.

We would listen in astonishment, Lee and I, as he played such complex patterns at such speed. And then he'd slow the whole thing down and play it to us phrase by phrase, until we had the whole piece by heart. After that it was a question of technique, which he left up to us. It is such a deep way to learn, and once you have learned music that way, it is almost impossible to forget; the intellect has had nothing to do with the process, so the memorizing takes place at the level of instinct and intuition. Put another way, the music is not memorized, it is absorbed.

I can't tell you how good it feels to be out of New York. There was nothing there for me in the end. Round here, most of the orange groves have gone. Don't know how long I'll stay. There are still a few things I haven't tried, and I'll try them at my leisure.

The house has more space than I need, so Carol found someone to take a room and share the kitchen, a Brazilian girl, student, not musical. The deal is she can't entertain here because I like to choose my own company. She's happy with that. She has her own entrance, so I don't see her much, which is fine since I like my private space. There's also a room for guests.

I practice mornings, teach afternoons and in the evenings work on a few ideas I have or go play with a few people because I'm thinking of putting together a group again and doing recitals.

At long last I have a full-size grand piano, a CD player and just the music I love. Often listen to Bartok's Second Violin Concerto and the Concerto for Orchestra, and then I'm back in the penthouse. As usual, there's not much by the way of furniture, except for what I have made myself, and a few gifts. It's pleasant to sit in the little courtyard at the back of the house - there's no view but I never was one for scenery.

Susan will be here soon, for a few weeks or couple of months. We have accepted invitations to do some concerts. We want to make another record together, etudes perhaps.

Someone bothered to reach me on the phone - I usually have the answering machine on and am not too reliable with returning calls. He wanted to let me know Lee was in town. Odd, isn't it, that you're not playing together? I said, well, yes, you have a point there, but really that's finished now and I'm into different things. If you see him, though, give him my best wishes.

You can be close, like the dancers who become the dance, and you can be alone together.

chapter thirty one **for the time being**

Intricacy of the dance, the duet as pas de deux, piano and saxophone, me and you, simultaneous.

Imagine the wind across a field of poppies, from the slightest puff that moves the petals barely to tremble, to the stirring wind that bends the stems this way and that in compliance.

Imagine the field of poppies on a lyrical day, clear blue sky above, a carpet of red beneath a canopy of blue.

Imagine the field of poppies flattened by a storm, the flecks of red pressed into the brown earth, oppressed by the massive grey mountains of cloud.

Motion and counter motion, ebb and flow, perfect equilibrium of the planets we are in perpetual counterbalance and compensating tension, where eruptive power appears as perfect stillness, like the pupil of the eye in which there may be light or darkness.

Our lives found such a harmony, an intuitive state, where words were no more than breath. We choose a theme, one we knew very well, and then the improvisation begins, without introduction, all of it as spontaneous as feeling, from the first note to the last, as the sky changes color at sunset, through a whole range of complexions, never the same for a split second.

We would follow the emerging form that arose from our joint and separate intimations, know without question its extent and magnitude, its limitations and frailties, its heart unfolding. I always felt we were painting a picture, like the myriad patterns that fill your vision when you close your eyes very tight.

And in those poems of sound, we exposed our deepest privacies and in the wholesomeness, the total honesty, attained seclusion. This music does not have an adjective; it was us, pure and simple.

They are poems without words and paintings without a canvas and dances without movement. The music is here and it is gone. Life, in a nutshell, is for the time being.

Powerful and delicate, aspiring to nothing and yet arising like the star over the horizon, jewels in the diadem.

Each piece complete, without rehearsal or second attempts, quite free of the slightest suspicion of doubt of arriving on the final note at the time ordained by the content of the journey. You could say that our lives are complete before we set out; all we do is reveal the substance and expire.

What did we need with an adjective? Just call it music.

For once in my life I had completed something - or rather we had completed something - independently and in total dependence. Finally I had brought to fruition what had started in the Capitol studios and been interrupted by that studio engineer. And an honorable calling it had been.

Whether the idea was commercially viable I really don't know. Part of the difficulty is that something that cannot be categorized is next to useless, at least in the short term, because it belongs only in its own space. However, it exists, on the Interplay label, also our own creation, and will always exist because anything that is complete exists for ever and yet does not need to exist anymore, so it would not surprise me if it is not obtainable in the short term. What else to call that musical offering but by our names.

If I now chose when to play, infrequently, and with partners only of my own choosing, a very few confederates, where to play was a choice less easily made.

There was no place for such music on a regular basis, because there was no profit in it, as there never has been in the true music that belongs to and speaks for the community.

But the community no longer has a heart or a place, being all fragmented and dispersed and the musician must be itinerant, on the look out for a place to rest.

There were open-air recitals, hotel lounges, college concert halls, few and far between. And inevitably there was recognition; the people heard what was meant, heard the stirring of the song, and I could feel the gratitude and affection returned to me. But there was not continuity, there was no place to cultivate this marriage.

And I would play now only with students, regardless of age, and people whose hearts were open. I myself was still a student. Or I did so on my own, hours and hours of solo recordings, from which one day - there was no hurry - I could select the best and make an offering to you once again, when there was money for such an uncommercial proposition.

There comes a time when there is little strength left for resistance, for holding out against the day. Content, then, to retire for the most part, let my path lead where it will, happy to have kept my side of the bargain.

And, inevitably, the curiosity persists. Always curious, alert to new possibilities, new variations on the continuo, the continuum, fresh combinations of voices.

And my choice was the guitar, so different from the piano, so much more the instrument of the people, of the mountains and the plains.

And so another partnership with another name that may never be more than the name Ron, fairly ordinary. And the customary months of preparation, exploring the changes latent in our differences and common ground, like the colors of a sunset, never the same from one flickering second to the next.

You might find me, on the odd night, on Sunset Boulevard or in

Pasadena or Oakland, never that far from home. But more often at home with Ron and Jim or sitting in the cool evening sun, by the white metal table in the courtyard, feeding the sparrows in between writing notes about the kind of place where the music might be heard to best advantage, just for future reference, on the off-chance that events might conspire favorably. My heart was not full of hope and neither was it pessimistic, because I now walk the path along the mountain ridge, a clearly visible silhouette, little more known than that.

And keeping touch, after a fashion, with Gerry and the boys, bereft of explanations as I am, and Gary or a letter to Bill the ornithologist.

Lee came to town. Shall I go to hear how it is now? I do not think he likes me. Perhaps the most I can do is sit outside and listen from there. I could not bear to be close and not respond: to sit at a table, hands in my lap, feeling the immense possibilities course through me and sit paralysed, well now, no, that I could not bear. So I stay at home and play my lines and imagine what his would have been.

I was driving along a road I know so well, and am suddenly in territory utterly forbidding and unfamiliar. Distraught by images sent to terrorize me, and wracked by vicious pains. No longer driving the car, I am like the poppies pressed against the earth, head forced against the window, arms rigid but unable to ward off the pain. I know the car is slithering about as if on ice, and my whole life is on ice, seared by an intense cold, and hear a whine of sirens and the gurgle in my throat and fear that I am about to burst.

I next hear the clink of something on what I take to be a metal tray, above me the fire sprinkler and Owen's face looking fondly down and I almost laugh at the irony of the memory of my gazing down at him under the sprinklers in the garden of the old house in the

Valley, croquet hoops pinning his ankles and wrists to the ground. I am in the County General hospital for indigents, which happens if you are not credit worthy and without health insurance.

They say I must not play again.

Convalesce, they said. Do not smoke. Avoid fats. Do not blow that thing. Rest. Only a gentle stroll. Rest. I am resting. I am not smoking. I am not playing that thing. And I stroll in the courtyard, feeding the sparrows, rather tatty specimens, once charming and homely, but now scavengers learning fierce competition.

I am resting on my bed, hands behind my old head, and I am resting on my bed, hands behind my head hearing the crunch of tires on the gravel driveway which was when the telegram boy delivered the condolences from Mr. Mayer.

The radio is on. There's a pile of books by the bed. Just back from seeing Gerry off at the airport. 'Why did you not come a little sooner, since I am already convalescing?' 'Your mother told me you did not want to see me, that you were well looked after. She called me at the supermarket where I work, but wouldn't tell me where you were. I don't understand how she could have done that. I mean, what was I supposed to tell the boys.' And there I was in the hospital for indigents, still lacking the power to protest.

Betty, I tell you I would rather wear out than rust out. Old phrases scuttling through for scrutiny.

And I look at that thing which has kept me faithful company for so many years and wonder how long it will be before I have to sing again for the glory.

chapter thirty two **foreground music**

"I hear nothing whatsoever today which expands the great music of the past."

On the most scenic railway journey in the whole of Norway. An old student travelling with younger students. There's some discussion going on which I can't understand. I'm quietly playing chess, but my opposing partner is concentrating more on the discussion than on our game. I'm used to that. It's his move. The carriage is mainly occupied by Japanese tourists. Every so often the train stops, at places where there are good photographs to be had, and the tourists all scurry off the train and take photographs of themselves against the back drop of snow covered mountains or precipitous waterfalls. Breathtaking views if that's your taste. There is something written in Norwegian on the window. So, being curious, I point at the words. My partner smiles, impressed that at last I have taken note of the grand scenery, and tells me the name of whatever it is he thinks I am looking at. I frown and draw his attention more specifically to the writing on the window. Ah, that says 'Emergency Exit'. He makes his move, a careless one, and looks at me as if to say, 'You come all this way just to read signs on windows?'

The tourists are all back on board. The train sets off again, and the musicians continue their discussion. One of them turns to me and asks in English, 'What's most important: rhythm or melody?' 'Well, you tell me.' 'I think it is melody because ... ' He stops short. I am looking at him very sternly. How can this guy call himself a musician? 'Is that what you've been discussing all this time?' 'Yes.' 'It's not something to discuss. Let's take a great melody, say "All The Things You Are". Now, I'll set a poor rhythm and you sing the melody to that rhythm.' He sings and very soon is struggling helplessly to give any feeling to the melody. 'Ok. Now pick a very ordinary melody, whatever you like. I'll set the rhythm, and we'll see what happens.' I beat out the rhythm on my knees, and a counter-rhythm with one foot, while he sings. Involuntarily, the melody starts to come to life: it has to, because the rhythm insists on it. A couple of the other guys join in, singing different lines, and the train trundles on. The tourists glance around furtively now and then, smiling bravely, and go back to watching the passing view. But I know very well where their real attention is. After the melody is all played through, I ask the younger students, 'So why do you discuss things when you can find the answers in the music? If you can't hear the rhythm of life, what have you got to sing about anyway?'

Then we have some fun working out polyrhythms against the rhythm set by the wheels of the train. Most musicians start to use their instruments before they even know what they are for. And I suspect most of them never find out. That's like studying wave motion and remaining ignorant of the power of the currents underneath.

I was happy teaching in Norway and would have stayed longer but do not relish the cold weather. I had been playing again for a few months, but always kept something in reserve, showing at least some care not to overtax myself. It was like being in the background, being a support more than anything else, maybe helping to give people a sense of the standards that have to be met. Even in a small town in Norway. Even in a small town in Texas County Missouri. There were a few moments when the feeling of the music got the better of me and then I just followed wherever it went.

A reporter came to visit me. We sat in the courtyard of my house, the sparrows for ever grateful for the breadcrumbs. What was I up to? I had finally come to the same realization as Lennie; that the music needed somewhere special, a place within the community, may be a community center of some description. I had seen a place advertised, near Cahuenga, where the Canteen Kids used to perform. A big place, big enough for recording studios, teaching studios and a small concert or recital hall. But I didn't hold out much hope. It was always a question of money these days.

I never had liked walking unless there was somewhere to get to. The advice was that I should walk. Fred came around to see that I took a walk every so often. After a while I began to feel like his dog, which was not a good feeling to have, so instead of walking we'd play for an hour or so and I'd try to ignore the faint dizziness.

I told Gerry that she needn't worry because the house was going to be hers. The house was in my mother's name, and she never had liked the girl from Carmel Valley, and would, she said, only agree to Gerry inheriting the house if I divorced her. That was not something I had any intention of doing; it had never been like that. I ask again and again. She is inflexible. My own man, but hardly self-sufficient.

I am overcome by moods of insecurity, and like to go then to be with the people I trust, people who don't ask questions. Then the mood passes, and I go back home. Even when I am in such company, I am preoccupied, and never admit it but know that I am afraid. I seem to have done everything.

At Gary's house for a meal and I notice that everyone else is eating and I'm smoking a cigarette, during the meal. I am confused by my own bad manners, but can't put the cigarette out. Sometimes I don't eat at all, and other times I eat like a greedy child and hope to God I don't choke.

I go to Fred's, get to feel ok, and go back home again. A few hours later, I'm back on his doorstep, wanting to play scrabble.

I think of writing to the record companies, to enquire about any proceeds, but I haven't kept the addresses. It's all a bit late in the day.

One day I phone Gerry and speak to the boys, and the next day phone Susan to see if she still wants to do the tour of China. I would like to be serious about the idea, but she's busy anyway. And I ask about the house. Always the same answer.

I have kept a few students. It is difficult to encourage them, knowing what the situation is. And the sparrows are always there.

I call Fred. Carol answers. What's for supper? Pea soup. Mind if I come round? No, you know you're always welcome. I eat a whole saucepan full of pea soup.

And still the old enthusiasm wells up in the good moments. Almost joyful.

And I think of putting another group together, maybe try singing instead of the saxophone all the time.

It is known that I like to play the occasional session. I get a phone call, asking, as a special favor considering I have not been so well myself, if I can sub for Conte who's called off sick. A gig at Dontes. That place has been my favorite place, after the Half-Note. How can I refuse? After all, I know them all so well. It's the closest I've found to my idea of a place where people can gather on a day to renew ....

I put the phone down and feel oddly elated at the prospect of making an appearance. Impatient to get there, even if it is only a Thursday night. Phone Susan in New York, suggest she comes to LA with her boyfriend. Stay at the house and, who knows, we could work on putting a group together, piano, guitar, tenor, alto, bass, drums.

Time drags. Phone Ron about doing another recording. Fine idea, he'd love to, but we haven't broken even on the last one yet.

I do not enjoy my own cooking, but will have to put up with it tonight because everyone is out or busy. I look at the pork chops in the cooling lard. Ugly, quite unappetizing, and I let them go cold. On the way out, I change my mind, take a bite and put the ugly thing back in the pan. Really ought to clean up. Wipe my beard with a napkin. which I screw up and toss into the sink.

Iron a shirt. Pick up the horn and eventually find the car keys.

I haven't felt so well in a long time. On the stand again, so much to look forward to or am I fooling myself I wonder. It's my call and without hesitation I ask for *Out Of Nowhere* because I'll never get to the bottom of that one and I am not disappointed because coming into the solo I hear another melody, shimmering ahead of where I am, still too far away to catch it, distant, only faintly in earshot as I strain to find a place for it, to let it come in.

Troubles me deeply, this almost imperceptible voice, lyrical and sweet, alluring, the singing of someone in the privacy of a room down a corridor. My fingers quiver over the keys, bubbling, and are going numb, and still I cannot find the place for this melody out of nowhere, so beautiful it chills my heart, ache as I do to find a place for it, as I would hope to catch the attention of someone I love but who does not see me.

My legs turn to soft wax and the joints start to give up as if I had overexerted myself running up this hill chasing an exquisite image that forever eludes my grasp, will not heed my call and come to me. There is no breathing, no cry as the song breaks off, this song out of nowhere that I hold onto, a mountain climber's rope, the last fibre twisting and twitched to breaking point under the strain of this falling life, the long fall of the memory of life in endless melodies floating away, untethered, a balloon drifting up above the child's disbelieving eyes staring after it, enchanted, sad, helpless, the once bright, bobbing spot of color shrinking into a spot of stillness.

The image fades and I am hearing silence, have released all the music, all the changes I'll ever remember, all the things, going over the changes, going over backwards, toppled over quite without grace of movement. It's no good, I've lost it, cannot hold on, cannot keep up, was standing and now going over and clutch, abandoned for dear life to this voice of mine, all music still to come, but out of time. Just do not let it go, do not let it fall, this instrument which has breathed all my life.

So hold it up, in final composure, slightly away from the body so that it does not hit the ground.

There is a rushing as of water through a culvert, swirling and churning sweeping all before it and it is passing through me and I am carried along into the great sea. There is a roaring and the heat of a desert wind and I stumbling in a cloud of sand, quite without bearings.

I am standing and I am falling and I hold on as I let go, lose my place, and I am all weight as something impedes me, breaks my heavy fall, a final crash quite without grace in a scattering of objects I no longer have names for, and there will be a crashing of cymbals, after you've gone out of nowhere. Lost time. Last time, the very last drop. Mute and without end. Take this from me, please; I gave it all, and eternally the song is....:||

my old flame

He was another D.O.A. for St. Joseph's Medical Center in Burbank, the first in the early hours of Friday December 18 1987. The paramedics slid the stretcher back into the ambulance, closed the doors, and went off for a break, chatting about their plans for Christmas.

Two days later there was a graveside only memorial service at Forest Lawn Memorial Park in Glendale. He was buried next to his father.

To say buried is not really appropriate. The ashes were held in a small wooden cigar box. A gust of wind rudely blew the lid off and scattered the ashes over the grass. So the modest headstone marks no more than a random spot.

The whole affair was badly organized and many people were not aware of the event until some days afterwards. The priest had never met him, but at least got his name correct. His mother did not show up. The owner of Dontes, Carey Leverette, died a few weeks later. The venue on Lankershim Boulevard then closed down. And that was that.

marshlight ○——+——

"He was my musical father and I shall carry his music in me all my life. I loved him and will always love him."

"In the late 1940s, I happened to be listening to a jazz program on radio. I had turned on the program in the middle of a recording and was completely taken aback by a cascading line of such utter complexity played by two saxophones that my jaw dropped in astonishment."

"He was my closest and dearest friend and I miss him unbearably much."

"I never received one word of condolence from the record companies, and have certainly never received a cent from them."

"He was a master of improvisation and completely redefined the parameters of improvised music. He has left behind a legacy that will serve as a rich resource for musical concepts for generations to come."

"I do not know of any other musician who surprised me as much as he did with his inventiveness."

"He was more totally dedicated to the music than anyone I've ever met."

"It is extraordinary that he is so little known and that makes me wonder what people use for ears these days."

"He was a gentle spirit, always courteous and kind, and never spoke above a whisper. He rarely spoke, but when he did, well, it was worth writing down."

"Watch that kid. He's got it!"

"I imagine he snuck around and found Pres and Bird and Lennie up there, and said, 'How about we play that in another key?'"

appendix a **acknowledgements**

The idea for this book came to life shortly after I accidentally 'discovered' the music of Warne Marsh in 1987. It was impossible to believe that someone who could create such intricate inspirations with such assurance and joy should be so little known. Even now, some 14 years later, each time I listen to him is like the first time. This of course is only personal, but the only other musician who satisfies my ears so much is J. S. Bach.

The research and writing took four years, during which time I received substantial help and encouragement from a steadily increasing number of people; some knew Warne Marsh well, some just love the music, and some have since passed away. I have tried to keep track of everyone, but if there is any error of omission, I hope you will forgive me.

My only wish in writing the book was to try to bring to life a man whom I greatly respect and to whom I owe the debt of gratitude for so many moments of happiness and for leading me to a deeper intimacy with the music that keeps the world young and hopeful. My hope is that the book may in some small way help to widen the audience for Warne Marsh's music and do something towards keeping his gift alive.

This also acknowledges my deep gratitude to George Ziskind for making the final checks on the manuscript. If any errors have survived, the fault is completely mine.

And for all the help and encouragement I received in the preparation for and the writing of this book, my sincere thanks go to:-

Jan Allan, Paul Altman, Roger Andrews, Jerry Atkins, Arne Astrup, Roland Baggenaes, J.A. Banks Jnr., Jeff Barr, Johs Bergh, Jack Block, Clive Bostle, Anthony Braxton, John Breckow, Alan Broadbent, Ted Brown, Wesley A. Brown, Clora Bryant, Rudolf Buchmann, Monty Budwig, Mrs C. Burchell, Ozzie Cadena, Rune Carlsson, Gary Carner, Safford Chamberlain, Susan Chen, Dave Cliff, John Craig, Martha Crawford, Steven Crouch, Zota Croughan, Michael Cuscuna, Roy Daniels, Hugo de Craen, Mils Edstrom, Gudrun Endress, Tom Everett, Kerr Ferguson, Gunnar and Sidsel Feydt, Daniel Fiore, Gary Foster, David Frishberg, Jack Goodwin, John William 'Bill' Hardy, Johan Heloo, Mike Hennessey, Mathias C. Hermann, Chuck Hersch, Jim Heymann, John Hicks, Paul Hoffman, Lorence Honda, Jan Horne, Randi Hultin, Ike and Moira Isaacs, Peter J. Jacobson, Randy Johnston, Jo Keith, George Khouri, Keith Knox, Martin Krivin, Ron La Rue, Rob Leurentop, Lloyd Lifton, Jack MacKinney, Robert Malmberg, Laurence Marable, Geraldyne Marsh, John W. Miner, Keith 'Red' Mitchell, Kevin Moore, Sal Mosca, Tom Nolan, Peter Prisco, Phil Schaap, Don Schitten, Betty Scott, Carolyn See, Don Sheridan, Kirk Silsbee, Dr. Stephen E. Silverman, Torgrim Sollid, Mark Sowlakis, Don Specht, Toshiya Taenaka, Bruce Turner, George Ziskind, Maurice Zolotow.

appendix b **stops along the way**

Warne Marsh Performances: Selected live and studio sessions

R Performances known to have been recorded
RNI Recording sessions not released on record or CD

00.05.42 USO, AT CAHUENGA, NEAR SUNSET, HOLLYWOOD
HOLLYWOOD CANTEEN KIDS. [Band led by Chuck Falkner]

23.06.43 ORPHEUM, LOS ANGELES
HOLLYWOOD CANTEEN KIDS:- Chuck Falkner, Johnny Cheek, Neil Cunningham, Harry Matthews (tpts): Dave Wells, Scott McKennon, Roy Hall (tb): Dick Selix, Warne Marsh, Betty Churchill, Morton Friedman, Don Walters (reeds): Karl Kiffe (d): Bob Clark (p): Hal Jacobs (g): Paul Gray (b)

PALACE THEATER, VINE STREET
A four month engagement in the BLACKOUTS REVIEW
HOLLYWOOD CANTEEN KIDS. [Band led by Karl Kiffe]

00.00.44 Jam sessions with Marsh, Kiffe and Andre Previn

00.00.44 FILM APPEARANCES
HOLLYWOOD CANTEEN KIDS appear in the first Jane Powell movie, Song of the Open Road, including a Marsh solo, and Junior Jive Bombers.

00.00.45 NORTH HOLLYWOOD
Marsh, Previn, Kiffe. [How High The Moon: Stompin At The Savoy]
Recorded on the family record cutter [R]

00.01.45 NBC RADIO. A weekly show with Hoagy Carmichael [R]
-00.06.46 THE TEENAGERS [Band led by Dick Allen Markowitz, then by Jimmy Higson.] Recorded Marsh solos include "Apple Honey".

SEPTEMBER 1945 - SPRING 1946: UNIVERSITY OF SOUTHERN CALIFORNIA

1946-1947 US ARMY

1946/47 SPECIAL SERVICES DANCE BAND [R]
[?: Just You Just Me: Exactly Like You: The Way You Look Tonight: Moten Swing: ?: ?: Opus: Adios: Prelude To A Kiss: I Don't Know Why: Where Are You?: Ghost Of A Chance: I've Got You Under My Skin: Cherokee: Somewhere In The Night: ?: ?: ?: The Very Thought Of You: Night And Day]

RETURNS TO LA SHORTLY AFTER LEAVING ARMY, HAVING MET TRISTANO

00.00.47 THE RED FEATHER, LOS ANGELES
BUTCH STONE BAND: John McComb (tpt): Dave Madden, Marsh (ts): B. Stone (bs & voc): Shelly Robbins (p): Arnold Fishkin (b): Karl Kiffe (d)

00.00.47 PALLADIUM BALLROOM, LOS ANGELES
BUDDY RICH BAND, including Terrence Gibbs, Doug Mettome, Hal McKusick, Johnny Mandell, Marsh, Buddy Rich

LATE 1948 MOVES BACK TO NEW YORK

1948/49 BIRDLAND, BASIN STREET, VANGUARD, TOP OF GATE

00.00.48 NOLA REHEARSAL ROOMS, NEW YORK [R]
Lee Konitz (as), Marsh, John Laporta (cl), Tristano (p), Bill Anthony (b) [Incl. Indiana: Fine and Dandy]

00.03.49 CLIQUE CLUB, NEW YORK [PNR]
Marsh, Konitz, Tristano, Bauer (g), Fishkin (b), Granowsky (d)

01.11.49 SILHOUETTE CLUB, CHICAGO

15.12.49 OPENING NIGHT AT BIRDLAND
Tristano, Marsh, Konitz, Bauer, Fishkin,Morton (d) [Incl. Lennie's Pennies] This performance was recorded and broadcast by Voice of America, after the live performance, but the tapes have vanished. Charlie Parker was also performing, amongst others.]

16.12.49 BIRDLAND, NEW YORK CITY

24.12.49 MODERN JAZZ ALL-STARS CONCERT, CARNEGIE HALL [R]
TRISTANO SEXTET [Incl. You Go To My Head: Sax Of A Kind]
Tristano and Parker were featured with their own working band, an honour not afforded the other stars.

00.00.50 WESTCHESTER WOMENS CLUB, MT VERNON
Marsh, Sal Mosca (p), Ferrara (tp), Dennis (tb), M. Roach (d)

00.05.50 BIRDLAND
Tristano, Marsh, Konitz, Bauer, plus various drummers and bassists

00.02.51 421 CLUB, PHILADELPHIA
Marsh, Konitz, Tristano, B. Jones (b), R.Haynes (b)

00.04.51 BLUE NOTE, CHICAGO
Marsh, Konitz, Dennis, Tristano, B. Jones, Mickey Simonetta

21.05.51 BIRDLAND, NEW YORK
Tristano, Marsh, Konitz, Shulman, Dennis, Ferrara, Roach
[Ella Fitzgerald was on the same evening]

00.10.51 BIRDLAND, NEW YORK
Marsh, Konitz, Dennis, Tristano, Clyde Lombardi (b), Roach

30.11.52 LOS ANGELES [R]
Shorty Rodgers (tpt): Milt Bernhart (tb): Marsh, Giuffre, Bob Cooper (ts): Hawes (p): Howard Rumsey (b): Manne (d)
[Incl. Moten Swing: Round Robin: April: Blues: Indiana: Jumpin' With Symphony Sid Topsy]

00.04.54 STORYVILLE, BOSTON
Marsh, Konitz, Ball, Teddi King (voc) plus others unknown

00.00.55 LENNIE TRISTANO SCHOOL OF MUSIC, NEW YORK
Marsh, Konitz, Ferrara, Dennis, Tristano, Mosca, Ball (p), Morton

11.06.55 SING SONG ROOM, CONFUCIUS RESTAURANT, MANHATTAN
Tristano Quartet

00.07.55 NEWPORT, RHODE ISLAND [R]
Marsh and Konitz

00.08.55 MOVES BACK TO LOS ANGELES

00.00.55 HOLLYWOOD BOWL JAZZ CONCERT
Konitz, Marsh and others unknown

1955-57 JAZZ CITY, LOS ANGELES
Engagements with Lee Konitz

07-1956-02.57 Marsh forms group with R. Ball (p), Ted Brown (ts), Ben Tucker (b), J. Morton (d), and sometimes Art Pepper

00.00.56 LOS ANGELES - TV SHOW: STARS OF JAZZ [R]
Marsh, Brown, Ball, Tucker, Morton
[Incl. Au Privave: Ad Libido: These Are The Things I Love: You Took Advantage Of Me: Softly: Background Music]

10.07.56-00.02.57 THE HAIG, LOS ANGELES
Marsh, Ball, Don Overberg (g), Al Cotton (b), J.Morton

00.00.57 LOS ANGELES [R]
Marsh, Brown, Ball & bass/drums
[Incl. All The Things You Are: The Best Thing For You Is Me: Au Privave: Feather Bed: Oops: Easy To Love: Limehouse Blues: Memories of You: Smog Eyes: Out Of Nowhere: Donna Lee: I'll SeeYou In My Dreams:]

00.00.57 AT THE BLACKHAWK
Marsh with Art Pepper

00.01.57 AT THE CAFE BOHEMIA [R]
Marsh, Konitz, Mosca, Wilson

00.03.57 BILL WHISLING'S HAWAIIAN CLUB, LOS ANGELES
Marsh, Brown, Ball, Tucker, Morton*
[incl. Somebody Loves Me: Smog Eyes: Long Gone: Topsy]
*This same group played at the club on Friday and Saturday nights between November 1956 and March 1957, with some Sundays and Thursdays.

14.05.57 NBC TV [R]
Marsh and Konitz

00.10.57 THE GALLEON ROOM, DANA POINT, CALIFORNIA
Marsh, Joe Albany (p), Bob Whitlock (b), Red Martinson (d)
[Playing Sunday afternoon sessions]

12. 1957 MOVES BACK TO NEW YORK

00.00.58 NEW YORK
Appears at THE CORK 'N' BIB (on Long Island), BIRDLAND and the HALF NOTE

00.00.58 NEW YORK - Venue not known [R]
Marsh, Konitz

14.05.58 RADIO/TV SHOW: "THE SUBJECT IS JAZZ" [R]
[National Education TV. Musical direction was by Billy Taylor.]
Marsh, Konitz, Don Elliott, Mundell Lowe, Billy Taylor (p), Ed Sofranski, Ed Thigpen [Incl. Move: Godchild: Ladybird: Ever So Easy: Subconscious Lee: Minor Blues]

00.07.58 HALF NOTE, NEW YORK Mutual Radio broadcast [R]
Marsh, Konitz, Knobby Totah (b), Motian
[Incl. Billie's Bounce: Will You Still Be Mine: Cheek To Cheek: 317 East 32nd Street: Round Midnight: Yardbird Suite: Topsy]

00.09.58 HALF NOTE, NEW YORK CITY
Tristano, Marsh, Harry Grimes (b), Motian (d)

00.10.58 HALF NOTE, NEW YORK CITY
Marsh, Tristano, Grimes, Motian
[Appeared weekends during late 1958]

00.00.59 HALF NOTE, NEW YORK CITY [R]
Marsh, Konitz, Bill Evans, Jimmy Garrison or Peter Ind (b), Paul Motian (d) [Incl. Subconscious-Lee: 317 East 32nd Street: Background Music: Will You Still Be Mine: Lennie's Pennies: Half Nelson: You Stepped Out Of A Dream: Round Midnight: It's You Or No One: How About You: Scrapple From The Apple: Baby All The Time: Palo Alto: Body And Soul: Blues: Back Home: How About You: Yardbird Suite: It's You Or No One: Scrapple: April: Just Friends: Will You Still Be Mine: April: Melancholy Baby: Lennie-Bird: Baby All The Time: How About You: It's You Or No One: Scrapple: Just Friends: Palo Alto: 317 East 32nd Street: You Stepped Out Of A Dream: Two Not One: April: Back Home: Half Nelson: You Stepped Out Of A Dream: It's You Or No One: Subconscious-Lee: What's New: Yesterdays: Yardbird Suite] [These are possibly the sessions which Tristano edited and which then became THE ART OF IMPROVISING albums.]

00.00.59 JAZZ CITY, TORONTO
Marsh, Konitz, Tristano, Sonny Dallas (b), Haynes

1961 MOVES TO LOS ANGELES

1961/62 Performs in Las Vegas with Don Overburg (g) & others

EARLY 1964 MOVES BACK TO NEW YORK

00.00.64 TELEVISION SHOW:- LOOK UP AND LIVE
Tristano, Konitz, Marsh, Dallas, Nick Stabulas (d)

00.06.64 HALF NOTE CAFE, NEW YORK [R]
Tristano Quintet. [Said to be the first time Marsh, Konitz and Tristano had performed together for three and a half years]

20.06.64 LE COQ D'OR, TORONTO
Marsh, Konitz, Tristano, Dallas, Stabulas

00.10.64 HALF NOTE, NEW YORK
Tristano, Marsh, Konitz, Dallas, Roger Mancuso (d)

00.00.65 RIVERDALE, NEW YORK (PRIVATE SCHOOL)
Marsh, Mosca and others unknown

00.00.65 JAZZ WORKSHOP, BOSTON, MASS
Tristano, Marsh, Konitz, bass and drums

Spring 1966 CELLAR CLUB, TORONTO
Marsh, Tristano, Dallas, Mancuso. [A one week engagement]

FALL 1966 MOVES BACK TO LOS ANGELES

02.12.66 BALBOA BAY CLUB
With the Keith William's dance band, along with Gary Foster.

00.01.67 DUALITY LP
Clare Fischer Band. Marsh on side two only. Recorded at CBS Studios, Sunset Boulevard, LA. Released on the DISCOVERY Label and not by CBS.

16.04.67 SESSION AT CLARE FISCHER'S HOUSE [R]
Fischer, Marsh, Foster, George Williams (b)
[Incl. April, I'll Remember: ? : Out Of Nowhere: You'd Be So Nice To Come Home To*: All The Things*: Love Me Or Leave Me* - * No Bass]

12.12.67 DONTE'S, 4269 LANKERSHIM BOULEVARD, NORTH HOLLYWOOD
First appearance at the club

SPRING 68 DONTE'S
CLARE FISCHER ORCHESTRA: Steve Huffstetter, Conteo Candoli, Buddy Childers,Larry McGuire, Stewart Fischer (tpts): Gil Falco, Charlie Loper, Dave Sanchez, Morris Repass (tbns): Marsh, John Lowe, Bill Perkins, Tom Scott, Foster, Kim Richmond (reeds): Clare Fischer (p/org): Chuck Domanico (b): Larry Bunker (d)

[Also performs during 1968/69 with the Matty Malneck band, along with Gary Foster, and the Clare Fischer Band.]

23.06.68 DONTE'S
Marsh, Foster and rhythm section

01.09.68 DONTE'S
As above

26/27.09.68 DONTE'S
As above

06.10.68 DONTE'S
As above

15.12.68 DONTE'S
As above

00.00.69 CALIFORNIA [R]
Marsh, Ball, Overburg, Tucker (or possibly P. Ind?), Morton
[Tapes made with Marsh's permission by a student of Peter Ind's]
[Incl. Three Little Words: Don't Blame Me: It's The Same Old Thing: You'd Be So Nice To Come Home To: Sweet and Lovely: Indiana: Slow Boat To China: Limehouse Blues]

23.05.69 DONTE'S

15.06.69 DONTE'S

06-13.07.69 THE LIGHTHOUSE, HERMOSA BEACH, California
Marsh, Foster

20.07.69 DONTE'S

17.08.69 DONTE'S

14.09.69 The NE PLUS ULTRA session. LOS ANGELES
Unissued material: You Stepped Out Of A Dream: Smog Eyes (2 takes): How About You: Bach Two Part Invention No.13 - 4 takes]

00.11.70 BACH DANCING AND DYNAMITE CLUB, HALF MOON BAY, CA
Marsh, Foster, Parlato (b), Tirabasso (d)

00.12.70 DONTES
Marsh, Foster, Parlato, Tirabasso

00.00.71 JAZZ WEST, SHERMAN OAKS, CA [Mondays]
Marsh, Foster, Pat Smith (b), Tirabasso

11.01.71 ICE HOUSE, PASADENA, CA [R]
Marsh, Foster, DeLaRosa (b), Tirabasso
Recorded by Lou Ciotti

26.03.71 STUDIO SESSION [Recorded, but tape may be lost]
Marsh, Foster, DeLaRosa, Tirabasso

29.03.71 ICE HOUSE, PASADENA [R] [Recorded by Ron Hoops]
Marsh, Foster, DeLaRosa, Tirabasso

28.04.71 CAL-TEC COLLEGE [R]
Marsh, Foster

23.07-07.08 71 THE GILDED CAGE, PASADENA
Marsh, Foster, DeLaRosa, Tirabasso

09.08.71 ICE HOUSE, PASADENA [R]
Marsh, Foster, Dave Koontz (g), Frank DeLaRosa, John Tirabasso
[Incl. You'd Be So Nice To Come Home To: If You Could See Me Now: Round Midnight: Fuzz Blues: Subconscious-Lee: How About You: Confusion In Dallas]

26.08.71 THE GILDED CAGE, NEAR PASADENA [RNI]
Marsh, Ronnie Hoops (p), John Terry, Paul Ruhland
[Incl. Lullaby Of The Leaves: It's You Or No One: Day By Day: I Love You]

28.08.71 GILDED CAGE, PASADENA [R]
Marsh, Foster, Braxton and others
[Incl. What Is This Thing Called Love: You Stepped Out Of A Dream: Lullaby Of The Leaves: 317 East 32nd Street: Donna Lee]

27.09-01.11.71 JAZZ WEST, SAN FERNANDO
Performed Monday nights
Marsh, Foster, DeLaRosa, Tirabasso

24.04.71 ICE HOUSE, PASADENA
Marsh, Foster, DeLaRosa, Tirabasso

09.05.72 REPORT OF 1ST ANNUAL SYMPOSIUM ON RELAXED IMPROVISATION [R]
[Unreleased material from this recording session includes: REEL 1:- Kary's Trance: "Square Theme" - a polka against Donna Lee: I've Got It Bad. REEL 2:- Stella By Starlight: There Will Never Be Another You. REEL 3:- Sentimental Mood: Cherokee: You've Changed: Watch What Happens. Approx 71 minutes]

27.05.72 ICE HOUSE, PASADENA, CALIFORNIA [R]
Marsh, Foster, DeLaRosa, Tirabasso
[Kary's Trance: Lennie's Pennies: 317 E. 32nd Street: You Stepped Out Of A Dream: Body And Soul & Two Not One - played as one: All The Things You Are: Bach Two Part Invention: Two Not One: If You Could See Me Now: Confusion In Dallas: How About You: Fuzz Blues: Background Music]

29.05.72 ICE HOUSE, PASADENA, CALIFORNIA [R]
Marsh, Foster, DeLaRosa, Tirabasso
REEL 1: Marsh & Foster duets:- All The Things You Are: Bach Two Part Invention No. 13. Others:- How About You: Everything Happens To Me: Confusion In Dallas: Background Music: Fuzz Blues: Lennie's Pennies. REEL 2: Lennie's Pennies: 317 E. 32nd Street: You Stepped Out Of A Dream: Body And Soul]

00.06.72 STUDIO SESSION [R] [Recorded by Peter Welding]
Marsh, Fischer, Foster, Ruhland, Tirabasso
[Incl. 1. That Old Feeling. 2. Strike Up The Band. 3. Indian Summer. 4. The More I See You. 5. Nardis. 6. The Best Thing For You. 7. After You've Gone. 8. This Can't Be Love (incomplete)]

22.10.72 PILGRIMAGE THEATER, LOS ANGELES
Marsh, Foster, Hoops, Cliff Hugo, Tirabasso

00.10.72 DOWNSTAIRS AT JIMMY'S, NEW YORK [R]
SUPERSAX

25/26.10.73 DOWNSTAIRS AT JIMMY'S, NEW YORK [R]
SUPERSAX [On reel-to-reel]

03.11.73 DONTE'S, LOS ANGELES [R]
SUPERSAX - Marsh solos

00.00.74 LIVE AT THE LEFT BANK [R]
SUPERSAX: Included Marsh, Rosolino, Flory, Migliori

00.00.74 LA BASTILLE, HOUSTON, TEXAS
SUPERSAX

14.07.74 BALTIMORE, USA [R]
SUPERSAX [Incl. Just Friends: Salt Peanuts: Moose The Mooche: Parker's Mood]

00.09.74 PHILADELPHIA

Late 1975 COLLEGE OF THE SISKEWS (?)
Marsh, Foster, Jake Hanna, Hoops, Fred Atwood

00.00.75 [CLUB DATE - Venue uncertain]
Marsh, Mosca

00.00.75 AMSTERDAM [R]
Marsh, Konitz, Ind, Levitt
[Incl. It s You Or No One: 317 East 32nd Street: Subconscious-Lee]

00.00.75 RADIO HILVERSUM, TV/Radio Broadcast
Marsh, Dave Cliff (g), Ind, Levitt
[Incl. It's You Or No One: I Want To Be Happy: Easy Living: Softly As In A Morning Sunrise]

00.01.75 DONTE'S [R]
Marsh SUPERSAX solos

09.01.75 YOKOHAMA SHIMIN HALL, JAPAN [R]
SUPERSAX: Rosolino (tb): Flory, Joe Lopes (as): Migliori, Marsh (ts): Nimitz (bs): Levy (p) Clark (b) Jake Hanna (d)
[Incl. Scrapple From The Apple: All The Things You Are: Salt Peanuts: Parker's Mood: Embraceable You: Moose The Mooche: Ornithology: Just Friends: Star Eyes: Be Bop: Lover Man: Blue n' Boogie: A Night In Tunisia: Ko-Ko]

00.01.75 TOKYO [R] [Tape held by Nippon Hoso Radio Company]
SUPERSAX

29.04.75 WYNNETT LOUNGE, THE CALTECH Y, PASADENA
Warne Marsh Quartet [Concert produced by John Breckow]

04.10.75 CARNEGIE RECITAL HALL, 154 W. 57th Str, NEW YORK [R]
Marsh, Crothers (p), Joe Solomon (b), Roger Mancuso (d)
[Concert partly sponsored by Harry Sewing, who recorded all Warne's SUPERSAX solos]

00.11.75 NORTHERN CALIFORNIA (CONCERT) and AT DONTE'S [R]
SUPERSAX

26.11.75 STOCKHOLM HOUSE OF CULTURE - CONCERT [R]
Marsh, Allan and others
[Sponsored by the Stockholm House of Culture. Produced by Johan Edsler]

27.11.75 FASCHING CLUB, STOCKHOLM [R]
Marsh, Allan and others

00.12.75 STOCKPORT, UK [R]
Marsh and rhythm section

00.00.75 JAZZHUS TAGSKAEGGET, AARHUS, DENMARK
Marsh with the Bent Erikson Trio
[incl. You Stepped Out Of A Dream: Walkin': Like Someone In Love: Moonlight In Vermont]

04.12.75 CAFE MONTMARTRE, COPENHAGEN [R]
Marsh, Konitz

06.12.75 BIM-HUIS, NETHERLANDS
Marsh, Konitz, Ind, Cliff, Levitt

11.12.75 [Venue unknown] [R]
Warne Marsh Quartet [with Ind and Laren]

12.12.75 NANTES, FRANCE [R] [Broadcast by French Radio]
Marsh, Konitz, Cliff, Ind, Levitt
[Incl. Wow: Background Music: ?: I'll Remember April]

17.12.75 QUEENS HALL, EDINBURGH
Marsh, Konitz, Ind, Cliff, Levitt

18.12.75 THE SEVEN DIALS, UK [R]
Marsh, Konitz, Ind, Cliff, Levitt
[Incl. Wow: Background Music: You Got To My Head: 317 E. 32nd: Subconscious-Lee: It's You Or No One: The Way You Look Tonight: Softly As In A Morning Sunrise: Out Of Nowhere: Bach Invention No. 2: Kary's Trance: Darn That Dream: Now's The Time]

21.12.75 QUEEN'S THEATRE, SITTINGBOURNE, UK [R]
Marsh, Ind, Cliff, Levitt
[Incl.Easy To Love: Little Willie Leaps: God Bless The Child: You Stepped Out Of A Dream: Donna Lee: The Night Has A Thousand Eyes: Foolin' Myself: It's You Or No One: All The Things You Are: Au Privave: Body and Soul:The Way You Look Tonight: Limehouse Blues: Darn That Dream: Softly As In A Morning Sunrise: Background Music]

22.12.75 THE CORNER HOUSE, WHITLEY BAY, UK [R]
Marsh, Konitz, Cliff, Ind, Levitt [Presented by Jazz North East]
[Incl. Wow: Subconscious-Lee: The Night Has A Thousand Eyes: Loverman Sound-Lee: Background Music: April: Star Eyes: God Bless The Child: Chi Chi]

00.00.75 JAZZHUS TAGSKAEGGET, AARHUS, DENMARK
Marsh with the Bent Erikson Trio

00.00.76 NEWPORT JAZZ FESTIVAL
Marsh, Konitz

00.00.76 VILLAGE VANGUARD, NEW YORK [R]
Marsh, Mosca, (unknown) (b), S. Scott (d)
[Incl. How About You: Featherbed: Time On My Hands: Sax Of A Kind: Sound-lee]

00.00.76 STOCKHOLM KULTURHUSET, SWEDEN [RNI]
Marsh, Jan Allan (t), Robert Malmberg (p), Roman Dylag, Red Mitchell (b), Rune Carlsson (d)

00.00.76 FASCHING CLUB, STOCKHOLM, SWEDEN [RNI]
Personnel as above
[Tapes were made of both these sessions, but Marsh never allowed them to be released.]

18-22.02.76 RATSO'S, CHICAGO [RNI]
SUPERSAX:- Gary Barone (tp): Lanny Morgan, Med Flory (as): Marsh, J. Migliori (ts): Bill Byrne (bar): L. Levy (p): Fred Atwood (b): J. Hanna (d)
[Incl. The Bird: Salt Peanuts: Koko: Ornithology: Now's The Time - 24 solos]

00.03.76 WARREN BULKELEY HOTEL, STOCKPORT, UK [RNI]
[Recorded by Peter Ind]
Marsh, Cliff, Ind, Levitt
[Incl.It's Only A Paper Moon: You Stepped Out Of A Dream: The Way You Look Tonight: I Want To Be Happy: Dizzy Atmosphere: Moose The Mooche: Little Willie Leaps: All God's Chillun Got Rhythm: Crazy She Calls Me: God Bless The Child: Now's The Time]

09.03.76 MIDDLETON HALL, HULL, UK
Marsh, Konitz, Ind, Levitt
[Incl.Easy Living: It's Only A Paper Moon: You Go To My Head: Lady Be Good]

13.03.76 BERGANO, ITALY [R]
Marsh, Konitz, Ind, Levitt
[This was part of a 2 week tour of Italy]

15.03.76 CAMDEN JAZZ FESTIVAL, SHAW THEATRE, UK [R]
Marsh, Konitz, Ind, Levitt
[Incl. Wow: Background Music: Body And Soul: It's You Or No One: Subconscious-Lee: 317 East 32nd Street: The Night Has A Thousand Eyes: You Go To My Head: Two Not One: Star Eyes: Bach Invention No.16: Lady Be Good:Easy Living: Cherokee: I'll See You In My Dreams]

24/25.06.76 RONNIE SCOTT'S, UK [R]
Marsh, Konitz, Ind, Levitt
[These were part of a week's engagement at the club]
[Incl. It's You Or No One: Wow: Subconscious-Lee: Embraceable You: Easy Living: Background Music: Chi Chi: Kary's Trance: Sound-Lee: Just Friends: All The Things You Are: Love Me Or Leave Me: April: I'll Remember April: She's Funny That Way: Limehouse Blues: Chi Chi]

00.06.76 SHAW THEATRE, UK [R]
Marsh, Konitz, Ind, Levitt

00.06.76 STORYVILLE [R]
Marsh, Konitz, Mosca, Gomez

21.07.76 VERONA JAZZ FESTIVAL, ITALY [R]
Marsh and rhythm section

00.08.76 AARHUS JAZZ FESTIVAL, DENMARK [R]
As above

00.00.76 CITY HALL, PASADENA
Marsh, Foster, Atwood (b), Peter Donald (d)

00.11.76 DENMARK [R] [Radio Broadcast]
Marsh, Ole Kock Hansen (p), N.H.O. Pedersen, plus drums
[Incl. Blue Lester: Two Up]
Preceded by brief interview taped during visit to Denmark in 1975

00.12.76 RONNIE SCOTT'S, UK [R]
Marsh, Konitz, Ind, Levitt

00.00.77 DONTE'S [R]
Marsh, Pepper, Levy, Monty Budwick (b), Nick Ceroli (d)
[Incl. I'll Remember April: Billy's Bounce: You Go To My Head: Easy Living: Lady Be Good: All God's Chillun Got Rhythm]
[Several reel-to-reel tapes were made of these performances with Marsh's permission.]

13.02.77 DONTE'S [R]
Marsh, Foster, Levy, Atwood, John Donte

05.03.77 GREAT AMERICAN MUSIC HALL, SAN FRANCISCO [R]
Warne Marsh and Bill Evans
[Four tracks recorded, including Every time We Say Goodbye]

06.03.77 GREAT AMERICAN MUSIC HALL, SAN FRANCISCO [R]
Marsh, Konitz [Three tracks recorded]

13.03.77 CENTENNIAL LIBRARY, EDMONTON, ALBERTA
Marsh, Konitz, Downes (p), Young (b), Gjerston (d)
[Incl.Things Ain't What They Used To Be]

Spring 77 KEYSTONE CORNER, SAN FRANCISCO [R]
Marsh, Konitz and unknown rhythm section
[Incl. Night And Day: You'd Be So Nice To Come Home To: Featherbed: What's New: The Night Has A Thousand Eyes]

28.04.77 DABNEY HALL, CAL TEK, CA [R]
Marsh, Foster, Alan Broadbent (p), Hughart (b), Ceroli
[Incl. Sipping At Bells: You'd Be So Nice To Come Home To: You Go To My Head: All About You: April: What's New:Yesterdays: All The Things You Are: Subconscious-Lee: Bach Invention No.16: You Stepped Out Of A Dream: What Is This Called Love]

[It may have been around this time that Marsh and Christlieb did a private studio session with Jim Hughart and Nick Ceroli - 16 tracks]

FALL 1977 THE PRESERVATION BE-BOP BAND
Marsh, Candoli (tpt), Frank Rosolino (tbn), Lou Levy (p), Fred Atwood (b), John Dentz (d)

FALL 1977 MOVES TO RIDGEFIELD, CONNECTICUT

00.00.78 APOGEE Recording session [R]
[There are tapes of alternate takes of this session, including Magnetism: Body And Soul: Rapunzel: Lunarcy: Love Me: I Could Have Told You: Tenors Of The Time: Solitude: Stompin At The Savoy]

00.00.79 KOOL JAZZ FESTIVAL,STORYVILLE, NEW YORK
Marsh, Mosca, Konitz, Gomez, Elliot Zigmund(d)
[Tapes exist of the rehearsals] [Appeared here at least for two nights]

01.04.79 LU LU WHITES, SOUTH END, BOSTON, USA [R]
Marsh, Mosca, Gomez, Scattaretico (d); Mosca solo

12.08.79 RED MITCHELL'S APARTMENT, STOCKHOLM [R]
Marsh, Mitchell Duo

03-10.09.79 VILLAGE VANGUARD, 178 7th AVENUE Sth, NEW YORK
Marsh, Mosca, Frank Comino (b), Tim Pleasant (d)
[Incl.Gone With The Wind: Body And Soul]

19.10.79 BEVERLY CAVERN, 4289 BEVERLY BLVD, HOLLYWOOD
[Now closed]
Warne Marsh Quintet

Early 1980s CONCERT AT STONY BROOK COLLEGE [R]
Marsh, Klopotowski, Dallas, Skip Scott
[Incl. Star Eyes: Background Music: You Don't Know What Love Is: Victory Ball: It's You Or No One: You Stepped Out Of A Dream: You'd Be So Nice To Come Home To: Foolin' Myself: Lennie's Pennies: Embraceable You: Kary's Trance: Strike Up The Band]

00.00.80 PEACHTREE'S, NEW ROCHELLE, NEW YORK
Marsh and various others, between 1980 & 1982.
[One performance with Betty Scott (voc), Steve Silverman (p), Mark Diorio (g), Frank Canino (b), Skipp Scott (d). This was a benefit concert for Sal Mosca whose studio at 4 South 4th Avenue had burned down earlier in the year.]

00.00.80 VILLAGE VANGUARD (1980-1983)
Marsh-Mosca Quartet, with Earl Sauls (g) and others

00.00.80 RED MITCHELL'S APARTMENT, STOCKHOLM [R]
Marsh, Mitchell
[Incl. It's You Or No One: You Stepped Out Of A Dream: These Foolish Things: Sorry Sou: Carioca]

26.01.80 ALICE TULLY HALL, LINCOLN CENTER
Marsh, Mitchell, Scattaretico (d)

07.01.80 VILLAGE VANGUARD
Warne Marsh/Connie Crothers

04.04.80 COPENHAGEN [R]
Marsh, Kenny Drew (p), Bo Shief (b), Age Tauggaard (d)
[Incl. Little Willie Leaps: Easy To Love: Star Eyes: Ornithology]

17.04.80 SWEDISH RADIO, STOCKHOLM [R]
Marsh and Swedish Radio Jazzgroup - B. Rosengren, R. Erikson, J. Allan, Nils Lindberg, R. Mitchell and others.
[Incl. Cubitz: As Your Are: Blues For Bill: Concerto for Tenor, Trumpet and Orchestra (Nils Lindberg)]

18-19.04.80 HOTHOUSE Recording session, FASCHING CLUB, STOCKHOLM [R]
[Enough material was recorded to make at least one more album.
[Unreleased tracks from a studio session include : ?: They Can't Take That Away: You're In Love With Me: These Foolish Things]

21.04.80 CAFE MONTMARTRE, COPENHAGEN [R]
Marsh Quartet

03-5.06.80 SWEET BASIL, WEST VILLAGE, NEW YORK [R]
Warne Marsh, Red Mitchell
[Tape 1 - Incl. Tea For Two: Slow Boat To China: I Can't Get Started:April: All The Things You Are: Subconscious-Lee: What Is This Thing Called Love: Embraceable You: How High The Moon: Ornithology]
[Tape 2 - Incl.It's You Or No One: Gone With The Wind: Everything Happens To Me: Cherokee]

[Michael Cuscuna did an interview with Warne Marsh preceding a live broadcast on NPR from Sweet Basil in June 1980]

00.06.80 VILLAGE VANGUARD. NEW YORK [R]
Marsh, Mosca

00.07.80 CHRISTIANSAND, NORWAY
Marsh did a week's teaching

26/27.08.80 PASQUALE'S, PACIFIC COAST H'WAY, MALIBU
Marsh, Levy, Christlieb, Pat Senatore (b), Dick Berk (d)
[Incl. Close Enough For Love: Love Me Or Leave Me: What's New: Love For Sale: Wabash: My Heart Stood Still: The Night Has A Thousand Eyes: My Foolish Heart: Lunarcy]

29.08.80 SWEET BASIL, NEW YORK [WKCR Radio Broadcast] [R]
Marsh, Mitchell Duo
[Michael Cuscuna also did an interview on this broadcast, for which the compere was Billy Taylor. Tunes broadcast included Sipping At Bells (Miles Davis), Easy Living: These Foolish Things:Topsy: It's You Or No One: You Stepped Out Of A Dream: Sorry Sue: South American Way]

25.10.80 LEONARD STREET JAZZ, 75 LEONARD STR, NEW YORK
Warne Marsh Trio

30.10.80 BERLIN JAZZ FESTIVAL, PHILHARMONIC HALL, WEST BERLIN [R]
1. Marsh, Mosca, Gomez, K. Clark (d)
[Incl. And Then There Is Music: Like The Angels: It's You Or No One: Leave Me: Family Song: Background Music: I'll Remember April]
2. Marsh, Connie Crothers [Lennie's Pennies]
3. Marsh, Konitz, Martial Solal [Invitation: 317 East 32nd Street: My Old Flame: All The Things You Are]
[There is also a video recording of the festival]

00.00.81 WILLIAM PATERSON COLLEGE, WAYNE, NEW JERSEY
[Concert arranged by Dr Marty Krivin.]

07-11.01.81 VILLAGE VANGUARD [R]
Marsh, Judy Niemork [voc], and rhythm section

12.02.81 TRONDHEIM, NORWAY [R]
Marsh, Inderberg, Sollid, Erling Aksdal (p), Terje Venaas (b), Espen Ruud (d)
[Incl. It's You Or No One: Background Music: Topsy: ?: ?: ?: 317 East 32nd Street: Ornithology: Lennie-Bird: ?: ? Subconscious-Lee: Ballad: Scrapple: What's New: Walkin': Lester Leaps In: ?]

15.02.81 CLUB 7, OSLO, NORWAY [R]
Marsh, T. Sollid (tp), J.P. Inderberg (bar), E. Aksdal (p), T. Venaas (b), E. Ruud (d)
[Incl. Sipping At Bells: I'll Remember April: 317 E. 32nd Street: ?: ?: Background Music: It's You Or No One: Body And Soul: Scrapple From The Apple: Star Eyes: ?: Lover Man]

08-15.06.81 VILLAGE VANGUARD
Marsh-Mosca

08-16.08.81 VILLAGE VANGUARD
Marsh/Mosca

00.11.81 VILLAGE VANGUARD [R]
Marsh, Mosca

27.12.81 CAFE MONTMARTRE, COPENHAGEN [R]
Marsh, Konitz

26.02.82 FAR AND AWAY CLUB, NEW JERSEY [R]
Marsh with guitar, bass and drums

12.08.82 NOS JAZZ FESTIVAL, DE MEERVART, HOLLAND [R]
Marsh, Mosca, Canino, Taruo Okamoto (d)
[Incl. Background Music: 317 E. 32nd Street: It's You Or No One: These Foolish Things: Body And Soul: Sax Of A Kind: Leave Me: High On You: All About You: Switchboard Joe: How Deep How High: Body And Soul]
[There are tapes of the rehearsals]

05.09.82 CHICAGO JAZZ FESTIVAL [R]
Marsh, Levy, Jim Raney (g), John Whitfield (b), Dick Borden (d)
[Incl. My Shining Hour: I'm Old Fashioned: 213 West 32nd Street: Subconscious Lee: Limehouse Blues: Lunarcy]

05-06.09.82 THE JAZZ SHOWCASE
Same personnel as above

01.11.82 HASTY PUDDING CLUB, 12 HOLYOKE STREET, HARVARD SQUARE, CAMBRIDGE, MASS. [R]
Marsh, Paul Altman (t), Joe Cohn (g), George Kaye (b), Taruo Okamoto (d)
[Incl. Stella By Starlight: Smog Eyes: Sipping At Bells: Subconscious-Lee: The Lonely One]

12.08.82 DE MEERVART, AMSTERDAM [R]
Marsh and others

1982 or 83 ONE STEP DOWN, WASHINGTON, DC.
Marsh and others not known

16.01.83 JAZZ FORUM, 648 BROADWAY, NEW YORK
Marsh, J. Klopotowski (g), Mraz (b), Okamoto
[Incl. Lennie's Pennies: Victory Ball]

00.03.83 DE KROOG, NETHERLANDS
Warne Marsh Quartet

25.03.83 'BIM HUIS', AMSTERDAM [R]
Warne Marsh Quartet

28.03.83 THE NEW MORNING JAZZ CLUB, PARIS [R]
Marsh, Levy, Lundgaard, Martin
[Incl. It's You Or No One: Star Eyes: Kary's Trance: I'm Old Fashioned: The Night Has A Thousand Eyes: Subconscious-Lee: Easy Living: April: My Old Flame: Airegin]

29.03.83 THE NEW MORNING JAZZ CLUB, PARIS [R]
Marsh, Levy, Jesper Lundgaard (b), James Martin (d)
[Incl. High On You: All About You: Switchboard Joe: 317 East 32nd Street:Limehouse Blues: Lunarcy: You Stepped Out Of A Dream: Star Eyes: Victory Ball: Easy Living: Background Music: I Can't Give You Anything But Love]

31.03.83 DE TOBBE, VOORBURG, HOLLAND [R]
Marsh, Levy, Lundgaard, Martin
[Incl. Speak Low: Star Eyes: I'm Old Fashioned: The Dolphin: Easy Living: Devannah: Lunarcy: All 'Bout You: If You Could See Me Now: Switchboard Joe: Emily: Sax Of A Kind: 317 E. 32nd Street]

02.04.83 BELGIUM [R]
Marsh, Levy

06.04.83 GRONINGEN, HOLLAND
Marsh, Levy

11.04.83 PIZZA ON THE PARK, HYDE PARK, LONDON [R]
Marsh, Levy
[Incl. Speak Low: Emily: High On You: Subconscious-Lee: Lunarcy: I Can't Give You Anything But Love: Limehouse: How High The Moon: I'm Old Fashioned: April: Kary's Trance: My Old Flame: It's You Or No One: Sax Of A Kind: Background Music]

12.04.83 PIZZA ON THE PARK, LONDON [R]
Marsh, Levy
[Incl. You Stepped Out Of A Dream: 317 East 32nd Street: Limehouse Blues: I'm Old Fashioned: I Can't Give You Anything But Love: High On You: Lunarcy: I'll Remember April: My Old Flame: Star Eyes: How High The Moon: Airegin]

13-16.04.83 AS ABOVE [R]
Marsh, Levy, Baldock, Clare
[Incl. Star Eyes: Speak Low: Out Of Nowhere: Lunarcy: I Can't Give You Anything But Love: 317 East 32nd Street: It's You Or No One: Loverman: Background Music: Emily: Subconscious-Lee: All The Things You Are: Lennie's Pennies: Limehouse Blues: High On You]

14.06.83 OSLO NRK - Radio Broadcast [R]
Marsh, Sollid, Inderberg, Aksdal, Venaas, Ruud
[Incl. 317 E. 32nd Street: Background Music]

26.07.83 VILLAGE VANGUARD [R]
Marsh, Hank Jones, George Mraz, Bobby Durham
[Incl. Star Eyes: On Green Dolphin Street: Emily: Don't Get Around Much Anymore: Sax Of A Kind]

07.08.83 VILLAGE VANGUARD [R]
Marsh, Hank Jones, George Mraz, Bobby Durham (d)
[Incl. Hot House: But Beautiful: Blue Bossa]

08.08.83 AS ABOVE [R]
[Incl. Cal Massie: Wave: Softly As In A Morning Sunrise: Star Eyes: Sonnymoon For Two: Would'n You: Memories Of You: There Will Never Be Another You]

23.09.83 WEST END CAFE, BROADWAY AND W. 114th STREET, NEW YORK [R]
Marsh, Klopotowski, Peck Morrison (b), Earl Williams (d)
Marsh performed here from 19-24.09.83.
[Tunes broadcast on WKCR: Blues For Trane: You Stepped Out Of A Dream: These Foolish Things: Anthropology: Sonnymoon For Two]

26.10.83 VILLAGE VANGUARD [R]
Warne Marsh, Hank Jones, Mraz, Tom Harrow
[Incl. It's You Or No One: Star Eyes: Moose The Mooche: Don't Get Around Much: Just Friends: I'll Remember April: Easy To Love: My Old Flame: Blue Bossa: Strike Up The Band: Subconscious-Lee]

02.12.83 WEST END CAFE [R]
Marsh, Randy Johnston (g), Nat Reeves (b), Earl Williams (d)
[Tunes broadcast on WKCR: It's You Or No One: Victory Ball: My Old Flame: Sax Of A Kind]
[The Quartet performed here 1-10.12.83. The broadcast on 9.12.83 was also recorded but recording was spoiled by technical problems]

03.12.83 WEST END CAFE [R]
Marsh, Johnston, Steve La Spina (b), Tim Horner (d)
[Tunes broadcast on WKCR:- Incl. All The Other Things: All About You: I Get A Kick Out Of You]

27.01.84 WEST END CAFE [R]
As Above
[Incl. All The Things: All About You: I Get A Kick Out Of You: ?: 317 E. 32nd Street]

04.04.84 STUTTGART, GERMANY [R]
Marsh, Hans Koller and the AAAG Saxophone Quartet

18/19.05.84 WEST END CAFE [R]
Marsh, Randy Johnston (g), Steve La Spina (b), Curtis Boyd (d)
[Tunes broadcast on WKCR: All About You: Embraceable You: Background Music]

00.00.84 EUROPEAN TOUR
Marsh, Chen, Canino (b), Pleasant (d)
[Included appearances at The New Morning Club, Paris, The Heineken Jazz Festival, Rotterdam, and the dates with Norwegian Radio, as below.]

11/15.09.84 SILVER SCREEN ROOM, THE HYATT, SUNSET BOULEVARD, HOLLYWOOD
Marsh, Talmadge Farlow (g), John Heard (b)
[Incl. All The Things You Are: Everything Happens To Me: There'll Never Be Another You: They Can't Take That Away From Me: Body And Soul: Fascinating Rhythm: Untitled Blues: I Wish I Knew: Emily: Sweet Lorraine: It's You Or No One: How Deep Is The Ocean: No Greater Love: I Can't Get Started: My Shining Hour: Green Dolphin Street: Easy To Love: What Is This Thing Called Love: Hot House]

11.10.84 OSLO, NRK BROADCAST [R]
Marsh, Chen, and others
[Incl. Bluin' Boogie: Lover Man: All The Things You Are: Night In Tunisia]

25.10.84 OSLO NRK TV [R]
Marsh and Norwegian Radio Big Band [Incl. A Time For Love]

25.11.84 OSLO - TV PROGRAM "Logic Lines" [R]
Marsh and others, includes Marsh teaching at Trondelag Musikkonservatorium

00.00.85 THE MARQUEE, DOWNTOWN LONG BEACH, CALIFORNIA
Marsh, Chen, Bob Maize (b), Tootie Heath (d)
[The concert was sponsored by radio KLON-FM, Long Beach, California]

00.00.85 HOP SINGHS, MARINA DEL REY, CALIFORNIA
Marsh, Larry Koontz (g)

10.04.85 SILVER SCREEN ROOM, THE HYATT, SUNSET BOULEVARD, HOLLYWOOD
Marsh, Harold Land (ts), Art Hillery (p), Bob Maize (b), Tootie Heath (d)
[Incl. I Love You: Star Eyes: If You Could See Me Now: I Can't Get Started: Oleo]

Summer 1985 OUTDOOR CONCERT, LONG BEACH
Marsh, Chen

00.06.85 SILVER SCREEN ROOM, THE HYATT, SUNSET BOULEVARD, HOLLYWOOD
Marsh and others

02.10.85 DONTE'S [R]
Marsh, D. Koontz (g), P. Corley (b), C. Burnett (d)
[Incl. I Love You: How Deep Is The Ocean: Joy Spring: Topsy: You Stepped Out Of A Dream]

18.12.85 HYATT ON SUNSET [R]
Marsh, Chen, B. Maize (b), Tootie Heath (d)
[Incl. My Romance: Wow: Love For Sale (?)]

21.12.85 As above [R]
Marsh, Chen, Hughart, J. Heath
[Incl. Joy Spring: How Deep Is The Ocean: Background Music: Sweet And Lovely (?): Darn That Dream: Once I Loved]

1986 MOVES TO VAN NUYS, CALIFORNIA

02.04.86 HYATT, SUNSET BOULEVARD, HOLLYWOOD [R]
Marsh and others

02.06.86 PASADENA CITY COLLEGE JAZZ BAND [Directed by Gary Foster]
Warne Marsh
Incl. Out Of Nowhere: Round Midnight: Cherokee: You Go To My Head: Body and Soul: Lennie's Pennies]
[Gary Foster accompanied Marsh on Lennie's Pennies and that was the last time the two played together]

00.12.86 NEW ORLEANS BAR AND GRILL, OAKLAND, CALIFORNIA
Marsh, Chen

00.02.87 ALFONSE'S, SAN FERNANDO VALLEY, LOS ANGELES
Marsh, Eschete, Hughart, Chiz Harris (d)
[Incl. I Remember You: Love for Sale: Besame Mucho: Close Enough]

18.10.87 MILLS COLLEGE [R]
Marsh Trio
[Incl. It's You Or No One: I Cried For You: Easy Living: 317 East 32nd Street: Gee Baby: After You've Gone]

17.12.87 DONTE'S, NORTH HOLLYWOOD
Warne Marsh Quartet: Marsh, Ross Tomkins (p), Larance Marable (d) plus Bass
[Including an interrupted "Out Of Nowhere" which was Warne Marsh's last solo]:||

appendix c **selected bibliography**

Baggenaes, R. Warne Marsh: Interview (Ca. 12.76)
Balliett, W. Jazz: a True Improvisor (New Yorker. 14.10.85)
Balliett, W. Obituary (New Yorker. 18.7.88)
Bernlef, J. Memories of Warne Marsh (JazzNu. 9.88:v.118 [Du])
Bernlef, J. Warne Marsh: The Perfect Solo (Source unknown. 1980 [Du])
Billard, F. Marsh: Retrospection et Digression (Jm. 4.83 [Fr])
Blomberg, L. Warne Marsh and Red Mitchell (Oj. 5.80)
Blomberg, L. Warne Marsh-Kompromissloes Individualist (Oj. 2.69)
Blumenthal, B. Warmed-up Cool (Boston Phoenix. 23.11.82)
Borg, C. Warne Marsh: Interview (Oj. 7.80)
Burns, J. Cool Sounds (Jji. 7.70:v.23/7)
Christlieb, P. Conversations with Warne (LA Jazz Scene. 8.88)
Concert Review: Around the World (Ca. 5.77)
Coss, B. A new Look at Lennie (Mne. 11.51)
Crouch, S. Riffs: The Swan and the Odd Duck (Vv. 11.83)
Davis, F. In the Moment: Jazz in the 1980s (OUP. New York, 1986)
Davis, F. Warne Marsh's Inner Melody (db. 1.83)
Delmas, J. Marsh et Konitz: Martial Solal a Nantes (Jh. 2.76)
Delmas, J. Tristano et son fils (Jh. 3.76:n. 326 [Fr])
Endress, G. Warne Marsh: Interview (Jp. 8.84)
Feather, L. Land and Marsh (LA Times. 12.4.85)
Flecker, C. Entre Complices: Konitz et Marsh (Jm. 2.76 [Fr])
Gardner, M. Marsh: Concert Reviews (Ca. 3.76)
Gieske, T. Saxman Marsh returns to his roots (LA Times. 1.87)
Gleason, R. Hollywood Jazz Notes (db. 31.10.57)
Goddet, L. Warne Marsh: Interview (Jh. 3.76:n. 325)
Heckman, D. Lennie Tristano Quintet at the Half Note (db. 5.11.64)
Hennessey, M. Obituary (Jji. 2.88)
Hennessey, M. Talent in Action: Marsh at Pizza on the Park (Bb. 5.83)
Interview with Per Husby (Ce. 6.89)
Lake, S. Concert Review: Konitz-Marsh at Ronnie Scott Club (MM. 29.5.76)
Lindgren, C. E. Den Maarklige Mr Marsh (Estrad. No.2/2.59)
Lock, G. Forces In Motion (Quartet Books. London, 1988)
Lock, G. Obituary (Wi. 2.88)
Maher, J. Sounds from Seclusion (Mne. 18.8.55)
McRae, B. Camden Jazz Week (Jji. 4.76)
Morgan, A. Warne Marsh (JM. 6.61:vii/4)
Morgan, A. Warne Marsh: All Music (Jji. 2.76)
Morgenstern, D. Dogin Around: A Night At Donte's (Jji. 6.77)
Muth, J. de. People-Chicago (Jm. 1977:[n.1])
Nolan, T. All That Jazz (LA Herald. 3.89)
Nolan, T. Playing in the Band (LA Herald. 14.7.85)
Nolan, T. Return of the Hepcats (LA Herald. 1.85)
Olsson, J. Sensationell aaterfoering (Oj. 1.76)
O'Neill, J. Personal Recollection of Marsh (Jji. 8.88)

Palmer, R. Return of a Radical (Rolling Stone. 20.3.80)
Palmer, R. Tristano: A neglected jazzman (Source unknown. 1982)
Pareles, J. Jazz: Marsh Group Appears at Forum (Unknown. 20.1.83)
Rosengren, B. Concert Review: Goteberg (Oj. 1.76)
See, C. One Soul Sings. Some Listen (LA Times. 9.1.88)
Shera, M. Konitz-Marsh at Middleton Hill Hall (Jji. 4.76)
Sheridan, C. Caught...Warne Marsh Quartet (db. 8.4.76)
Silsbee, K. Farlow & Marsh: Mr Gentle & Mr Cool (LA Reader. 21.2.84)
Silsbee, K. Obituary: Jazz '87 (LA Reader. 8.1.88)
Sturdevant, J. Tristano Tributes (Jm. 1979:[n.2])
Tirro, F. Silent Theme Tradition in Jazz (Mq. 1967: Vol LIII/n. 3)
Tomkins, L. The Warne Marsh Story - Part 1 (Ci. 5.76)
Tomkins, L. The Warne Marsh Story - Part 2 (Ci. 6.76)
Tynan. Hollywood Jazz Beat (db. 4.4.57)
Tynan. Marsh Quintet at Bill Whisling's (db. 21.3.57)
Ulanov, B. Lennie Tristano at Birdland (Mne. 6.50)
Ulanov, B. Tristano-Master in the Making (Mne. 8.49)
Ulanov, B. Tristano-Tardy Triumph (Mne. 12.50)
Ulanov, B. Tristano-The Means of Mastery (Mne. 9.49)
(Unknown) MCA Sponsors draft-proof band (db. 1.6.43)
(Unknown) Obituary: Final Bar (db. 3.88)
(Unknown) Obituary (Jh. 1988)
(Unknown) Obituary (LA Times. 19.12.87)
(Unknown) Obituary (Newark Star Ledger. 20.12.87)
(Unknown) On the Lennie Tristano School (Mne. 10.52)
(Unknown) Schoenberg of Jazz (on Tristano) (Time. 27.8.51)
(Unknown) Tristano-The Mature Artist Confronts Modern Jazz (db. 30.10.58)
Voce, S. Late Warne ing (Jji. 4.70:v.23/5)
Westin, L. Masterful, amazing Marsh (Oj. 1.76)
Wilson, J. S. Jazz: Quartet Revives Spirit of Tristano (Unknown. 9.9.79)
Wilson, K. Concert Review: Konitz and Marsh (Ca. 6.77)

Reviews

All Music (db 6.77)
All Music (Jji 9.77)
All Music M. James (Ca 10.78)
All Music R.W. (Mm)
Apogee J. Atkins (Ce 12.78)
Art of Improvising, First Annual Symposium of Relaxed Improvisation, Ne Plus Ultra J. Atkins (Ce 5.78)
Back Home J. Roberts (db 12.87)
Back Home V. Schonfield (Jji 4.87)
Back Home K. Whitehead (Ce 4.87)
Ballad Album (Jm 5.85)
Ballad Album, Blues for a Reason, Music for Prancing J. Norris (Ca 10.85)
Cross currents (db 4.79)

Hot House (Jji 12.86)
Hot House R. Cook (Wi 9.86)
Hot House B. Rusch (Ce 10.86)
How Deep, How High (Jji 1.81)
Jazz from East Village V. Schonfield (Jji 2.86)
Konitz and Marsh Meet Again M. Luzzi (Ca 4.77)
Live in Hollywood (Jji 9.80)
Live in Hollywood K. Silsbee (BAM 14.7.80)
Live in Toronto J. Balleras (db 12.83)
London Concert A. Macintosh (Jf 1977: n.49: 46-7)
London Concert A. Morgan (Jji 12.77)
London Concert J. Postgate (Jji 2.86)
Marsh and Konitz Vol 3, Marsh/Mitchell: Big Two, Marsh and Susan Chen J. Balleras (db 6.87)
Marsh and Konitz Vol 3 N. Coleman (Wi 2.87)
Music for Prancing (Ce 7.85)
Music for Prancing (Jt 5.85)
Music for Prancing J. Barr (Jt 20.5.85)
Music for Prancing D. Gelly (Jji 6.85)
Ne Plus Ultra M. Gardner (Ca 8.71: Vol 9. No. 2)
Ne Plus Ultra H. Pekar (db 10.70)
Ne Plus Ultra-The Best is Yet to Come Steve Voce (Jji 10.70:v.23/10)
Sax of a Kind (Jm 6.86)
Star Highs (Jm 7.85)
Tenor Gladness (Jji 3.81)
Tenor Gladness J. Atkins (Ce 4.80)
Tenor Gladness Sohmer (db 11.80)
Warne Marsh and Susan Chen A.Bergebuhr (Ce 5.87)
Warne Marsh and Susan Chen M. Fish (Wi 7.87)
Warne Out J. Atkins (Ce 6.76)
Warne Out S. Voce (Jji 1.80)
Warne Out Welding (db 12.78)

Bb=Billboard. Ce=Cadence. Ca=Coda. Ci=Crescendo International.db=downbeat. Jh=Jazz Hot. Jji=Jazz Journal International.Jm=Jazz Magazine. JM=Jazz Monthly. Jp=Jazz Podium. Jt=Jazz Times. Mne=Metronome. Mq=Musical Quarterly. Oj=Orkester Journalen. Vv=Village Voice. Wi=Wire International.

978-0-595-51090-0
0-595-51090-6